A BASQUE STORY

A Novel

BY

M. Bryce Ternet

Second Edition. Fist Published 2009, United States of America

To the Basque people, who make the world a more interesting place.
Etorkizuna, kontakizuna.

And

To my wife, Renata, who makes my world a better place.

Also by M. Bryce Ternet

Diplomatic Weekends in Africa

Strohm Alley

The Yellow House on Maloney Grove

The American Middle Class Revolution

Rock Creek

The Stevenson Plan,
A Novel of the Monterey Peninsula

Author's Note

This story is set in early to mid 2000s. News briefs from the 1990s and 2000s concerning Basque affairs are included at the end of most chapters. These news articles have been included to highlight headlines of the Basque nationalist movement during this time period, especially concerning the often overshadowed French Basque Country. However, the news briefs are not directly related to this fictional story itself.

In references to geographical locations in southwest France and northwest Spain, I most often refer to places by their French names. Referring to place names in French has no deeper connation and is only a reflection of my initial introduction to the Basque Country.

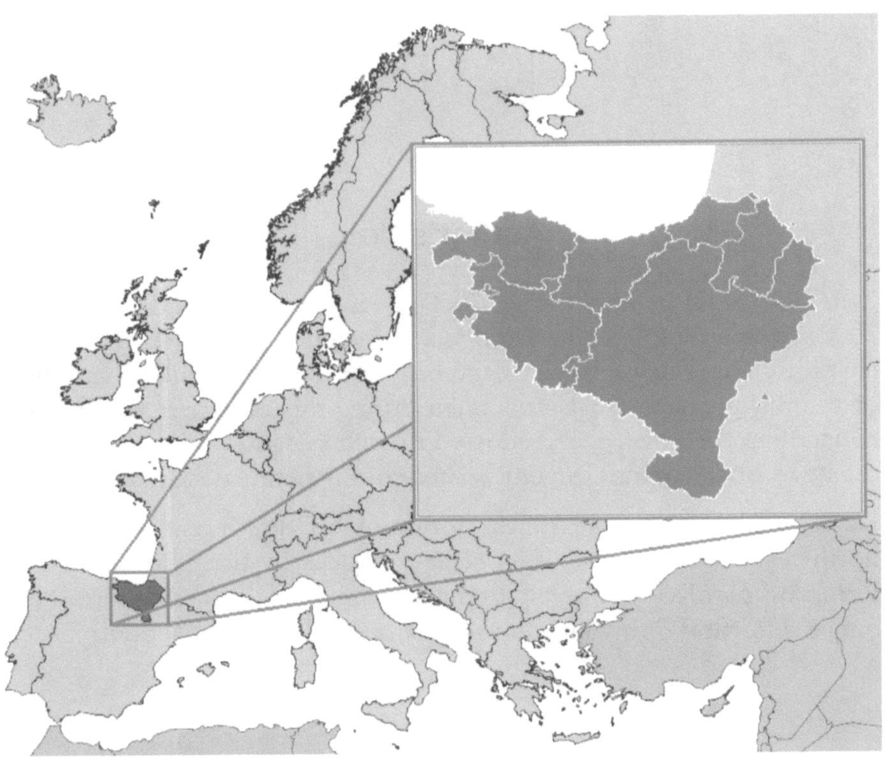

The Basque Country

Bay of Bizkaia
Lapurdi
Behe Nafarroa
Zuberoa
Bizkaia
Gipuzkoa
Araba
Navarre
Euskal Herria
Basque Country

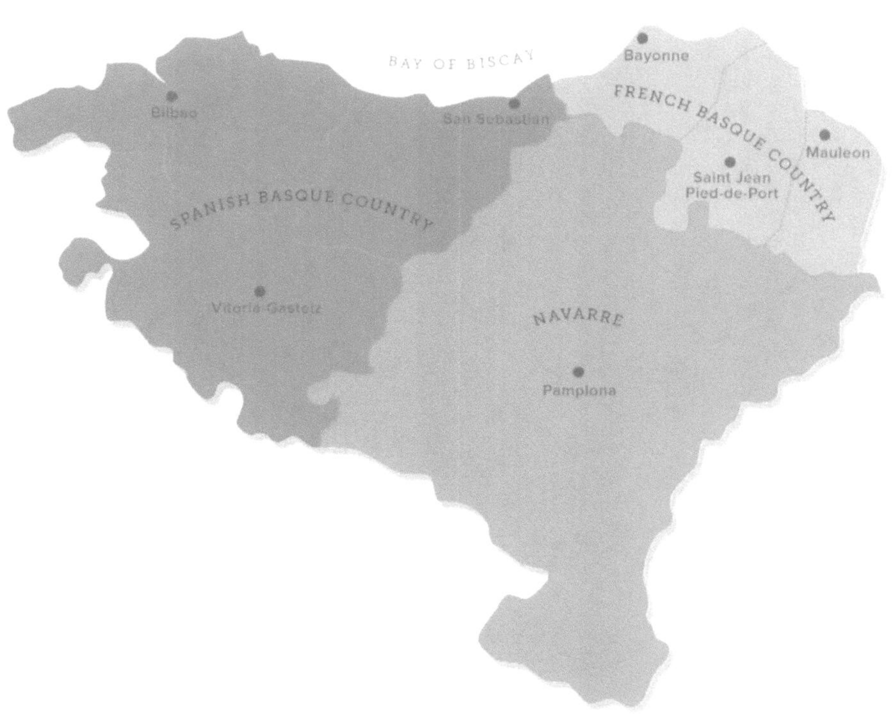
BAY OF BISCAY
Bayonne
FRENCH BASQUE COUNTRY
Bilbao
San Sebastian
Mauleon
Saint Jean
Pied-de-Port
SPANISH BASQUE COUNTRY
Vitoria-Gasteiz
NAVARRE
Pamplona

1

San Francisco, California

RAINDROPS STREAMED OFF THE DARKENED rooftops overhead onto the people below as they stared down at the still, lifeless body. Their black ski masks were now rolled up above their eyes, resting high on their foreheads. Water dripped from their faces. It ran down their bodies onto the pavement where it diluted the puddle of blood forming in the center of the dark alley into a crimson colored mix. The blood blackened water channeled through cracks in the concrete. It formed a thin stream, gently flowing in the center of the alley between the buildings. Captured in a silent flow, the water slowly moved to an unseen end somewhere off in the distance. Waves of fog moved in, surrounding the scene.

They gazed in terrible fascination upon the death they had administered. No one spoke, each feeling something different. The realization hit them that this man would never speak again. This father would never see his children again. This husband would never see his wife again. Yet, of foremost importance to those surrounding the body was the fact that this traitor would never turn his back on his people again.

One shivered as a thick cloud of fog moved through the alley and appeared to swallow the five bodies. The one with longer hair than the others fiddled with the hair coming out of a ponytail that jutted from the back of a ski mask. This one interrupted the solemnity of the moment by reaching up to pull loose strands back into place. The shortest of the group kept shifting weight from leg to leg like a pendulum.

Nervously, the one who shivered darted his eyes into the wall of fog engulfing them. The only thing that could be made out was a large dumpster a little ways from them that, for some unknown reason, seemed out of place. Probably because it was large and permanent, while everything else about the situation was not.

The eerie, unreal atmosphere made the group feel they were almost invisible until suddenly the silence was broken as words, spoken in an ancient language, pierced through the thick damp air.

A voice boomed from one who stood taller than the rest. This deep voice came from the member of the group who had a face with a strong chin, thick eyebrows, and a small wispy moustache. He told them they should feel proud of what they had done. No longer would this country ignore them. His words assured them they had done a great deed for their people and their homeland.

The others heard him without moving or saying a word. When he finished, his words hung in the air and seemed to float above them like a cloud. Of their group, only he had ever been involved in a killing. Rarely would he speak of it because, according to him, the man he killed did not deserve to even be mentioned again. Since he was their leader, no one in the group ever doubted or questioned his actions.

Usually the group was assigned minor vandalism jobs and the occasional roughing-up of a businessman for the revolutionary tax that helped fund the cause. Now things would be different. Prior to tonight they had known, in theory, what would happen after they'd completed the task. Now the blood on their hands left no doubt as they reflected thoroughly on what would become of them. To their people they would be heroes.

At least that's what he told them. They all sincerely wanted to believe he was right.

Hoping he wouldn't notice, they held their hands out into the light drizzle so the water would wash off the blood. They felt proud, alive and sickened all at the same time. The short one had to choke back the bile he felt building in his throat.

After reciting something that sounded like a prayer, the one with the thin moustache told them once again that they had done a great deed for their cause. His voice was full of pride and it sliced through the air like a sharp steel blade. Though the others didn't initially understand what he said, they could not ignore his words as he spoke the language of their ancestors. The language they wanted for their future. Three other voices softly joined his.

Nire aitaren etxea
Defendituko dut,
Otsoen kontra,
Sikatearen kontra,
Lukurreriaren kontra,
Justiziaren knotra;
Harmak kenduko kizkidate,
Eta eskuarekin defendituko dut
Nire aitaren etxea;
Ni hilen naiz,
Nire arima galduko da,
Nire askazia galduko da,
Baina nire aitarne etxeak
Iraunen du zutik.

I shall defend
The house of my father,
Against wolves,
Against draught,
Against usury,
Against the law;
They will take my weapons,
And with my hands I shall defend
The house of my father;
I shall die,
My soul will be lost,
My descendants will be lost,
But the house of my father
Will endure
On its feet.

As the last word sank into the fog, a moment followed of unintended silent reflection—now it would really begin. Turning from the death scene, they followed behind the one with the thin moustache as they hurried toward the street. They quickly piled into a blue Volkswagen waiting for them at the end of the alley. The plan was for all of them to be separately moved out of the country. Their fabricated passports already had been prepared. So had their travel arrangements. If all went according to plan, they would all be back in the homeland within a week.

The Volkswagen sped off into the foggy night. The one with the thin moustache smiled as he lit a yellowish cigarette and blew out a line of blue smoke. He was more than pleased with the way things had gone. In the back, the one who had shivered thought about playing pelote in his home village. Lighting a cigarette as well, the one with the ponytail shivered with delight, feeling a quiver deep inside her. Thinking of an old girlfriend and feeling like crying, the shortest one bit his lip and forced back his emotions. At the wheel, the driver of the car didn't speak to the passengers. In fact, she did not even look at or acknowledge them.

Relentlessly, the rain continued to beat down on the body of the fallen man in the dark alley. The lonely body was sprawled at impossible angles as gravity pressed it against the broken pavement. As the Volkswagen sped off into the night, the body continued bleeding. But the blood that oozed from the body into a now stronger current of rainwater was not the only thing that moved in the alley after the ensemble departed from the scene.

2

Washington, DC

THE CLOCK READ 5:27 A.M. For twenty minutes, he'd been lying in bed, gathering his will in order to get up and face another day as Federal Agent John Gibson of the Federal Bureau of Investigation. Before the clock could begin its loud screaming, he reached an arm over and turned off the small alarm clock on the table beside his bed.

Though the little machine was set to clear its lungs at 5:30 a.m. every morning, he couldn't remember the last time he had given it the chance to startle him awake with its unbearable screeching. He thought to himself, how astonishing it is that one little plastic clock can do so much damage to a person's morning. How can anyone have a good day when they've been startled awake by such an awful noise?

Leaning over, he hit the button to turn on the radio. A typical standard radio voice, that sounded the same on any station, was giving the weekly weather forecast. The expressionless voice coming from the radio predicted high temperatures, with a peak in the 80s, plus considerable humidity levels.

It was only the beginning of spring and already there seemed no end in sight for the hot, humid weather. An early summer was pushing forward, probably because winter had been very light with only about an inch of snow that lasted for a day. Though in some areas an inch of snow is hardly noticed, that inch of snow had caused chaos in and around the city, with school and business closings. To top it off, panicky drivers ramming into one another caused a thirty-car pileup on Interstate 90.

Even considering the already uncomfortable weather, Gibson loathed DC's true summer weather. Over two hundred years ago the great city planners, the noble and wise founding fathers of the United States of America, had decided to place the capital of the country at the juncture of two rivers, in an area encompassed by low, mosquito-infested marshland. In hot weather the city's concrete absorbed the heat and the shield of pollution above kept heat from escaping and created a brownish glow above downtown. At times, being in DC felt like being in a swamp.

The voice on the radio continued beyond the weather forecast, announcing the Cherry Blossom Festival that coming weekend. Thousands and thousands of tourists would be flooding into the city to see a group of flowering trees surrounding the small area of the Tidal Basin. Each year, the event resulted in campers with Wisconsin or Ohio license plates trying to park on Constitution Avenue and loads of baseball cap wearing tourists flooding the Metro system, not understanding that when the doors of the train opened, people must move so passengers can either get off or onto the train. Of course, the masses on the Metro would be nothing like they were at the peak tourist time in summer. In summer, there would be lines of people waiting to jam into the already packed train cars full of the regular commuters. When the train stopped at such places as Arlington Cemetery, no commuters would move, and the tourists would be left to feverously try to get on or off a Metro car.

Also in summer, one had to take into consideration the added numbers of summer interns. They were easy to spot on the Metro, as they usually were overdressed, overconfident, and discussing Capitol Hill politics as if they did anything else except give Capitol tours and sort mail. Give them a couple of years to become disillusioned, Gibson always thought.

While riding on the Metro he sometimes wondered what people, who have never ridden on a metropolitan subway system, think of the whole experience? What did they think of the germaphobics who were so scared to touch anything that they ended up *metro-surfing* by waving their arms trying to keep their balance as the cars swayed? Did they realize there were seriously disturbed people who rode on the most crowded cars for the sole purpose that they got off on rubbing against other people?

He supposed, city or no city, there were sick people everywhere. At least when tourists came to Washington DC and rode on the Metro they wouldn't have to worry about sitting in piss or on a half-eaten hamburger, or getting mugged or raped, as they would in other U.S. cities. At least DC's Metro system was clean and, for the most part, effective for getting around. They had even recently arrested a ten year old for eating fries on the Metro just to prove their strictness on keeping it clean. If only everything else in DC ran so efficiently.

The voice on the radio switched subjects and took on a sad sounding tone. Two children had been killed in a drive-by shooting last night in Prince George's County. The police mistakenly shot an unarmed man at a drive-through restaurant, thinking he was the culprit. Tragic, but not an uncommon theme for the DC area.

Time to end this morning reflection, he thought. He got up from his bed and with uneven steps, headed for the sink. Another day, another government dollar spent.

After he splashed water on his face, he stood in front of the mirror and looked at himself. Not bad, he assessed. He'd managed to get past forty-five without acquiring a gut that so often comes as a package deal for so many other men. Also, he still had a nice thick batch of dark hair on his head. Not bad at all, he thought as he walked away from the sink. Sometimes he compared his looks to the FBI agents on television shows. He thought he measured up fairly equal.

Often he thought how things might have been better for him. His wife could have stayed with him, instead of running off with the CFO of the company where she worked. It had been eight years. At times, it seemed like ages ago. Other times, it felt like just yesterday.

Then were times when he thought about living in an actual house in the suburbs with a dog, kids, a yard and a barbeque grill, instead of his small apartment near Eastern Market. He could even have chosen a more lucrative profession than devoting his life to being a government employee. Oh well, his life was his life.

Finished with has daydreaming, he stepped into the shower and turned the knob all the way to the far side. He listened as water noisily crept through the pipes in the walls then the cold water, just how he liked it, burst from the showerhead as if the pipes had never been used. As John Gibson stood under the stream of freezing cold water, he thought of all he needed to get done in the day.

* * *

Officer Jackson and Officer Williams considered themselves good police officers. In most cases they were. Not only were they partners on the force, they were good friends, both having served numerous years as patrolmen in the San Francisco Police Department. Neither minded watching kids, half their age, join the force and quickly pass them on the rank scale. Both men agreed the most important duty in life was to make it through a day alive, then go home to their wives and kids. It was also important to have a steady paycheck coming in and to eat out at Burger King whenever the wives didn't cook. Like many other Americans, and quite a few other policemen, they were overweight. They lifted weights once a week though and their arms were a fleshy combination of fat and muscle. Jackson and Williams believed having big arms and big chests made up nicely for big bellies that hung over tightened belts.

On this particular morning, the two jovial officers were on their normal everyday drive, patrolling the south side of downtown San Francisco, having their usual morning banter.

"You wanna go get some doughnuts and coffee?" Officer Jackson asked without turning his head.

"I'll take the coffee, but no doughnuts," Williams replied.

"What, no doughnuts? You're a cop, aren't you?" Jackson shot back at him.

"Yep, I sure am a cop," Williams assured his partner.

"Well, cops are supposed to like doughnuts. Don't you ever watch TV?"

"Yep, I do. And that's what I hear. But the thing is, I don't like 'em."

"I guess they're too fattening for a fit guy like you," ribbed Jackson. "I'll bet you like that fake meat stuff. What do you call it—tofu?"

Williams burst out laughing. "Tofu! Who would ever want to eat that cardboard tasting shit?"

Joining in the laughter, Jackson said, "I was thinking I could really go for one of those breakfast croissant sandwiches over at BK. He turned away from the steering wheel to glance over at Williams in the passenger seat.

Rubbing his stomach and frowning, Williams asked, "Are they fattening?"

"I'm sure they are," chuckled Jackson.

"Hell, they'll taste good then. Let's go!"

Just as Officer Jackson pulled into an abandoned lot to turn the police car around, a woman's voice crackled over the radio. The voice from dispatch reported: "A body has been discovered in an alley off Bryant Street by some deliverymen. The closest squad car is requested to the scene in order to check out the report."

Realizing they were only a few city blocks away, the two big men pouted like little boys because their fast food trip was interrupted. With a sigh of resignation, Williams picked up the radio and responded with their location and said they would be there right away.

"Guess our favorite little morning snack is going to have to wait, old buddy," Williams said to Jackson, who looked like he was about to throw a fit and proclaim he quit the force.

* * *

She didn't talk during the entire drive east from San Francisco to Stockton. He questioned if they could trust her as she pulled into a parking lot with only three cars in it. Obviously, she had Basque origins in her family line. One could see that from just looking at her facial features—dark hair, large ears, and a long nose.

He was told that her family had been in Stockton for over 150 years. Until recently, they had primarily been involved in the sheep industry. Even if she was an American, she was still an *Amerikanoak*, which put her high above all other Americans on the evolutionary scale. He decided to trust her.

No time was wasted after she stopped the Volkswagen next to the three parked vehicles. As soon as they had climbed out of the small car, they were surrounded by a group of people and led to different vehicles. All the people tried speaking Basque to them. They had horrible accents, seeming to eat their own words. But at least they were trying.

Looking around, he wished there was a chance, once more, for him to tell his brave soldiers how proud he was of them. But he didn't have the opportunity. As he glanced out the back window of the Land Rover he was ushered to, he saw the others were also being led to respective vehicles. It was too dark in the parking lot for him to even give them a respectful parting nod.

As was his habit, he stroked his moustache lightly then lit one of his yellow cigarettes. So far, all had gone as planned.

The plump man driving the Land Rover stepped on the gas and they sped out of the parking lot. The equally plump man in the passenger seat turned to speak to him. "You have done a great deed for our people, Lopé," he said in pretty good Basque.

* * *

Brotherly Love Helps ETA Suspect Escape

A leading Basque separatist has managed to escape from one of France's best-known jails after his brother took his place in his prison cell. The escaped man is regarded by Spanish authorities as one of the leading members of ETA.

The two managed to swap places during a prison visit. A local correspondent commented this was no small feat in one of the highest security jails in the country.

Earlier this year, the escaped prisoner was arrested in the Ardeche region and was being held in connection with a series of car bomb attacks in the Basque region of Spain.

The incident is viewed as embarrassing for French authorities.

3

Reno, Nevada

A TREE WITH WORDS CARVED into its trunk was displayed on the large screen at the front of the classroom. Under the picture, a caption noted the tree was in a forest somewhere in California. Some of the carved words were in Spanish, but most were in Basque with the language's typical surplus of Xs and Zs, which to Anglophones appear strangely placed. None of the carved inscriptions on the tree were in English.

"Now, who can tell me why these Basque-American herdsmen, or *Amerikanuak* herdsmen as they were known, or *Vascos*—a derogatory name for them used by cowboys, carved inscriptions into trees in various places around the high plains of California, Nevada, Idaho and Oregon?" asked the Professor as the lights in the room gradually brightened.

A blonde, ponytailed girl wearing a scandalously short blue skirt crossed her legs slowly as she shot her hand high into the air. No one else even had a chance to think about lifting their hand to attempt an answer.

Professor Miller, wearing a light blue collared shirt and tan chinos, pointed to the Blonde in the front row. As he noticed her breathing increase, he imagined her breasts popping open the buttons of her already tight pink blouse. If anyone had been paying attention, they would have noticed the twinkle in Professor Miller's eyes as he called on the purring, young Blonde.

"Yes."

The Blonde blushed a moment before answering. "They were recording their language because they thought that Franco would erase it completely in their homeland." She tried to quietly pop the gum she was chewing, but failed.

The Professor caught himself staring at the pair of gleaming legs under the desk and smiled at her response to his question. How charming college girls are, he thought. Bringing his thoughts back to the business at hand, he regrettably raised his head from the area below the desk. He looked out into the mass of faces staring at him from the ascending levels of the room.

"No. As good as that answer is, it's not the correct answer. Although true that General Franco did try his best to rid the planet of *Euskera*, what we call the Basque language, and he did indeed do serious damage to it, that's not why these fellows were carving inscriptions into trees in the vast American west. Does anyone else care to take a stab at it?"

Glancing at the Blonde, he noticed she was intently watching him. She must like the smart, older types, he told himself. He sucked in his stomach and lifted his chin as he paced in front of the projected computer screen that was displaying his PowerPoint presentation.

A hand raised in one of the back rows. He pointed to the hand. "Yes?"

"There wasn't another human being within a hundred miles of them when they carved into the trees," answered a firm, young voice.

Nodding his head in agreement, the Professor replied, "Yes, that's absolutely true. And?" Out of the corner of his eye, he saw the Blonde was watching him again and he turned quickly to reveal his profile, chin raised.

"And, they got tired of talking to their sheep and picked up a new pastime?" queried the voice from the back.

The Professor strained to focus on the face from which the voice spoke on the back row. It was blurry and he could not really make out a face. The face looked vaguely familiar, but it was too far away for him to see with the lights still partially dimmed. Professor Miller mentally muttered to himself that he should be wearing his glasses, but they made him look older.

"That's right. They were lonely out there by themselves." As he pronounced the word *lonely,* he moved his eyes from the back rows to the front in the hopes the Blonde noticed the gesture. Professor Miller also hoped she had intentions for a private lesson after class.

"Of course," he continued, "for this reason sheepherders were also to acquire the insulting rumor of being, let's say, very sexually attracted to their flocks of sheep." He let his eyes meet the Blonde's to convey his desired intentions as the classroom laughed at his joke.

"But let's back up for a moment so I can clarify something that occasionally gets confused regarding the Basque Country. When we say the Basque Country, we're referring to two regions within the modern day countries of Spain and France, referred to as the Pais Vasco and Pays Basque, respectively in each. The Basque terms for their homeland can be either Euskal Herria or Euskadi."

After providing the clarification, the Professor continued with his lecture, analyzing the history of the Basques from the turn of the 9th century to the end of the Franco regime in Spain, and how the identity of the Basques had been altered by events during this time period. During his lecture, the Professor noticed the Blonde following his every move. This made him feel slightly orgasmic. If he lifted his arm, her eyes followed. If he bowed his head in silent contemplation, she did the same.

Whoever said being a professor was a hard life? Sure, his wife left him after catching him banging one of his students, but there would always be young women wanting higher grades in his classes.

He dimmed the lights and hit the space bar on his laptop, causing a new image to be displayed on the screen, as he continued his lecture. "There are somewhere around fifty thousand Americans living in the United States today who can trace their ancestry to the Basques. Of course, out of our population of two hundred sixty million, that's not a great percentage. But considering there are only three million or so Basques in Euskal Herria, literally translating as 'the place of Basque speakers,' this number is significant."

A picture of a stout man with a tanned face wearing a black beret appeared on the screen, followed by a light chuckle from the crowd. Professor Miller turned to see the picture and allowed himself a grin before continuing. "California has the highest percentage of those with Basque ethnic origins in the United States. In fact, one third of the nation's ethnic Basque population is in California. Idaho ranks second, and this great state of Nevada comes in third. Reno, this wonderful city, has the highest percentage of Basque-Americans in the state. If you're wondering why I'm praising Nevada so much right now, it's because somewhere out there among you there is a representative from Carson City and I'm tying to suck up to get you to give our school and my program more money!" The class again broke into laughter. The Professor grinned. He knew he was good at his job.

"Don't worry. I'm just joking around everyone. I doubt anyone from the capital would want to spend their afternoon listening to me babble. Anyway, let's get back to it." As if a light switch was turned back on, his expression went from playful to serious in an instant. "A recent census proved there are Basque-Americans in each and every one of the fifty states."

The screen changed to show a graph of the states with the largest Basque-American populations. In descending order, the states listed were: California, Idaho, Nevada, Oregon, Washington, Utah, Arizona, New York, Texas, Florida, Colorado and Connecticut.

"Now, it's not so easy to identify these people. Many of them were born here in the States, but can easily trace their heritage back to Spain or France. Almost all of them have given up the traditional ways, like sheep herding, and taken on mainstream jobs. Looking at this list of states and knowing the longstanding presence of Basques in America's sheep herding industry, it's not hard to realize why most are in the western states. New York has always had a large presence due to it being the first stop when coming into this country. For many, it is also the last stop on their trip across the Atlantic.

"However, that leaves two states on this list that don't have sheep and aren't major ports. Does anyone know how to explain this?" Professor Miller asked, looking expectantly around the room, though not really wasn't expecting an answer. "This is due to the beloved American pastime of gambling. You see, Florida and Connecticut both allow forms of gambling, and a sport that is widely bet on is the Basque sport of *jai alai*. Although this fast-paced and considerably dangerous sport is now played in major capital cities around the globe, after the Basque Country, the most popular destination is arguably Miami. And just as when considering sheep herding, the Basque people seem to be the world's best at playing *jai alai,* which, by the way of explanation, we tend to spell as Hi-Li here in the States."

Suddenly, the classroom of people was staring at the screen with a picture of a short, powerfully built man with a huge moustache that seemed to almost connect with his equally huge eyebrows. On his head he wore a red beret. In the picture he was standing outside a restaurant with a fifteen letter name above its window. He looked extremely merry and jovial as if he'd consumed a bottle of red wine for breakfast.

The class laughed with the man in the photo, but the Professor ignored their response and continued his lecture. "This picture is of the owner of a Basque restaurant in San Francisco. Basque cooking is legendary and many Basque-Americans have taken advantage of America's somewhat newly found interest in foreign cuisine by starting their own restaurants in western cities."

The man and the restaurant faded into a dusty photograph of a man carrying a *makila,* a Basque walking stick with a secret knife built into the handle, following alongside a herd of sheep. "However, we can still find, even today, Basques in America herding sheep on vast ranches in California, Idaho, and here in Nevada. But why be sheep *bergers*?" he asked. He waited for the voice to echo from the back of the room, but no response came, so he continued with an explanation.

"Because the Basques have been sheep herding in the Pyrenees of Spain and France for centuries. They are probably the best sheepherders the world has ever seen. When they migrated here to America, they soon realized they could continue the trade they had mastered in Europe right here in the western states. No one else seemed capable of spending weeks on end, alone, on the high plains with a herd of sheep. But the Basques could do it..."

"However, Professor," the voice rang out once again from the back of the small auditorium, "isn't there also the possibility that it wasn't just because they knew how to be *bergers* of sheep," the voice pronounced the French word for herdsman much better than the professor had, "but because there simply was the opportunity to take over the sheep industry and the Basque settlers took it as those before them had already done earlier in the Rio de la Plata region of South America?"

The Professor peered through the dim lights in the direction of the voice, the same voice as earlier. It bothered him he'd been caught off guard and wasn't prepared to deal with such direct questioning. Worse, the voice obviously belonged to someone holding a decent degree of intelligence. "You make a good point," the Professor answered.

Before Professor Miller could continue, the voice interrupted him, turning slightly condescending. "And isn't sheep herding in the Basque Country entirely different from the new world? I mean, over there they tend to have small local herds that pretty much stay in the same area. Here, however, sheep flocks are, and pretty much always have been, very large in number and the herders must move them across hundreds of miles of land to pasture."

He began to feel flushed. This little bastard was making him look bad in front of the hot Blonde in the front row! "Yes, these are all good points you're making and I've studied them before. However, unfortunately, I'm not going to have time to debate the entire theory on Basque sheep herding in the western hemisphere today." He paused, purposefully.

"For now, we'll just say that there were numerous factors at play that led to the Basques dominating the sheep industry in the western United States. After all, perhaps they preferred this simply because the lifestyle allowed them to easily guard their own culture while minimally exposing them to the culture surrounding them that was attempting to swallow it." Everyone in the room noticed the touch of annoyance in his voice.

"I thank you for your insight though." The manner in which he spoke the word *though* conveyed the finality to the short debate. Professor Miller cracked his neck by turning his head sharply and stretched his shoulders backward.

A large abstract sculpture took over the screen. With a little imagination, one could see the image of a man carrying a sheep in the sculpture. A caption at the bottom of the screen read: National

Monument to the Basque Sheepherder. After letting them gaze at the screen a few moments, the professor provided further explanation. "This sculpture is right outside Reno, if any of you would like to see it. There are also some of the reputed Basque tree carvings, like the one we saw earlier, not far from it. That is, if some punk hasn't gotten tired of spray painting walls downtown and gone out into the woods to paint trees."

A soft laugh rippled through the room as he paused for a glance through the darkness at the set of perfect legs now gently rubbing against one another in the front row. Whoever it was in the back row had rattled him a bit, but now he felt much better. After taking a deep breath, he continued.

"Immigration of Basques to the United States has largely tapered off in the last decade. With the end of the Franco regime, many Basque-Americans have actually returned to the Basque country in Europe to live. Knowing this, I ask you if they ever really were Americans?"

The screen changed once again. Now it showed a group of people dancing in traditional Basque clothing—men in white pants and shirts with red sashes and berets, women in white shirts with lace fronts, decorated bonnets, black skirts and high laced leggings. The caption didn't say the scene was from Europe, as would be expected at first glance, but that the picture had been taken at the San Inazio Basque Festival in Boise, Idaho. The Professor raised his eyebrows in mocked disbelief, but it was too dark in the room for anyone to see his well-practiced expression change.

"I might add that a poll done in the mid-1980s revealed, when asked to describe their ancestry, nearly eighty percent of Basque-Americans identified themselves first as Basque, second as Americans. Another fascinating sociological issue this poll raised is over what the Basques think about being Basque. Just under half the Basque-Americans questioned for this poll didn't identify themselves as just Basque, but as either distinctly Spanish or French Basque. So we must now ask ourselves, what it is to be a Basque-American? For is it not a different person who has lived their entire life in America, but had a grandparent come over from the Basque country, from someone who was born in say, Bilbao, and is new to this country? Or maybe we should identify people who are Basque solely by whether or not they speak *Euskera,* as the Basque language is called in Basque, which is quite possibly the oldest living tongue in Europe, and is arguably unrelated to any other known language. Or maybe, no one should be called Basque unless they can trace a pure Basque bloodline? Or maybe, the only people that should be labeled as Basque are those who have an O blood type and Rh-negative blood. Blood becomes important when discussing the Basques, because Basques have the highest concentration of type O blood of any other ethnic group. Basques also have the highest percentage of Rh-negative blood of any people in the world. This rhesus factor is what proved many scholars wrong who believed the Basques were related to other ancient European groups, such as the Scots, Irish, and Corsicans. These groups are indeed ancient, but the Basques are even older. But a really good question is: Who do Basques identify as other Basques?"

The vibrant scene of the dancers on the screen faded into a flag with a red background crisscrossed by a white and green cross. It was the *ikurrina*, the flag of the Basques.

Professor Miller stopped talking to pace back and forth in front of the flag on the screen with his head bowed in apparent deep thought. Then he said, "These are all hard questions, but they're of the caliber we have to ask when we study the sociology of ethnic groups around the world."

Suddenly the lights in the room were turned on. Everyone's eyes instinctively reacted from the sudden change in lighting. "And these are the kind of questions I want you all to address when we break up into discussion groups this afternoon for a while," the Professor announced.

He turned abruptly and seemed to talk directly to the Blonde as he spoke. "Let's take a quick break. I'll see you all back here in fifteen minutes."

The Professor smiled at the Blonde and the she openly smiled back.

* * *

Although daybreak brought more light into the area, it was still gloomy from the rain and fog that had not yet departed with the night. When two men in a delivery truck found the battered body in the alleyway, they called it in as if they were ordering take out.

Flashing lights bounced off the walls of the alley as the first police car arrived. Officers Jackson and Williams arrived to a scene they had witnessed many times before.

The first thing the officers did was to confirm the man was dead. Then they cordoned off the area and called for backup. All they could do was then wait for the other police cars to arrive.

Detective David Chiles was sorry to have taken his time getting to the scene. Sometimes it was so hard to rush to the scene of a crime like this one. Before he arrived, he assumed it would turn out to be another random homicide like most they came across.

Looking down at the victim, the face staring blankly back at him, instantly revealed his mistake. Briskly, he walked back to his unmarked detective's car and spoke into the radio. "I think we'd better get some more people out here."

Going to be a long day, Detective Chiles said to himself.

* * *

The Great Salt Lake did not look so great to him. They had driven all night and most of the day across a barren desert and now he was looking out the car's window at a dead, shallow lake that had even more desert for its beaches. He wanted to ask the others in the car why the Mormons had stopped here as he'd read that this was their place. He didn't speak though, because he was not sure how well he spoke English. And from the way they talked to him in Basque, he doubted they would understand much of what he would say if he spoke Basque to them.

Leaning his head back, he thought of his girlfriend, Marie-Hélène. She may not have been the most beautiful *fille* to other guys, but to him she was the most beautiful girl in the world. What Aurelion Irazoqui wanted most was to get back to her soft touch.

Marie-Hélène was extremely pro-independence for the Pays Basque and he knew she was going to be so proud of him. His only regret was that he had not been able to tell her of his mission beforehand due to the oath of silence he'd been forced to take.

A man and woman sat in the front of the car and, beside him in the back, was an elderly man. The old man looked like he'd not spent a day of his life indoors. His skin appeared as if the wind and sun had carved their initials into it over time. Though the old man had not said a word to anyone in the car, Aurelion noticed him muttering something to himself as they crossed the high desert of Nevada. This man had been a sheepherder in this very desert passing by the windows and it was here that the sun and wind had left their marks on him. Aurelion knew this from just looking at the old man. Looking sideways at him, Aurelion liked that the old man proudly wore his black beret on his head. Maybe these American Basques weren't so bad after all, he thought.

Suddenly, the lady in the front seat turned around and handed him a passport. Though she said something intended to be in Basque, Aurelion shrugged and, in Basque, excused himself for not understanding her.

She said in broken French, "This is your passport to get out of the United States. Try to memorize as much of this as you can before we get to the airport. You're flying to Montreal where you will be picked up by another group and, from there, you will receive another passport before you fly back to Europe."

"*Bon. Merci beaucoup, Madame,*" he softly replied.

* * *

When he hurried out of the building, after sitting in the dim room, the light enveloping him outdoors was blinding. He nearly dropped the lighter in his hand when he stepped out from the building. He'd been dying for a cigarette for over an hour. In the past, college students had actually been allowed to light up during lectures. Right now, he was wishing they still were allowed that privilege. As he took a long, soothing drag on his cigarette, Parker thought to himself how wonderful it felt not to wear a tie. He had dressed down as much as he possibly could—T-shirt, jeans, and sneakers.

He was proud of himself for not sneaking out earlier. Thanks to his self-discipline, he'd kept still instead of missing any of the presentation.

Parker reflected on the waves of countryside hills that grew into mountainous foothills, then becoming a line of jagged mountains called the Pyrenees. That was the Pays Basque and he recognized his familiar longing to be there once again. Ever since having attended lycée, French high school, in Bayonne, Baiona in Basque, for a year, he made a habit of returning on an annual basis. The Basque Country was the only place Sebastian Parker truly felt at home. He missed that feeling.

The seminar had been good so far. Nothing new for him, but he enjoyed hearing his old teacher speak on Basque issues. Professor Miller had been his teacher for many classes in Basque nationalism while he was doing his undergraduate studies here at the University of Nevada. Now that it had been a few years since having finished his Master's degree at George Washington University in International Affairs with a focus on terrorist studies, Parker often thought of his past professors in undergraduate and graduate schools. Some were good, others bad, while a few had been decent. The smallest group had been excellent. Those that fell into this category, like Professor Miller, made college worthwhile. Unlike the others, these select few went beyond merely presenting material from a textbook and actually taught their students. They were the professors who years later you still remembered being excited about attending their classes.

In the span of four hours, Professor Miller basically summarized two years of classes to the group attending the special lecture. Parker had been able to convince his boss that the lecture would reveal new information to him on the intentions of the Basque nationalist movement. He laughed to himself at how he'd been so convincing that his boss would not let him attend the daylong seminar on his own vacation time. Instead, his employer, the Central Intelligence Agency, was paying him to be here.

Just as he was gleefully exhaling a cloud of smoke from his cigarette, he heard a familiar voice from behind. "Sebastian Parker? Is that really you?"

He turned to see the familiar face that he'd been watching all morning—wide blue eyes framed by delicate wrinkles and light brown hair. "Hello, Professor," he replied.

A wide smile appeared on Professor Miller's face as he approached Parker. "Well, goddamn, you didn't tell me you'd be here for this one," the Professor exclaimed, holding out his hand.

"I didn't know I was going to be here until just a couple days ago," Parker said. He received the offered hand in a long, firm handshake. "I'm here officially, so paperwork had to be approved and all that bullshit. You know how it is. Anyway, sometimes I just really need a break from DC. Even when you're outside of downtown, you're still swimming in the *merde* just as much as if you were standing on Pennsylvania Avenue."

"You're the one that went to work for the federal government, even when I advised you that it wasn't the right place for you," the Professor reminded his ex-student.

"What can I say? They've got interesting jobs."

"But what about teaching? You could do it," Professor Miller said, as he waved a hand backward toward the lecture hall.

"Teaching, huh? Why? So I can leer over and take advantage of easily persuaded young *belles filles*?"

The Professor looked at him for a few seconds before giving him a playful wink. "Hey, you've got to take advantage of the benefits of your job, right? Just look at you. You're here due to a benefit from your job. So, how's that much different from giving, *guidance*, to some of my students that seek my personal help?"

"You helped me and gave me guidance, but it didn't include getting me naked," Parker retorted.

Taking on a dignified air before responding, the Professor said, "Guidance comes in many forms, my dear young Sebastian Parker. And it's not my fault that most people seeking my guidance happen to be beautiful young women."

Parker chuckled. "That's only because you allow one in ten males into your office who come to your secretary looking for you."

"Well, you should feel privileged then, because you were one of those ten. And I'll feel thankful for my secretary. After all these years, she always seems to know who I'll want to see."

"You should make sure to buy her more of that cookie dough ice cream she likes so much."

"That's a good idea. I don't know what I'd do without her," admitted the Professor.

"Maybe you'd realize that more guys are in your classes than girls."

The Professor looked briefly troubled then said, "Yeah, you're right. I need to buy her more of that ice cream." After making that decision, he appeared happy and content with life again.

Parker silently, but thoroughly, observed the Professor as he took a drag.

"But did you see that girl?" the Professor deftly changed the subject. "Damn, she's a knockout. By the way, mind if I get one of those heart darts from you?" he asked, pointing to Parker's cigarette.

Parker choked on the smoke rising from his lungs as he shook his head while laughing at the Professor's comment. He pulled out his box of cigarettes from his jeans pocket and the Professor grabbed one and placed it between his lips.

"That was you in there, wasn't it?" the Professor asked, as Parker held a lighter to the cigarette hanging in his mouth.

"Yeah. I thought you were looking a little too confident up there."

"I knew I recognized the voice, but couldn't see your face."

"Since you weren't wearing your glasses, I knew you wouldn't be able to make me out in that light."

"I know. I know. I'll start wearing them one of these days." Professor Miller paused for a moment then asked, "Were you really trying to bust my balls back there, Sebastian?"

Parker waved a hand in the air and shook his head back and forth. "Ah, you handled it just fine. Besides, we both know that if someone really would have asked every Basque sheepherder out here why they were sheepherders, they would have given you too many different answers to label one as predominant."

Smiling, the Professor nodded his head. The young girls and having his summers off were nice, but he just witnessed the real reason why he enjoyed teaching.

Standing in the brilliant sunlight, the Professor and his former student remembered some of their past late night conversations as they enjoyed their cigarettes.

* * *

Five ETA Suspects Held in France

Police in France have arrested five people suspected of belonging to the Basque guerilla group ETA. The four men and one woman were detained in the western town of Niort.

Police say they were traveling in a stolen car and were allegedly preparing to steal another vehicle. They were all carrying shotguns.

The arrests come one day after ETA said it was responsible for two car bomb attacks in Madrid, outside the landmark Europa Office Tower and Santiago Bernabeu Stadium, in which more than a dozen people were injured.

4

San Francisco, California

"ARE WE SURE IT'S HIM?" the Captain asked, as he filled his mug with coffee.

The Captain was in his early 60s; his skin and hair best revealed his age. On his face, the skin looked like tightly stretched brick, while his hair was the color of old cement. Actually, the gray stubble on his face made sandpaper look soft. Too many years of late nights with fast food and bad coffee had taken a toll on his body and the abuse showed. He was wearing a thin, short-sleeved, white shirt with a plaid tie that looked as if it had been on sale at a thrift store.

"Yeah, it's him. Chiles even found his wallet on him," Detective Jacobs responded, as he sipped his own coffee. Jacobs also wore a short-sleeved white shirt, but his had pizza stains on it and today he had not bothered with a tie. Despite his choice of apparel, he desperately wanted the Captain to like him better than the other detectives.

"Chiles! Shit! He'd better not screw this one up trying to be a goddamn hero again!"

Jacobs didn't try to hold back the noticeable grin at hearing the Captain speak negatively of Chiles. The reason he hated Chiles was because he was nothing but a sissy do-gooder. *Fuck Chiles.*

Though Jacobs was twenty years younger than the Captain, he had a gut twice the size. He, too, had abused his body with the same fried fat and cheap coffee combo, but his vices also included sugar-laced doughnuts, cheap cigarettes, San Francisco's famous garlic fries and beer.

Since the Captain always became fiercely demanding with high-profile murder cases, Detective Jacobs prepared himself to deal with an irate boss.

"Damn, José Aldarossa Arana! He's probably the most popular city councilman this city has ever had," the Captain said, more to himself than to Jacobs.

Both men knew the mayor would probably be calling the Chief of Police soon. That meant the Chief would then be calling the Captain. Naturally, the Chief would ask about the progress of the case even though it had only been an hour since the body was identified. Jacobs wanted to try his best to keep the Captain calm because whenever he got pissed off, he took it out on whoever was closest to him. At the moment, that was Detective Jacobs.

Slightly squirming, Jacobs wished he could light up a cigarette. Those damned hippies and their health codes had made it illegal for him to smoke anywhere in the building.

"Was there anything missing from his wallet?" the Captain asked.

"No, it doesn't seem so. His driver's license was even placed to fall out as soon as it was opened, according to Chiles."

"Shit!" the Captain said, as he looked up from dumping a small mountain of sugar into his coffee. "What goddamn else, Jacobs? I know you're keeping something from me."

Jacobs followed the Captain into his large office and closed the door. The Captain sat down in his weathered chair, waiting for his detective's response. Jacobs thought the Captain deserved a bigger desk and a nicer chair, like the Chief.

Just inside the door, Jacobs remained standing. "Well, sir, some of his fingernails and toenails were ripped off," Jacobs said. The coffee mug began to feel heavy in his hand. He wished the Captain would give him permission to sit in one of the chairs next to him.

Giving Jacobs a hard glance, the Captain asked, "What the hell're you talking about, Jacobs?"

Jacobs placed his mug of coffee down on the small table by the door. He didn't want to drop it if the Captain made an explosive outburst. Then he straightened himself, squared his shoulders and said, "It appears he was tortured in some, ahh...different ways, sir."

"What the hell do you mean, in some different ways?"

Detective Jacobs stood steadily and met the hard gaze of the Captain. He ran a hand back through his greasy black hair before he added, "Chiles believes this was an execution of some sort, sir."

The air between the two men was suddenly quiet and tense. Jacobs stood waiting as the Captain tapped his slender fingers quietly on his desk.

The Captain broke the silence by unsteadily saying, "I want you to get out there, now! I'm sure the TV crews will be there soon if they're not already. Make sure the scene is completely roped off and don't let anything slip out!"

He took a deep breath and moved his eyes to an unfixed point outside the window. "I want to move his wife and kids to a safe house until we can determine that they aren't in any danger." Pausing to take a breath he continued, "I'll go to meet with her myself. Then I'll join you at the scene with that goddamn Chiles!"

* * *

"I should have gone to Miami to play *cesta punta* professionally," he muttered to himself, thinking of his favorite form of the game of pelote. The Basque name for it was *jai alai*, but he secretly preferred the French name. Many times he heard stories of a boy from a village across the valley from his family's in Navarra who had successfully done it. Whenever Peio Antonio Camino thought about pelote, he had to force his mind to remember his father's deep, stern voice telling him he was not good enough at the game of pelote in any form. His father had always told him he was destined only to become a factory worker. Peio couldn't help but wonder: Would my all-knowing father approve of his son now that I am going to be called a terrorist and murderer?

Peio loved Euskadi more than pelote, but wondered if he loved the homeland enough to begin killing others in its name. Looking out the window of the car, he noticed the stars overhead and saw how still and serene they were in the night sky. It made him wonder why Euskadi couldn't be the same.

When the original group split up, he was led into the boxy mini-van. The man driving told him in Spanish that they were going to

Reno, where he was to catch a flight that would eventually take him to Mexico City. Though the man was polite during the entire drive from Stockton, he insisted that Peio try to sleep. Peio wished he could fall asleep, but it was as if all his nerve endings were on fire.

To indulge the man driving the car, he had turned his head and pretended to be asleep. Instead, he stared out at the gleaming array of stars and tried to form a constellation of a fronton among them.

* * *

Detective Chiles looked up and saw his Captain walking briskly toward him. For an older guy, he sure could move fast when he had someone to yell at. Though Chiles was confident he had done nothing wrong in his investigation of the crime scene, he mentally braced himself for a tirade.

He'd watched the Captain get out of the squad car and bolt through the line of reporters and cameramen without a sideways glance. Obviously, the Captain's course was set straight for the lanky frame that belonged to Detective Chiles, but he stayed in his crouched position in the alleyway. Chiles couldn't help but feel like a target of an incoming missile, knowing the missile's intent was to destroy him.

Since Jacobs arrived at the scene before the Captain, he filled Chiles in on what was happening, although Chiles had to nearly pay Jacobs to tell him anything. It was unfortunate that Jacobs possessed the two characteristics Chiles hated in a person—an ass-kisser and a racist. Whenever he saw Jacobs, far too often in his opinion, he was constantly reminded of a case they had worked together four years ago.

At that time, Jacobs was partnered with him on a case of an inner city gang killing. Jacobs' previous partner had just retired and the Captain was looking for a replacement. Since Chiles had recently made detective, he was the most likely candidate to fill the void. Before then, Chiles had never really been exposed to Jacobs. When first meeting him, Chiles didn't like Jacob's greasy looks, but told himself not to make a judgment on appearances alone.

But the first day working the case together revealed to Chiles how much he despised Jacobs. The man had a racist, slanderous remark about everything. In addition, whenever they drove by an attractive woman wearing somewhat revealing clothing, Jacobs would blurt out something like: "Wow, I'd like to frisk her in a back room. Look at her, you know she's dirty. She'd like it if I cavity searched her with my baton." It took all Detective Chiles' control to ignore everything that came out of Jacob's filthy mouth.

By their second day on the case they already had a suspect positively identified by witnesses. Finding the person responsible for a crime was not too difficult anymore, but everything in between the identification and being able to lock them away in a cell was where most of the problems in law enforcement came, Chiles came to quickly learn while on the force.

An informant told them where they would find the twelve year old African-American boy who they were searching for. His name was Jabar Wilson. Jabar, who should have been reading library books and playing basketball, had murdered two members in a rival gang. He made the two other boys get on their knees while he stuck a .9 mm in each of their mouths, simultaneously pulling the triggers.

Chiles ruled out the possibility it had been an initiation act because the gang Jabar belonged to, the Black Hoods, only took on new members who were ten or under. Chances were this had not been Jabar's first serious crime and possibly not even his first murder. Though only twelve years old, Jabar was no longer a boy.

When Chiles and Jacobs found Jabar, he was hanging out behind a convenience store in the Sunset District selling cocaine to upper middle class white kids. Jabar was wearing huge basketball shorts pulled down to his thighs and a T-shirt that said: "Fuck the Police." As soon as Jabar saw the police light in the windshield, which was not turned on, he took off through a blocked-off back alley. Detectives Chiles and Jacobs jumped out of their car and pursued on foot. At the time, Jacobs was forty pounds lighter and able to keep up with Chiles, always remaining just a few paces behind.

Detective Chiles never lost sight of Jabar even when the kid turned into an open door of an old crumbling building. Chiles was running at a full sprint when he turned into the doorway and his forehead slammed into a thick steel bar. The blow knocked him off his feet and his slender body slammed down hard on the crackled pavement. A few seconds later, Detective Jacobs caught up to him.

Though blood was running into his eyes, Chiles motioned Jacobs into the building. Shakily, he used the side of the building to help get himself standing and leaned against the open doorway. Then, for a moment, he lost consciousness. Those few seconds of unconsciousness were interrupted by three thunderous bangs from somewhere above him. There was one single bang, then two quick bangs a few seconds after. All he remembered from that point to when he awoke in a hospital bed was a jubilant grinning Jacobs crouching in front of him saying, "I got the little nigger! I got the little fuckin' coon!"

Jabar Wilson would never have the chance to become a man.

The next day, Detective Chiles forcibly requested from the Captain that he never again be assigned on a case with Detective Jacobs. He never had been.

At the time, Chiles thought about making an official complaint against Detective Jacobs, but knew he would never be able to prove anything since he hadn't actually seen what happened. It burned him to know Jacobs got away with murder and they both knew it.

Jacobs always claimed he had no choice, but Chiles never believed him. Secretly, Chiles hoped to one day have the opportunity to knock Jacobs on his fat ass.

Nonetheless, there were times when Jacobs was needed—like now. He told Chiles how the Chief had called the Captain, demanding the murderer or murderers be caught immediately. Then the Chief promised the mayor swift justice and the Captain promised the Chief even swifter justice. Even the normally non-astute Officer Jacobs remarked, "With such a buildup of promises, someone is bound to be let down. After the Captain talked to the Chief, he opened his door just to slam it shut as loud as he could."

The murder of José Aldarossa Arana, the loved and highly respected city councilman and possible next mayor, was now public knowledge thanks to the news crews that were still trying to get across the yellow, taped-off crime scene police lines. Chiles was impressed and annoyed with their apparent resourcefulness. Often he wondered how they found out these things so quickly. They had somehow sensed this murder was more than an everyday homicide even before the San Francisco Police Department knew for sure.

Watching the Captain heading his way, Chiles instinctively knew by the expression on his Captain's face that his day was about to get a lot worse. Chiles knelt over the wrapped body when the Captain approached and stood directly over him.

Though the Captain thought highly of Detective Chiles' abilities, he would never let it be known. Chiles was thirty or so, but to the Captain he was still an over-idealistic kid who took too damn long to cover a crime scene.

"Goddamn it, Chiles! You better have something for me or I'm going to sling your balls so hard you won't be able to walk for a week!" the Captain barked at him. "Well, Detective, you've been out here all morning. You've got to have found something by now."

Chiles swallowed hard before he replied. "No, sir. Not really."

"What the hell do you mean, not really?" the Captain growled.

"I've got the area secure. I've got officers out questioning anyone they can find around here. But, I'm sure you've noticed that this isn't much of a high traffic area. There's a fish canning plant at the end of the alley and a restaurant around the corner, but neither would have been open late last night. The rest of these are just abandoned buildings. We're hoping to come across any transients that may have taken shelter in one of these buildings last night. Even if they were here, they could've missed everything since there are no windows facing this alleyway. I've been combing this place from end to end and still haven't come up with anything. It just doesn't make any sense, Captain."

As he spoke, Detective Chiles didn't look at the Captain. He glanced up from the puddle he'd been watching as rain dropped lightly into it, creating miniature tidal waves. He realized he'd said more than he should have. The Captain darted his cold eyes between him and the tape body outline. Even though obviously angry, Chiles could see the Captain was interested in hearing what he had to say.

Looking away from the Captain, Chiles' focus fell on a dumpster down the alley. He knew it was empty because he opened the heavy, rusted, metal lid when he first arrived on the scene, looking for anything carelessly discarded. No such luck. There'd been nothing inside it.

Detective Chiles felt he now had the floor and should continue. "He wasn't killed here. He was already dead when he was dumped in this place. The wounds that killed him must have been inflicted hours before he was brought here."

Chiles had not raised his eyes, but instead spoke to the body of the dead councilman. All the time he spoke, he could feel the Captain's intense presence bouncing off the wet pavement, trying to slap him in the face. The weather and circumstances made him feel cold before the Captain had arrived. Now, with the Captain menacingly standing over him, he felt too warm in his long trench coat.

Doggedly, he continued with his assessment, "What doesn't make sense is…why was he left here?"

Promptly, the Captain interrupted him. "What doesn't make sense to me is why someone took the time to pull his damn pants down to his ankles and take off his damn shoes!"

Clearly the Captain had been informed of the body's condition when first found, Chiles thought. "I suppose for the same reason whoever did this made sure his face was pointed at the ground. It was to shame him as much as possible, even in death. But what really doesn't make sense to me, sir, is why didn't they just dump him at the end of the alley. Not too many cars would fit down here, so he was most likely dragged here." At the end of his explanation, Detective Chiles had to raise his voice due to the rise in commotion coming from the other side of the taped-off area that was being guarded by uniformed officers.

"What are you saying, Chiles?" the Captain asked, slapping away the accumulation of raindrops from his face as if they deserved the death penalty.

Detective Chiles reflected on his answer for a moment before speaking, something he told himself to do more in life. Then, he said, "I mean whoever did this, did it for some sort of a symbolic act, but they meant for the body to be easily found and identified. Also, they wanted us to easily see that they slowly pulverized and sliced this man to death. They then dragged him down this alley, pulled down his slacks, took off his shoes, turned him face down, and left his body to bleed out whatever blood was left."

When Chiles paused, just as he'd expected, the Captain spoke before he had the chance to continue. "So what doesn't make sense about that?"

Looking up, Chiles accepted the invitation to join the Captain in a tense stare. He felt water from the rain moving under his shortly cropped hair down the back of his neck. This added to his annoyance.

"What doesn't make sense is why, if this was a symbolic execution, for whatever reason, and we were meant to find this body so easily, then why did they leave it here in this part of SoMa? They could have dumped it in numerous other dark places just as easily without being seen that would have been much more certain for the discovery of the body. We're only here now because a couple of delivery guys took a wrong turn and then happened to see this body down here. This could have easily gone unnoticed for days, especially with this fog and rain we've had lately," Chiles puzzled, running a finger through the air.

Though Detective Chiles respected his Captain, he didn't appreciate how he had to spell some things out for him that, to him, seemed perfectly logical. He tried to adjust his voice as best he could so that it would not come out as condescending when he explained, "The killer, or killers, aren't familiar with San Francisco, sir." Still, seeing a blank stare from the Captain, he continued. "Sir, they're not from here."

* * *

French Arrest Six ETA Suspects

French police have arrested six suspected militants of the Basque separatist group ETA and seized a cache of explosives just outside the southern city of Bordeaux.

Members of the French anti-terrorist squad and a police special weapons squad raided the flat in Bouscat where two handguns, a homemade rocket-launcher and several detonators were seized in the raid, police said.

One of the six detained at the flat is considered by police to be the head of an ETA reservist cell. It is the third time

in less than a week that French police have cracked down on alleged ETA activities.

Last Saturday, police seized some 700 kilograms of dynamite believed to belong to the group on the outskirts of the southern city of Pau. French police say the group stole the dynamite three years ago. The dynamite was located close to where a suspected ETA member was arrested by anti-terrorist police. The police suspect the dynamite was originally stolen from Brittany in northern France with the help of Breton nationalists.

On Monday, the French authorities also found suspected ETA documents and equipment used to make car license plates in a van near Pau.

5

Washington, DC

AS SOON AS GIBSON spoke, he realized he shouldn't have made it sound so much like a question. "You wanted to see me, sir?" He was standing at attention in front of the desk of the Deputy Director for the Federal Bureau of Investigation's Counter Terrorism Department because he'd been ordered to be there. Even though Agent Gibson didn't like it, he would have to deal with taking orders from the little prick. There was no question about it.

The Deputy Director didn't acknowledge his existence, as he had his nose stuck in a dossier when the secretary led Gibson into the large office. He made Gibson wait for a full two minutes before responding. Gibson had seen this tactic many times in his twenty-year plus career with the FBI. He was being "iced" before having something big laid on him.

"You may sit," came a cool, practiced voice. Everything about the Deputy Director looked stiff to Agent Gibson—even his expensive looking three piece, light gray suit looked uncomfortable.

John Gibson didn't like being iced by anyone. He was also wearing a suit, a dark brown one, but he had the satisfaction of knowing his was loose and comfortable. Refusing the offered chair, he responded in a firm tone: "I prefer to remain standing, sir."

A pair of narrow eyes rose from the dossier strewn on the oversized desk. Who needs a desk that big? Gibson asked himself as he met the somewhat irritated look with his own unblinking gaze.

By now, he no longer cared for the rules of politics that told him he should bow down to anyone in a senior position. Yes, he would take orders, but he refused to kiss anyone's ass. He figured it would one day most likely cost him his job. If it did, he could always be a security guard at the Smithsonian.

A career as a government employee had many downsides. Living in the capital of the overrun bureaucracy exemplified them ten-fold. As far as Gibson was concerned, Washington DC drowned itself in its own piles of stinking horse manure. The little prick in front of him had probably never even fired a gun, yet he'd been rewarded with this current position for having done some political deed.

Peering over his small, gold rimmed glasses, the Deputy Director finally looked at the man before him. He couldn't help but feel somewhat uneasy in the presence of one of the Bureau's most decorated and respected agents. He decided to ease his attitude. "As you wish," he said as he adjusted his position in his overstuffed leather chair. Then he continued, "We've got a delicate matter that you've been recommended to take care of." The Deputy Director gave a grave nod with his head in the direction of the bulging file on his desk.

Gibson darted his eyes at the file before bringing them back to rest on the Deputy Director's meticulously arranged head of hair. He didn't like the man's eyes. They were too small and dark. He was doing his best to avoid them. Clearing his throat he said, "I thought everything we do here at the FBI is delicate, sir."

Probably placed too much emphasis on the *sir*, but too late now to do anything about it, he immediately thought to himself.

The Deputy Director flashed his perfect, gleaming teeth before agreeing, "Of course, everything we handle is delicate. But not everything we handle is as much concern to the Director, or the people upstairs, or to the people in that big house over there on Pennsylvania Avenue. And now that we have the overriding objective of defending Homeland Security, you should consider everything as a delicate matter…"

Pausing, the Deputy Director knew he now had the full attention of this obviously bitter field agent. Of course, he realized he was stretching the line of concern a little too far, but figured Gibson wouldn't know. It was well known that Gibson was not political. But he was one of the Bureau's best—everyone agreed on that point.

Actually, it had been the Director of their division himself who actually picked Gibson to handle the affair in San Francisco, overstepping the Bureau's agents that were already posted in California. Those agents were ordered to stay away because the Director knew Gibson was a man that could take care of things without the fuss and commotion most other overly showy agents would cause. If there were more like him, the country would run as smoothly as the Director's Duke University graduation ceremony, he often told people.

Curious, Gibson asked, "Did some reputable politician get drunk and kill someone again with their car?"

Sneering at the remark, the Deputy Director admitted to himself that so far the meeting wasn't going well.

The Deputy Director remembered that his boss, the Director of the Counter Terrorism Division, had smiled when he told him he would be able to handle Agent Gibson without any problems.

The Deputy Director had corralled many difficult men in his still billowing career and figured this one would be no different. Remembering back though, he recalled hearing the Director laugh when he closed the door to his office. He figured he would need a new strategy for this particular agent. Instead of responding to the sarcastic remark with the usual smirk on his face, he tried a grin. "No, that's not why you've been called here. But it does have to do with a politician and a killing. Not here. In San Francisco."

Immediately, the Deputy Director noticed a change in Agent Gibson's demeanor.

"Who?" Gibson asked, easing his guard.

"His name was José Aldarossa Arana, a very popular city councilman. Many believed he would become the next mayor of San Francisco. This morning his body was found by the San Francisco Police Department. The San Francisco Chief of Police has promised full cooperation with us and we want you to get out there as soon as possible. They've secured the scene where the body was found, but at our request have left the scene as it is for us to have a look. A flight has been arranged for you that leaves from Dulles in three hours."

"Dulles? On a commercial flight?" Gibson asked.

"Yes, Dulles. Unfortunately, it seems we don't have any jets available to fly you out to San Francisco early this afternoon. Therefore, we have to get you out there by way of a commercial flight. As you know, we have a lot of agents on the Midnight Stalker case in Chicago and Detroit right now. That means we have a lot of our jets standing by in those cities." A mischievous grin took over his face as he continued, "Since this is a top priority, we have to get you out there as soon as possible, however possible. This is all we have available," he said as he flashed his bleached white teeth.

Gibson accepted he'd been beat for the moment and there was no way of changing what had already put into place. He decided to put an end to the little bastard's moment of glory and move on. In spite of himself, he had become interested. Everything sounded so mysterious, even for the FBI. Yet, he was suspicious and his tone reflected it when he asked, "We have tons of people out in California. Why aren't they taking care of this?"

Since first laying eyes on Agent John Gibson, this was the part the Deputy Director had been dreading. In his heart, he figured this man didn't deserve the amount of praise he was now forced to bestow onto him.

"You're right. Normally, in an affair like this they would handle it. They were notified shortly after the discovery of the body, but a call from here ordered them to stand down as someone high up wants you to handle it." He paused and exhaled heavily, blinking his eyelids hard before continuing, "The division Director himself has asked for you to take care of this investigation."

"You mean Bob told you to have me sent out for this?"

Silently, the Deputy Director fumed inside as he realized Gibson was close enough to the Director to call him by his first name.

"Yes, Director Robert Smith asked for you," the Deputy Director mumbled.

"That's great, but why, sir? City councilmen are dusted all the time in this country, even ones that are prospective mayors. Who cares so much about this one?"

Gibson was aware of the cruelty of his words, but justified them in his head. He'd seen too many mutilated corpses. Also, beneath the tough image the Deputy Director fondled so carelessly, Gibson could see he wasn't the only one in the room that had noticed his harsh words. The face in front of him looked almost hurt from his apparent lack of humanity. If this guy wants to continue in a career of politics, he'd better forget that humanity crap, Gibson thought.

The Deputy Director cleared his throat before he spoke. "The difference is that we believe this…" he paused to clear his throat, "we believe this execution may have been committed by the Basque terrorist group, ETA."

The Deputy Director leaned back in his chair for the first time since the meeting began. Even a man as hardened as Gibson could not hide his curiosity. He knew he now had Gibson's full attention.

"ETA, I hate those guys," Gibson said under his breath. "So, that's why you've called on me," he said out loud.

"Well, you're the most seasoned agent in our Counter Terrorism Department and you do have first-hand experience with ETA. Remember Miami?" A sideways grin crossed the Deputy Director's face.

This sniveling little bitch needs to get out more, thought Gibson to himself. Out loud, he said, "Of course I remember Miami."

Even though he tried hard to dismiss the Miami affair, the mention of it now brought back a sudden flash of vivid images.

* * *

Ramon Maria Azpiroz had lived in Miami working as a used car salesman for over two years when he was finally tracked down. In the 80s, he'd been one of ETA's key gunmen. For years, the Spanish government tried to pin something solid on him, but he always managed to slip away. But when El Fusil, as he was known in Spain, walked up to two Spanish policemen in a central Barcelona square and fired a total of ten bullets into them, nearly twenty people were able to identify him. More than likely the reason for so many witnesses was that the crime was committed in broad daylight, on a popular city street. But also due to the fact that El Fusil had not bothered to even wear the typical black ski masks that he and his ETA compatriots so often wore.

Agent Gibson hated terrorists, but he especially hated these kind of terrorists. Some kid surely witnessed the horrible scene that day and would never be able to forget seeing such evil in humanity. It was a cowardly execution. Maybe they all were.

What had those two Spanish policemen done to be killed? They were just doing their jobs like everyone else. Did this Basque Homeland and Liberty group, or whatever the hell it was that they called themselves, think that policeman weren't necessary in modern society? Gibson greatly enjoyed slamming El Fusil's face into the ground when they finally arrested him.

Azpiroz was the first known Basque terrorist arrested in the States. He also then had the privilege of being the first Basque terrorist extradited from the United States. Gibson hoped the Spanish government would fry his cowardly ass. It turned out though that for all their hard talk, they didn't even give him a life sentence. However, they did make sure to lock him up in a shithole of a prison in a far corner of Spain, away from the Basque Country.

Gibson felt this served the bastard right. They should make it as difficult as possible for anyone Azpiroz cared about, or who cared about him, to visit him. But he wondered what sort of person could even care for a person like that.

At the extradition trial, Gibson watched Azpiroz when two Spanish authorities, probably some sort of governmental lawyers, presented evidence to the American judge of Azpiroz's involvement in eight known murders. Azpiroz must have given up trying to run from his crimes, because he did not deny any of the allegations. Carefully, Gibson watched the murderer's face as the Spaniards read off the list of charges against him in Spain. He couldn't believe what he saw. An unmistakable expression stretched across Azpiroz's arrogant face—pride. Azpiroz noticed Gibson watching him at the time and turned to deliberately give him a big grin.

* * *

John Gibson now knew that Ramon Azpiroz had come to Miami via Mexico City, where he spent six months getting by somehow. Then in Cancun, when a cruise ship made its scheduled daytime stop before eventually heading to Miami, someone arranged to smuggle him aboard. For the rest of the trip around the Caribbean, Azpiroz worked aboard the ship as a dishwasher. Exactly who got him his fake passport and arranged for him to get on the ship remained a mystery. Though the Mexican police pledged to "get right on the investigation," it would most likely remain a mystery.

According to the Spanish Police, Azpiroz first slipped across the Pyrenees after killing the two policemen in Barcelona into France before moving on to Mexico. This was, of course, back when there were still actual borders to be crossed between France and Spain. He hid out in the city of Bayonne for about a month before being transported to Brittany, where sympathy for the Basque nationalist cause is deeply rooted, Gibson was told by someone. From Brittany, he was smuggled on a transatlantic cargo ship going to Mexico.

Evidently this guy stepped off the cruise ship in Miami with a fake passport, a new name, and probably a smile on his face. Azpiroz then penetrated the mighty fortress of America without breaking a sweat. All those Haitians in their crude rafts dreaming of nothing else but to come to America and be nothing more than a janitor would be jealous. Once in the States, Azpiroz rented a modest townhouse, found a job, and even obtained a Florida driver's license.

It secretly amazed Gibson at how fast and easily these well known and recognized terrorists could move and disappear in the world. He'd spent his career going after these terrorists and it was usually the same story. Though the world was becoming a smaller place, these guys would always have their ways of eluding multiple countries' top security forces.

Gibson remembered the stakeout on Azpiroz's house. He'd noticed the house's back yard looked as if it hadn't been mowed in a year. He also noticed a beautiful vase full of bright flowers in a window. It was puzzling why an international terrorist would have a pretty bouquet of flowers in his front window.

The Spanish government pleaded with the U.S. to help in apprehending Azpiroz. Probably because once traced to Mexico, he then boarded the Florida bound cruise ship.

Gibson was briefed by the Director on his assignment. With great emphasis, the high profile concerns of the case were made aware to him. It was imperative that the case be conducted smoothly, quickly, and as quietly as possible.

Being a seasoned member of the Bureau's Counter Terrorism Unit, Gibson was aware of the Basque nationalist movement, even if the group had never set foot in the States, to anyone's knowledge. Even so, he devoted an entire day to studying ETA and the organization's history before heading to Miami. His assignments normally were focused on domestic terrorist groups and, in a normal situation, the assignment would have gone to some other agent more involved with international groups. But the Director sent his most reliable man instead of his most qualified.

When the Director explained the case held delicate importance, he also explained to Gibson that the American government wanted to remain on the sidelines of the Basque conflict in Europe.

"The United States has a firm standing relationship with both France and Spain. We need to stay as far away as possible from the Basque conflict in these countries," he said. "The most desirable political position is to take neither side on the issue. Of course, we should lean heavily toward helping the French and Spanish governments, but it cannot be forgotten that there are thousands of Americans with Basque heritage. The best position to take is to take no position at all. Let the French and Spanish deal with their own problems," the Director concluded.

In this case, however, a terrorist had crossed into the United States and an example needed to be sent that the U.S. would not be a safe haven for Basque terrorists. Proving political asylum would be one matter to consider in specific cases, but not if the person had just murdered two innocent people and laid down his gun before proclaiming to be a politically persecuted refugee. *El Fusil* needed to be apprehended and sent back to Spain, but the operation needed to be conducted discreetly and thoroughly. Even the press was going to be shut out of this one as best as legally possible on grounds of national security, Gibson was informed.

Agent Gibson forwarded a profile of Azpiroz he received from the Spaniards to the Miami Police Department. It didn't take them long to match the picture with the driver's license of a man working on a used car lot, a man with no criminal record. He appeared to be a short, stocky, dark skinned man who coworkers described as friendly and hard working. A man whose neighbors described as polite and quiet, even though he spoke Spanish with a different accent than they did. In fact, he even used different words in Spanish for some things.

With the help of a Miami Police Department SWAT team, Gibson took Azpiroz while the fugitive was coming home from work one day. Azpiroz looked like any other working man in the U.S. with a T-shirt tucked into a pair of jeans. When Gibson called out to him using his real name, Azpiroz responded in heavily accented English that he did not understand. Seconds later, Azpiroz had his face smashed into the ground.

Azpiroz told Gibson he was surprised to have been found, but would not resist arrest. Gibson didn't intend to give him any chance to resist. While ramming Azpiroz's face into the steaming pavement, he thought of the two young Spanish policemen.

When a call was placed to Spain, a group of Spaniards from the Spanish Embassy arrived in Miami the next day to identify El Fusil. The Spanish government was given forty-five days to prepare a case for the extradition of Ramon Maria Azpiroz. They only needed a couple of days.

* * *

"That's the reason you're being assigned this one."

Gibson heard a shrill voice snap him from his reflection. He realized he'd been staring at the vase of flowers on the Deputy Director's table. That nice secretary of his must have put them there. The Deputy Director hadn't even noticed them, he was sure.

"Gibson!"

"Yes, sir," Gibson responded.

"Are you paying attention?"

"Yes, sorry," Gibson said, as he forced his gaze away from the vase of flowers and tried to focus on the Deputy Director's ear instead of his eyes.

"Continuing—your assignment is to go to San Francisco and investigate the murder, and then track down the killers by whatever means you deem necessary. First off, you need to determine whether or not the murder was indeed done by any Basque group. And if that's the case, determine if foreign nationals are involved. If you prove, without a doubt, that there is zero chance of the murder having not been done for political motives, we will take you off the case immediately and turn it back over to the San Francisco PD. You'll have anything you need at your disposal. The timeframe for the assignment is open-ended, but don't mess around out there, you hear me?" the Deputy Director asserted as he raised an accusing finger at Gibson.

"Yes, sir. Thank you for the assignment." Gibson always looked forward to an opportunity to bring down terrorists. He could even put up with a pompous ass such as this one when, in the end, he would have the chance to go out and bust some bad guys. Now these bastards were going after politicians in the U.S. He planned to make them pay for it. Having gotten one of them already, he was now going to get another. Probably would even get a chance to rough them up a bit. The thought of it strengthened his motivation.

Sensing eagerness in Agent Gibson, the Deputy Director now enjoyed the cooperation and attention he was receiving. "Now, as you are aware, this organization, if it was indeed ETA behind this, is known to be very, how would one say, *brutal* to those who come after them." The sideways grin returned. "And they may remember you." The Deputy Director made extra sure to emphasize the word *you* and followed it with a menacing stare.

"To hell with the bastards!" Gibson said as he turned, not asking if he was dismissed or not, before walking out of the office.

* * *

Basque Militant Ejected from Court

A former leader of the Basque separatist group, ETA, accused of organizing an assassination attempt on the Spanish king, was thrown out of his own trial yesterday after declaring he did not recognize the court.

The accused man, whose trial began amid fresh violence in the Basque country, had been specially extradited from a French prison to answer the charges in Spain.

The accused was ordered to leave after refusing to take his place in the dock and shouting in the Basque language that he refused to take part "in this circus."

Spanish prosecutors allege the individual recruited for and planned numerous assassination attempts on the king.

French authorities want the accused back in France within four months to serve out an eight-year sentence for terrorism.

Hours before the trial got underway, a car bomb, believed to be the work of the ETA, exploded in the Basque town of Sestao, injuring two people. One man was a leader within the Socialist Party. He had to have a leg amputated.

6

Reno, Nevada

SEBASTIAN PARKER GLANCED AT THE COVER of the booklet everyone attending the seminar had been handed by the troop of rail-thin attractive girls standing post at the room's exits. The title was: *Basques in America.*

Looking out over the audience in the room, he noticed the stunning blonde girl in the front row. Her gaze was fixed on Professor Miller as he prepared his notes at the podium. It made Sebastian Parker want to gag.

The Professor raised his head from his notes. "Okay, everyone, let's split into groups of four or five to conduct a few exercises. My lovely assistants here," he pointed at his volunteer girls, "will hand out the exercises I want you all to be working on. I'll make my way around to talk with every group individually."

Chairs squeaked and creaked as a hundred people turned to find with whom they would group. The noise gradually settled into a muffled hum after the brief explosion as people moved and adjusted to their newly formed groups. Parker found himself in a group with a girl with braces, who looked like she was twelve; a red-headed woman with 80s hair-sprayed bangs about his age; and, a twenty-year-old guy with a shaved head and a small patch of facial hair on his chin. He realized sitting near the back was not such a good idea as he was stuck with the kind of people those in front had made sure were not in their group.

Parker wished he were in the group with the Blonde in the front row. After all, the Professor did have very good taste. Though, without the distraction of being so close to a knockout female body, he knew he would be able to better concentrate on the issues to be discussed.

One of the Professor's beauties handed him a sheet of paper on which were a list of questions. He quickly noticed she had on a tight, light green skirt topped by a white, short-sleeved sweater that nicely displayed the roundness of her breasts. Just as she walked down the aisle past him, he felt a vibration against his inner thigh. He pulled out his cell phone to see who was calling. It was his boss at the main offices of the CIA in Langley, Virginia. Obviously, the call was important.

Quietly, Parker gathered his things and politely excused himself from his odd group. Since his boss knew his passions, he would not have disturbed Parker during anything related to Basque affairs unless absolutely necessary. Therefore, this had to be something serious. Even before answering, he knew his getaway was prematurely canceled.

* * *

A cloud of smoke escaped out the cracked car window before the stub of a cigarette landed in a flash of embers on the highway. Her legs ached from sitting in a car for such a long time. People in America were crazy to drive such long distances. Why didn't they use trains more? They passed a road sign saying they were still 75 miles from Boise. Mentally, she calculated that must be about 120 kilometers. A 120 kilometer trip by itself was a considerable journey by car in Europe, but here it was just another drive on a highway. "Americans are all *fous*!" she said to herself.

The man driving the old car told her he was taking her to the Boise Airport. From there she was going to fly to Denver, and from Denver to Buenos Aires. He told her the Basque presence in Buenos Aires was still strong. She was certain she knew much more about the Basques in South America then he, and even considered telling him so, but didn't because she didn't want him to start thinking she might be interested in him.

As he drove, the man tried talking to her in French a few times, but she merely responded with *oui* or *non* or a shrug to his efforts at conversation. Graciana Etceverria preferred to stare out the window at nothing while puffing away at her cigarettes. She figured he probably was a decent *mec.* After all, he did have Basque ancestry, but he was too young and too good looking of a man for her to engage in conversation. In her experience, young, good looking men always wanted more from her than just conversation. They would get to a point where they would tell her how she was sexy, hot, or *belle*; but she already knew she was all of these things and hated for men to remind her. They always missed the point: she had no intention of wasting her time with penises. Graciana used men for what she wanted from them and that was all. She'd encountered very few men who seemed worth the time to become better acquainted. Lopé, Aurelion, and Peio were rare exceptions.

Stealing a quick glance at the man driving the car, a small car by American standards but huge by European ones, she noticed he was looking nervous and disappointed. He probably felt blessed to be assigned to her. She was wearing black leather pants and a skin-tight red top revealing her small nipples. More than once, when she glanced at him, she caught him attempting to drop his eyes to check her out. At these times, she always met his quick glances with a stare of pure hatred. Every once in a while, though, she would tease him by gently running her long, French-tipped fingernails along her taunt upper thigh of her leg propped up on the dashboard. Maybe he even fantasized about getting some action on the trip between Stockton and Boise. Looking at his face, Graciana Etceverria knew he had.

Some strands of her hair had come loose from her ponytail, resting on the sides of her face. She used both hands to tuck them behind her ears. Sorry to disappoint you, guy, she said to herself.

Her lighter appeared in her hand and another cigarette hung from her mouth. The snapping sound of the lighter made him turn to look at her. In the light of the flame, he met her piercing green eyes. Though she knew he was waiting for her to offer him one, she delicately blew out a thin line of smoke from her tightly pursed lips into his face and turned her head away from him. *Stupid men.*

* * *

As the Captain walked away from Detective Chiles, he stared at the bare brick walls that entrenched the narrow corridor between them. Jacobs strutted down to inform the Captain of a call for him from the Chief on the walkie-talkie. It was common knowledge that the Captain dreaded talking to the Chief. In fact, the Captain hated the Chief more than anyone hated the Captain.

Chiles watched him walk back toward the ever-growing crowd of people in the street. He had to focus through the thickening fog to see anything. Idly, he wondered if there were other places like San Francisco where fog could actually be thicker in the afternoon than it had been in the morning. There were none that he knew of, but he'd only been to a couple other states and to Tijuana, like a lot of Californians.

Now that the Captain was not going to bark at him anyone, he moved much slower. Jacobs lingered longer than necessary after the Captain started for the call. He looked down at Chiles bent over the body shape outlined in tape on the pavement and enjoyed feeling taller than him.

Jacobs eventually left and made his way toward the street. Chiles returned to his investigation of the area directly around the tape body. Just as he was picking up a rusty nail with his gloved hand, he heard an authoritative command from the Captain. Looking up, Chiles saw his Captain moving quickly back in his direction.

"Chiles! Chiles! Stop what you're doing right now!"

Chiles gently replaced the nail on the pavement. He waited patiently, still crouching, for whatever was coming down the alley.

"Get up, Chiles. The Chief just informed me that we've been ordered to stand down. The FBI is taking over. We're just supposed to keep the perimeter secure and continue questioning whoever we can find around here." The Captain took a couple of deep breaths and eased his attitude. "We've been out-ranked."

Chiles knew the routine, but still didn't like it. "I could have handled this one, sir," he said, as he stood up.

"I know you would have, son," the Captain said as he patted him roughly on the shoulder.

"Are they on their way?" Chiles asked.

"Yes and no."

Chiles gave the Captain a puzzled glance as the Captain turned and motioned for him to follow.

As they walked, the Captain told Chiles, "They're sending in a local unit to make sure the body is secure at the coroner's, but it seems that even they are being over stepped on this one. They're actually sending some people out from DC."

When the Captain looked over at the tall, young detective walking next to him, he felt a tinge of paternal pride. "You did a good job here. How about letting me buy you a cup of coffee, Chiles? I'll even splurge a little and take us to one of those fancy places."

"Will Jacobs be there?" Chiles asked.

Smiling, the Captain said, "No. No Jacobs. I need a break from him myself."

"Sounds good then, sir."

* * *

Strong coffee. After fighting through the Metro just to travel a few miles, Gibson was back in his small apartment and more coffee was his first order of business. There was not much time to pack, but he made time to sit still for a moment with a full mug of his special brew to think things over. When he turned on his small radio, the weather forecast was on again. The cracking voice of a man announced it was going to be unbearably humid for the next few days. The air quality index was going to be creeping dangerously high for the DC metro area.

Gibson began to think about Azpiroz. To him, Azpiroz represented a destructive element that needed to be stopped. He thought some politicians were also destructive elements, but they were much harder to put away. As he stared into his coffee mug, the weather report ended and the soft trumpet of Miles Davis crooned from the radio.

Suddenly his phone sprang into action. Regrettably, Gibson doused Mr. Davis and picked up the phone.

"Hello."

"Hi, John, this is Bob."

"Good morning, sir."

"To you too, John. Is the cell phone they gave you not working? I just tried calling you on it and you didn't answer."

"Oh, that damn thing. Sorry, I haven't turned it on yet," Gibson explained as he pulled the plastic, folded phone from his pants pocket, staring at the contraption as if it had fallen from another planet.

"Why don't you turn it on now, John. Giving you a cell phone to take isn't going to do us much good if you don't have it turned on," the Director chided.

"Okay, okay," Gibson said between clenched teeth. He opened the small phone and gazed blankly at it. "So, how do you turn it on?"

The Director laughed loudly into the landline phone. "You really are getting old, buddy. Just hit that little button in the bottom right-hand corner."

Doing as he was told, Gibson immediately saw a light go on at the top of the phone. "Okay, the damn thing's on, now leave me alone about it, would ya? You know your Deputy Director is a real jackass?"

"I know, I know. I don't like him much either. But he's kissed the right asses to end up getting my job one these days, so we're stuck dealing with him."

Changing subjects the Director said, with noticeable tension in his voice, "John, I've got to tell you something."

"I'm listening."

"Well, you're not going to be alone on this one." The Director paused.

"What are you saying, Bob?"

"Listen, it's out of my hands, John. I told them you could handle it by yourself, but I don't think even they are calling the shots on this one."

"Who are *they*?"

"Never mind, John."

"So, what are you saying: that someone else from the Bureau is going to be looking over my shoulder while I'm out there?" Gibson bit his tongue for raising his voice. He thought of his division Director as an old and trusted friend.

"No, John. It's not someone else from the Bureau. You're going to be working with a guy from the CIA. He'll be meeting you in San Francisco."

Gibson no longer tried to keep the annoyance out of his tone. "The CIA! You've got to be kidding me, Bob! How the hell am I going to work with someone from that place? They're all a bunch of paranoid freaks!"

"I'm sorry, old buddy. Like I said, there's nothing I can do."

A silence came over the phone and Gibson noticed the faucet of his sink was gently dripping. Taking a deep breath, he finally asked, "Who is it?"

"His name is Sebastian Parker."

"Do you know anything about him?"

"He sounds solid, John. He's not a field man, but an analyst."

"Wait, you paused before you spoke. What else aren't you telling me about him, Bob?" Gibson almost demanded.

"Nothing. It's nothing," the Director quickly assured his agent.

"Bob!"

"All right, all right. It's just that he's younger than us," confessed his superior.

"So?"

"So—quite a bit younger."

"What's quite a bit younger?"

"Well, about half our age."

"This can't be happening! First you tell me I have to share the spot with some desk jockey from the CIA. Now you're telling me he's just a goddamn kid? What the hell's going on here, Bob?"

"I admit that it's strange and that most people over at the CIA think they're goddamn James Bond, but we were asked by Homeland Security to collaborate on the investigation. Parker's young, but I spoke earlier with some people and supposedly he's one of their future stars. And he's one of the leading specialists on the Basque nationalist movement and ETA over there. First, he's going to be there to help you prove Basque involvement. Second, to decipher political motive. Third, to help identify the group responsible. You're just going to have to deal with it."

Gibson rolled his eyes, wishing the Director could see his action through the phone.

"Let me know when you've got something and have a nice flight, John."

Gibson was about to disconnect the call when he heard his boss add, "Oh, and John, if the kid is old enough, buy him a beer after a good day." Gibson could picture the Director's beaming smile.

"If you weren't the Director of my division and my boss, I think I would tell you to go to hell, sir." Gibson responded.

There was a chuckle as the Director replied, "Don't let that stop you."

"All right then. Go to hell, sir."

The Director laughed loudly into the phone as he broke the connection.

Gibson put his coffee mug in the sink and rinsed it before quickly going into his bedroom where he threw some clothes into a small suitcase. He was used to packing in a hurry. Within minutes he was out the door, headed for Dulles International Airport.

* * *

As Parker expected, his short vacation away from work was definitely over. He felt as if he'd pinched a bit of his scrotum in his zipper by what his boss told him on the phone. He was assigned to a field case.

When his boss said that he was to leave Reno immediately and get to San Francisco, Parker sneered into the phone. He blurted his first thought, "The joke is funny, but I know I'm being called back because some high honcho in the agency needs a report done yesterday or sooner."

His boss did not find his response amusing and simply said, "I am very serious." So it was off to San Francisco for Sebastian Parker.

Parker stood alone in front of the large window of the terminal in Reno's airport. He could see in the distance the arid desert that began where the runways stopped. Tall, lonely looking mountains loomed beyond.

There were not many other people waiting for the short flight to San Francisco, and they were all seated behind him. All except for a little boy and girl who kept running up and down a boarding ramp laughing each time they passed one another. If only happiness remained that simple to hold on to, he thought.

Parker took a long drink of the double espresso he picked up from a coffee stand and tried to focus his thoughts. There was a large coffee stain on the front of his shirt that made it even more difficult for him to concentrate.

Just as was walking from the coffee stand, a locomotive looking young man about his age rammed into him, dumping a nice portion of his coffee down the front of his shirt. In Spanish accented English, the young man simply said, "Pardon'a me," and nervously sped off. Though Parker was momentarily stunned by the brief encounter, he quickly put it out of his mind. There were more important things to ponder, although he could still feel the wetness of the spot on the skin of his chest and it irritated him.

Being assigned to his first field case was exciting, but he was also extremely curious about the circumstances. He reflected on what his boss told him.

Working with the FBI? Nothing of the situation made any sense. Besides that, he was going to be working with some hard-ass agent with a reputation of being a pain. *Fantastic.*

Parker couldn't help but wonder though why a more senior member of his unit was not assigned this case? Then he realized his own question was the answer. He was assigned because it was likely no one else would have accepted the assignment. Also, he was the youngest and newest member of his division, resulting in him having very few choices in any matter.

But perhaps he would like a little action instead of his usual routine of monitoring web sites, reading newspapers, and writing reports at his desk. Besides, he realized the importance of the case and in his mind that erased his doubts. The possibility of ETA bringing its campaign to the States oddly fascinated him.

"Now boarding for flight number 322, non-stop to San Francisco," a light, feminine voice echoed from speakers hidden somewhere out of sight. Parker mentally said good-bye to the high desert and joined the line forming to board the plane.

* * *

ETA Suspects Held after Chase Drama

Two armed suspects from the Basque separatist group ETA have been arrested in France after a high-speed car chase.

Police said the two men were stopped in the town of Aubusson in the Creuse area of central France. The men failed to stop for a traffic check while driving a car with false number plates.

The chase through Aubusson ended when the men's vehicle hit a parked car. Two guns were recovered from the vehicle.

The group is believed to have had a number of key operations in France this year, including a training camp.

7

Washington, DC

THE CAB RIDE TO DULLES International Airport was just how John Gibson preferred—without conversation. He gazed out at the sprawl that now led all the way from the White House to Dulles.

When he stepped out of the cab and paid his fare to the Ethiopian driver, he heard a voice call, "John Gibson?" Turning, he saw a young, skinny man approach him with hair so stiff it looked like it hurt. Gibson nodded his acknowledgment.

"Hello, sir. I'm Paris Fletcher."

Gibson accepted a firm shake. Of course, Gibson noticed the somewhat bizarre name for the young man, but he never enjoyed jumping into someone else's business without a proper invitation. Besides, why give the kid a hard time? He'd passed his first test with him by not calling him *agent* out loud in front of a group of angry looking men that were standing nearby. Gibson wondered if Fletcher actually enjoyed what looked to be his first position at the Bureau: finding transportation and escorting agents at the airport to their planes.

Fletcher gave him a sideways glance as he grabbed Gibson's small suitcase from the back seat of the cab. Handing the suitcase to Gibson, he said, "You mean, you really aren't going to ask me how I ended up with a first name like Paris?"

Gibson slammed the cab door shut and gave a quick wave to the Ethiopian driver. Maybe his fare would help pay for his family's dinner that night, he hoped. He imagined them crammed in some filthy, health code violating apartment in suburban Maryland.

Turning to look at Agent Fletcher when they neared the automatic doors, Gibson noticed the group of dark skinned men watching their every step with increasing hostility. They were gesturing toward them with muffled whispers. He thought to himself why foreigners seemed to stare so much? And if they are so angry about living in the United States, and apparently with every single white American, then why don't they just go back to wherever they came from? America may not be so much of a land of equality anymore, but at least there was no worrying about the military taking over leadership of the government every six months in a bloody coup like in other places. These people should learn some damn respect, he thought.

He felt an urge to whip out his big .45 mm handgun, point it at the group of men, and see if they still wanted to stare. However, chances were they would be better armed, so he decided to put aside the dark impulse.

Bringing his thoughts back to the young agent, he said, "I'll bet you get asked that question all the time. I just thought I'd give you a break."

Fletcher laughed and shook his head. "I appreciate that, I do. But I'm so used to being asked that I don't know what to do when I'm not." Darting a look at his own reflection as the automatic glass doors opened, he continued, "My mom was watching a show once while she was pregnant and there was a boy named Paris on it and she decided she liked the name. So here I am. Believe me, I wish there was a better story—like maybe if I had been conceived in Paris on the banks of the Seine or something. But no. My mom was just watching television." Fletcher shrugged and Gibson saw it made him look ten years younger.

"Well, I think it's better than John, anyway," Gibson said, as they entered the long hall of the terminal. Fletcher smiled.

"Tell me something, Fletcher, did the Deputy Director of my division give you this assignment?" Gibson asked.

"Yes, he did, sir."

"Did he ask you to check if we had jets available before having to find an alternate source?"

"No, sir. He actually told me he wanted you to be on an alternate source."

Gibson clenched his teeth and growled, "That rat bastard!"

"What's that, sir?"

"Forget it. I'm sure you've done a fine job. Let's just get to my *alternate source.*"

As they walked, Gibson noticed one of the airport's moon-cruiser looking transport vehicles traversing the area between the terminal and the entrance building. The sight of these gigantic wheeled buses snapped him from his inner thoughts. The huge wheeled buses looked like something you would see in a sci-fi movie set on Mars.

"So what did you put me on—Delta, Northwest, United?" he casually asked Fletcher as they continued to walk.

"Nope, United Parcel Service." Fletcher appeared proud of his achievement.

"UPS?"

"Yep, UPS. There is a jet leaving in twenty minutes. You won't have to worry about going through security with your piece or dealing with all the tourists and businessmen. You'll actually get there faster too. Don't worry, I've traveled this way before myself and it's gone over perfectly every time. When you arrive in San Francisco, you'll receive a vehicle, hotel reservation information and instructions on where you will meet your contact tomorrow morning."

"So much for peanuts and a movie," Gibson grumbled.

"The pilots might have some beef jerky or something," Fletcher replied, trying not to grin.

* * *

Other members of ETA were meeting him in Caracas—that much Lopé knew. It bothered him though that he didn't know much more than this one simple fact out of the entire operation. For security purposes, none of them were to know where the others were going. Yet, how could he look after his team if he didn't know where they would be?

Still, he had agreed, while knowing he would disagree with the circumstances as soon as the time came. Lopé had done so because he wanted to be a part of the mission, under any conditions, even if it meant biting his tongue in half and ripping out his hair.

Taking out a Basque-American politician who publically spoke out against ETA and the cause—this was huge! Finally, they brought the fight to America and now America would have to face the issue of the Basque independence movement. The fascist governments of Spain and France would no longer be able to hide the issue from the people of the United States. The Basque cause desperately needed outside support, financial as well as moral. Basques in America would now realize the true power and reach of ETA. How could they not after what had been done?

Lopé was taken to Seattle's Sea-Tac Airport where he now sat in the terminal's lobby, waiting to board his flight to Caracas, Venezuela. Surrounding him was an American tourist group, wearing shorts with tucked-in shirts and sneakers.

Why do Americans have to talk so loudly? Do they think the person next to them really can't hear them when they are practically screaming? And why are so many of them fat? Young beautiful Italian people always seemed to grow plump with age, but that could be blamed on a lifetime of eating pasta dishes as appetizers that at a certain age begin to add up. But so many Americans were beyond plump by the age of ten! *Mon dieu*! *C'est dégoûtant*! Does the greasy fat in fast food transfer to babies through breast milk? It must somehow, he concluded.

The fatness surrounding him annoyed him. Lopé wanted to yell out that they all needed to put down their remote controls and get their fat asses outdoors. He wanted to move far away from them, but there were no other empty seats. He was stuck.

It frustrated the hell out of him knowing he would probably be stuck among them on the plane as well. This would only remind him how much he despised Americans and he hoped he would be able to restrain himself from putting one of them out of their overweight, disgusting misery.

To put their excess flesh out of his mind, he tried to picture the faces of his team members. There was Graciana—beautiful, furious, and ruthless. Her fierceness even surprised him at times. Aurelion—smart and determined. And last, there was Peio—strong, athletic and loyal. Peio may not have been the brightest person he'd ever met, but he would never want to get into a fistfight with him. Growing up playing handball and with four mean older brothers had made Peio's hands and body tougher than nails.

Lopé rarely told them how thrilled he was to have been assigned to them by the council as a unit, but considered these three to be the epitome of all that was great of the Basque race. He prayed all would return home. After this, they would probably get the high profile assassinations in Madrid and Barcelona, possibly even Paris. Maybe they would even be made the new anti-tourism unit for the Basque Country? He was already anxious for a new mission. They would become the next legendary commando unit of ETA. He was sure of it.

* * *

Before boarding the small jet, Agent Fletcher handed him a file to review on the way to San Francisco. Gibson had the file open in front of him before the plane taxied onto the runway. He saw that the file had been assembled by a division within the CIA, and that the primary author was a one S. Parker. He'd soon know how thorough of a person had been assigned to the case with him, he thought.

Instead of looking through the contents of the file right away, he stared out the small window next to him at the concrete below. He had his own seat behind the two pilots and was glad the extent of conversation he would have to deal with on the flight was the nod of the head he gave them when he boarded the plane.

Agent Fletcher said something to the two pilots and something to him, but Gibson wasn't listening. He didn't even notice the plane was taking off until he realized he was no longer transfixed on a crack in the concrete, but looking down upon perfectly lined rows of newly built large houses that all looked the same. Glancing below at the planned housing communities that speckled the gently rolling green Virginia countryside reminded Gibson of something he recently read. The article reported that Loudon County in Virginia, which they were currently flying over, was one of the fastest growing counties in the country.

Then looking down, he noticed the bulging file on his lap and remembered he had work to do. In the file was information regarding terrorist activities in the previous year, suspected to have been the work of Euskadi Ta Askulduna, or ETA (Basque Homeland and Freedom), or its French counterpart Iparretarrak, IK (Those of the North). There were even records of activities from the youth wing of Haika (Rise Up) in Spain and France. Following and monitoring the activities of domestic terrorist groups, even those seen as potential threats, had detoured him from keeping up with current activities of foreign terrorist organizations.

But he'd learned a fair amount about ETA, the organization and its activities, from his Miami experience. In his opinion, ETA was like most other terrorist groups around the world. They were typically paramilitary, on the extreme end of left or right wings, in this case Marxist, predominately unpopular with the masses they represented, and often ruthlessly dedicated to a lost cause they had long since lost sight of. Even so, Gibson was surprised to be holding a folder so thick with documented activities covering such a short period of time. The headlines, that never seemed to be covered in the American nightly newscasts or newspapers, bled from the pages before him.

Spain: A bomb planted by ETA in a cemetery fails to explode. It was planted in a flowerpot and was intended to go off during a memorial service for one of ETA's victims.

Spain: Two people suspected of being in ETA's Barcelona commando unit are arrested in that city by Spanish police.

Spain: ETA publicly threatens all signatories of the anti-terrorist pact between the Popular Party (PP) and the Spanish Socialist Party (PSOE).

Spain: Several buildings are destroyed in the Spanish Basque Country. The businesses targeted had reportedly disregarded paying their "revolutionary tax," a major source of ETA's funding. Spanish police arrest the editor of the Basque magazine *Ardi Beltza*. The editor is charged with identifying assassination targets for ETA in the magazine.

Spain: A car bomb attempt fails in central Madrid. Thirty-five kilograms of dynamite are discovered in pressure cookers in a vehicle that caught fire when the detonator went off but did not explode. Soon after, a car blows up in a nearby city, thought to be the getaway vehicle used in the operation. ETA is known to dispose of evidence by blowing up cars used in attacks and members of the group often place their explosives in pressure cookers.

Spain: Just two days after the Basque government in Spain announces an early election for the region, a powerful car bomb explodes near a railway station in San Sebastian, Spain. A town official, a member of the PSOE, was walking by at the time of the remote detonation. He was injured and two others were killed by the blast.

France: In a joint operation, French and Spanish police arrest two members of ETA in Anglet, France. One of them is suspected to be ETA's top military leader. He had disappeared in the French Basque Country for nearly ten years, thought to be running ETA's military activities from France.

Spain: A Spanish army officer narrowly escapes from his car before it explodes from a bomb attached beneath his feet in Navarre, Spain. A sentry post of the paramilitary Spanish Civil Guard is demolished from a planted bomb.

***Spain*:** Spanish police discover a flat that is referred to as an ETA "bomb factory" in Barcelona.

***Spain*:** A crudely made bomb explodes in the post office of Hernani, Spain. A bomb explodes in a gas station and another in front of a Spanish bank in Ondarroa. A barrage of Molotov cocktails is thrown through the windows of the Bilbao office of the Spanish newspaper, *El Correo Espanol*, destroying the office.

***Spain*:** Nearly twenty youths are arrested by the Spanish police under charges that they were members of the Basque youth organization Haika and have illegal links with ETA.

France: French police claim to have prevented an escape plan by ETA. Three members of ETA being held in French prisons were to be transferred from a prison in central France to one in Paris. The French anti-terrorist agency, La Division Nationale Antiterroriste (DNAT), had been informed of a planned attack on the vehicle that would have transported the three inmates and rescheduled the transfer.

France: A report by the French anti-terrorist analyst group, L'Unite de Coordination de la Lutte Antiterroriste (UCLAT), leaks information into the French magazine, *Le Figaro*, stating terrorist threat to be rapidly rising in France due to an increase of terrorist activities concerning the

Basque Country. It reports a fear that Iparretarrak is on the verge of increasing their activities on French soil.

France: ETA members steal 1.6 tons of explosives, 20,000 detonators and fuses from a warehouse outside of Grenoble, France. The group is suspected of being members of ETA's reserve groups responsible for rebuilding the organization's arsenals after its fourteen month cease fire ended. Checkpoints on roads leading into Spain from France are immediately installed, but the explosives are not uncovered. The affair is reminiscent of the incident a year and a half ago where ETA stole more than eight tons of explosives from a factory located in Brittany.

Spain: A car explosion kills a member of the Ertzaintza, the regional police of the four Basque provinces in Spain. The policeman was lured to a rigged car that had been pushed into the middle of a street. The vehicle had been car-jacked on a nearby highway by someone posing as a hitchhiker.

France: French police arrest two ETA activists in the Landes region of France. The two men were wanted by the Spanish police in connection with the murder of a Spanish politician in Madrid.

Spain: ETA issues a warning for tourists to stay out of Spain, claiming tourist attractions are to become targets. Spain is the world's third top tourist country after France and the United States, but Spanish authorities dismissed the statement as a weak threat.

Spain: The deputy mayor of Lasarte, Spain, is shot and killed. He was a member of the PSOE and known to be anti-ETA. Two men entered the bar where he was having a drink and shot him in the head.

Spain: Explosions in two Mediterranean coastal resorts in northeastern Spain killed one Spanish policeman and caused extensive damage.

France: French police arrest a woman in Biarritz, France, who had been banned by the French government from returning to the Basque Country. She had reportedly helped ETA hide arms in the past. Spanish police arrest a woman in Hernani who they linked to ETA's Sugoi commando unit. She is a teacher of the Basque language and had been expelled from France by the French government.

Spain: A Spanish-born popular movie star received a threat on his life from ETA. The actor keeps a house in Marbella, Spain. He had openly condemned ETA's past assassination of a PP official.

Spain: A public bus is firebombed in San Sebastian. Four hooded youths tossed Molotov cocktails into the bus, setting it on fire.

Spain: In the old quarter of San Sebastian, regional police seize close to fifty Molotov cocktails that are abandoned after a street battle between police and a group of youths.

Spain: The night before elections, a bomb explodes in central Madrid. The bomb had been left in a car in front of a Spanish bank on a crowded street. Thirteen people were injured by the blast and one was gravely wounded. In a separate incident, four ETA suspects were detained in Saintes, France, for carrying automatic weapons. One of the detained was wanted for the murder of a Basque police officer in Spain a year ago.

Spain: The day after the Basque parliamentary elections, a member of the PP was killed by repeated gunshots to the head in the Aragon region of Spain. The only evidence found at the scene of the crime were shells from a 9 mm pistol, which Spanish police state is a weapon of choice by the ETA.

A sudden dip by the plane jolted Gibson. The bundle in the file slipped out of his hands and dropped to the floor. As he leaned forward to pick it up, he saw the file had opened to a memo on Ramon Maria Ezpiroz, a.k.a. El Fusil. It concerned a recent article in the Basque newspaper *Black Sheep.*

He saw that Ezpiroz had recently published a statement claiming: "The Spanish prison guards often beat me in my cell. The guards pushed me down a staircase, causing me to break my ankle the same day of my appeal. Therefore, due to the fall, I missed my opportunity to appeal my case to a Spanish judge and will have to wait another year before my next opportunity."

Gibson smiled as he read the memo.

Although Gibson knew ETA was still active in Spain and France, he was shocked after reading all that had been going on even in the last year. It seemed to him that ETA, and its northern partner IK, were without a doubt waging a small war against the Spanish and French states. He also noted that both France and Spain had quite effectively kept the rest of the world in the dark on the actual status of the Basque struggle. The events occurring bore a striking resemblance to the much better known struggle in Northern Ireland. The FBI sure could have used that kind of control on the press after some recent encounters, Gibson thought.

The sky was brilliantly blue and clear outside his window. He saw rugged mountains in the distance and desolate desert stretched in every direction beneath them. They were approaching the Sierra Nevada range.

Gibson had only driven through this western region once. After the incident in Idaho. When it ended, he decided he needed to be alone and just drive. After he botched the Idaho affair, the landscape fit his mood perfectly—vast and empty. He remembered thinking how the area was such a wasteland and how he could not imagine anyone living there. Now, as the plane flew over the area he'd once driven across, the same thoughts entered his head.

Agent John Gibson had not known if he would have a job after Idaho. But instead of returning to DC to face being fired, he returned to be privately honored by the Bureau.

That was a story *the press*, therefore the public, and therefore the world, would never hear.

* * *

The air in the room was thick with blue smoke. California's law prohibiting smoking in public places obviously didn't apply in this bar. Gibson wished every public place in the country was smoke-free. He didn't understand why these selfish smokers didn't slowly kill themselves in their own private homes or cars instead of trying to shorten every one else's lives around them with their second hand smoke.

Due to the location, not on a street, but down a back alley, the bar must be able to get away with breaking the somewhat newly instated state law, he concluded. Gibson had trouble even finding the place, let alone the punk-ass CIA kid whom he was to work with. Apparently the kid arrived in San Francisco before him and made their meeting arrangements. He thought it was odd that this Parker kid had chosen an ethnic Basque bar in the city for the location of their meeting.

Especially since tensions among the Basque-Americans in San Francisco were sure to be running high after the brutal murder of their own much loved politician. Besides that point, he and this kid would certainly have no chance of concealing themselves as this was definitely not just another bar.

The establishment he walked into was the kind of place where tourists never ventured. The kind of place only a select few even knew about. In fact, there wasn't even a typical sign over the doorway proclaiming the existence of a bar. There was only a simple wooden sign next to the heavy wooden door that said something in a language he supposed was Basque.

Looking around the interior, the present patrons appeared to be mostly rough looking older men. Gibson set his doubts aside for the moment with the excuse that everyone who worked for the CIA was a little *off* somehow.

Due to the lack of any front windows, it was dark at the entrance. But at the rear of the room there was a window looking out onto a small courtyard. There was a dark bar counter against one of the walls, but it lacked a bartender. When he opened the door, all eyes in the room automatically turned toward him. Gibson imagined hearing a record screeching off track. After a few seconds of judgment, the occupants returned to whatever they were doing before and ignored him. Though he was unaware, the conversations in the room that had been taking place as he strolled in through the entrance actually switched to a different language.

Not knowing what else to do, Gibson walked up to the bar. There were no stools, so he stood and waited for something to happen. No bartender appeared to ask him if he wanted a drink. It was then he realized there was a lot of talking going on in the small room, but he couldn't seem to make out any words or even what language was being spoken.

Gibson took the opportunity to quickly scan the room. Most of the men were playing some sort of card game that he didn't recognize, but the game looked similar to poker. Later he would learn they were playing a Basque card game called *mus*.

Nearly all the men were bronze skinned and quite a few of them wore black berets. How could this Parker be one of these people who looked as if they were fresh off the boat? It pissed Gibson off knowing that Parker was probably there among these men, playing a childish game on him. So the guy can fit in, big goddamn deal, Gibson remarked to himself. He noticed someone moving from one of the back corner tables and figured this had to be Parker.

Through narrowed eyes, Gibson watched the young man approach him. He was the typical tall, dark, and handsome model that most women seemed to love, but his appearance was much more relaxed than he would have expected from a CIA employee. This guy wore blue jeans and a sloppy shirt, clearly had not shaved in a week or so, and his hair looked as if he had just rolled out of bed. The young man looked somewhat annoyed at having his game of cards and conversation interrupted.

As he walked up to Gibson, the young man said in overly-pronounced English, "How can I help you?"

"Are you Parker?" Gibson responded.

Gibson was rewarded with a harsh smirk from the young man who smartly replied, "No, I'm Gastion, the bartender here. So if you want a drink you had better ask for one it now, or I'm going back to my game." Looking into the bartender's face, he noted the large, brown eyes looking through him as if they were looking at nothing.

For a brief moment, Gibson felt like a fool. Absently, he patted his gun under his jacket for the reassurance and confidence this move always brought him. The feeling quickly passed as he said, "Listen here, pal, I'm not here for a goddamn drink. I'm here to meet someone named Sebastian Parker. Now why don't you cut the damn attitude and tell me if you know who he is or not?"

The bartender didn't flinch as Gibson talked. Instead, he casually produced a pack of cigarettes from his shirt pocket and placed one in his mouth. By the time Gibson finished speaking, the bartender had slowly lit his cigarette and exhaled a breath of smoke in Gibson's face. His demeanor spoke the words he was clearly thinking: "Where the hell do you think you are?"

"He's right over at that table," he calmly said, out loud, as he pointed to a table near the door.

Gibson was now beyond furious. He turned in the direction of the table. Fuming, he thought: How does this jackass have the nerve to do this to me? Whichever one he is, he has been watching me be humiliated this entire time. But which one is he?

At the table sat a group of five men. When Gibson walked to the table, no one in the group even raised their eyes from their cards to notice his approach.

"Parker!" he snapped as he stood over the table.

"Yup, that's me," a voice said in crystal clear English.

Gibson looked at each of the faces buried in cards they were holding in front of them, but still couldn't identify from where the voice had originated. The European features in the faces looked the same to him.

"*Merde, je suis foutu!*" The same voice as before, only now in French. However, this time a hand of cards being thrown on the table followed the voice.

Sebastian Parker pushed his chair back and rose to his feet, still not acknowledging Gibson's presence. Parker shook hands and said something in a language Gibson couldn't identify with each man at the table before facing him. Parker didn't offer his hand to Gibson, but motioned for him to move back to the bar with a slight nod of his head.

Gibson was more surprised by the appearance of Sebastian Parker than he had been by the bartender. In a swift glance, he noticed the young man had longish, sun-bleached blond hair and a tanned face. He was wearing jeans and a brown sweater. In comparison, Gibson was wearing a dark blue suit. Going on his first impression, Gibson was very worried. He had at least hoped for a clean-cut type in a suit who would be easy for him to control. This one looked wild.

Parker leaned on the bar counter as if he'd done so a thousand times. Almost instantaneously, the bartender appeared behind the bar, waiting for Parker's order. "*Deux Izarras, s'il te plait,* Gastion," he said.

The bartender promptly set two extra large shot glasses in front of them filled with a thick, brilliant green liquid. Parker picked up the glass in front of him and held it up, anticipating a toast. He waited for Gibson to pick up the other glass as well, but the glass remained sitting on the bar.

"I'm buying us a shot to inaugurate our new partnership, okay?" Parker said. It was the first time he really looked at Agent Gibson. He noted the FBI agent looked older to him than he had expected.

"I don't drink while I'm at work," Gibson said matter-of-factly. It was the first time he really looked at Parker. He noted the CIA employee looked younger than he had expected.

"C'mon, this is Izarra! This is straight from the Pyrenees. Do you know how hard it is to find this stuff in the U.S.? Trust me—practically impossible to find."

"Well, I don't want it. Give it to one of these guys. They all look like they've been drinking for a few hours. As do you, by the way."

"Me? Oh, no. I've only been drinking for an hour or so. So you really aren't going to take this?"

"No."

Parker raised his glass in a silent salute and quickly drained it. Then he picked up the glass in front of Gibson and downed it as well. After closing his eyes and releasing a soft moan of delight, he turned to face Gibson and held out his hand. "Sebastian Parker. Nice to meet you."

Gibson was taken aback by the firmness and strength of Parker's shake. Sebastian Parker was not going to be an easy person to figure out.

Parker said something to Gastion before he led Gibson out the door to the enclosed alleyway. It sounded to Gibson like Parker said "*adio*" to the man. It also sounded like Spanish to him as he heard a lot of Spanish spoken on the streets of DC, but he'd never heard this word before. He assumed it was a Basque word.

* * *

Policeman Dies in Spanish Gun Battle

A Spanish policeman has been killed and another wounded in a gun battle with two suspected members of ETA. The incident occurred near a petrol station 40 kilometers northwest of Madrid, after the two suspects opened fire on a policeman as he approached their vehicle. He was killed after being shot at point-blank range. A colleague was also wounded and is in critical condition in a hospital.

Spanish authorities said the suspects were on their way to Madrid to carry out a bombing attack, which may have been planned for the next day. Police arrested one suspect, who was wounded in the shooting immediately after the incident, and captured a second suspect in San Sebastian a few hours later.

Following the shooting, a bomb squad also blew up the suspects' vehicle, which Spanish radio said contained explosives.

8

Caracas, Venezuela

LOPÉ GLANCED OUT THE CAR'S window at the people walking along the streets of Caracas. This was his first time in the Venezuelan capital, and the faces he studied on the sidewalks genuinely confused him. He expected to see mostly dark, tan faces in Venezuela, but instead he saw all shades: light tan, dark tan, brown, white, light black, dark black. It was like being in America again, he thought.

But he knew it was definitely not the United States, simply from the architecture of the buildings surrounding him. It was a very pleasing mixture of classic European and colonial styles with a touch of neglect. These factors made it a distinct style all to itself— South American.

Lopé noticed they were approaching a large cathedral. Just as the car was getting near, the driver abruptly turned onto a street leading in the opposite direction. Although he could no longer see the spires of the cathedral, he could now clearly see the low, green mountains enclosing a long valley that was home to the city of Caracas. When Lopé told the driver he wanted to see the cathedral, the driver responded by saying he would have to walk there if he wanted to see it for it was in a pedestrian-only zone. Although Lopé was disappointed to hear this, since he felt a strong urge to kneel and pray to the saints, he fully understood and appreciated the idea of pedestrian zones.

The driver, who seemed to be a good, honest Basque-Venezuelan, still retained some typical Basque features, Lopé noticed. He had dark hair, large ears, thick eyebrows, and a long nose. It was impressive that after nearly seven generations, present day genes still maintained

Basque qualities. The Basques are the greatest people in the world, Lopé said to himself.

The driver recited to Lopé a story. "When Spain wanted to open commerce with the province of Venezuela in the 1600s, it looked for, but could not find a way to do so at first. Eventually Spain found an answer in the proposal of a group of Basque businessmen in the province of Guipuzcoa, who claimed they could install and operate a trading company in Venezuela. The name of the company they formed was the Royal Guizpocoan Company. It dominated trade in Venezuela for over a hundred years."

The driver also explained how the square by the cathedral they had passed closed to vehicles was named Bolivar Square, after Venezuela's great liberator, and perhaps the liberator of all South America: Simon Bolivar. The driver asked Lopé if he knew that Bolivar had Basque blood in him?"

"Of course," Lopé responded, even though he did not. Yet the information made him feel even more proud. Then he repeated to himself once again: the Basques are the greatest people in the world.

* * *

José Aldarossa Arana lay on the table in all his glory and mortality. The fluorescent lights from above bounced off the pale body on the examination table. During his long career, Gibson had rarely seen a body so drained of blood. It made the skin look almost translucent.

Silently, Gibson observed the horrified expression on Parker's face and then realized the extent of Parker's inexperience. Clearly the young man had never seen a dead body, and definitely not one in the condition before them now. Parker was staring squint-eyed at the cruel craftsmanship of murder.

The coroner led them to the table in the center of the room under a low hung light. He explained that no other prints had been found on the victim's wallet, nor were there any external pieces of hair or spots of blood found on the body or clothes. He added that the victim could not have had any skin under his fingernails, because the fingernails had all been torn off. It was the coroner's stated opinion that whoever had murdered the councilman had not been an amateur killer.

When the coroner lifted the sheet covering the man's body, Gibson could see for himself before the coroner uttered a word, that the man on the table had not died happy. All the fingernails and more than half the toenails had been ripped off with what must have been a pair of pliers. There were large rips in the skin of the fingers and toes from were nails had once been attached. A few of the fingers had been broken from the way they unnaturally were set on top of others.

It would have been difficult for anyone not to notice the testicles. They were a deep bluish color and looked as if they had ruptured. When the coroner noticed Gibson looking at them, he commented, "I believe the testicles were squeezed very tightly."

"Why do you think that?" Gibson asked.

The coroner responded, as he pointed to a few marks on the skin of the testicles that looked like fingernail indentures, "Someone with very large fingernails did that. Unfortunately, whoever did it was bright enough to wear gloves, because there were no other skin cells found on the genitals."

"Notice the large dark blue bruises spotting the body's ribs and shoulders. And one wrist has definitely been snapped back in the wrong direction. You can see by the loose position of the hand on this wrist that it gives the impression it wanted to fall off the arm. Now look at the face. It has been beaten so badly that it is barely recognizable. One eye is completely swollen shut, while the broken jaw has forced the mouth to remain hanging open. Now notice the smaller cuts made with a blade of some sort, in two places, behind the knee and on the inside of the elbow, which would have caused him to bleed out profusely."

Though Gibson agreed about the cuts, he personally believed they had been done as a warning before a final blow, which had indeed come. Obviously, the councilman had not done as told, because the final blow had been delivered with a fierce slashing cut across his jugular. Looking at it, Gibson noticed the deep neck wound created a gaping crater in the skin. It was, in fact, the only wound on the body that did not look calculated. To him, the rest of the wounds were administered deliberately, gruesomely, in a meticulous manner of which any sadist perfectionist would approve. The death strike, however, was uneven and jagged. As if whoever had done it had hesitated while delivering the strike.

Glancing at Parker, Gibson noticed his eyes halted on the fierce neck wound. It was no small thing for an amateur to witness. Movies may be realistic as hell these days, but nothing is as realistically profound as the real thing. Seconds later, a pale blue color flushed Parker's face and his stance became unsteady. Gibson told the coroner, "That's all the viewing we need for now, but I would like to see the complete autopsy report once completed." Then he turned to grab the arm of the now very wobbly Parker.

Once they were out of the room and into a hallway, Gibson asked Parker, "Are you all right?"

Parker gave him a nod, but then suddenly turned in the opposite direction to throw up. Watching the young man cough up vomit into a garbage can completely changed Gibson's impression of Sebastian Parker. He was no longer the hard-ass punk in the bar. Now he was little more than a kid.

"I'll bet that green stuff you downed earlier doesn't taste so good now," Gibson idly commented.

With his head still buried into a half-full garbage can and stinging bile dripping from his nose, Parker responded to the comment by slightly raising a middle finger.

Gibson asked, "Feeling better?"

Parker's face grew slightly red as he stood. "Yeah, thanks," he said, not realizing how much embarrassment he revealed in his tone.

For a brief instant, Gibson felt sorry for how apparently innocent Parker was in the truths of the world. Momentarily, he reflected on all the bad shit he'd seen in his career, and a flash of vivid images burned behind his eyes. He saw Tommy Smith. A young boy in Idaho who had taken a bullet in his chest that ended his life with a splatter of blood out his back. He saw the face of Lamar Williams, his former partner, who had coughed up a puddle of blood on him and died as he held his head in his arms. He saw the bodies of ten people who had been killed by a man who had committed suicide and taken them with him after he walked into a crowded New York City subway station and pulled the switch on his backpack of explosives.

These were the images Gibson saw in his head as he drove to the dead body site. He admitted that perhaps Parker's innocence wasn't such a bad thing.

"Listen, Parker. I know it's rough the first time, but don't worry about it too much," he said.

"Oh, yeah, sure. I'll bet you went out and had a beer after your first experience with one of…*those*," Parker bitterly responded.

Parker noticed Gibson's face twitch a little, and his eyes roll upward as if he were actually remembering his first encounter with a dead body. After a few seconds, Gibson said, "No. Actually I was pretty shaken up after my first. Not quite as bad as you, but still rattled quite a bit."

Although Parker heard admission to something beyond the ordinary in the voice of Gibson, it was over-powered in his mind by the fact that this old man was still saying that he was tougher than him. Parker wanted to call him an arrogant bastard to his face, but he held back his burning words. He decided to just let the big, tough FBI man feel as if he was so superior. *For now anyway.*

"Parker, back there at that Basque bar…"

"The Amerikanoak?"

"Whatever it's called. Did you find anything out about the murder?"

"What do you mean?"

"Well, weren't you there to ask questions to see if anyone knew if Basques killed the city councilman?"

"No, I wasn't. I was there to have a nice conversation, play cards, have a few drinks, and if you wouldn't have showed up, to get a nice Basque meal," Parker calmly answered.

"We're on a case here, kid! You're job out here is to connect with these damn sheep people and find out what they know. If I had my way, I'd go back in that bar and put a gun barrel in all their mouths and see who knows something. Anyway, they're all just terrorists anyway, in my opinion."

"I know what my job out here is, Agent Gibson. But what you don't understand is that I'm not going to start accusing these people of anything until we can prove Basques were actually responsible for this.

How far do you think I would be able to get with any one of them if I just went in and started asking why they murdered one of their own? I can tell you—not far. And these people are better connected than you can imagine. If I pissed off one of them here, we can kiss our chances a fat *au revoir* for any cooperation from the Basques from Bakersfield to Boise. You also don't understand that it's not polite in Basque culture to speak of the dead. They're one of the most culturally-bound people the Earth has ever seen, and we're not going to be able to change that. Even though I'm sure most of the men in that room were sympathetic to the loss of Arana, not one of them would have mentioned his name in a public place. It's simply not in their nature to speak of the dead in a public setting." Parker turned and glared at Gibson. *Suck on that, tough guy.*

He continued: "And I think we're going to get nowhere in this case if you keep that bigoted, xenophobic attitude of yours. The Basques are not an evil people and, in fact, some of my best friends in the world happen to be Basque, and are probably the most genuinely kind people I know. And, by the way, you old fart, I'm twenty-five years old. I suppose I appear to be a kid to you, because it's been so long since you were anywhere close to remembering what it felt like to be twenty-five. I don't expect you to think of me as one of your big-balls FBI meatheads, but I do expect you to treat me like I'm your partner on this case. Because, like it or not, that's what we are."

Gibson took the lecture without making a comment. He could see that Parker was on the verge of leaning out the car window and hurling again at any minute; he respected the fact that he'd obviously choked it down in order to finish speaking his mind. So the kid, or, young man, is not as worthless as I originally feared, he commented to himself.

Parker tried to calm himself by looking out the window at the passing crowds of people. "I also want you to know I think this whole mission is a bit of a farce to begin with."

"How so?"

"Because it seems we're just doing this to show that the FBI and the CIA can work together in this new world of interdepartmental cooperation. Yet, they obviously aren't taking it overly serious, because if they were they would have sent you someone besides me who does this kind of stuff. I'm just a desk analyst for fuck's sake!"

An image of the body they had just seen popped into his head. He had to pause to choke back a sudden upheaval in his stomach. "And besides, Basque stories don't normally have happy endings," he added, trying to close his eyes to shut out the terribleness of the world for a brief moment.

From that moment, Gibson was sure of something about Sebastian Parker. He was a smart-ass and was going to be a major pain to work with, but he sure had balls. A brief grin even crossed his face as he drove the Ford Expedition through the steep streets of San Francisco.

* * *

Graciana already loved Buenos Aires. With its grand avenues, Victorian houses, and classic-style facades, there were places in the city that were indistinguishable from any European capital. But the city had its own particular charm. And to her, the people were fabulous. They held everything great about European people and added a glimmering touch of South American flair. This sexy concoction had created a people who left their mark by creating the most sensuous of dances—the tango. Graciana fanaticized about finding a nice, sleek, and dark Argentine *femme* of her own with whom to tango.

Just as the thought crossed her mind, a vision presented itself. She was medium in height with long, flowing, dark brown hair cascading from under a wide-brimmed hat that perfectly framed her small, tanned face. She was wearing a white cotton dress that accented her lightly tanned skin and casually came down to her mid-thighs. She walked like a model, one foot straight out, pointed toe and down, and then the other foot came out and repeated the delicate process. Her breasts bounced gently as she strolled along, not noticing the countless sets of male eyes transfixed on her.

Graciana was sure the tantalizing woman brought her deep brown eyes to meet her gaze as they passed one another on the sidewalk. She tried her best to make it obvious, in that split second, that she was undressing the woman in white with her creative imagination. But why didn't the woman check her out as well? Despite the long flight from the western United States, Graciana looked as wonderful as ever dressed in a short, white and blue polka-dotted skirt with matching blue heels and a skintight, sleeveless white camisole.

Unfortunately for Graciana, the woman in white passed by her without noticing. Therefore, she was stuck walking with the silver haired woman who had picked her up at the airport.

The woman had to be in her late fifties, but she still wore her hair long, in a ponytail, and wore a pair of dark sunglasses. Though she had been brief in her conversation with Graciana, she liked this silver haired lady. They were walking to the house of a couple that would be arranging Graciana's departure back to the Basque Country.

Graciana glanced down the city's streets and noticed how big a city Buenos Aires had become. Every street was lined with rows of pale white buildings. Soon they came to a square that marked an intersection of roads where a statue of a man and a fenced-in tree were in the middle of the square. She knew the statue was of the founder of Buenos Aires, but she was solely interested in the tree. The tree was strong, yet delicate. Its branches just like the Basque people. A swelling of pride overcame her as she stared at the tree.

The silver haired woman noticed Graciana slow down and become entranced by the sight of the tree. Just as the woman was about to say something, Graciana held up her hand and nodded her head to show she already knew very well the object holding her attention so profoundly. She was gazing on a tree that had been planted by Basque settlers in Argentina over four hundred years ago. It had been transplanted from an offshoot of the sacred tree in Guernica.

* * *

"I called ahead to make sure the detective who first examined the scene meets us at the site," Gibson said.

Parker, still looking a bit peaked, raised an eyebrow in acknowledgement.

"It should be right around here somewhere. Hopefully our guy is one of San Francisco's best, but I'm personally expecting a jackass," Gibson said, as he parked the Expedition on the side of the street.

There were two police cars parked, blocking the alley. One was marked, the other was not. A scrawny, nervous looking uniformed police officer sat in the driver's seat of the squad car. Another man, who was younger and tall, wearing a brown trench coat, paced in a circle at the entrance of the alleyway.

After exiting the car, Gibson and Parker ducked under the yellow crime scene tape marking off the area and approached the officer in the trench coat. As they did, the scrawny officer reluctantly pulled himself out of his squad car. Before the police officer had even closed his car door, Gibson had his FBI badge out and pointed in his direction. The scrawny police officer returned to his seat in the car, unhappy to have had to move.

It was the sound of the squad car's door closing that made the trench-coated detective look up from his feet and notice the two men walking his way.

"So, you must be them," Detective Chiles said in way of a greeting.

"I suppose that depends on who you mean by them, but if you're referring to the federal agent taking over this investigation, then that's me, or us," Agent Gibson replied, nodding toward Parker. "I'm Agent Gibson and this is Parker."

Detective Chiles shook both their hands. Parker wanted to tell Gibson to lighten up and quit being such a federal asshole, but he held back.

Underneath his long coat, Chiles was wearing a white dress shirt with small brown stripes, a plain brown tie, and straight brown slacks.

"I'm Detective Chiles and it's all yours," he replied as he waved sideways down the narrow alley.

During this interchange, Parker slowly eased away from the other two. He noted another yellow line and another police car at the far end of the alley. There was a taped-off area, where the body must have been found. But the only physical object in the alley was a rusty dumpster about halfway down the alley. Oddly enough, there wasn't even the typical garbage present in most alleys like soda cans, fast-food wrappers, newspapers or cardboard boxes. None of it. It was too clean for an alley.

"You, of course, already checked out that dumpster down there?" Parker asked Chiles. The churning sickness that Parker felt in his stomach moved aside due to a new sensation rising inside of him. He was interested.

Both Chiles and Gibson turned to look at Parker as if he were a child butting into an adult conversation. "We looked at it, but didn't find anything. It's completely empty and we couldn't find any traces of blood or hair inside. But, of course, our investigation was cut a little short by higher powers," Chiles replied as he shot Gibson a glance.

Gibson understood the jabbing comment, but merely shrugged his shoulders in response. He'd heard it all before. Actually, he was annoyed with himself, not at Detective Chiles, or the San Francisco Police Department, or even the Federal government. He was annoyed that Parker had butted in to ask a dumb question. Turning and glaring at Parker, he hoped the kid got the point to shut the hell up. In turn, like a boy might do after an order from his father, Parker stuck out his tongue after Gibson turned his back on him.

"What did you find, Detective Chiles?" Gibson asked.

"Besides the broken body of one of our most popular city councilman? Nothing. We interviewed people all around this area and came up with nothing. The nearest residence is a new loft apartment building three or four blocks from here, and not too many people ever drive down these streets at night."

"And the body was found just as you described in your statement?"

"That's right: face down, pants down, bare foot, wallet opened. Right over there. Some of your people were here earlier looking for samples."

"Yeah, I know. I talked to our lab and they said they didn't find much in their scan and probably nothing to go on." Gibson paused a moment to look up at the gray sky before he continued, "Okay, Detective Chiles. Sounds like you did all you could do. We'll give you a call if we have any more questions or need anything. I understand you're going to leave us your watchdogs here to guard the crime scene until we're done with it."

"Yes. This officer and the one at the other end will stay until you reprieve them. But don't you want to come down to the station to talk with the Chief?"

"No, I don't think we need to. In my experience, it's people like you who know more about a situation than their bosses."

Parker watched with a touch of amazement at how the outward expression of Chiles changed with Gibson's last comment. When they first arrived, Chiles, who could not have been much older than him, had been somewhat hostile with their presence. Gibson even encouraged this attitude by being his typical hard-ass self. Now, he'd turned it all around and made this young police detective feel that he was on the same team. The two shook hands again and as Chiles walked to his car, Parker saw a slight smile on his face.

Gibson motioned with a snap of his wrist for Parker to follow. "Listen. You don't know shit about investigating a crime scene. So I just want you to stay out of my way while we're here." Gibson barked at him.

"Whatever, Agent Rambo," Parker quipped.

Gibson stopped at the taped-off area where the body had been found. He knelt down on his knees and stared at the wet pavement in front of him. "We're never going to find anything here."

Parker rolled his eyes at Gibson and started walking further down the alley. Gibson noticed Parker walking off without raising his head. *Good. Maybe I can think now.*

As Parker walked, he looked up at the walls of the buildings surrounding him and felt the gloominess of the place. There were hardly any windows in the decaying walls of what must be warehouses. At each end there was only one window. That was all. He may not have been experienced in crime scene investigation, but he sure had enough common sense to realize this site had been picked for offering dark obscurity. He then found himself standing next to the rusty dumpster.

It looked as if at one time it had been painted a dark color, but now it was mostly the color of rust. Time had eaten holes out of the metal. Half the lid had long since dissipated and what was left had worn away to a thin sheet. Besides decaying pieces of metal that had fallen into its center, there was nothing inside the dumpster.

Parker tried to imagine himself as someone on the street. To a person wandering the damp, empty streets of San Francisco, this dumpster might not be a bad place to seek shelter from the rain—one side of it anyway. He carefully lifted up the creaky lid and balanced it against the brick wall behind. Then he lifted himself up and jumped inside. As he did, his movement knocked the lid free from its place propped against the wall and it came crashing down over his head. Quickly, he reacted by crouching down and was covered by a shower of rusty metal shards.

The bang of the door startled Gibson and he instantly yelled out, "Parker! What the hell are you doing?"

As Parker tried to shake the pieces of metal off of him, he called back, "Looking for evidence, sir!"

Gibson started walking heavily toward the trash dumpster. "God-damn it, Parker! I don't care what those assholes back in DC say. I'm not going to let you ruin my investigation!" He put a hand on the edge of the dumpster and peered inside to see Parker's body covered in a layer of blackish grime. Parker didn't seem to mind his furious presence. Instead, he was intently looking at something in a corner of the container.

"Well, Agent Gibson, you can go back to staring at that tired piece of pavement out there, or we can start searching for a homeless person wearing this ridiculously ugly shirt." Parker pointed to a three-inch tear of purple, red and yellow fabric that had been covered by a rusted pile of decayed metal. An impish grin crossed Parker's dirty face as he looked up at Gibson.

Gibson had been surprised very few times in his career. He admitted to himself that Sebastian Parker had just surprised him.

* * *

Jimmy Walker's dad had beaten him almost daily for years before Jimmy finally left. A couple nights a week, his father would go to the bowling alley with his friends and then come home late and find a reason to beat his son. The dishes hadn't been washed. There was a mess in the living room. His supper had not been left out for him. Or one of another various reasons.

One night, Jimmy realized he didn't care whether or not his father beat him anymore. That was the night he decided to leave. If he was going to live in this world, it was not going to be like that.

He considered trying to find his mother, who left years before and didn't take him with her, but decided living with her would probably be no better than living with his dad. She drank too much. As soon as she would get home from her job at the supermarket, she would get out her bottle of vile smelling whiskey and start drinking. The more she drank, the harsher her eyes became. His father would usually get home later at night from having been wherever and they started fighting as soon as he stumbled through the door.

Sometimes they would hit each other and scream and break things in their trailer. Other times they would fight and then start kissing each other right in front of him and move to their bedroom where they would not even bother to shut the door. Jimmy had seen his parents screwing each other more times than he wanted to think about.

One time, he walked by after listening to loud heavy metal music in his room and, not knowing they were there, walked into the living room of the trailer and found himself face to face with his mother's bouncing bare breasts. She was straddled on top of his dad on their pale green and yellow striped couch. Her eyes were half-closed, her mouth wide open in a silent scream.

Jimmy just stood there in the hallway, not knowing what to do. For a moment, he couldn't move his eyes from their position on his mother's enormous, dark nipples. He shook his head and knew he was going to puke. Just as he tried to silently move back into his bedroom, he saw his mother's eyes open all the way and look directly at him. She smiled slyly and winked at him. He never hated her as much as he did at that moment.

That was all over now. His life was in his hands. He left Fresno for San Francisco because he had heard it was a popular destination for street people as he was to become. He went to San Francisco to scrounge, scrape, and survive. But he also went to San Francisco to live his own life.

In a shelter he found clothing after the clothes he had literally began falling apart on his body. He even liked how unattractive the shirt was he found. It was a button-down, collared shirt with a red background and purple and yellow stripes crisscrossing on top.

He quickly learned that living on the streets was no walk through the park. But he liked the sense of freedom the lifestyle gave him. Usually, he stayed away from groups of other street people and did his own thing. Jimmy liked to walk through the business districts of downtown in the mornings and watch the stressed-out businessmen rushing to their busy, important jobs. They always looked as if they were about to burst a vein in their foreheads. Thinking about his parents and watching the unhappy looking business people only made him appreciate his chosen life all the more.

Everything had been going just fine until the other night.

As usual, Jimmy had spent the early evening hours walking the streets of downtown. When he first arrived in the city, he would always stroll around Union Square or Fisherman's Warf. He liked to see the flashy dressed people avert their eyes when they passed him, in fear he was going to ask them for some of their hard earned money. He also liked walking by restaurants with funny French looking names, where people were paying over a hundred bucks a person for dinner—later he would get their leftover steak and lobster for free out of the restaurant's trash dumpsters. However, after a few months of this, he grew tired of being constantly surrounded by people looking down their noses at him because he had to deal with this enough during the day. Due to this change in heart, he began to walk the less popular streets of San Francisco at night. Normally, he would just keep walking until he found a good place to sleep at night in the non-touristy areas of the city.

These streets always seemed to lead him to areas where strung-out looking men and women would ask him if he wanted to have some fun. Some were no older than he was. It reminded him of when he was in sixth grade and a tall, black haired girl in his school, who was two grades above him, told him to pull his pants down in the woods behind the trailer park one day while they were walking home from the bus stop. Though he didn't want to, she said she would tell everyone at school he was a fag if he didn't. So he did. Then she pushed him to the ground and grabbed his penis. She held him down so he couldn't move. He told her to stop and let him go, but she pushed him back down.

Jimmy was small in size, always had been. The black haired girl was bigger than him. He thought he probably could push her off and get away without tripping on his pants down at his ankles, but he didn't even try. Instead, he tried telling himself that he was supposed to like what was happening because now his penis felt as if it was too hard and going to break in the black haired girl's hand.

Then she quickly took off her pants. She left her shirt on and sat on top of him. At first it rubbed and hurt really bad, but then something happened and he felt her warm insides surrounding him. For a second, it was the most unbelievably incredible feeling he could ever imagine. Then something else happened.

Jimmy felt a surge run through his body that scared him. It hurt and felt like he was dying, and then like he was bleeding. Bleeding out of his penis and into the black haired girl. In horror, he looked up at the girl to find she was grinning devilishly down at him.

From that point on, Jimmy didn't ever want to look down at his penis again. That one experience with sex had left him feeling devastated and frightened. He couldn't understand why people like it so much.

The night of the city councilman's murder, Jimmy Walker had been walking the wet, dark streets south of the Financial District near the bay. He was in somewhat of a daze with his head bent low. He often walked like this and would awaken from his trance-like stupor and not know where he was or how he'd gotten there.

On the night in question, he found himself standing in a narrow, dark alley when he snapped alert. Though he had no clue where he was, he felt the constant pouring of rain hitting him. A dumpster down the alley caught his eye. Jimmy figured it would be full of garbage, and he refused to sleep on garbage, but it was worth a look.

To his surprise, the rusty dumpster was empty. Glancing around at the emptiness surrounding him, he saw there were no lights in either direction. He climbed into the dumpster and curled up in the back corner. Before he closed his eyes he said to himself, "Tomorrow will be a new day with new challenges. I'll get through it all just as I always do."

Sometime later in the night, the sound of strange voices speaking in unison startled him from his damp slumber.

* * *

Mexico Holds ETA Suspect

Police in Mexico have arrested nine people with suspected links to the armed Basque separatist group ETA.

Six of the suspects are reported to be Spaniards and the other three Mexican. The Mexican and Spanish police carried out the operation jointly.

Those detained are said to be responsible for channeling funds to and from ETA and also helping exiled members of the group.

Most of those detained fled from Europe after involvement in previous ETA operations.

9

San Francisco, California

"HELLO, DETECTIVE CHILES? This is Agent Gibson. Look, I, or we, need your help. Parker actually found something out here."

Chiles was surprised. "Sure, Agent Gibson. Honestly, I hadn't expected to hear from you again, but that's great news," he said.

Parker watched as Gibson spoke into his phone. It was clear that Gibson had done his best to avoid using cell phones. He kept trying to use it like a CB radio.

"Where can we meet you, Chiles?" Gibson asked the small plastic box he held awkwardly.

"There's a little coffee shop diner on the corner of 3rd Street and Gilman Avenue. All you need to do to get there is get on Gilman and turn right and you'll come across the diner shortly. I'll meet you there in twenty," Chiles said.

"Great," Gibson said. He looked at the phone and then at Parker.

"You hang it up by this little button right here," Parker slowly explained as he demonstrated on Gibson's phone.

"I've done just fine my entire career without these damned things," Gibson said, more to himself than to Parker.

Parker rolled his eyes as Gibson stuck the cell phone in his coat pocket. "Well, times do change, Gibson. Whether you change as well is entirely up to you."

* * *

Why does it seem the rivers in North America are so much wider than rivers in Europe? Aurelion Irazoqui asked himself as they crossed over the St. Lawrence River on the Jacques Cartier Bridge into the city of Montreal.

The skyline of the large city prompted Aurelion to believe it was a city caught between two worlds. It had tall, concrete and glass skyscraper buildings, but also had the towering church steeples and rows of old buildings like Europe.

While in California, he overheard a tourist guide proudly telling a group of people that a certain building was very old, built in the 1870s. Aurelion actually laughed out loud at the ludicrous statement. One hundred and thirty years was not old for a building! The small house in Saint-Jean-Pied-de-Port, where he grew up, was old. That house was built in 1610.

Despite its modern looking buildings, the city of Montreal did look old to him. After all, even Paris had those hideous skyscrapers on one side of the city. Aurelion remembered reading somewhere that Montreal was over three hundred fifty years old. This was not really very old for a city in his mind, but it did demand some level of respect.

Every sign they passed was in French and English, and sometimes not even in English below the French words. Seeing signs *en Français* made him feel good. Of course, if they were in Basque as well, it would be better, but he could live with seeing just French in any American or Canadian city.

The French weren't always his favorite people, but more often than not, he would rather have a Frenchman than an American or Canadian. At least a Frenchman would know how to shake hands properly. Aurelion was half-French himself, but he didn't like to admit it. As far as he was concerned, he was all Basque.

Aurelion had been to Montreal a few years ago on a student trip and he was happy to see not much had changed. He gazed at the city they were rapidly approaching as his driver was obviously trying to find out the maximum speed of the car. He liked how the forested hill of Mont Royal could be seen from anywhere in the city. He searched for a glimpse of the façade of the enormous Basilique de Notre Dame. He also liked the converted Vieux-Port area that he remembered used to be abandoned warehouses, but now was a trendy art center. If he had to live anywhere outside of the Basque country, maybe it would be here.

When the driver introduced himself in Basque, he told Aurelion he was an ETA member in exile. Aurelion was too young and too new to the organization to remember the names and faces of those exiled or expelled from the Basque Country. Momentarily, he considered asking the man why he was exiled, but from the rough looks of the *mec*, he assumed it had something to do with an assassination. The man had a deeply scarred face and small black eyes that never stayed in one place. He harshly smoked his cigarettes. Though shorter than Aurelion, his build could best be described as a resembling a tank. Aurelion told himself that the driver was someone he'd never want to get into a fight with.

His driver told him how Montreal was the center for the Quebecois Separatism Movement and that he knew many of its leaders. Most of them were far too conservative, the driver said. "They don't want to kill anyone or blow anything up anymore. They used to do that in the 60s here. Now they are just a bunch of weak-hearted politicians," he spat out in French. "But at least they know how to get an election called to decide self-determination for Quebec. They get one every few years, but so far it hasn't gone their way," he added.

"Perhaps we could learn something from them," Aurelion commented.

The man puffed deeply on his *clop* and shrugged. "Now you won't have to ask why I was sent here," he responded.

* * *

Parker watched Gibson hard at work across the table. Gibson was explaining the situation to Chiles in rapid fire military fashion. "We need men questioning everyone again in that perimeter. We need men questioning people in homeless shelters and under bridges and wherever else one finds homeless people. We need you to be in charge of these men. We need to be looking for someone wearing this shirt."

This man was a natural leader, Parker thought.

"More coffee, sweetie?" the stringy, older, ashen blonde haired waitress asked him, waking him from his reverie.

"Yes, please, Madame."

"Madame! Well aren't you just full of sugar and honey. I ain't never been called no fancy name like *Madame* before," she said through a wide smile that revealed tobacco stained teeth. She filled up his cup with dark black coffee.

"I'm sorry to hear that, because you should have been long before today," Parker said.

"My, my, what a charmer I got here! If I were twenty years younger you'd be in trouble." Parker smiled at the waitress. "You must not be from around these parts," she added.

"No. I'm from the other coast. The east coast."

"The east coast, huh? I've always wanted to go out that 'ways. But I've only made it as far as Reno," she laughed at herself.

"You'll make it someday," he said with a smile.

The waitress looked hard at him for a long moment. Parker thought she looked far older than she probably was. "Why are you down here at a place like this? You should be at one of those fancy coffee places uptown," she said, now embarrassed.

Parker took a second to consider his answer. "I like it here better. You see and meet real people at a place like this. And besides, the service and the coffee are better."

The waitress turned and walked down to the next table to repeat her routine of jabbering heartlessly and filling cups with coffee. Parker thought maybe she was smiling after she left their table. He hoped so.

Gibson and Chiles didn't even seem to notice the other conversation that had taken place at their table. The two of them just kept talking and planning out a strategy.

But Parker was wrong. Gibson had kept a watchful eye on him the entire time.

* * *

"There are a lot of bad shirts in this room. I just walked up and down every isle and unfortunately though, no one is wearing our particularly ugly shirt," Parker said as he approached Gibson. "You look like a general standing like that."

"What are you talking about, Parker? How am I standing?"

"How I picture a general overlooking his chosen battlefield would stand."

"I didn't choose this battlefield. You remember that, Parker. I'm just taking it over. There's a difference." Gibson glared at him before he continued, "Now, go back down all those isles and take this with you." He held out the piece of cloth Parker had found.

"What do you want me to do with this?" Parker asked.

"Ask people if they know anyone who wears a shirt like that. If so, ask where we may be able to find this fashion king," Gibson replied with a grin. "It's not like they change their clothes very often. This is what an investigation is all about."

Parker snatched the cloth scrap from Gibson's hand and returned to the rows of shabbily dressed men and women eating soup at long tables. "I think I'd almost rather be back staring at my computer," he muttered, just loudly enough for Gibson to hear as he walked away.

* * *

"Do you like Mexico?" the little man driving the rusty blue pick-up truck asked him in Spanish.

"*Si*," Peio Camino answered. "Looks like a very nice country."

"Mexico is a great country, but I'm talking about this city," the man said back to him.

Peio was confused and wanted to tell the man to just leave him alone. All he wanted to do was to get back home and play pelote. *Why won't they just stop asking me so many damn questions!* Aloud, he replied with dripping impatience in his thick tone, "I do not understand what you say."

The darker, smaller woman in the front seat with the driver looked back at him with comforting, brown eyes. "It is okay that you do not understand."

Peio had never heard someone speak Spanish as she did. Her tone was very smooth, but her words were rough. Later he would learn she was a descendant of the ancient Mayan people. "You see, in Mexico we sometimes forget we are the only ones who call our great capital city by simply *Mexico*, instead of Mexico City. Carlos is only asking if you like this city."

Peio was put at ease by her kind words and expression. He felt extremely tense and nervous during the entire plane trip from the United States. But now he was beginning to feel better. Perhaps everything would be okay after all. He glanced out at the enormous city they were driving through and said, "Yes, it is very big."

"*Si*, bigger than Los Angeles! Mexico is the greatest city in the world!" Carlos cried out as he honked the horn of the little pick-up truck driving through the crowded streets of Mexico.

* * *

"This is hopeless, Gibson." Since reconvening that morning, they had been to nearly ten shelters, down about fifty streets, and in about twice as many back alleys. "All we've got to show for it is that guy spitting in your face." Parker had to force himself not to laugh at the memory of the cranky old man spitting in Gibson's face when he showed him the scrap of cloth.

"I should have given him a good heart attack," Gibson said through clenched teeth. He shook off his temporary anger and tightened his grip on the steering wheel of the Expedition. "This is how it is. We can't give up, no matter how hopeless it seems. This isn't a very big city to someone on the streets and eventually we'll come across something. Because of you, we could be way ahead in the game here."

"Don't try bullshitting me, Gibson. I know you think I'm worthless."

Gibson looked sideways at Parker and saw a look on his face that he hadn't seen before. "Look, Sebastian," he was just starting to speak when the cell phone in his jacket pocket began blaring some sort of a song. Awkwardly, he reached inside his coat and pulled out the small box. "Parker! How did this annoying goddamn noise get on my phone?"

"Somehow, you must have hit the button that changes the ring tone. I'll change it for you later." Parker turned away from Gibson and bit down on his tongue to keep from laughing. Earlier, when Gibson wasn't looking, he changed the ring tone on the phone.

"Good, because that noise is goddamn awful." Gibson was saying even after he turned on his phone.

"Agent Gibson, sir, I wasn't making any noises," the voice of Detective Chiles came from the phone.

"Never mind that, Chiles. Sorry. Have you got something?"

"Yeah, you'd better get over here to Mission Street. I think I've found something."

* * *

As they climbed out of the car, they noticed Chiles standing with a blue haired young girl on the sidewalk. Parker thought how it really made quite a scene. Uptight Chiles talking with a spike haired girl with holes in her jeans and a black T-shirt that had "Anarchy Rules" written across the front. Observing more closely, he realized the girl was doing little to conceal her mounting desire to kick Chiles in the groin and make a run for it.

"I hope you've got some good news for us, Chiles," Gibson said, as they walked up to the oddly matched pair.

"I don't, Agent Gibson, but she does," Chiles said. He nodded his head down at the girl, who was at least two feet shorter than him, even with her spiked hair.

Gibson approached the girl and leaned down to look her into the eyes. "So, what can you tell us, sweetheart?" he asked.

"I can tell you to go fuck yourself. There ain't nothing sweet about me, so why don't you get off my ass," she snapped at him.

Chiles stiffened and looked as though he would slap the girl for showing such disrespect. Parker laughed at the girl's response and turned away so Gibson wouldn't see him. The girl just stood and sneered at Gibson.

Gibson cracked his neck and ground his teeth together without taking his eyes off the blue haired girl scowling in front of him. "Listen here, missy, you tell me what I need to know and we'll leave you alone with your ass. Or, you can keep being a mean little bitch and we can take you to the station and we'll keep you there until we can find something you did that would put you there anyway. One of these options will have you on your way in two minutes from now. The other will have you stuck in a cell with a bunch of women that will want to beat you while no one is looking. Now which one is it going to be?"

The blue haired girl stood her ground and didn't flinch while Gibson threatened her. When he was done, she stared back into his dark eyes and calmly replied, "Let me see that again." Chiles held out a Polaroid photograph he'd take of the torn fabric for her to look at. She glanced at the photo. "Yeah, I know a kid who wears a shirt that looks like that."

Hearing her words, Gibson's pulse quickened. "What's his name? Where can we find him?"

"His name is Jimmy, but he lives on the streets like me, so I don't have any fuckin' clue where you'd find him."

Gibson and Chiles both shook their heads. "Can you tell us anything more that might help us locate him?" Chiles asked.

"I've only run into him a couple of times and to tell you the truth, he's not much to talk to. He's also not much to remember. But I can try." The blue haired girl stood still and closed her eyes.

"Let's see, he's kinda short and has long, dark brown hair. He doesn't like hanging around with the rest of us. He goes off and does his own fuckin' thing like he's fuckin' better than us or something."

Gibson was beginning to get annoyed. "C'mon, think. You've got to be able to tell us something else more."

The blue haired girl twisted her face in thought. She closed her eyes again for a moment. "He likes music. He's always hanging out by metal music stores so he can hear the music playing inside," she added.

"What the hell is *metal* music?" Gibson said with a confused look as he straightened himself.

Both Parker and the girl rolled their eyes. The girl spit on the sidewalk. "Man, you're a fuckin' dinosaur." She pulled out a pack of cigarettes and popped one into her mouth. As she lit the end she explained, while waving one of her small dirty hands, "You know, like heavy metal music and hard rock shit."

Parker noticed Gibson clench his teeth before he pulled Chiles aside to discuss a plan. Neither of them even thanked the blue haired girl for her help.

"Thanks a lot," Parker said to her.

The blue haired girl looked at him. "Hey wait, he in trouble or somethin'?"

"No. We just think he saw something and can help us."

"That's good. Even though I don't like him much, I don't want him to get in any trouble or nothin'. We gots ta look out for each other out here, ya know?"

"I can imagine. Here take this," Parker said, handing her a twenty dollar bill that made the blue haired girl's eyes widen. "Only condition is that you first buy yourself something to eat, use the rest for whatever you want."

She snatched the bill from his hand. "Man, I don't do that fuckin' stuff. Just because I live on the streets don't make me no fuckin' addict. Besides, I'm fuckin' starving." She narrowed her eyes on him as if to see him clearer. "You don't seem like those other pricks." Then the blue haired girl thanked him, crossed the street, and entered a diner without looking back.

Parker watched her a moment then turned back to where Gibson and Chiles had been conversing only to find they weren't there any longer. "Parker, get in the damn truck!" Gibson yelled at him from the Expedition that already had Chiles in the passenger seat.

I'm definitely not like these guys, Parker said to himself as he settled into the back seat.

"So what's the plan, then? Stake out every heavy metal record store in the city?" Parker inquired from the back seat.

"Something like that, yes," Chiles replied.

Chiles is even getting an attitude with me now, Parker thought.

"There really aren't too many music stores in the city that specialize only in hard rock. If you haven't noticed by now, most of the greater downtown area of San Francisco is full of a lot of rich white people, conservative Asians, and what we'll call free-spirited people. Gentrification moves others farther and farther out of the downtown itself. What's good for us is that these groups of people living here don't tend to like hard rock music. With my men, we should be able to cover every store in the city rather quickly. There's one right down this street that we're going to now. Who knows? Maybe we'll get lucky," Chiles said.

Gibson parked the Expedition in front of the dark storefront of Mayhem Mike's. The heavy guitar chords of a Metallica song escaped through the window of the store covered with concert posters. Gibson and Chiles settled in to analyzing the group of kids standing in front of the store and everyone entering or leaving.

"This is stupid. He doesn't have any money and he isn't going to be buying any CDs," Parker stated as he leaned over the seat of the truck. The two men in front both looked at him like he was a child misbehaving in the back seat. "I'm getting out to have a look," Parker said as he opened the door and jumped out from the car. Just as he closed the door, he heard Gibson start to tell him not to, but he kept going anyway.

The store was on the corner of two streets. Parker noticed an alleyway behind. Our Jimmy seems to like alleys, he said to himself, as he walked down the street to the back alley. When he poked his head around the corner, he saw there was a back door to the store and the loud guitar music from inside oozed from its cracks. Sitting near the door was the ugly shirt and the boy wearing it.

Instead of taking the boy directly to the police station, Parker insisted they take the boy out for lunch. Gibson and Chiles voiced their strong objections, but eventually gave in. After all, Parker did find him.

They drank coffee and watched Jimmy devour his plates of food and waited. After convincing him nothing bad was going to happen to him for telling the truth and letting him finish his food, they were able to discover he had indeed been in the empty dumpster the night the body was dumped in the alley.

"I would have gone back there every night for months if it weren't for what happened my first night there. It would have easily become my favorite sleeping place because I liked how quiet it was. I'm disappointed to have to give it up as a sleeping spot," he confessed.

"Did you poke your head out of the dumpster or look through any holes to see the people in the alley?" Gibson asked Jimmy.

"I froze up when I heard the voices. I waited until long after I heard a car drive away before climbing out of the dumpster. And then I saw the body," Jimmy replied.

"Why didn't you call the police to report the body?" Chiles asked.

Parker thought Jimmy's response to this question was especially clever.

"If I'd called the police, I woulda been dragged into some place and asked a ton of questions I couldn't answer…kinda like now."

A bright redness came over Chiles' face.

Parker didn't see the reasoning that the seasoned investigators were following by asking the boy the same questions over and over. As soon as they took a break from their line of questioning, he said, "Jimmy, try to think about the voices you heard that night."

"Since I was in a dumpster and it was raining, I couldn't understand anything they were saying."

"Could you guess how many different voices you heard?" Parker encouraged.

"I only remember maybe three different ones, but it sounded like there were more. I don't know. The voice I heard the most was deep, and also there was a woman's voice."

Parker glanced across the table at Gibson who appeared to approve of Parker's questioning. Gibson nodded to Parker, encouraging him to continue. "Could you at least tell us what language the voices were speaking?" Parker asked.

"I have no idea, but definitely wasn't English. Living out here one hears a lota different languages all the time, but I don't remember ever hearing that strange language."

Parker's eyes began to narrow as he asked the boy. "Close your eyes and listen for a minute." He spouted off a few phrases in Basque.

Immediately Jimmy's eyes shot open. "Yes, that's it!"

Parker made sure to beam a smug grin in Gibson's direction.

Chiles handed his business card to Jimmy. "Don't leave the city for awhile, Jimmy. Just in case we need to ask you a few more questions."

Jimmy put the card, along with the money Parker palmed him, in his pants pocket. He looked up at Chiles and asked: "How would you or anyone ever be able to find me if I did leave?" Then Jimmy shrugged his shoulders and started walking back to his seat next to the back door of Mayhem Mike's.

As Parker watched Jimmy walk away, he thought to himself how incredibly tough a kid can become when they have no other choice.

"I'm going back to my office to do a search of Basque-Americans with criminal histories in San Francisco," Chiles said.

Parker didn't see the logic in what Chiles was planning to do. For one thing, Basque-Americans were such a small ethnic group in the United States that even with today's modern computers, it would be difficult to do any kind of a search based solely on Basque-Americans. Secondly, the Basques never seemed to hang around the same place where they committed a serious crime. They tended to go to another city or village. Or cross a border.

When Chiles left, Parker wasn't disappointed. It was possible Chiles would get in the way with what they had to do next. Parker told Gibson they should return to the Amerikanuak.

* * *

Bomb Blast Hits Spanish Hotels

A bomb has been defused in a hotel in Pamplona while thousands of tourists are in the city for the annual bull-running festival. The device was left in a women's toilet in a hotel located in the town's center.

A Spanish news agency reported the bomb had been left because the hotel had refused to pay a revolutionary tax to ETA.

Two suspected Basque separatists, wanted in connection with the planned bombing, have been arrested in a town near Pamplona. Explosives, guns, timers and detonators were found in their flat and Spanish police believe another attack was about to be attempted.

ETA's other recent attacks in Navarre have included the killing of two policemen in a car bomb. A series of attacks, blamed on ETA, has been carried out since recent elections in which Batasuna was banned from taking part.

In another region of Spain, two bombs went off minutes apart in the Spanish resort cities of Alicante and Benidorm. The bombs, which were planted in hotels,

injured thirteen people, including foreign tourists and police officers. Police received a warning call, but the devices went off well before the stated time. The front left corner of one hotel was demolished and a bar across the street has its front entrance blown in.

10

San Sebastian, Spain

HE KNEW HE WAS HOME as his dark, narrow eyes scanned the long beach bordering the esplanade of Donostia, the city the Spanish called San Sebastian. From high above the city, on the steps leading to the remains of the old fortress that used to guard the city from invasion attempts by sea, he tried to see everything as if seeing for the first time. Waves from the ocean crashed against the huge rock outcropping that marked the entrance into the bay, producing a soft spray of ocean mist that gently faded in the air. Round, green mountains guarded the city on land and between them and the ocean, the city of Donostia looked impenetrable.

Lopé had grown up in this city and didn't ever want to leave again. He knew though, he would have to. As soon as he arrived back home, he was given immediate orders to lie low and then meet with someone the next day. Now, sitting on the steps with the bright sun illuminating him, he waited for whoever was meeting him with details of his next assignment.

Instinctively, he knew what was coming—they were going to send him away from his beloved home. Aware of this eventuality, he savored every second of the view. Until he heard the sound of heavy boots approach from behind.

A pair of thick legs accompanied the boots. The legs belonged to an equally thickly built man who sat down on the stone steps next to him. The man silently produced a pack of Turkish, non-filtered cigarettes from his shirt pocket and offered one to Lopé, who took it and lit the cigarette with his own lighter.

"They are worried about your presence in San Sebastian. Too many people know you here," the man said in Spanish, after lighting a cigarette of his own and stepping on a group of tiny red ants scurrying along the stone at his feet.

Lopé considered the statement and eventually nodded his head in acknowledgement after releasing a long, slow cloud of thick smoke.

"There will be a lot of questions around here after what happened in America. You need to go to Madrid. There you'll become a member of a commando unit until further notice." The man rose slowly and walked down the stone stairs. Lopé never saw his face.

He was not congratulated on his successful mission in America, but he knew not to take it personally. After the heat settled, he figured he and his crew would be reunited and properly placed on a pedestal above all other commando units. They would be the ones remembered for taking the Basque struggle to an entirely new global level. This thought brought a feeling of joy inside him he'd never felt before.

* * *

"It's early evening and the bar will have a nice crowd of people enjoying a cocktail before dinner," Parker suggested.

"Too late for people to be having before dinner drinks," Gibson replied.

"Many Basque-Americans still retain a European attitude for meal times, which means long lunches and late dinners, by American standards." As Parker pushed open the heavy wooden door to the bar, he turned to Gibson and said over his shoulder, "Don't talk while we're inside."

Immediately, Gibson started to say something but didn't, recognizing that Parker was probably right. *This time anyway.*

The air inside was even more clogged with heavy blue smoke than it had been on his first visit. Gibson wondered if the same group of men that had been in the bar yesterday had even moved. But now there were more men in the room. He noticed new faces at the dark wooden tables, and that the long bar was now lined with men standing next to it, holding drinks and smoking.

Gibson realized that Parker was looking for someone in particular. Before Gibson was aware he was gone, Parker was heading for a far corner. Not sure what to do, Gibson stood at the entrance a moment before walking to an open space at the bar.

"Can I get a glass of water?" he politely asked the bartender, who was busy pouring glasses of red wine.

"Do I know you?" Gastion asked, noticeably annoyed.

"Yes…well, no, you don't. But I was in here yesterday with someone. Do you remember me now?" Gibson said, pointing to his face.

Gastion narrowed his eyes and let them go up and down the front of Gibson. "No, I don't," he curtly replied.

"Okay, fine. That's just fine. But how about that glass of water?"

"Why do you come into a bar and ask for a glass of water?" Gastion grumbled.

Some of the men standing next to Gibson looked over at him and then turned their backs, laughing at the bartender's comment.

Gibson felt the weight of his .45 mm in its shoulder holster. His hand, below the bar, clinched into a fist. "I'm here with Sebastian Parker. I know you know who he is. He's over in that corner right now," he said, raising a finger and pointing in the direction he'd last seen Parker.

Gastion followed Gibson's finger to the corner. "Yes, I know Sebastian, but I do not see him over there."

Quickly looking himself, Gibson noted the bartender was correct. He glanced around the room, but didn't see Parker anywhere. *Damn him!*

The bartender interrupted his thoughts by saying, "Our wine is much better here than our water. It is good wine, from Southern France and Spain, and is not the fruity *merde* from California. No one drinks the water, but everyone drinks the wine."

Gibson peered at the mocking smile on the face of the bartender. "I never drink that grape juice shit. I hardly even drink beer, but if I buy a beer, will you leave me alone?"

"You may order a beer if you like, but I am not doing any thing to you to have to leave you alone. Remember, you walked into my bar," Gastion spoke to him in a calm, careful voice.

"All right, give me a Bud then."

"I'm sorry, sir, we don't have that."

"Well, then give me a Miller."

Gastion just shook his head instead of repeating himself.

"Then, what do you have?" Gibson said rather testily.

"We have 1664. It is a good French beer."

"A good French beer, huh? Germany has good beer. How can French beer be any good?"

"Because this beer is made in Alsace, a region in France on the border with Germany that has, at times, been occupied by *les Boches*," Gastion explained, filling a pint glass from a keg tap. "It may be French and have nothing to do with the Basque Country, but it's still better than American beer."

"What are you supposed to be, some kind of history teacher?" growled Gibson.

"No. Unlike in this country, though, we in Europe are taught to learn our own history and geography. Most of you don't even know what wars your country has fought in or even where your own states are on a map." He grinned, placed the beer in front of Gibson, and made his way to the other end of the bar where a group of drunken men were tapping their empty glasses.

"Shove it up your French ass," Gibson said under his breath as Gastion walked away, even though he didn't disagree with the bartender's outlook on the American educational system. He took a long gulp of the beer and admitted to himself that it was, in fact, a good beer. Not heavy enough to remind him of a micro-brew. There was just a taste of quality that was rare in most domestic beers he'd tasted. For a few minutes, he forgot to be enraged at Parker, forgot the cloud of smoke he was standing in, forgot the turned backs and whispered comments being made about him, and just enjoyed his beer.

Just as he drained the last of his glass, he saw Parker's surfer looking hairdo over the top of a line of bent heads at the bar. Parker sauntered up to Gibson and softly said, "If you're through making new friends, we should go now."

"Aren't we going to talk to anyone?"

"I already have. Now, please. Let's go. I'll explain later."

Gibson followed him out the exit into the alleyway. Once they had turned the corner onto a street, he grabbed Parker and pushed him against a wall. "You'd better start talking right now, Parker," he demanded.

"Listen, Gibson, I don't know if you understand or not, but the trust I've gained took years to obtain. I fly out here to SF for long weekends all the time and that's the place where I hang out. How long do you think it would have lasted if I had taken you in with me?"

Gibson took his hands off Parker and stepped back from. "Okay, I guess you're right. Sorry. So what did you find out?"

"Let's get off the street and then I'll tell you." Gibson nodded in agreement and the two walked in silence until they were inside the large SUV.

"First off, I think it'll be safe for us to assume now that we are dealing with a unit of ETA from the Basque Country. Secondly, we need to drive out to Stockton tomorrow morning. There's someone there who should be able to help us," Parker reported.

"How do you know?"

"Basque-Americans here are similar to the Basques in the Basque Country. Some are very supportive of ETA's activities, some are very much against them. The man I spoke with back at the bar told me that that a small unit of ETA had been sent to kill Arana to try and raise awareness and support for the movement here in the States."

"So the situation is just as everyone feared?"

Parker let out a deep breath. "Exactly. But they're not here anymore and they probably aren't even still in the country. But it's possible that they haven't returned to the Basque Country, yet. A group in Stockton helped them get away.

"So you think we should go there and find who helped them so we can find out where they are now?" Gibson asked for clarification.

"No, I'm not thinking that at all, actually. These people are too well organized and too smart. I'm sure they all had passports under different names and all left from different cities or something. We'll never catch them that way and we're not going to find anything else here. But this guy out in Stockton might be able to lead us in the right direction to find them in the Basque Country."

"Woa, woa. The Basque Country? You mean for us go to Europe?"

"Yup," Parker said. He cracked the window and lit a cigarette.

Gibson scowled and said, "I can't stand Europeans. Haven't they ever heard of deodorant?" He paused a moment then added, "Where did you go back there anyway?"

"There's a room that is not exactly open to the public. Some of them like to play cards with money, and since organized gambling is illegal in the state of California…"

"Oh, I see. Just as they don't seem to recognize that smoking in enclosed bars in California is illegal as well. I don't suppose you'd let me report it to our friend Detective Chiles would you?"

Parker turned an icy stare on Gibson.

Gibson laughed. "Relax, Parker. I'm only joking. I wouldn't want to betray your trust. You know, you've got a pretty evil look about you at times."

Parker didn't respond.

* * *

The scores of tourists pouring through the hotel lobby on their way to discover San Francisco didn't fail to notice the young man looking like death slumped over on one of the couches near the entrance. His eyes were half closed and his head kept falling from its perch on his hand. Gibson handed him a steaming cup of coffee in a white Styrofoam cup and told him to get up. Parker took the cup and stood up, fighting the urge to fall back down on the couch.

Gibson waited until they were in the SUV before he said anything. "So what the hell happened to you last night?"

"After you went up to your room, I went back to the Amerikanoak."

"What the hell did you do that for?"

Parker glared at Gibson for a moment, then placed a cigarette in his mouth and lit it. "Why do people usually go to bars at night? I went to hang out with some old friends and get trashed. Apparently that's what happened."

"This isn't a vacation. You're no good to me if you're drunk."

"I'm not drunk now and besides, I kept my ears open for anything of interest."

"And you probably ran your mouth too."

"I never discuss work when I'm drinking," Parker said, not really believing his own words.

"I sure hope not. Aren't they suspicious of talking to someone who works for the CIA? And how do you know so many of them in the first place?"

Parker sipped his coffee and took a long drag on his cigarette before answering. "I did undergrad in Reno and spent a lot of time here and still come out often, as I mentioned before. I tell them I work for George Washington University."

"You know, that could really come back to hurt you, Parker. I work around these terrorist groups all the time and they don't particularly like it when people from the CIA lie to them."

"They don't like people from the FBI either. So don't worry about it. I can take care of myself."

"Okay, you're the boss on this one."

"No, you're the boss. Right now I just want to be hungover. It's eighty miles or so to Stockton. I'm going to try and get some sleep. Wake me up when we get close and I'll tell you where to go."

Parker gulped down the cup of coffee and flicked his cigarette out the window. He closed his eyes and fell almost instantly into a heavy sleep.

* * *

"Hey, Sara!" the older gentleman called, trying to get the young woman's attention. "Sara Gamboa!" She turned her head to look in his direction. "You want another one of those?" he asked.

She responded with a nod of her head, indicating she'd take another vodka on the rocks. The gray, stout man went behind the bar and returned with a full glass of top shelf vodka, taking it to the table where she sat. "Here you go, Sara," said the man, as he looked at the woman sitting in front of him with a look of deep concern. He set the glass down and then sat in a chair next to her.

"What's wrong, *chérie*?" he asked. Her eyes were fixed on the centerpiece of flowers on the table. She didn't acknowledge his question. He decided to try again. "Sara, I have known you all your life. As you know, your father and I are the best of friends. I've watched you grow up into the wonderful person you are now. But I've never seen you like this. Whatever it is, you can tell me and I will help you."

She raised her dark brown eyes. "You can't help me," she said in a chilling tone.

What she wanted to add was that no one could help someone who had aided a group of murderers escape from a crime scene. She wanted to also add that no one could help someone who had seen a tortured body in an alley and then drove away with the people who had done the torturing. Worst, she wanted to add how she felt she had betrayed her father's wishes. He always told her their people, the Basques, should not be involved in the armed struggle.

She picked up the glass and swallowed the contents in one large gulp.

* * *

A mist hung low in the still air. Waves of it floated by him. Sebastian Parker wanted to stop walking, but knew he couldn't. He was on a mission of some sort, wasn't he? Looking around, he smelled the air as he stepped on the long grass beneath his feet. The air was damp and earthy-smelling. The murky mist clung to the ground, rising to his knees thick as snow. Behind a round mountaintop, he saw the brilliant glow of the moon. Everything was quiet. Not even the noises from the summer bugs that thrived in the low mountains could be heard.

Soft light from the slivered moon landed gently on the blanket of fog. He could barely make out the dark form of the mountain peak they were treading on. Looking around, he noticed a dark line of mountains surrounding him. A shock of realization came to him and he knew exactly where he was and what he was doing. It wasn't a good night to be smuggling horses across the border.

Pascal insisted they go on with the plan. The horses had been brought all the way from Alava, and Pascal wanted to get them across the border into France as soon as possible. Everyone else in the group of five men wanted to postpone the trip until a night when the moon wouldn't be so bright, but Pascal was their leader and he told them they were going regardless. Pascal was a powerful man with huge arms and broad shoulders. He knew how to put a man down quickly. Not one of them would dare disagree with Pascal.

They moved silently across the still landscape. They weren't high enough to be above the timberline. Since these low mountains were basically just the foothills of the Pyrenees, they traversed in and out of numerous forested areas. Parker noticed one of the other men walking not far from him. He couldn't remember the man's name, but seemed to remember the man being really good at pelote. Closest to him was Pascal. Even through the night and mist, Parker could feel the man's determination to succeed. Another of the group was next to the pelote player. That man had a small face and always covered half of it by wearing a black beret pulled over his forehead. Jean, he recalled, was the man's name.

When Parker stepped on something hard and the sound was different from the usual rock or piece of wood, he quickly knelt down to have a look. His hands felt the outline of a shotgun on the ground. The moisture from the veil of mist filled his senses and dampened his face. *What was a shotgun doing way up here?*

Knowing that the French *douanes* would surely be out looking for smugglers crossing the border with contraband, he felt an urge to pick up the weapon to carry. The thought was rapidly suppressed, however, after he reminded himself that Basque smugglers had always taken an unspoken vow never to kill a customs official if caught. You could run from them, indeed it was expected for you to do just that if the time came, but resorting to violence against them was strictly forbidden unless absolutely necessary. Smuggling was a lucrative business for the Basques. Also a dangerous one.

He rose and continued to hike across the serene landscape. Parker felt as if he had done this before. He felt as if he'd made this trek across the mountains into Spain and returned back again into France with new acquisitions many times before tonight. But, at the same time, it felt as if this were his first trip across the mountains. Looking around, he asked himself, how can the mist at my knees be so thick and how can the moon above be so bright?

Something soft and mushy squished beneath his feet. He was sure it wasn't mud, since the earth all around was dry. He figured it must be *pottok* droppings. For the small mountain ponies they were, they sure could produce large piles of shit. Parker halted to try and scrape some of the dung off his shoe on a rock. Then he felt a hard nudge on his shoulder. Turning, he saw the moonlit face of Pascal staring at him, wide eyed and crazy. Pascal's eyes looked too big for his face.

"Keep moving," Pascal's gruff voice told him in Basque. Pascal didn't wait for him. The big man just kept moving along through the brush at his steady pace. Parker followed.

After hiking on the gentle slopes drenched in moonlight for some time, they reached an old stone building built into the side of the mountain. It looked like the roof came straight out from the mountainside. Even though Parker couldn't remember ever seeing the structure before, he knew this was their destination. He also knew that somewhere back in the mist they had crossed the border and were now in Spain. The stone structure was a sheepherders' cabin that Basque herders used during summer months when they took their flocks into the higher mountains to graze.

Deliberately, Pascal had led them in a wide circle so they would be walking in the direction of the front of the building as they approached. The thick stone that made up the building's walls was aglow from the bright moonlight. There were a few windows at the front of the structure, but they could see no light coming from them.

Pascal glanced behind to note the position of his men. They were exposed on a slope with no trees and few rock outcroppings for protection. In addition, the moon was bright, so they could all clearly see each other even though they were spread out. Raising his hand, Pascal motioned for the others to stop. They watched his broad shouldered frame slowly walk up to the cabin.

When he reached a distance of about twenty meters from the cabin, he stopped and crouched down. Then Pascal made a noise that sounded like a cat having its tail ripped off. There was a pause after Pascal's call that bothered them all.

The silence was heavy. It made Parker feel a surge of fear gushing through his limbs. His hair began to rise. A sharp screech emanated from the stone cabin piercing the night. All five men breathed a sigh of relief.

The cabin was really just a room with a small fireplace on one end and a stone table in the center, around which sat four men on wooden benches. There was a kerosene lamp on the table, six or seven bottles of red wine and some scattered glasses. Light from the lamp couldn't be seen from outside the cabin because thick wooden boards had been placed over the open windows. When Pascal's group stepped through the narrow doorway, the men at the table were playing cards and laughing.

"What's so funny?" Pascal asked in Basque.

"You're face is still pale, Pascal. Did we scare you a little?" one of them asked.

"This is no time for games, Miguel. We were about to start running." Pascal's face went from white shaded to red as he spoke.

Miguel set his cards down on the stone table and stood up with a wide grin on his dark face. "Pascal, Pascal. We're sorry, okay." He grabbed one of the two full bottles left and held it up in the air. "Here, sit down and have a drink with us before you go."

Pascal still looked angry. "I don't drink until after the job is done," he said. He cast a glance in the direction of his group and added with a wave of a hand, "I'm sure they'd appreciate a good drop though."

The others, including Parker, nodded their heads in agreement and thankfully took the short glasses full of wine handed to them.

"Are you sure you want to go on tonight? Considering the moon? It's true the French are all stupid, but even they could find someone on a night like tonight." Miguel commented.

Pascal shot a stern glance at Miguel, answering his question.

Meanwhile, Parker savored every drop in his glass. He swished the liquid around in his mouth and thought he could taste all the flavors of the Pyrenees in that one gulp of red wine—*pottock*, sheep, grass, trees, earth, and herbs.

They finished their glasses of wine and gladly accepted the offer for a refill. During this time, Pascal remained uneasy, pacing the dirt floor of the cabin. One glass was okay with him, but everyone in the room noticed the second glass was not. Instead of saying anything, he merely walked by them out the door and back into the night. The rest of his group quickly drained their glasses, placed them on the table, and followed his lead. Since they'd done this before, they knew where they were going.

Just east of the stone cabin, the slope of the mountain grew steeper and became the edge of a cliff that framed a small area, making obscuring it from the vision of anyone walking in the nearby mountains. It was in this place that the Spanish Basques, led by Miguel, would leave the herds of horses they brought from further south in Spain. Tonight there was a herd of about twenty horses. They were all tied together with loose rope and appeared calm.

Twenty horses on a night like this would be no cakewalk. Parker noticed the outline of a small framed man sitting on a rock above the horses. The little man acknowledged their presence by standing up and walking off in the direction of the cabin.

Whispering, Pascal told his men to spread out along the line and that he would walk in front. Within a few minutes, they were walking with the horses in the direction of the border.

Parker gazed at the ominous shadows surrounding him. He felt like he was breathing the mist into his lungs and it was turning him into a veil of mist as well. Momentarily closing his eyes, he breathed deeply as he walked.

Suddenly, he realized he was separated from the horses and the other three in the group. Parker frantically looked in every direction. All he could see was moonlight and a gentle slope to his side. Something told him to walk up to the top of the low mountain. Following his intuition, this is what he did.

He hung his head and watched the stiff grass as he walked. Though he couldn't explain, he could now see his feet below him as he walked, even though the mist still clung just as heavily on the ground as before.

He walked and walked, but didn't feel tired. In fact, the higher he went, the better he felt. It was like a great surge of joy rising in him with every step. When he finally raised his head, he saw that the slope was about to end and realized he was almost to the summit of the mountain. A fresh burst of energy pulsated through his veins and he began to run.

As he ran, his legs suddenly gave out and he began to feel as if he were floating through the air. Just as he was reaching the summit there was a brilliant flash of light and the moonlit night turned into a blue sky and sunny day. Parker looked out upon the green, rolling, hilly countryside speckled with white farmhouses framed in red and green that led to the ocean. It was such a breathtaking scene, emotions welled up inside him and he felt burning tears streaming down his cheeks—

His shoulder was being roughly shaken. Opening his eyes, Parker saw the face of Agent John Gibson.

"I just saw a sign that said we are getting close to Stockton," Gibson said. "You were really out of it there, kid." He stared out the side window at an abandoned pick-up on the side of the road that caught his eye. "You were even speaking a little Basque in your sleep. At least I think it was Basque."

Parker glared at Gibson while placing a cigarette between his lips. "The way you just said that made it sound as if you think me speaking a little Basque automatically makes me no better than the terrorists we're after," he said, lighting the cigarette.

Gibson's expression conveyed that Parker's comment caught him off-guard. He tried to regain his composure as quickly as possible. "Ah, well, that's not what I meant. It's just that everyone I've ever been around that spoke Basque has actually been a terrorist."

Parker cracked his window and blew out a choppy puff of smoke. "If I were a terrorist, Agent Gibson, I sure as hell wouldn't be here with you," he said, looking out the window. "Turn left at the next road," he instructed.

* * *

Basque Party Ban a Step Closer

The upper house of the Spanish parliament has passed a law that clears the way toward banning Batasuna, the political wing of the Basque separatist group, ETA. The law passed overwhelmingly, with a 214 to 15 vote. Besides the Popular Party of the Prime Minister, the opposition Socialist party backed the bill.

The government holds Batasuna and other logistical support groups partly responsible for ETA's campaign. Formerly known as Herribatasuna, then Euskal Herritarok and now just Batasuna, in the future it says it wants to be known as the Socialist Nationalists.

An earlier attempt to crumple Batasuna by locking up its leaders failed.

The moderate Basque nationalists, who control the Basque regional government, voted against the bill. Many critics in the Basque region warned that the new law could deepen confrontation rather than end it.

11

Stockton, California

THE OLD MAN PEERED at the men through his thick glasses and cleared his throat. He looked at them, noting that one was middle-aged and the other much younger, but did not speak right away. It wasn't his habit to begin conversations and since these two had come to *his* ranch house, he figured one of them should speak first. He leaned back in his rocking chair on the wooden porch and waited.

His name was Pierre Urbano and he had left his family's village in Basse-Navarre when he was fourteen years old to come to the United States to be a sheepherder. He'd endured a hard and lonely life on the desolate plains of Nevada and California, but through good fortune and wise financial decisions, had been able to become the owner of a large herd himself. When the sheep industry began to slow down, he converted to being a cattleman and prospered ever since. At one time, Pierre Urbano had the largest spread around Stockton.

Today, just as he was about to head inside for a mid-day nap, he noticed a cloud of dust moving down the road leading to his ranch. His wife opened the screen door, poked her head out and asked, "Are you expecting visitors?"

"No," he told her.

The old man remained seated in his chair, watching as Gibson and Parker walked along the path leading from the driveway to the porch. Now he was staring at them as they stood before him. Pierre Urbano thought they were an odd pair in spite of their obvious age difference. He observed that the older one looked tense and disagreeable, while the younger one, though friendly looking, was too pale around the eyes as if he had a bad case of *la grippe*.

As the silence lengthened, they felt uneasy. Finally, Parker looked over at Gibson, deciding he would be the one to break the ice. "Mr. Urbano, we're sorry to bother you, but I was told you might be able to help us." His head felt like a mallet was pounding a blue crab's shell inside.

The old man looked hard at him. "Help you? I don't even know you. Why would I help you?" he said as harshly as his weakened throat would allow.

Parker opted to try his luck and be frank with the old man. He didn't want to be standing there any longer than they had to since he felt a pressure building in his stomach that could lead to a mass exodus, at one end or the other. "I understand the oddness of the situation, sir. But we are after a group of murderers who killed José Aldarossa Arana in San Francisco a couple of days ago. I was told you might know who did it."

Pierre Urbano's round, wrinkled face didn't twitch in the slightest at the mention of the councilman's murder. He kept his small eyes fixed on Sebastian Parker.

Parker tried again. "Frank Sanders told me to come to you."

At the mention of the name, Pierre Urbano's eyebrows rose in interest. "You know Frank?" he asked.

"Yes. I met him five years ago through a friend of mine who is very good friends with him."

Gibson silently eyed Parker suspiciously.

"I haven't seen Frank in about a year. How is he?" Pierre Urbano asked, his tone now growing significantly warmer.

"Mean as ever," Parker replied.

"Ah, you're not lying then. You do know Frank! That Frank, he's a good man. It's only because of him that I'm alive today. One day, when I was out in the desert with a herd, some cowboys came with rifles pointed and wanted to shoot me just because I was a dirty *Vasco* sheepherder to them. But Frank Sanders was with them and told them cowboys he'd shoot'em dead if they touched me. Those other two cowboys looked like dogs that'd been kicked and they rode off."

The old man rose to his feet with a grin and a throaty chuckle. He extended his hand to Parker and introduced himself. Parker shook the old man's hand and noted the astonishingly strong grip for a man his age. Then Urbano turned and introduced himself to Gibson. He invited them to have a seat in the other chairs on the porch. Once they were sitting, he asked, "Would you like something to drink?"

Gibson began saying, "N—"

But Parker quickly spoke over him. "We'd love a drink." He threw a quick glance at Gibson, hoping he would understand.

Smiling, the old man called out in Basque into the house and within a few moments, a short, shriveled woman came out carrying a tray with a bottle of wine, three glasses, and a small bowl of crackers. Urbano placed a small table between them and she set down the tray on top. He didn't introduce his wife to them, and she didn't stay around long enough to be introduced. From one of the pockets of his jean overalls, he produced a folded corkscrew and effortlessly pulled out the cork from the bottle and poured the glasses full of the bright rosé wine.

As it was still before noon, Gibson had no desire to have a drink of anything. But a slight elbow nudge and nod of the head from Parker told him he was going to have to choke down the glass of wine, whether he liked it or not.

Parker, on the other hand, was actually quite excited about the prospect of a glass of wine. He hoped it would help relieve his hangover.

Pierre Urbano held up his glass and looked across the little table at them. They held up their glasses as well.

"*Ching, ching,*" the old man said with a mischievous grin.

"*À vôtre santé,*" Parker said. He and Urbano tipped back their heads and swallowed their wine in two gulps. When they were done, they set their glasses back on the table and stared at Gibson, who had taken one small sip of his wine.

Parker rolled his eyes and it made the old man smile. They both ate a few crackers and then the old man refilled their glasses. Gibson was still only halfway through his first glass.

Parker got out his pack of cigarettes, offered the pack to the old man who politely refused, but lit one of his own he retrieved from a pack stuffed into the front of his overalls. They nodded at one another with a grin.

Now it was time to talk.

"So, you are looking for who killed the councilman?" Urbano asked.

Parker shook his head in acknowledgement.

"You will not find them here," the old man said, turning his head to glance over the horizon.

"Yes, I know. Mr. Urbano. We didn't come here to ask you if it was a group from ETA who did this, because we already know it was. I'm also not here to ask you if you know anything about the killers, because we know you don't. But we know you are connected to practically everyone with Basque heritage in California and Nevada. Also, we know you are against ETA. In order to pull this off, whoever did this had to have help here. Our theory is that whoever helped this group in San Francisco wasn't from there either. Since the Central Valley is one of the largest enclaves of Basque-Americans in the west, I believe someone from here may have helped them, and I'm hoping you will know of some people or groups out here that are involved with ETA."

The old man dropped his eyes to the wooden floor of the porch. "Do you know why I am anti-ETA, as you say?"

"No, Frank didn't explain that to me," admitted Parker. The old man's expression changed from a cheery grin of a moment ago into one of sadness. Gibson forced down another gulp of rosé.

"I actually hate ETA. You see, I left the Pays Basque before most of this movement for independence started and I was out walking when many of the killings were taking place. So, I didn't really know much about it and didn't really care. But I never believed in killing people."

"My first born, Joshua, decided as soon as he was old enough he would go live with our relatives in the Basque Country. I thought it would be good for him to see where his people had come from. If I had known what was going to happen, I would have never have let him ago," Urbano paused for a moment.

"Joshua was a good boy who never did anyone harm. He saw what evil the ETA was doing and made the mistake of telling everyone he met over there his views on the struggle. Later, I was told he had convinced an entire village they should not support any of ETA's activities. One dark night, ETA decided to come for him. A group of men kidnapped him in front of his aunt, uncle, and cousins. They took him into the mountains and tortured him to try and make him stop speaking against them. Though they tore off all his fingernails, my boy was strong and stubborn. Weeks later, his body was stumbled upon by a *berger* looking for one of his lost sheep. That is why I hate ETA. That is why I will help you today." Urbano lifted his eyes.

Gibson and Parker waited intently for what he would say next.

Urbano continued. "Not too many people around here know what happened to my boy. Most of the other Basques in this area are from Labourd and don't know anyone from my family's village. I've always tried to stay out of politics, but everything that happens seems to get back to me, one way or another. I've been here for a long time and know pretty much all the other Basques. Some of the people here are supporters of independence at any cost, and there's been some talk lately about some people working with ETA." Urbano paused to take a large swallow of wine.

"Jean Gamboa owns a hotel downtown. It's a typical Basque hotel like in the old days, with a restaurant on the ground floor. It's located near the railroad tracks and is called the Pyrenees Hotel. Gamboa himself is an old man like me who has no respect for ETA. His daughter, Sara, is a different matter. Sara is a pretty, petite Basque girl with radical views and a fine talent for public speaking. She's actually on the city council. I went in to town the other day to have a pastis with Jean at his hotel and he told me something about her."

"What'd he tell you?" Gibson blurted out, receiving dirty looks from both Urbano and Parker. "Excuse me," he apologized.

"We were talking about our families and when I asked about Sara, he told me he thought something strange was happening to his daughter. Normally, she has dinner with them every Wednesday night at the hotel, but last Wednesday she didn't show up. She didn't even call them to say she wouldn't be there. The next morning, Jean tried to call her at work and was told she hadn't come in yet. Worried she might be sick, he went to her house and found her still in bed. Though she wasn't ill, she told him she just had a late night. When he asked her what she'd done, she just said she'd driven to San Francisco. She told him nothing more."

"Where can we find this woman?" Parker asked, suppressing a feeling of accomplishment.

"She spends a lot of time with her family at the hotel. If she's not there, you can ask anyone there how to get to her house."

Gibson was out of his chair and striding for the Expedition before Urbano finished his sentence.

Parker slowly stood and extended his hand. "It's been a great pleasure meeting you, sir. I thank you for your help. *Et pour le vin*," he said with a smile.

Pierre Urbano looked at the young man's hand. "You understand, I don't mean to do the girl harm. She's a nice girl. I just can't defend anyone who helps ETA."

Parker nodded, and the old man crunched his hand in a firm shake. "I can tell you are a good person…almost Basque," he added with a smile.

* * *

Gibson and Parker drove into downtown Stockton and easily found the Pyrenees Hotel. The hotel's large red façade dominated the block and was near the railroad tracks as they'd been told. The hotel had two large picture windows on each side of the entrance and a balcony lined the second floor.

Parker entered first and from the moment he stepped into the hotel, he felt as if he was back in Europe. They stood in a narrow entryway with a staircase at the back of the room. There was a room on either side of them. One was the hotel reception desk and the other a restaurant and bar room. The smell of richly flavored food cooking somewhere in the building made them hungry.

A portly man called to them from behind the bar. "Can I help you?"

Parker walked through the room up to the bar. About half the tables were occupied by people working their way through a hearty lunch. The clientele looked to be mostly older people, but there were a few middle-aged professionally dressed people mixed in as well. Two older men were sitting on stools at the end of the bar. They were drinking white wine out of short glasses and disputing something in French. Loud talking and clanging silverware filled the room.

Glancing at the bartender, Parker decided to risk assuming the man spoke French. The bartender had hawk-like eyes that sharpened on one as though they were a piece of carrion. "*Nous cherchons* Sara Gamboa. *Nous avons un rendez-vous avec elle à midi.*" He held up his wrist and looked at his watch, explaining that they were looking for Miss Gamboa as they had a meeting with her at noon. Simultaneously, the bartender and he glanced at the clock on a far wall that read 12:15. Raising his head, he did his best Gallic shrug. "Women do not like waiting for men. *Les femmes n'aiment pas quand les hommes sont en retard, n'est-ce pas*?"

Running his hands across his protruding belly, the bartender gazed hesitantly at Parker. Seeing the man's expression, Parker thought, for an embarrassing moment, that he made a mistake in his guesswork and had spouted French for nothing.

The chubby face produced a voice and explained that they were in luck. She was sitting at a table near the back of the room. "*Elle est là-bas.*" The bartender waved a finger to a back corner of the room.

As the three of them looked in the direction of the dark haired girl sitting alone in the corner, she glanced up from a magazine she was reading. Her eyes seemed to double in size and she dropped the magazine as every muscle in her body tensed. She was about to make a dash for the back door of the room when the look in her eyes turned from adrenaline rush to fear.

Sara eased back into her chair and gently, slowly placed her hands on the table in front of her. The tense moment happened so fast that Parker hadn't noticed the veil of silence that had overcome the formerly cheery room.

Then he realized what Sara Gamboa and the other diners had seen—Agent Gibson's drawn .45 mm caliber pointed directly at her.

"You might want to get these people out of here," Parker suggested to the bartender.

"*Putain flic*," the bartender replied.

Parker turned a penetrating look on the man and told him to shut up. "*Ta guelle.*"

Gibson peered over from the sights on his gun at Parker and the bartender with a speckle of amusement on his face. "Parker, that sure sounded like an insult to me," he said.

"Yeah, I don't like rude people," Parker said. He started walking to Sara's table. A couple sitting near her quickly rose from their seats and walked away. When he was close, Parker grinned and asked, "May we join you?"

Her large brown eyes watched him sit down across from her. Parker looked at her without saying anything.

Most of the people had cleared out of the room by now, except for the two old men drinking wine at the bar. These two hadn't even noticed what was happening behind their backs.

For some reason, Sara was more uncomfortable with the young one's stares than by the gun pointed at her. He had a look in his eyes that she didn't understand. Surely he knew what she had done and must despise her, since he brought the big man with the gun to her. Yet, a sense of caring shone through his eyes. His eyes pulled hers into looking directly at him. There was something else behind those eyes and that handsome face, she was sure of it. Now he was speaking to her, but she couldn't hear the words.

He smiled at her and spoke again. "Sara, you're going to have to stand up for a minute to let Agent Gibson here frisk you. Then you can sit back down and we're going to talk."

Somehow, the man with the gun was now standing right next to her, the big gun pointing at her. "Please, I don't have any weapons and I won't cause any trouble," she managed to say. The man ran a hand across her sides. He pulled her purse across the floor and motioned for her to sit.

"So, how do you prefer your piperade?" Parker asked her after she was seated.

"Pardon me?" she asked, with a look of complete confusion on her face.

"You know, Basque piperade with eggs and peppers and tomatoes. Do you like it better all scrambled together or solid like an omelet?"

Gibson would have berated anyone else for beginning an interrogation of a suspect in this crazy manner, but in the short time he'd known Sebastian Parker, he'd seen him succeed more than most. He decided to give Parker the benefit of the doubt.

Sara looked just as confused as Gibson. She pondered over the question for longer than was needed solely because she couldn't understand what was going on. "Like a thick omelet," she finally answered.

Parker shook his head in agreement. "I agree. That's the best way." He noticed a little color returning to her face and an easing of the muscles in her face and neck. "I'd love nothing more than to sit here and chat with you about Basque cuisine, Sara, but unfortunately we've got to talk about something serious now. Since we already know you, I think it's only fair that we introduce ourselves. I'm Sebastian Parker and this is Federal Agent John Gibson."

Gibson gave her a stiff nod, his gun still pointed at her.

"We know you were involved with the killing, Sara. And, I'll be honest with you, you're in trouble no matter what. I mean, they're going to nail you for being an accomplice any way you look at it..." Parker let his voice trail off.

Sara's thin neck tensed again and a screen of regret filled her eyes. Since Parker didn't take his eyes from her face, he didn't see Gibson gently grinning in pride at Parker's performance.

One of the older men at the bar slammed a wrinkled hand on the counter, spouting a mouthful of disgust in Basque over something. The outburst jarred Sara from her momentary lapse. She snapped awake as if she just woke from a terrible dream. Seeing the barrel of a gun pointed at her confirmed she wasn't dreaming. "What can I do?" she asked.

"Tell us everything," Parker replied.

She shook her head in agreement and took a few deep breaths.

"Gibson, be a gentleman and sit down and put your gun away."

Gibson sat down stiffly in a chair next to, but slightly behind, Sara Gamboa. He kept an eye on her and one on the entrance into the room, his hand on his gun. "Okay, Sara," Parker said.

"You know, even if I tell you something to save myself, they'll come after me," she said.

"Who will come after you, Sara? ETA?" Parker asked.

"No, that's not who I mean. You don't understand. ETA didn't do this by themselves. We were just waiting for them to ask for our help. Oh, *bordel*, I shouldn't have listened to him! I knew he was lying when he said we'd never get caught." She was shaking slightly and having trouble pulling out a cigarette from the box on the table in front of her.

Parker touched the back of her hand and moved it from the box. He pulled out two cigarettes from the box and handed her one. He lit hers once she had it in her mouth. The other he lit for himself. Out of the corner of his eye, he noticed Gibson's disapproval, so he decided to get back to the questions.

"Who told you that, Sara?" Parker asked.

She sucked harshly on the cigarette and quickly released the smoke from her mouth. Parker had only seen speed freaks smoke so violently. "There is a secret grassroots organization here in the U.S. that raises funds and weapons for ETA's fight. I'm a member of this organization. We communicate with one another and stay connected with those in the Pays Basque through the internet by only writing in Basque, which is difficult to monitor."

Taking a quick glance back at Gibson, she then continued. "I'm sure you know of ETA's revolutionary tax?" Parker nodded his head. "About a year ago we were told to up our efforts in the U.S. by not just requesting donations for the fight for independence, but by demanding them. Many prominent Basque-Americans in this country have already been approached, and many have paid. Arana was the first to refuse to make a contribution and you saw what happened to him." She leaned back in her chair and sucked on her cigarette. Parker noticed that talking about her cause gave her new confidence.

Eyeing her closely, Parker glanced over at Gibson who looked as if he wanted to ram her face into the table. "He had a wife and kids, Sara. He was a city councilman in a large, symbolic U.S. city. His family hasn't lived in the Basque Country for over a hundred years. The only connection he had to the cause was his Basque name." In her eyes, Parker saw nothing in response.

"It's a war, Mr. Parker. Did the Fascists consider these things when they massacred our people at Guernica? Did General Franco keep these things in mind when he brutally repressed our people for decades while receiving aid from the United States, just because he wasn't a communist? You can't understand. You're not Basque!"

Looking at Parker, Gibson noticed something change in him as Sara spoke. It was as if someone were holding him to the floor and covering his mouth while lecturing him on an issue he couldn't wait to comment on. Parker forcefully rammed the cigarette into the ashtray on the table. This was the first time Gibson had seen him pissed off.

Parker's usual soft eyes turned to ice. "I understand the Basques perhaps better than you do," he said to her in Basque. She looked at him in silent surprise.

"And I know many Basques who are proud of being Basque, yet they don't agree with the deadly tactics of ETA," he added in French.

"Now tell us about this organization and everything you know about that night!" He had raised his voice and finished by speaking in English, mostly for the sake of Gibson who was staring blankly at him.

She took two cigarettes from the pack and handed him one. After they were both lit, she said, "We call ourselves *Those of the New World,* but you won't find anything about our group anywhere."

"How clever. Just like *Those of the North* in France," Parker added.

Sara looked at Parker for the first time as if he actually knew his stuff. "Everything was kept purposefully vague for that night. I was to pick up a group at a destination in San Francisco and bring them to a drop off destination here, where they were split up. The night I was to go, I found out the location was in the city by an anonymous e-mail. I didn't know where I was to drop them off until I received a call just before I was about to pick them up. I didn't talk to any of them and don't know where they went after I dropped them off or who they went with. All I really know is that eventually they were all going back to the Pays Basque, but by different routes."

She pulled fiercely on her cigarette once again, then added, "There. That's all I can tell you. Even though it's nothing, I'm sure I'm going to pay for telling you even that."

Softly, Parker asked, "Who's going to make you pay, Sara?"

"These people are ready to explode! We've been waiting over half a century to join in the fight and now's our chance. There's more of a following for ETA here than you could ever imagine. And they have ways of finding things out. Who knows—maybe one of those old men up there at the bar was put there to watch me. And now they'll know everything," she said as she pointed her cigarette at the old men.

"Sara, you're being paranoid. Just calm down. We can get protection for you," Parker promised, nodding in Gibson's direction.

"Protection!" She thrust her arms in the air. "Are you fucking kidding me? Why not just put a big sign on me that says traitor!"

"Okay, okay. Listen, Sara, can you just give us a brief description of the group you drove from San Francisco to Stockton? Anything at all, even the smallest details would be helpful." Parker pulled out a small notepad and pen. Gibson nodded his approval.

"There were three men and one woman. The woman is very pretty with long blonde hair. The one I took as the leader is tall and thin, and I think I remember seeing a small scar below the corner of one of his eyes. He had black hair. I didn't get much of a look at the other two guys. One was average in height with light brown hair. The other was short, dark skinned, and strong looking."

Parker made a few notes in his notepad. "Anything else?"

"Both the girl and the tall one smoked cigarettes. He smoked non-filtered Gauloises and she smoked half a pack in an hour. Besides that, all I can really add is that they were young, probably all in their early twenties."

"All right. Now are you sure you didn't know any of the people who took them once you dropped them off?"

She dabbed out her cigarette in the ashtray. "When it came to any sort of illegal activity, we never saw one another. We communicated through fake email accounts with fake names. I doubt they were from around here anyway."

"How about their cars that night? Do you remember any of those?" Parker pursued.

"It was dark and I was exhausted. I wasn't supposed to look anyway—just drop them off and drive away, as discreetly as possible."

In a softer tone, Parker asked, "But would you recognize any of them if you saw them again?"

Sara looked directly into Parker's eyes and spoke softly. "Definitely not the two in the back. But the tall one had a face one wouldn't forget. The woman had too beautiful of a face not be jealous of it. The two of them would make an interesting couple—him looking fierce and reptilian, and she looking like an angel."

Leaning back slightly, Parker winked at Gibson.

Jean Gamboa suddenly burst into the room with his arms in the air. He angrily demanded, "What do you think you're doing to my daughter?"

Parker raised a hand to Gibson, indicating he not whip out his gun.

"You leave my *petite fille* alone, you hear me!" He grabbed Sara's arm with a shaking hand and pulled her up from her chair. "What they bother you for, Sara?" he asked his daughter.

She wouldn't look at him.

Gibson spoke pointedly, but respectfully. "We have reason to believe your daughter was involved in a crime, sir."

"A crime!" He over-pronounced the *r,* making it sound like a painful letter to speak. "What crime? My Sara is a good girl. She has nothing to do with no crime." He paused for her to add something to his statement of her innocence. But his pause was met with silence from his daughter. Looking at her again, but differently now, as a father slightly ashamed by his child's actions, he breathed deeply with his weakened lungs.

"You here to arrest her?" he asked.

Gibson considered the question before answering. "No, we're not going to arrest her. Not yet, anyway. We don't have enough proof to take her in. We just came to have a word with her."

A smile crossed Jean Gamboa's face, revealing the perfect line of his dentures, as he explained that their interview with her was over. "*Eh bien, alors c'est fini maintenant*," he said definitively.

Gibson looked questioningly to Parker who translated. "He says no more talking."

"Listen sir, she'd be better off with us. If she cooperates, we can protect her," Gibson pleaded.

Jean Gamboa puffed his chest out. "I will protect her," he said in the deepest voice his throat could muster. He put his frail arm around his daughter's shoulders and led her out of the room. She placed her head on his shoulder and remained expressionless. Just as they left the room, her father poked his head back around the entrance. "You come back if you have warrant. Otherwise, *allez-vous faire foutre*!"

The bartender had been busying himself washing glasses behind the bar. Now he made his presence known by chuckling at the comment from the older man. The pair of old men at the bar continued their argument, without giving the slightest acknowledgment of anyone else in the room.

Parker was about to translate the French expression for Gibson, but it was Gibson's turn to raise a hand. "I think I got that one. Get the hell out of here, right?"

Parker palmed his pack of cigarettes on the table and popped one in his mouth. "Pretty much," he agreed. He lit a dangling cigarette in his mouth.

* * *

Gibson slammed on the brakes of the Expedition and steered the vehicle onto the dirt shoulder of the highway. He snapped off his sunglasses and turned in his seat to face Parker. "All right, Parker, what's next? Our principal witness, that you ably supplied, just left us. How are we ever going to find these bastards now?"

Parker looked at him calmly while he cracked his window and lit a cigarette. "You know, I really should have asked you if it was okay if I smoke in here, but now it's too late. So I'll just have to assume you don't really care." With that said, he blew out a thin line of smoke through the small opening of the lowered window.

Gibson continued staring at him. "We've got all we need. There's no point trying to track them down here. We'll just go and wait for them to return to their homeland, if they are not already there," Parker calmly remarked.

"Homeland! You mean in Europe?"

"Yes, Agent Gibson. The Basque Country is in Europe."

Gibson slammed a clenched fist down onto the steering wheel. "Goddamn it! I don't want to go to Europe!" he bristled with frustration.

Casually, Parker inhaled and exhaled smoke a few times before turning to look Gibson in the eye. "Trust me, the Basque Country is like nowhere else in Europe, or even in the world for that matter. The hydrangeas will be about to bloom in Biarritz, and the green of the rolling hills of the countryside will be its greenest. And when we're not tracking down these bastards, we'll be enjoying everything about the enchanting place."

Parker had closed his eyes as he visualized his description. When he opened them, he saw Gibson looking at him like he was an escaped lunatic from an asylum. "Let me remind you once again that this isn't meant to be a vacation, Parker," Gibson said through gritted teeth.

"You've got to learn *la joie de vivre* a little bit, Gibson. You know—the good things in life. I know this won't be a vacation, but we might as well make the most of it. Right?"

Gibson eyed Parker without responding. He put the SUV back into drive and stepped on the gas pedal before commenting. "You really like these Basque people, huh, Parker?"

"What's that supposed to mean?"

"Oh, nothing. You just seemed to be a bit overly concerned for Miss Gamboa back there."

Parker practically bit through the filter of his cigarette. "Are you implying that just because I have a vested interest in the Basque culture, I'm automatically an ETA supporter?"

"Never mind, forget it," Gibson said.

"I'll try, whatever that shit was. Why don't you get your boys out here to watch over Sara. I think she'll cooperate once we show her we're serious about protecting her."

"When we get back to the city, I'll tell them to send some people out here." Gibson cracked his knuckles on the steering wheel. "I guess I'll also need to tell someone to get us airline tickets to Europe."

"*Mais oui, elle nous attend,*" Parker replied, saying that Europe was waiting for them.

* * *

Basque Groups on U.S. Terror List

The government of the United States has added Batasuna, the alleged political wing of the Basque armed separatist group ETA, to its list of terrorist groups.

This decision makes the group liable to sanctions in the U.S. After the Spanish Prime Minister, currently in Washington for talks, pressured the American President, this decision was made. The Spanish Prime Minister was an early ally of the U.S. President in the war against Iraq, supporting U.S. moves to seek U.N. support.

Batasuna is already indefinitely banned in Spain, the first ban of a political party since the death in 1975 of dictator General Francisco Franco. The U.S. Secretary of State signed the order, adding three Basque nationalist groups: Batasuna, Euskal Herritarrok and Herri Batasuna to the U.S. terrorist organization list. ETA is already on the U.S. State Department's list of foreign terrorist organizations.

The U.S. Secretary of State signed the statement one day before he visited the Spanish capital, but the announcement was delayed to ensure that the organizations named would not have time to escape financial sanctions by moving funds out of reach of U.S. authorities. The decree prohibits all financial transactions, including donations. Members of the groups placed on the list are also subject to a U.S. visa ban.

European press sources are claiming the move as a reward for Spain's support for the United States in the Iraq conflict. Many Spanish newspapers point out that it has taken the U.S. and many other countries quite a long time to recognize that ETA, in all its multiple arms, is a

terrorist organization. However, the Spanish newspaper, *El Pais*, has warned against the belief that the fight against ETA can be won in the international arena.

The European Union has already blacklisted Batasuna by adding it to its list of terrorist organizations. Inclusion on the E.U. list obliges all European Union countries to cooperate with officials investigating the prosecution of the party. News of the E.U.'s announcement was met with a car bomb planted in Madrid, killing two policemen.

ETA claimed responsibility, reminding the world of its existence and unimposing persistence, proving that although it is down, the organization is by no means defeated.

12

Basque Country, France

FIELDS OF LEAFY VINEYARDS piled on top of each other passed beneath them and Parker recognized they were flying over the Bordeaux region. He had two small bottles of a full bodied Bordeaux red, after a small bottle of French champagne. Dreamily, he wished the plane could land for an extended wine tasting.

The stiffness emanating from Gibson sitting next to him quickly knocked the pleasant reveries from his mind. He knew Gibson was upset at him for drinking so much on their flight across the Atlantic from San Francisco to Paris, and now on their short flight from Paris to Biarritz. In his mind, Parker could easily justify his indulgences. He wouldn't have been able to sleep on the first flight without getting a bit lit up, and he couldn't be asked by anyone to refuse a few glasses of a fine French wine while traveling to France. Besides, not being able to smoke was bad enough. Gibson could go screw himself for being such a lame ass.

Below them the long, spaced rows of vines soon changed into lines of tall, thin pine trees. They were now over the famous forest of the Landes. Parker remembered reading that it was the largest man-made forest in Europe. Napoleon III ordered it planted on top of the marsh lands that the region had once been. Now it was a land of flat fields of grain, thick forests, and wonderful beaches. Parker considered sharing these facts with Gibson, but decided against it in favor of waiting in anticipation for the flat fields below to transform into the rolling hills that would mark their entry over the Pays Basque. He closed his eyes.

When he opened them he saw an ocean of green hills freckled with white farmhouses bordered by a dark blue ocean, back dropped by a line of jagged mountains. Instantly, Parker felt the familiar, warm feeling he always felt when arriving in the Basque Country. It was like returning home.

* * *

Sara Gamboa was beyond frightened—she was petrified. Her father, bless his soul, assured her she had nothing to worry about. He told her other Basque-Americans would never think of harming her, no matter how militant they were. Looking at her father's crumbled face, she had difficulty believing him. After the incident at the hotel, he brought her to her house and refused to leave. She knew he would offer minimal protection. Even though he was old and had lived a good life, she didn't want her father killed with her.

Eventually, she was able to talk him into leaving when she mentioned her mother would not be able to give herself her nightly shot. That was what finally convinced her father the best thing for him to do was to go home. After he left, Sara double checked all the doors to make sure they were locked and all the windows were latched. Then grabbing a large steak knife from a drawer, she clung to it while she stared out her front window at the quiet street. She felt the touch of the cold metal of the knife on her cheek.

A clock chimed in a distant room, prompting her to look down at her watch. Midnight. As she crouched in the corner of her living room, staring at the street outside, she felt her eyes grow heavier and heavier. She tried her best to keep herself awake by slapping her face, but it was a hopeless cause. Exhaustion finally overcame her and before long she was lightly snoring with the large knife pressed against her face.

Something crashed. The loud sound pierced through the calm of the house and woke Sara. Staying in her crouched position, she nervously moved her eyes around the room. Then glancing down at her watch, she saw the time was 3:30 a.m. *Did I dream the noise?*

Looking again, she saw nothing, but then another noise came from the kitchen. She was torn between knowing she had to get up and the fact her mind had great difficulty in forcing her to do so. Her body felt like clay and she didn't know where the energy or force came from that helped her rise and stand next to the entrance into the living room from the kitchen—the big steak knife still in her hand.

Footsteps. The undeniable sound of footsteps walking across her kitchen sent a chill through her body. Her breathing uncontrollably increased and every nerve in her body seemed to be pulsating. In her head she counted the steps. When the steps lead to where she knew was just to the left of her, she sprang from her hiding place, intending to automatically drive the large knife into the chest of whoever had intruded into her home. But Sara Gamboa was not a killer and fell short from where she intended to strike.

She rapidly turned to face the intruder. Instead of driving the knife into a body, she merely stood in silent confusion. She knew the man standing before her, knew him very well in fact. Sara never realized that her own weapon of choice for her defense had actually been turned against her and used to pierce one of her lungs. As she felt her last breaths leave her body, a warm sensation overcame her.

* * *

Gentle sunshine danced on their faces as they walked through the doors of the Biarritz Airport. Everything around them held a glow. The plants seemed greener, the trees fuller, and the flowers brighter. Even the pavement appeared to shine. They watched a boy pull up in the blue Peugeot Parker rented inside the airport. Parker said something in French to the driver and motioned for Gibson to get in. Soon they were driving at a rapid speed away from the terminal.

Parker gunned the car in second gear until the loud grinding noise coming from the engine sounded as if something was about to break. Gibson noticed how he didn't even check his mirrors when changing lanes. Without a word, Parker turned on the radio and played with the knob until he settled on a station with a woman singing a sad sounding song. Then cracking his window, Parker lit a cigarette from one of the three packs of Chesterfield Lights he bought inside the airport. He mumbled something about a different taste from those in the States, and turned up the volume of the radio.

Gibson didn't understand a word of the song, but he thought the woman's voice was sexy. He noticed Parker looked content and relaxed as he drove. Gibson also enjoyed the moment of calm. He gazed out the window at the new, confusing land around him. It looked like it was a land wanting to remain rural, yet modernization was creeping in on its frontiers. One minute he was enjoying the view of charming farmhouses graciously spaced on a wavy green landscape, the next they were passing a French version of Home Depot. The song ended and suddenly the voice of a man screaming something from the speakers of the car made him jump in his seat. Eventually, the loud Frenchman stopped yelling and the melodious voices of an American boy band filled the car.

Parker nearly choked on the smoke he was exhaling as he raised his shoulders in an exaggerated display of disgrace. "What is this *putain merde*? Like we don't hear enough of this crap in the States to come over to France and hear it!" He turned the knob to a different station. Gibson thought it was awful sounding music on the new station. Since the singing was in French, that seemed to be enough for Parker.

"Did you just turn fifty degrees more French in the last twenty minutes?"

Parker glanced at Gibson in response to the question. He lit another cigarette and shrugged abruptly.

In the far distance, Gibson could see the gothic spires of a cathedral. Parker told him he would get them rooms in Bayonne and Gibson remembered him mentioning there being a large cathedral in the city. Although Parker said something more about where they would stay, he couldn't quite make it out and had been too upset with him for drinking too much on the planes to talk. It had sounded something like little Bayonne. He decided to inquire further on the subject once they arrived at the hotel.

Fixating on the spires jutting above the line of trees on the highway, Gibson contemplated how different Europe was from the United States. Mainly he noted how one saw skyscrapers when approaching a city in the States; here one saw the tops of cathedrals.

They passed through the downtown area. Parker explained it was referred to as the *centre ville*. Gibson noticed many inner city streets were medieval looking—worn cobblestone, narrow, dark, and blocked off to automobile traffic. Then they drove over a river on a small bridge. Traffic on the street came to a stop, leaving them on the bridge. Looking down, he saw the river was murky and slow flowing.

While they were halted in traffic on the bridge, Gibson looked in disbelief at the serene beauty of the scene before him. Each side of the winding river was bordered by a line of white buildings with red and green shutters that were actually row houses with storefronts on the street levels. In the background was a rolling green countryside that gradually grew into a thick line of mountainous peaks in the distance. There were a few other weathered, stone bridges crossing the river that looked only wide enough for one vehicle to pass over at a time. A narrow walkway ran along each side and there were people standing along it, staring down at the gently flowing water.

Glancing at Parker, Gibson noticed he was also admiring the scene. Taking a closer look, it seemed to him that Parker now appeared different. From their first meeting, he found Sebastian Parker to be easy going and likable. But now he looked even more relaxed and comfortable in this surrounding.

Parker turned halfway in his seat to talk to Gibson. "Over there, to the left, is the Hotel De Ville," he said.

Gibson turned the opposite direction and saw an inviting square in front of a large, classic style, stone building. There were flags flying from the building and he recognized the French flag among them. The square had a fountain in the center and there were a few cafés that had tables and chairs around the periphery of the square. Despite his dislike for most things European, he admitted that some things were nice about Europe. This square for instance, with a view of the charming buildings bordering the river, would be a nice place to sit outside and have a drink.

"You'll see one in every city here. They are like our city halls and usually mark the center of a city," Parker explained.

"Doesn't seem like a bad place, for being in Europe that is," Gibson admitted.

Parker ignored the disdain in Gibson's voice. "I haven't seen much better. Ernest Hemingway even once wrote: *Bayonne is a nice town.* What more of an expert opinion is needed after that?"

After driving across the bridge, they entered a different part of the city. The buildings weren't so nice here and the narrow streets didn't look as inviting as across the river. Later Gibson would learn that this was Petit Bayonne. Parker brought the Peugot to a screeching stop in front of a building that to Gibson looked like a large, neglected house. Over the door there was a small sign that read: Hotel Baiona.

* * *

She loved sitting on the low beach wall in Hendeye and staring out at the blue mass of the Atlantic Ocean. Sometimes she would sit in the same spot, entranced by the swirling water for hours. It was the only place she ever felt as if she were actually meant to be alive instead of just waiting for an end. Sometimes she thought anyone seeing her might think she made quite an interesting, yet bizarre, scene—a very attractive young woman sitting for hours by herself looking at nothing. But Graciana didn't care what people thought of her. Actually, she didn't care about much at all. The cause didn't mean as much to her as she knew it was supposed to. It was supposed to give her purpose, supposed to make her feel a part of something as it did for Lopé.

In the end, it was just something more exciting to do with her life than going to university and doing whatever afterward. Probably every year she would join her colleagues and strike for some reason or other—because they didn't get paid enough, or didn't have enough vacation time, or because they didn't have a good enough café next to their office. Then she would marry a husband who would cheat on her and drink too much. Then she would have a kid and sit at home and masturbate while her husband was off banging some other *meuf.* It was all bullshit and she wouldn't have it. She could never think of denying herself the right to be herself. If she couldn't live exactly the way she wanted, she wouldn't be able to live at all. It annoyed her that she could never sit in her favorite spot and not be bothered by hordes of *drageurs,* but she could usually promptly divert their pointless efforts with a look of death in their direction. Graciana wasn't going to let penises ruin her favorite spot in the world.

The smooth beach of Hendeye, Hendaia in Basque, bent inwards into the ocean. She liked to sit more toward the right end of the beach where she could look over the inlet and watch the fishing boats from Spain. Fonterrabi, the Spanish Basque town also known as by its Basque name of Hondarribia, with its rows of dark wooden balconies dangling over its streets, was directly across the inlet from Hendeye. In the center of the city the old castle still stood watch over the harbor, over the border, and over all of Fonterrabi. Though the French had always been skeptical about trusting their Basque population, the Spanish always had trouble even considering trusting the Spanish Basques.

Graciana lit a cigarette and tossed the lit match at Spain. She watched as the flame went out in the air and a flutter of black smoke jumped from the match before it slammed into the ground. To hell with the king, she thought to herself. Then glancing at her watch, she recognized that she was supposed to meet with some people.

Though she was excited about receiving orders for her next mission, she also knew she would be reprimanded for not locking herself in a room. Blatantly disobeying direct orders wasn't her motive. She just didn't want to be caged up like some kind of animal for however many days it would take the command to remember her.

Assuming she would be moved out of France, she hoped to be added to one of the more active cells in San Sebastian or Madrid—somewhere with lots of action. With a deep pull on her *clop,* she swung her thin legs over the wall and gracefully landed both feet on the sidewalk. She blew a delicate line of smoke from her barely parted lips and threw away the butt. The café where she was meeting the two penises, as she referred to most males in her mind, was a walk up a street. She decided to have another cigarette while she walked.

* * *

"Okay, I was told this guy from the Anti-Terrorist Division of the National Police, Capitaine Nivelle, would meet us when we checked in. By the way, is Capitaine the same as our Captain?"

"Pretty much. Nivelle, huh?" Parker said as they began to climb the winding wooden stairs that were so old and worn they tilted inwards. "That's a great start."

"What does the guy's name have to do with anything? Jesus, Parker, you're such a little shit sometimes. We haven't even met the guy yet. My boss told me he's top notch."

Parker stopped on the stairwell, causing Gibson to nearly run into him. "Oh, I'm sure he's a ground shaker and a body counter." He rolled his eyes and shook his head.

"What the hell does that mean?"

Parker kept walking up the stairs and only slightly turned his head to say, "*la Direction de l'Antiterrorisme*, called DNAT for short, is notoriously just as corrupt and brutal as its Spanish counterpart. The French just have better capabilities and the sense to hide it from the outside world. Actually, the French are even very good at hiding it from the rest of France. And as far as the name Nivelle, didn't you ever take a European History class that covered World War I?"

Gibson hated the way Parker could make him feel like he was being quizzed at times. The kid knew too much for someone his age. "Sure, when I was in tenth grade. Why? What's the name Nivelle have to do with World War I?"

"I'll tell you later. This is our floor."

* * *

Both men went into their own rooms, showered, and changed. Parker was lying on the edge of the bed in Gibson's room with a cigarette dangling from his lips. Gibson asked him not to smoke in his room. In response, Parker opened the room's window.

Gibson anxiously paced the room. "You're a smart guy, Parker. Don't you know those damned things are going to kill you?"

"Yup. If not lung cancer, it could be mouth or throat cancer. Or even heart failure or emphysema," he smartly quipped through a cloud of smoke, slowly released from his mouth.

"Then why do it?"

"I could walk out onto the street tomorrow and get hit by a bus and that would kill me too. I'll quit someday. Right now I like smoking."

"You've got a morbid philosophy there, kid," Gibson said as he jammed his .45 mm into his shoulder holster.

Parker leaned up and stared at the gun. "You know, it was pretty nice traveling with you since we were able to get around all the security lines due to your badge." He fell back heavily on the bed. "What I don't understand is how this Nivelle guy is going to know we're here?"

Gibson cracked his neck. "There was someone on us from the moment we stepped off the plane. I saw him radio us in and then there was a small black car trailing behind us until we pulled off on this road."

"Really? Wow, I guess they really do make some good use of tax dollars to train you all."

"I've been doing this for a long time, kid. I don't understand though why it's taking him so damn long to get here."

A small laugh came from Parker. "Ah, that's where I come in. You see, this guy's French and he's just letting us know that he is French." Gibson looked blankly at him. "He's just being fashionably late," he explained.

Ten minutes later, there was a loud knock at the door. Gibson instinctively drew his gun and moved to the side of the door, motioning for Parker to get off the bed.

"*Oui, c'est qui*?" Parker asked who it was at the door.

"*C'est le Capitaine Nivelle*," responded a direct and firm sounding voice. Gibson nodded his head and Parker opened the door a crack to see a tall, thin man in plain clothes with a pointy moustache and dark plastered hair. His eyes were small and dark.

Nivelle stayed with them for less than fifteen minutes. The entire time he acted as if he'd been there too long and it was a waste of his time. He was stern and unfriendly, causing Parker to dislike him more each minute. He told them he had orders from his superiors to be of any assistance necessary to them, but made it clear that if any action was going to be taken, he would absolutely have to be informed and included.

Immediately, Parker was opposed to the arrangement and claimed that any kind of a large move would surely blow any cover they had. He insisted they could only move in after they figured out who they were looking for.

Nivelle quickly brushed him off. "You don't know how to deal with these terrorists."

Parker wanted to tell him to fuck off, but Gibson's look told him not to be confrontational. "Do you have any leads on who we're looking for?" Gibson asked Nivelle.

Pointing out the window, Nivelle waved his hand in the air. "They are all guilty of something."

Parker had to clench his jaw to keep from asking who exactly he meant by his statement. Did he mean the entire Basque population? Just the French Basques? The Spanish Basques? The seventy-five percent of the Basque population who desired more autonomy? The forty-five percent who wanted complete independence? The less than ten percent who actually supported ETA and violent action? Or did he mean the French and Spanish people living in the Basque Country who, even though they weren't Basque, supported some level of independence for the Basque Country?

After he left, Parker provided some explanations to Gibson. "Nivelle was the name of a French General at the battle of Verdun, where he mercilessly was responsible for the climatic ending of tens of thousands of young French boy's lives in the name of *la belle France*. I strongly suspect Paris didn't send Nivelle to bring in the group alive and he has a history with the Basques already from events in the 80s. After all, France doesn't have a death penalty. The possibility of French terrorists committing murders on American soil and then returning to France would be a bright blemish on the country of France, especially since France is trying so hard to prove its prominence in this new Europe."

* * *

They had been walking for a few minutes and stopped in front of a hand-painted wall mural. It was a painting of six people—five men and one woman, in front of the Basque flag with a declaration written in Basque beneath the figures. Gibson turned to look at Parker and had no doubt Parker understood what was written on the wall. He patiently waited for the explanation that never came.

Parker stared blankly at the painting and then suddenly began walking away with no explanation. Gibson watched the lone figure of Parker walk with his head down across the rough pavement. He didn't want to feel helpless, but as he looked around the empty streets surrounding him, he decided it was indeed a good idea to follow. Gibson couldn't help but admit that even though Bayonne was not that big of a city by most standards, there were still parts that he'd seen in his short visit where a foreigner felt completely lost and isolated.

Parker walked like a soldier returning from a war he wasn't proud to have fought. Parker looked elated to be here, yet so sad at the same time. Gibson considered pressing him on the point, but decided to hold off and just follow in silence. A dark thought crept into his mind. *If Parker is so torn going after some of his old buddies, maybe I should be careful not to put too much trust in him.*

Soon after leaving the mural, they were crossing the river into the center of the city. They walked through a large open building that Gibson supposed was the city market, due to the stands of freshly butchered meats, fish, and cheeses. Even though it was a structure without walls, the odors underneath the roof were overpowering. He thought it smelled like a farm, a fish processing factory, and a refrigerator of sour milk all rolled into one heavily invading smell. Gibson followed Parker as he forced his way through the crowd of people shouting at the stall vendors. It didn't disappoint him that they were not staying.

They climbed up a steep, winding road that led to the cathedral towering over the city. Actually it was not really a road, by American standards anyway. There were cars parked on both sides, leaving only enough room for a very compact car to pass through the center. The sidewalks were more of a concrete strip, meant merely to separate the edge of the buildings from the road. A few people obviously decided open space on a sidewalk equaled a parking spot and left their little cars with one half blocking the walkway. Gibson also noticed there were piles of dog shit every few steps. Parker told him the French word for shit, but he couldn't remember it.

Personally, he didn't know how anyone could learn another language. He figured his mind just didn't work that way. Even though he was mildly enjoying glimpsing the colorful storefronts and old stone buildings they passed, he made sure to always keep one eye on where he was stepping. Having dog shit on your shoe is never a good thing.

Abruptly, the road spilled into an open square that was dominated by the immense presence of Sainte-Marie Cathédrale. The cathedral was a large edifice by itself, but seemed even more grandiose due to its location. Gibson had seen cathedrals in Europe, but the only one he truly could picture in his head was Notre Dame in Paris, which he'd been to with his ex-wife many years ago. This cathedral wasn't as large as that one, but its gothic look reminded him of that one in Paris.

A few years ago, during a period when he felt totally lost after his wife left him, he had gone to the National Cathedral in Washington, DC to try and find some deeper meaning in life. However, his visit to the National Cathedral left him feeling cold and even more lost. Though it was an impressive building, it was too clean and too perfect for him to find any otherworldly presence.

Parker pushed on the huge wooden door in the tall, stone entrance. The door seemed to glide open. When Gibson stepped into the dark interior of the cathedral, he was shocked to instantly doubt his theory on the worldly presence of God. If possible, he felt he was witnessing it.

Gibson was vaguely aware that Parker moved away from him. He didn't mind being left to wander on his own. The place almost felt magical, like stepping through a doorway back into the middle ages.

First, he noticed the smell inside the cathedral—like damp stone. Then, he noticed the soft sounds of Gregorian chant echoing around him. The setting was perfect.

As his eyes adjusted to the dark interior, Gibson could make out rows of wooden benches in the center. Two raised pews jutted out over the benches from massive stone columns. At the head of the benches was a large stage area. As he turned to walk to his right, he realized he was in a side area of the cathedral, because he could no longer see the high ceiling. He walked through a low area on the outside of the immense columns that must have been the supports for the ceiling far above. On his left side was the center of the cathedral. To his right were small adjoining rooms.

When he poked his head inside one of the small rooms, he saw the Virgin Mary staring back at him. It was a simple room with only one stained-glass window. A row of candles was lit in front of the statue of Mary and there was a wooden bench. At one end of the bench sat an old woman with her head lowered deep in prayer. He quietly moved on.

There were a few other small rooms on this side of the nave and he could see confessional pews inside each. He reached his hand out to touch the last stone pillar before turning to witness the full effect of the cathedral. The stone was cold and rough. However, the view he now saw was anything but cold. It was breathtaking.

Giant columns climbed higher and higher into the ornately carved, painted ceiling overhead. Individual panes of stained-glass lined the top of the ceiling leading to the rounded back of the cathedral where an image of Jesus was surrounded by other saints in beautifully colored glass.

Gibson had seen the image of Jesus in stained-glass many times before, but never felt so close to the image. But he figured it was the entire setting of the place. There wasn't as much stained-glass here as he had seen at Notre Dame, and the windows weren't as large or impressive, but he had trouble appreciating the beauty of Notre Dame while surrounded by rude, picture-taking tourists. Here, he had all the time he wanted to bask in the ethereal lure of the cathedral. As the soft music washed over him, he couldn't imagine a better place to be.

The few figures sitting on the benches with lowered heads in front of him seemed lost in the vast openness of the center of the cathedral. He stood in complete and total awe of his surroundings.

His moment was broken by the muffled footsteps of someone entering through the entrance behind him. Looking behind him, he saw a hunchbacked old man remove his black beret and place two fingers into the stone bath of holy water and make the sign of the cross across his head and heart. Gibson let go of the column and continued his tour around the cathedral.

There was a pile of rubble in one corner where the wall had begun to crumble. Instead of a roped off area, as he would have expected, there was merely a sign in front of the corner that he guessed correctly said to keep away. Gibson walked slowly away with his head raised, staring at the colorful ceiling. He felt guilty for the slight noise his shoes made as he walked on the centuries worn, stone floor.

Glancing to one side, he noticed a small anti-chamber that was, in fact, a side room for church services. There was a small podium in front of a few wooden benches. No one was in the room. He passed a doorway that looked as if it led to another part of the cathedral, maybe a courtyard, but the door was locked. Approaching the nave from a different direction, he noticed an ornate stone wall that had individual spaces for paintings of saints.

Gibson had never before seen saints in a Catholic church this close. In other places he'd been, a gate restricted one from getting too close. Here one was within a few feet of the deeply concerned faces of the saints.

White candles burned quietly on small tables in front of each. He stopped to look at one of the saints more closely. The stained-glass behind the old, bearded man was dark and needed cleaning. Even so, Gibson liked the stained-glass not looking brand new like in American churches. Nothing should look new in a place like this, he thought.

The deep blues and yellows in the glass outlined the old man perfectly. Gibson was transfixed by the expression on the face. Something about this place was making him feel as he never had before.

Maybe it was the fact there were only a couple of other people in the cathedral that made him feel as if the place was personable and all to oneself. Maybe it was the shock on the senses of the place—the damp smell, the light ethereal music, the gritty feel. Whatever it was, Gibson realized he was having a spiritual experience that he would never forget.

Throughout his life he had never felt like a religious person and was almost uncomfortable with this new feeling. As soon as he realized these feelings surfacing, he forced his eyes away from the bearded saint and decided to search for Parker. After entering the cathedral, he forgot all about Parker.

Parker was seated on a bench that could be considered the center of the cathedral. For a few moments, he'd forgotten Gibson's presence as well. This was one of his favorite places in the world and he didn't want Gibson to ruin it. When he lived in Bayonne as a student, he spent many hours lost in thought in this cathedral.

He noticed Gibson frantically looking for him in the darkened interior and couldn't understand how anyone could look so uncomfortable in such a place. One last glance upward at the majesty engulfing him and he rose to head to the door leading outside.

Gibson saw Parker walking to the doorway and followed.

"So what did you drag us in there for?" Gibson asked, as soon as they stepped away from the last step leading to the entrance of the cathedral. All of the jubilance he felt inside the cathedral was now gone.

Parker knew Gibson was now just being a hard-ass. He'd seen the serene look of peace fall on that hard face earlier inside the cathedral. Not even bothering to look at Gibson when he spoke, he said, "Because, I love that place."

Gibson's hands rose in mock protest, but he silently thanked Parker for bringing him there. Parker would later tell him that in the 1980s family members of imprisoned Basque nationalists conducted a two week hunger strike within the cathedral. He couldn't imagine a better place to starve oneself.

* * *

There she was. He watched the slight frame of Marie-Hélène cross the street with a covered bundle in her arms. They told him not to even look out the one small window in the room, but Aurelion couldn't resist watching her when she crossed the narrow corner from the boulangerie every morning to bring him food. Aurelion didn't have to look at a clock to know when she was on her way. He could feel her getting closer. She was so beautiful and he wished he could tell her so. Whenever he tried to gather up the courage to tell her how he felt, he began to feel strange inside, as if he was going to throw up in front of her instead of confessing his love.

He watched her and was still fixated on the street below, even after she disappeared into the building. She was getting really close now, and he sensed the familiar feeling of bile rising in his throat with every anticipating beat of his heart. There was a knock at the door followed by three other quick knocks. Sometimes he wanted to tell her there was no need for her to codify her knocks, as he always would know it was her, but he couldn't. At times, he even thought he could smell her coming down the dark hallway that led to his room.

* * *

Basque Demo Fails to Disrupt Summit

Police detained groups of Basque nationalists who held demonstrations in the French town of Biarritz at the start of the European Union Summit, but the talks have not been disrupted. The summit is taking place in the heart of the French Basque Country.

Some 40 protestors were detained in the center of the resort city and later released. Nineteen others were briefly held in another area.

The French police have taken exceptional security measures, sealing off the entire city center and cordoning off the main coastal road.

Thousands of Basque nationalists crossed from Spain into France to stage the protests at the informal summit, which is intended to focus on institutional reforms.

About a dozen journalists working for Basque-language media said they were refused accreditation to the summit, apparently on the orders of the French Interior Ministry.

It is just weeks since French and Spanish police arrested more than twenty suspected members of the Basque separatist group ETA, including its alleged leader, following a summer of violence in Spain.

Controls at the Franco-Spanish border were stepped up. Nearby Bayonne has seen violence. Basque separatists set fire to a building that housed two Spanish radio stations. Overnight, there were further clashes between French police and hundreds of demonstrators who took to the streets.

Basque nationalists want to use the summit to highlight their demands to decide the future of their region.

13

Bayonne, France

"WHERE TO NEXT? And let's cut out the sightseeing and get on with our job," Gibson commented.

Parker stopped in the middle of the narrow cobblestone road they were crossing and shrugged his shoulders heavily. "All right, have it your way. I was going to take you to a place called Chez Cazanove where you could have the best damn cup of hot chocolate in your life—seriously it tastes like you're drinking a bar of fresh chocolate. But since you've got your panties in a ruffle about getting down to business, we'll just cross back over to Petit Bayonne and find a good dark bar to duck into." Parker began strolling in the opposite direction.

For a moment Gibson stood, perplexed. Then he screeched, "A bar! You've got to be joking. How is it going to help us if you get wasted again?" He angrily stalked to the now unmoving Parker. The younger man refused to respond and his silence enraged Gibson further. Gibson's face was bulging and red by the time he made it to Parker. Parker remained calmly staring at him. Gibson spoke quietly, but his words were still fringed with anger. "Don't forget that you take orders from me on this assignment, kid. Now don't make me have to send you back."

Gibson's face came close to Parker's and he didn't move. To the surprise of Gibson, Parker moved his own face to within a few inches of his. This was a bold move for the kid, Gibson thought.

Parker spoke steadily, not raising his voice above a whisper. Since he was an inch or two shorter than Gibson, he had to tilt his head back slightly for his sharp eyes to meet Gibson's furious gaze. "When you call back to the States to tell on me, make sure and mention that you would have never gotten a lead to get this far without your intoxicated CIA kid, and that you're not going to find out anything here without him!"

The muscles in Gibson's face relaxed a little. He quickly glanced around to see if anyone was watching. Parker smiled and winked before pivoting on his heel and walking away. He followed a road down a steep, turning incline. Within seconds, Parker had vanished.

Gibson glanced around at the surrounding area. There were little shops with decorated window fronts on the street level of every old building in the small square. A flank of the cathedral blocked most of his view in one direction, but he could vaguely make out the ramparts of some sort of a crumbling fortress in the distance. Many other little roads led away from the cathedral like the one Parker had chosen. All seemed to lead to the center of the downtown area. Gibson realized how many of the roads looked similar, and he had to concentrate to remember where Parker had gone. He flexed the muscles in his arms and ground his teeth, selecting the road he was fairly sure Parker had taken.

Walking through the small city was a lot different without Parker walking in front of him. With Parker leading, he didn't pay as much attention as he should have. He silently cursed himself.

Once he left the open square next to the cathedral, the road dropped off into lines of buildings. Even though they were not physically tall buildings, as he was used to in the States, they looked so alike in shape and form it made them appear taller somehow.

As he walked, he didn't see many signs. He noticed the concrete pillars blocking off the road to traffic and leaving the area solely for pedestrian use. Even though it was the middle of the afternoon, there were scores of people on the streets, young and old. Hearing snatches of conversation, he thought he distinguished at least five different languages around him—none of them English.

The storefronts seemed to alternate every few windows from shoddy looking to nice and classy. In the center of the cobblestone road was a narrow strip of concrete that he assumed was intended for drainage. Whereas it had been sunny in the square of the cathedral, once among the buildings the sunlight was cut off and it was even a little dark. Though he kept walking, he wasn't sure if he was heading in the right direction. Surrounded by this atmosphere, Gibson felt like an outsider.

When he came around a tight corner in the maze of buildings, he was elated to see an opening through. He saw what may have been the river they had walked across earlier. The speed of his steps increased as he grew nearer the cascading sunlight. As he stepped into the shower of light, he forgot to watch where he was walking and rammed his midsection into one of the stone pillars blocking off the road. Grimacing silently in pain, he straightened up and the first thing that came into his view was Parker's slim figure, leaning against the rail of a bridge, cigarette in hand.

Parker didn't notice Gibson until he walked up next to him. With a look of surprise, Parker turned and said, "Where the hell have you been? I was about to send a search and rescue squad." He laughed as he looked closer at the expression on Gibson's face. It was one he hadn't seen. "You don't look so hot, Gibson. Are you all right?"

Waving a hand in the air, Gibson turned to look back at the dark roads he'd traversed. "I just got kind of lost back there, I think. Then I accidentally slammed my balls against one of those concrete things in the road."

"Wow, that is kinda rough. You want one of these?" Parker asked, offering Gibson his pack of Chesterfield Lights.

Surprisingly, Gibson looked at the pack and actually considered accepting one before refusing. Parker nodded his head as he pulled out his lighter. After dropping one cigarette he lit another. "I think we need to get some things straight here. I'll do my best to follow your rules, but you're going to have to give me some amount of trust and let me do things my way. Otherwise, we're never going to get anywhere here."

Parker stopped and took a drag of his cigarette before continuing. "Now, ETA is one of the most secretive organizations in the world. You hear of Spanish and French police forces making a lot of arrests, but most of the time they're just arresting people and trying to pin something on them they probably didn't do. It's not too difficult to find out who is actually a member of the organization in some form or another, but it is extremely difficult to find out who exactly carried out the attacks. Finding the location of these people is also complicated, because they are sheltered in so many untraceable places throughout the Basque Country and beyond."

Parker took a long drag and exhaled two even streams of smoke from his nostrils. "Right over there, where we're staying in Petit Bayonne," he pointed across the river to the opposite bank, "is one of ETA and IK's main hideouts." Gibson looked at him questioningly. "I'll explain IK later," Parker added.

Nervously pausing, Parker took another drag of the cigarette. "Here's the deal. If you want me to find out any information, you're going to have to back off, and most of all, keep your mouth shut. This organization has eyes and ears like you wouldn't believe. Even though their direct support is relatively small throughout the Basque Country, their indirect support is huge. This indirect support is detoured thoroughly, and Spanish and French authorities spend most of their time attempting to trace these sources."

"Oh, but unlike them, you can identify these sources," Gibson sarcastically said.

Parker flicked the cigarette into the slow river. "I doubt the actual leaders of ETA themselves could identify every source of support they receive. And I've never claimed to know all the sources…" He took a reflective pause before adding, "But I do know some, and what is more important, I know people who know many."

The last statement by Parker shot a burst of energy through Gibson. "What are we waiting for then? Let's go get these bastards!"

Glaring threateningly at Gibson, Parker said, "Haven't you been listening to anything I've told you about the Basques and ETA? The only reason ETA exists is due to their broad range of support from the Basque people. Not every Basque donates money to ETA's cause, but rarely will a Basque person report an ETA member. No one can just march into a place and demand an ETA member be surrendered. You'd only get menacing looks, turned shoulders, and curses in Basque. Now, quit being so damn American about this."

"What the hell's that supposed to mean?"

"It means that the cowboy approach of busting down a door and charging in with guns blazing isn't going to work. The Basques are a proud people and we're going to have to respect that and do this delicately. No one here will really help us, but maybe they can lead us in the right direction. I also have a theory I'm working on about all this, but I need time to work it out."

"Theory? We don't need goddamn theories right now Parker, we need results. What I don't understand is if people don't agree with the tactics of this terrorist organization—why do they protect it?"

"Because, the way many of them see it is that ETA and its allies are the only ones committed to fighting for Basque independence. In some ways, they're right."

Gibson thought Parker had reacted rather defensively. "You're sure sounding a little sympathetic to these murderers, Parker," he said, tauntingly.

Parker looked away from Gibson. "I'm not sympathetic to ETA, but I am to the Basque people and culture."

Taking a deep breath, Gibson puffed out his chest. "I just hope you remember the difference."

Parker turned back to meet an accusing stare from Gibson. His fists were clenched into tight balls at the side of his thighs. "Now what the hell is that supposed to mean, John Gibson?"

Gibson decided perhaps his jab went too far. It was time for them to move on before one of them threw the other over the side of the bridge. "Nothing, Parker. You said something about getting a beer. That sounds good."

The tension running through Parker eased and he unclenched his fists. "All right, but we've got to be more than cautious. Don't mention anything, even if you think there's no possible harm. We have to be careful over there in the *centre ville*," he pointed in the direction of the gothic spires of the cathedral peaking above the rest of the city, "but over there, in Petit Bayonne, it's a different story. Over there we are in an ETA haven. I'm not even sure about our hotel rooms."

"Not sure about our hotel rooms? What do you mean you're not sure about our hotel rooms?" Gibson was careful not to raise his voice, but he wanted to so badly he had to crack his knuckles while talking.

"Relax. Relax. I'm almost sure they're fine. The Basques are famous for being good businessmen," Parker responded in a casual tone. “I just thought it would be intriguing for you to realize that we could be sleeping a few doors down from the very people we’re looking for.”

Gibson cocked his head in disbelief. Parker had a smirk on his face, as if inwardly laughing at him. “How do you keep from getting kicked out of…” as he was about to say the name of the CIA, Parker raised a hand to stop him. “Out of that organization,” Gibson finished.

A large grin crossed Parker’s face. “I ask myself that same question all the time. But I normally just sit behind a desk, so it’s hard to get into too much trouble.” The grin changed into a brief smile then Parker’s face turned serious again. “Here’s our story: you are an old family friend who just happened to be traveling in Western Europe and you found out from my parents that I was here visiting my old exchange student families. Now I’m showing you around the Basque Country. Got it?”

Gibson was amazed by how quickly Parker thought. “Family friend. That makes me sound old, like I’m really friends with your parents,” Gibson complained in a mock, hurt tone.

Parker threw him a quick glance and started walking across the bridge. In a voice just loud enough for Gibson to hear, he said, “You’re too old to be just my friend.”

Gibson glared. “Asshole!” he said out loud, not caring if anyone heard him or not.

“I heard that, Gibson!” Parker called out over his shoulder. He slowed his pace to let Gibson get closer to him. “Since we’re in France, you might as well learn a good French way of saying that. It’s *trou de cul*.”

Gibson repeated the phrase, horribly mispronouncing the French translation. What Gibson said came out more like *throw do cow*. It made both men smile as they walked across the bridge over la Nive River and into Petit Bayonne.

* * *

The small hard ball surged off his taped fingers and slammed into the stone fronton of the pelote court. Peio’s shot was expertly placed. The spin he put on the ball with his swing coerced the ball to deflect off the wall to the far right side of the court. One of the players on the team he and his friend, Juan, were playing against, scrambled across the pavement of the court to try and return Peio's shot. The dark haired man lunged forward and was just able to make contact with the ball. But Peio's shot had been too good.

The player was only able to make minimal contact with the ball, foregoing spin, placement, and power into his return. Fortunately, Peio was perfectly placed for the weak return and was able to take his time to gauge the position of the opposite team's players before wailing the ball with his hand. There was a loud smack, followed by the ball moving seventy miles an hour across the far left side of the court. All the other team could do was watch in dismay. In utter joy, Peio watched his successful maneuver. He loved winning a game of pelote, even if it was just a pick-up game organized at the village café.

Hands were shaken and *bien joué* was said. Peio told the others he would shortly join them at the café for a drink. He needed to be alone to rejoice in his grand victory, smoke in peace for a few moments, and look around his little village. The three young men, having grown up with Peio, decided not to make a fuss about his request. It wasn't so much due to the fact that Peio was bigger and stronger than any of them and could, if he wanted to, pound them silly without much trouble—they left him alone because not one of them had ever seen Peio smoke.

If he had become a smoker, then something had made him become a smoker. Not one of them was willing to take the chance of angering Peio by asking him about the reason. They walked down the length of the court, crossed the little street that was the main one of the village, and then walked into the only café within ten miles.

* * *

It was now clear to John Gibson that just whenever he began to feel Sebastian Parker was a valuable asset on the investigation, the kid did something to change his mind. As soon as they went inside the bar, Parker went straight to pounding back glasses of pink liquor from a dark bottle. The label on the bottle was Patxaran. Gibson watched in amazement as Parker downed his drink, lit a cigarette, and then began drinking from the fresh glass was placed in front of him by the bartender. The bartender clearly recognized Parker.

Gibson figured that Parker had most likely spent many of his nights while in Bayonne at this particular bar. Parker announced the place's name as they entered, something sounding like the *Petit Bar*. Though Parker tried to get Gibson to have a drink, he adamantly refused, telling Parker one of them had to stay sober and he'd take a Coke.

The bartender and Parker rolled their eyes. Parker shook his head and turned away. Parker began conversing, in French, with a scruffy, rough looking man seated on a stool next to him, the same scruffy man who'd given them a dirty look when they entered the bar. Now he looked as if he was enjoying talking with Parker.

Taking a moment, Gibson examined his surroundings. Once one walked through the doors, the bar counter was directly in front, stretching to the back of the room. There were booths with tables and benches on one side of the room, and in the back was an open area he imagined was used as a makeshift dance floor. Inside the room was dark and smoky. The wooden walls had long since been smudged from the smoke of a million cigarettes. Gibson noted several booths were filled with people, and another man sat alone at the far end of the bar.

A few pictures had been hung around the room—old black and white pictures of what looked to him like Bayonne. One picture stuck out in his mind, which he later planned to ask Parker to explain. It had been placed above a row of liquor bottles behind the bar. The picture was of a group of men in tattered clothing and berets, shaking hands with what looked like an American officer around the time of the World War II, judging by the uniforms. All the rifles, slung over the shoulders of the men in berets, resembled guns he knew had been used in World War I. The American officer looked very pleased to be meeting the small group of Basque resistance fighters, if that's what they were. Yes, he decided, he would definitely ask Parker about this particularly interesting picture.

The scruffy man slammed his glass on the wooden bar and began almost screaming in a flurry of words to Parker sitting right next to him. Gibson reacted quickly. In an instant, he had risen from his stool, knocking it to the floor, and had his fingers firmly gripped around the handle of the .45 mm strapped against his chest. Parker, the scruffy man, and the bartender, all stared at him. The scruffy man looked at him with hate, the bartender with curiosity, and Parker with annoyance. Parker said something in French to the other two and turned back toward the scruffy man. Whatever Parker said made the other two men laugh and return to ignoring Gibson. But Gibson didn't remove his hand from the handle of his gun and return to his seat until he saw a discreet movement of assurance from Parker. Without losing the attention of the scruffy man or the bartender, Parker dropped a hand from atop the bar to his side and moved his flattened hand in a gentle side to side motion to indicate everything was all right.

Gibson picked up his tall stool from the floor and returned to his seat at the bar. He hated not knowing what was being said, not knowing what was going on, and he felt like an idiot just sitting there drinking a Coke, which finally appeared in front of him. But he remembered what Parker had told him and tried his best to sit back and be calm. After a few minutes, he even asked Parker to order him a beer.

Parker continued to gab with the scruffy man and the bartender. There were two men speaking Basque at a corner table. A young woman came in, sat at the bar, ordered a glass of wine, and then began eating a sandwich she pulled from her purse. Everyone in the bar appeared happy to be there. Under different circumstances, he would actually enjoy being in this bar during the middle of the day in this atmosphere, Gibson admitted.

* * *

A cruel looking face stared back at them from the stone wall. The black face with red eyes was slightly distorted, giving the impression of an enlarged forehead. Gibson felt uneasy looking into the red eyes, even though it was merely paint on a wall. For some reason, the eyes were unbelievably red and their stare was penetrating. A large spray-painted red glob was next to the face, giving the impression the face was coming out of the red mass. The overall effect was haunting.

Gibson couldn't decide whether the dark face with red eyes or the picture next to it stirred Parker.

On the drab, stone wall, next to the face, was painted a view of the Bay of Biscay with the Atlantic Ocean on one side and the meeting of France and Spain on the other. The ocean was painted bright blue and the land a dark green, except for the upside down, vibrant, yellow triangle that was the Basque Country. A large magnifying glass with a wooden handle was placed directly over the region. There were seven obscure objects within the outline of the Basque Country that symbolized the seven Basque provinces—Viscaya (Bizkaia), Guipuzcoa (Gipuzkoa), Alava (Araba), Navarre (Nafarroa), Labourd (Lapurdi), Basse-Navarre (Nafarroa Beherea), and Soule (Zuberoa)—within France and Spain. To indicate the border of the water and the land between France and Spain was a broad black line. There were no lines dividing borders within the outlined Basque Country.

Looking over the lens of the magnifying glass onto the Basque Country were four little men—two were on the French side, two on the Spanish side. The French men held the French flag and were wearing long black coats. The Spanish men were holding the Spanish flag and wearing army uniforms. All four of the little men held guns. Far behind the two Spanish men stood a holy man of the Catholic Church, who looked to be a bishop. On the faces of the two French men, looking over the magnifying glass were grim expressions of concern. The two Spanish men gave the clear impression of being angry. The bishop appeared sad and worried.

After quietly reflecting on the picture for a moment, Gibson was unable to say for sure whether one was meant to see the picture first as the predominate image on the wall, or if one was meant to initially see the evil face staring at you.

Gibson didn't need to ask Parker if he'd seen the picture before. From the concerned expression on Parker's face, he knew it was the first time seeing the image for both of them. It actually was a shock for Gibson to see feelings or emotions ripple through Parker when they first rounded the corner and were startled by the image in front of them.

When Parker's eyes caught sight of the image, he instantly focused all his attention on it, coming to a complete stop. But there was a problem, as Parker had too much to drink back at the bar and his motor functions were not fully functioning. One foot instantly received the message from his brain to stop walking, but the other didn't receive the message quite so quickly. The result was that he nearly tripped himself.

The only reason Gibson did not burst out in laughter at the wobbly Parker was due to the fact that the painted images on the stone wall in front of them actually startled him as well.

Parker was so absorbed in the scene that he didn't even show signs of breathing. The fluidity, prevalent in him just moments before, vanished. He went from borderline drunk to stoically sober in a matter of a few moments. Now he stood straight and stiff. After a few minutes of absolutely no movement, Parker walked up to the stone wall and placed a hand on the dark face with the bright red eyes. He let his hand stiffly slide across the red eyes as he turned to walk away.

Gibson followed.

* * *

Parker walked stiffly with his head hung low. He didn't feel drunk or even happy to be back in his favorite place. All he knew was that he needed something to lift his spirits and needed it fast. He felt like a junkie needing a quick fix. After a few moments, he came up with the answer—good food. They were in the proclaimed capital of the French Basque Country, meaning restaurants serving heavenly French-Basque cuisine were on every street. He decided it was time to introduce Gibson to the delicious allure of Basque food. In fact, one of the main reasons he chose their hotel was due to its proximity to his favorite restaurant in Bayonne.

He led the way until stopping in front of the restaurant's uninviting doorway. He could feel Gibson's questioning gaze burning into the back of his neck. "I think it's time for you to have a proper Basque meal," he announced as he opened the door.

* * *

Once inside the building, a pleasant looking young woman led them down a short flight of stairs into an open room dotted with round tables. Few of the tables in the restaurant were empty. The room was full of smiling faces and conversations. Since the Basques were reportedly suspicious of outsiders, Gibson thought it strange that no one obviously seemed to notice their entrance as they were led to a table in the far corner of the dimly-lit room. Soon after though he realized Parker had taken them to a restaurant only known to locals. No tourists would ever "accidentally" stumble into this establishment. Perhaps also their presence had not been odd to the hostess due to Parker only speaking Basque to her as soon as they entered.

As they seated themselves, Gibson observed a pair of old men on the opposite side of the room gesturing in their direction and discussing something. His instincts made him suspicious. Whether or not Parker acknowledged and registered the apparent suspicion from the opposite side of the room was not clear. What was perfectly clear to him, however, was that Parker was ready to eat.

After Parker greedily accepted a menu from a dark haired young man who would be their waiter, he spoke a barrage of words in French to the waiter. Gibson assumed he was ordering wine, because he picked up on the word Irrelouguy, which he remembered Parker telling him was a Basque wine. Then Gibson watched Parker's eyes devour the menu held out in front of him. In a barely audible voice, Parker read off items in French. As the menu was only in Basque and French, Gibson stared blindly at the words on the pages and waited for guidance from Parker.

"The way in which most restaurants in France, and this part of Europe operate, is that they give you a fixed price menu and within it you have different choices for the courses. It really turns out to be a nice deal. We're going to eat like Basque kings tonight. For the first course we have the choice of country paté, red pepper mousse, duck liver mousse, or salmon rillettes." Parker paused to mentally consider the choices.

"The next course will be a choice of soups. There's fish soup, pea and sorrel soup, or, how do you translate that into English again—oh, yeah—cream of chestnut soup. There's no *soupe de l'oignon* here, because onion soup is definitely French and not Basque. Personally, I prefer the *soupe de poisson.* It's not really all too Basque, but it's unreal. I always know I'm in the south of France when I have a good fish soup," Parker said, closing his eyes and inhaling deeply.

The returning waiter, carrying a bottle of red wine, snapped Parker from the feast already commencing in his head. He offered a quick glance of the bottle to Parker, who responded with a slight nod of his head. The waiter flipped out a folded corkscrew from his pants pocket. In a rapid blur of movements and a loud pop, the cork was out of the bottle and Parker's glass partly filled with the deeply colored wine. Parker took a small sip from his glass and grinned in approval. The waiter poured wine into each of their glasses, only filling Gibson's half full before he was able to motion he didn't desire any. After placing the bottle on the table, the waiter disappeared through the doorway into the kitchen of the restaurant.

Without looking at him, Gibson could feel the accusing eyes of Parker telling him he needed to at least try the wine. The label on the bottle indeed had the name Irrelouguy on it.

Taking his wine glass, Gibson slowly raised it to his lips and tipped it just enough to let a very small amount of the wine into his mouth and swallowed. The first reaction he had to the wine was that it was terrible. He looked to Parker, who'd been watching him, and openly displayed his disgust.

Parker spoke warmly to him. "Most people don't get a good taste for a wine with their first sip. There's too much of a shock to your senses for your taste buds to recognize anything, and you end up thinking the wine tastes like vinegar." Parker closed his eyes and took a large swallow from his own glass, savoring the after aroma of the wine with a deep breath before reopening his eyes.

"Then why do people only take one sip of their wine in restaurants when the waiter is having them taste it?" Gibson asked.

"Frankly, I have no idea why people only taste their wine once before nodding approval to the waiter. I'm sure most people secretly think what they've tried tastes awful, but don't want to admit it."

"But you only tasted your glass of wine once just a few minutes ago when the waiter was standing here," Gibson insisted.

Parker gave a small laugh. "Ah, yes. Well, for one thing, I don't care for the wine show and…"

"And what?"

"Well, Irrelouguy has never let me down," he replied as he grinned into his glass of wine. "It's a robust wine with a lot of character."

Gibson raised his glass once more, but before he could take another drink, Parker interrupted him. "Hold on, Gibson, I want you to try something different this time." Parker readjusted in his chair to better display the glass of wine held in his hand. "Okay, Irrelouguy is a big and fragrant wine so what we have to do is help release these fragrances however we can."

"How do you do that?" Gibson asked.

"First you take your glass in your hand and gently swirl the wine around." Parker proceeded as he instructed and they both watched the red liquid languidly swirl in his glass. "Now you can do this fairly discreetly and don't have to make a big ordeal out of it like many do who only want others to see them as wine snobs."

Gibson picked up his glass and tried to swirl the wine as Parker had done. At first, he thought it was awkward and felt as like he would spill the red wine on the white tablecloth. But gradually he eased his wrist and the action became more fluid. "That's it, good. Now smell your wine," Parker encouraged.

By following Parker's instructions, Gibson was amazed to smell the bundle of scents arising from his glass. He was surprised. He detected an assortment of scents he wouldn't have believed were present in wine, such as different fruits, spices and even oak. He was honestly impressed, but he held back from revealing his joyous discovery.

"We're ready to taste now. But when you go to take a sip, don't swallow the wine right away. Gently swoosh it around in your mouth a bit and let the flavors release before you swallow," Parker further instructed.

Doing as he was told, he was able to taste the different fragrances he previously smelled in the wine. Afterward, he looked at the glass of wine in a new light. "There really is more to this stuff!" he exclaimed.

After making his proclamation, he was instantly embarrassed by his outburst. Gibson guiltily glanced around the room. Instead of seeing accusing looks, he only saw joyous faces either involved in animated conversation or in deep concentration of the food on their plates.

Parker acted as if he hadn't noticed. He returned his focus to the menu. Gibson gazed at him imploringly. "Glad you like it. Now we can move on to the important decision concerning the selection of our feast."

Before Gibson could pick up his menu again, an arm suddenly appeared to his right and dropped a basket of sliced bread and two small butter dishes on the table. Suddenly, he felt very hungry. Taking a small slice of the bread, he spread a moderate amount of butter on it and took a bite. It was crusty bread with a fluffy interior and real butter. To him the bread tasted better than any bread he ever tasted back in the States. He wondered how it could taste so different as he finished the slice in two large bites.

"Okay, we've gone through the first course and the soup serving. Now there will be a salad. Normally in any household in France the salad serving would come after the main course, but in restaurants it seems to always be the other way around. Here we will have the choice between *salade au fromage de chèvre*, which is goat's cheese salad, *salade au foie gras*, basically goose liver salad, or *salade au viande de canard*, a salad with duck meat." Parker lowered the menu slightly and found a blank expression on Gibson's face confronting him. "What do you think?" Parker asked.

"They all sound kind of, I don't know, exotic for salads to me. Especially that goose liver one. Is that really any good?"

"It's the best. That's what I'll order then."

"All right. I'll give it a try," Gibson agreed.

"I'm proud of you," Parker said as he lifted his wine glass to Gibson and took a long drink. When finished, he said, "It's time for the main course. The choices are *poulet basquaise*, Basque chicken, *piperade*, a Basque omelet, *confit de canard*, which is basically duck cooked in its own fat, *rognons de veau a l'armagnac*, veal kidneys in armagnac and *lapin aux pruneaux,* rabbit with prunes. And, by the way, all of these are extraordinarily delicious."

Gibson stared into his glass of wine. "I've never had rabbit before."

"Bravo, John!" The mentioning of Agent Gibson's first name for the first time by Sebastian Parker brought both men to attention. "I mean—bravo, Gibson!" Parker quickly added.

Having made their choices, Parker gestured to their waiter who was busy opening a bottle of wine for a table next to theirs. "*Très bien.* Now we can get down to business. There will be cheese and a dessert too, but that can wait until later. Right now, *je crève de faim*!"

"What does that mean?"

"It means time to eat!"

* * *

Sebastian Parker sat alone at the bar inside the Euskauldun with his head held low over his *demi.* His blondish hair fell down over his eyes. A burning cigarette held loosely in his hand dangled close to one ear. After dinner, and a final warm shot of Armagnac to help with the digestion, Gibson was more than ready for bed. Parker made sure he was down for the night before he left his own room and walked down to the Euskaldun. He was waiting for Alaitz Etxegaraya.

Earlier in the day, while Gibson was wandering around the city, he ducked into a phone booth to call her. She had been excited to hear from him and they arranged to meet at the Euskauldun around 10:00 p.m. To Parker, the bar held soft and hazy memories of his days at lycée in Bayonne. It was the perfect meeting place since he and Alaitz had spent so many nights seated here discussing everything from the existence of the devil, to the innocence of childhood, to the complexities of marriage. They were friends by definition, but Alaitz did something to him that few other girls were capable of accomplishing. She made him want to see her more.

A set of thin arms suddenly surrounded his neck. Even through the dank smell of the bar, his nose instantly recognized and savored her scent. As her soft lips brushed against his cheek, he felt an unfamiliar and frightening feeling. It was a feeling he adored and feared at the same time. Parker wondered if everyone felt this way around people when they were in love.

Alaitz squeezed his neck tightly and a few strands of her fine brown hair fell softly against his face. He didn't want to talk, to think, or move. He just wanted to smell her lovely fragrance and feel her warm body pressed against his own and forget everything else in the world. But the moment was abruptly broken by the sound of a glass crashing on the floor.

She eased her grip on him and moved to his side so he could see her full profile. For a moment, he made a conscious effort not to say anything and just looked at her. He looked at her highly raised cheekbones and deep brown eyes guarded by long eyelashes. He looked at her small chin that looked too delicate to touch. Her hair fell perfectly straight down the sides of her face, creating a painting worth framing. She looked hard into his eyes as if she was searching for the answer to a question she had not yet asked.

"You're not happy to be here, Sebastian." She stated, not questioned. Parker hated a little that she could read him so well.

"I'm always happy to be here, *chérie*, especially with you."

"Yes, but not for the reason you're here."

Parker pulled two cigarettes from the box in his jacket pocket, placed both in his mouth, and lit them with his lighter. He placed one in her mouth and kissed her once on each of her cheeks.

"*Merci*," she said. "Don't change the subject."

He loved the way she had difficulty pronouncing the "ch" in change so the whole word came out slurred. She stared at him intently, waiting. The bartender came toward them and he ordered her a draft of Kronenberg as well. He waited until she had a pint glass of beer in hand before continuing.

Exhaling a stream of smoke, he shrugged. "All right. All right. I didn't want to bring you in on this, but I'm here on an assignment for work. I wasn't going to ask you for help unless I absolutely had no other choice. You're very important to me, and I don't want anything to ever happen to you." He purposefully stressed the last sentence in the hope it would do something to lighten her expression. Maybe cause a small smile, or a twinkle of her eyes. But it didn't.

She leaned so closely to his face that all had to do to kiss her would be a slight puckering of his lips and moving forward a few inches. Her closeness made him almost lightheaded. "What kind of an assignment is this?" Alaitz quietly, yet forcefully, asked into his ear.

He took a drag of his cigarette and rolled his head to her ear. "The secret kind."

She slowly pulled back from him with an obvious pout on her face. "How could you say that to me? Besides, you know I can take care of myself."

Briefly, he had a flashback of a night Alaitz kicked a piss drunk *mec* in the balls who wouldn't keep his hands off her on the dance floor. The guy didn't know what hit him until he was curled up in a puddle of spilled beer and cigarette butts on the floor.

Alaitz was a special girl, all right. Parker looked at the way the corner of her eyes and mouth had turned downward. He remarked to himself how effective the French woman's pout could be on men—even the French-Basques ones like Alaitz.

"C'mon, let's get out of here," he said. He stood and casually grabbed her hand. She let him lead her through the group of people standing in the middle of the room. Once they were outside, she didn't pull away from his grasp, but strengthened her grip around his hand. Parker considered pulling his own hand away, knowing well that the simple act of holding hands meant so much more to him than to her, but he couldn't bring himself to resist. He enjoyed how nice her touch felt. To him it was much, much more than just two hands in an embrace—it was a connection between two bodies.

They walked through the streets of Petit Bayonne without saying a word, content with the silence between them. Parker led the way without having a final destination in mind. Walking with her was enough.

Eventually, they took a seat on the medieval stone ramparts that surrounded the city. With their feet dangling over the edge, he placed two cigarettes in his mouth and after lighting them, handed her one. When he turned to look into her eyes, he was shocked by their brilliance even in the minimal light reaching them from a sidewalk lamp on the pathway below.

"You look like something is bothering you," Parker commented.

She closed her eyes and turned away. "No, nothing is bothering me, Sebastian."

"You wouldn't turn your head like that if nothing was bothering you."

Sucking hard on her cigarette, she harshly exhaled a cloud of smoke. "Why are you doing this? Have you become one of those *connards*?"

"Alaitz, you know I'm not one of them."

"Are you sure? And who's that older American you're here with?"

"He's nobody. Don't worry about it. How do you know about him anyway? Have you been following me?"

"Don't be such a fool, Sebastian. You know you are in Petit Bayonne where even the stones in the streets have eyes."

Parker felt burned by her comment and a cold shiver ran through him. "Listen, can we not talk about this?" he requested.

She snapped to her feet and threw her cigarette over the edge of the ramparts. "*Tu espèce d'imbécile*! You think just because you know some people here, or because you speak some of the language, that you're not in danger?"

He stared at the glowing ember of her discarded cigarette lying in the grass far below and didn't answer. Not looking up at her, he knew she angrily turned and stormed off into the night, leaving him alone to watch the glow of her cigarette fade away.

* * *

ETA Leaders Caught in France

Police in France have arrested a man and a woman suspected of being top leaders of the militant Basque separatist group ETA. French and Spanish police arrested the couple near Bordeaux in southwestern France in a joint operation.

Spanish media said the two suspected ETA leaders had fled from Spain to France in 1996, from where they formed part of the leadership of the outlawed armed group.

ETA is thought to have killed over 800 people and injured more than 2,300 since 1968, in a campaign for an independent Basque homeland in northwest Spain and southwest France.

These were the first high-profile arrests of ETA suspects this year. The Spanish authorities are calling it a major victory for the government of the Prime Minister.

The man is suspected of being ETA's current military head following the arrest of the group's previous military chief last year.

The woman is accused of taking part in one of ETA's most notorious killings: the murder of the former chief justice of the Constitutional Court in 1996.

The Prime Minister's government has been leading a campaign to outlaw the radical Basque Nationalist Party, Batasuna, the political wing of ETA, since it was banned by a judge three years ago.

When Batasuna refused to condemn a car bombing in the resort of Santa Pola, in which a six-year-old girl was killed, the Prime Minister was furious.

According to Batasuna, the Prime Minister's conservative government causes the continuing violence.

14

Bayonne, France

SOMEONE WAS POUNDING hard on the door of Gibson's hotel room. As he opened his eyes to investigate who was rudely interrupting his sleep, the pounding grew louder. It could only be about five o'clock in the morning or so, he thought. Struggling, he got up from the bed and as he put his feet on the cold, wooden floor of the room, he was faced with an abrupt realization that slapped him across the face. From the small clock on the nightstand, he could see that it was not five in the morning like he expected. The clock read nine thirty. Seeing the amount of sunlight penetrating through the thick window curtains concurred with the clock.

Annoyed, he shook his head to make sure he wasn't dreaming. The pounding on the door didn't stop. He wearily stood up and found his second unpleasant greeting of the day—no one was pounding on his door, the pounding was coming from a hammer banging away at the walls of his head.

Gibson fell back hard on the bed, cursing himself for having slipped and given in to the pleasures of French wine. He couldn't remember how many glasses he had at dinner with Parker the night before, but obviously too many.

It had been over ten years since he'd been in bed past six in the morning. He told himself that if Parker were there in front of him at that moment he would gladly give him a few punches for being so damned persuasive. Closing his eyes, Gibson wished he could fall back asleep and hopefully sleep off his dreadful hangover.

Just as he was about to achieve his goal, he heard a new knocking. This time it did come from the door. Due to the fact he now heard two sets of knocking, Gibson knew the pounding at the door was real. With concentrated effort, he got out of the bed, pulled the .45 mm from the nightstand drawer, and crept as noiselessly as he could in the direction of the door. He held the gun to where he judged anyone's head would be once entering the room. He slowly lifted the chain.

"Gibson, it's me! Open up you slacker. I'm getting bored out here." It was the all-too cheerful voice Gibson least wanted to hear at present—Sebastian Parker's.

He opened the door so that Parker could step into the room. With a big smile on his face, Parker strutted into the room, shutting the door behind him. "Are you going to sleep all day or are we going to get to work sometime?" he cheerily asked, even though Gibson had yet to lower the weapon aimed, with two hands for accuracy, at his forehead. "What? Are you mad because I introduced you to what proper dining is all about?" Parker carelessly asked.

"I'm mad because I'm hung over as hell! I haven't had a hangover in twenty years and then along comes aimless little you and see what happens!" The gun began to shake in Gibson's hands. He finally lowered the gun and set it on the nightstand with a loud thunk. He fell back onto the bed and held his head with his large hands.

Parker moved to the window and threw apart the curtains, allowing a cascading barrage of sunlight to fill the small room. "I think I'll take that as a compliment, Gibson," he turned and said.

Gibson replied through his hands, now shielding his face from the hurtful sunlight. "I wouldn't take it as a compliment if I were you. Have you not enough brain cells left to remember that just a minute ago I had a gun pointed at your face?" The raspiness of his own voice surprised him. He thought it must have been due to a combination of all the red wine and the smoke in the air at the restaurant the night before.

Sitting down on the bed next to him, Parker said, "Oh, I know you like me more than you'll even admit to yourself. You wouldn't shoot me."

"How is it you're so damn chipper this morning? I remember you having a lot more booze than me last night."

"Believe me, I still get hangovers. I'm not young enough anymore to not. I wish I realized how fortunate I was before my liver refused to bounce back. What used to only be a few hours the morning after, has now become a full day of recovery. But as far as today goes, I choked down a couple cups of coffee doused with shots of cognac at a bar across the street."

Gibson peered from between his fingers at Parker for the first time since he seated himself on the bed, long enough to let Parker see the disgusted look on his face at the mention of any form of alcohol. "Trust me, the first couple of sips are rough, but after that it's smooth sailing," Parker assured him.

Gibson felt an oncoming gag, which Parker registered by his facial expression. He quickly rose from the bed to stand next to the window.

"You should really close those curtains and quit standing in front of that window, Parker," Gibson said, trying to forget any association with alcohol.

"Oh, yeah, I suppose you're right," Parker said, with what Gibson viewed as far too little respect for the danger at hand. Parker snapped the curtains shut and crossed the room to flip on the light switch. "You know, I didn't force that stuff down your throat last night. I may have nagged you on to get you to try some wine with dinner, but especially after you had that *trou normande,* there was no stopping you."

Gibson tried to think hard, but couldn't figure out what in the world Parker was talking about. "What's a true Norman?" he demanded.

A wide grin crossed Parker's face as he broke out into a fit of laughter. When he was able to speak again, he replied, "Not a true Norman, a *trou normande*." Gibson stared at him, far from amused.

Parker quickly retorted. "But I can see you're in no mood for a French pronunciation lesson, so I'll just get to it. A *trou normande* is a mid-meal shot of strong liquor that is supposed to hollow out your already near full stomach so one is capable of finishing the latter half of the *repas*—I mean, meal. It basically translates as the Norman hole because the tradition is said to have begun in the Normandy region of

France, where calvados was used as the elixir of choice. We actually had calvados last night as our *trou.*"

Hazily, Gibson recalled a short glass that tasted like apple firewater from the three-hour long dinner, and although the drink undoubtedly pushed him beyond his alcohol tolerance, he did remember it actually making his stomach feel empty and ready to take on another onslaught of food.

"We've got a lunch meeting today, so I suggest you start to get yourself ready because lunch will start without us if we're not there at noon," Parker instructed.

The thought of food made Gibson's already churning stomach twist even more. "I should be all right after a long shower," he said, not fully trusting his words.

He slowly headed for the bathroom when Parker quietly added, "Ah, Gibson, have you seen your shower yet?"

Gibson turned back around to look at him for a moment. Parker thought Gibson looked older and weaker than ever. Even though he knew Gibson was upset at himself, upset with him, upset with French people, upset with Basque people, and pretty much upset with the world because of the heavy hangover clinging to him like a sweaty cotton T-shirt, he was also witnessing that even hard-ass Agent John Gibson had his weaknesses. Parker almost felt sorry for him. Almost.

The annoyed gaze plastered on Gibson's face openly conveyed that he didn't want to hear anything else come out of Parker's mouth. Gibson shook his head and was muttering something to himself as he slowly closed the bathroom door. *Just wait and see, old man.*

About three minutes later, Parker heard the water turned on and then what he was waiting to hear came from behind the closed door of the bathroom. "Parker! What the hell is this supposed to be!" The bathroom door cracked open and out shot Gibson's head. "Where's the damn shower?"

"That's what I was trying to tell you about before," Parker calmly replied.

Gibson shook his head angrily. "No, that back there," he nodded his head indicating behind him, "that's not a shower!"

"A lot of the showers in Europe are like that, especially in older places."

Gibson's eyes closed then opened wide again in bewilderment. "But that's not a shower. That thing is a bathtub with a portable faucet on it!" He lost his grip on the door and it creaked further open so that he had to quickly reach for a towel to cover himself.

"Listen, really not that big a deal. I'll be the first to admit that it's not as convenient as the stand-up showers in the States, but it's really not that bad once you get the hang of it. You just kind of take a bath and wash each part separately." Removing a pack from his jacket pocket, Parker flicked a cigarette between his lips.

"What? How's that going to work?"

Parker lit his cigarette and replied through an exhale of blue smoke. "Hey, if you do that, wear deodorant, don't wear too much cologne and wear a different set of clothes each day, you're going to be better off in the personal hygiene department than a lot of people here."

"You're a pain in the ass just as much as these crazy old world people, Parker," Gibson snarled, shutting the door.

"Maybe," Parker replied, laughing.

* * *

Parker drove the small Peugot on a road that followed the river out of Bayonne to the ocean. Gibson watched the darkened spires of the cathedral disappear behind them in the rearview mirror. They passed a sign indicating they were entering the city of Anglet, which is not so much an actual city as it is an area between Bayonne and Biarritz, Parker explained. Parker added that the Basque names for Bayonne, Anglet, and Biarritz are Baiona, Angelu and Miarritze, but said the Basque names for the cities are rarely used.

Before long, they saw the busy activity at the Port of Bayonne across the river. A sizeable forest of pines gradually appeared behind tight rows of houses. Parker flung his cigarette butt out the cracked window and turned down a small road that led to the edge of the forest. Small houses lined the short road, but there wasn't a house at the end of it, giving the impression one could drive straight into the trees. Parker explained that this was the *Forêt de Chiberta*, the Chiberta Forest. He stopped the car in front of a small blue house and told Gibson they had arrived.

"So, are you going to tell me who we're meeting here?" Gibson finally asked.

"An old friend. Don't worry—he's an Anglophone. I would say he's an American, but that's not how he thinks of himself."

Gibson sighed, annoyed. "Great, a crazy expat."

"He's not crazy. He's just not really an American anymore," Parker said defensively, as he opened his car door.

A tall, bronzed man with long brown hair pulled back into a ponytail met Parker at the white wooden fence in front of the house. Gibson slowly stepped from the car to watch the two men—one in his mid-twenties, the other in his mid-thirties—embrace by kissing one another on the cheek four times: once on one side, once on the other side, once back on the first side, then back to the other side. Parker was grinning widely and obviously happy to see this man.

Gibson thought this was a strange custom for men to joyfully be kissing cheeks with other men. Before he knew what was fully happening, the ponytailed man, that moments ago had been smooching Parker, was grabbing his hand and almost violently shaking it while muttering something in a creative mix of French and English. The man's voice was deep and full of confidence. Parker spoke in the same invented tongue and Gibson was able to pick up that the man's name was Patrick Holm.

Patrick looked him over with inquisitive eyes as he shook his hand longer than Gibson was used to. Patrick let go of his hand, turned, and began walking through the small yard in front of the house to a back patio area. They followed.

Once inside the short fence, intended to keep in a small dog named Niska, they seated themselves around a square patio table with four chairs that had been set with plates, silverware, glasses, a wicker bowl of cut pieces of bread and two carafes of *vin rouge*. Just the sight of the wine made Gibson instantly nauseous. Frantically, he looked for the one and only liquid he was prepared to drink—water. He was more than relieved when a thin, dark haired woman appeared through a door leading into the house, carrying another carafe filled with water. Much to his embarrassment though, his searching had not gone unnoticed by the other two sitting at the table. The two looked at him as if they were seeing a creature they'd never witnessed before.

"You are in France, John. In France we drink wine when we eat. *C'est normal,"* said the deep voice of Patrick.

Gibson's response was a glance of distress in the direction of Parker, who muttered something in French, receiving a round of laughter from the others as they toasted glasses of red wine to the word *topa*. Gibson's first instinct was to react at being the victim of a joke he didn't understand because of the language in which it had been spoken, but the pounding in his head told him to leave it alone and drink more water.

Patrick then introduced his girlfriend by blowing her a kiss and saying that her name was Sandrine. Sandrine said *kaixo* and *ongi etorri*, kissed Parker, then Gibson, four times on their cheeks before disappearing back into the house.

Gibson took a drink of water and leered at the carafes of red wine that were being rapidly drained by Parker and Patrick. He felt his stomach turn a somersault, so he put a piece of bread in his mouth. The baguette was warm, fresh from the boulangerie Patrick noted, and he let the fluffy interior melt around his tongue.

Two hours passed with nothing but cheerful toasts, wonderful food, and the rumbling of Gibson's stomach. Sandrine brought out thick country paté, a plate with at least four different slices of ham that she called *une assiette de charcuterie*, grilled fillets of salmon on a bed of lemon infused rice, a wheel of camembert and fruit. She ate as well, but the lunch was clearly mostly for the two old friends at the end of table. She kept refilling carafes of red wine.

"I knew Sebastian was coming so I got out many bottles of wine," she struggled to say in English to Gibson as she placed a new carafe on the table.

It seemed Sandrine spent more time bringing and removing plates of food than she did actually sitting at the table with them. She only ate small portions. Gibson had to break his gaze away numerous times from the mesmerizing image of a beautiful French woman delicately folding and bending food with a knife onto a fork, then brushing it past her lips, and placing it gently into her mouth. The whole idea was so foreign to him—that eating could be such an art form instead of just a means to survival. But for Sandrine, it looked as natural as blinking. And Sandrine also made the act appear so sensual, and even sexy, Gibson thought.

When she once again disappeared into the house, Parker looked up from the depths of his wine glass to find Patrick watching him with an air of curiosity. "When you come here for a visit, you don't bring friends, Sebastian…" Patrick said, nodding at Gibson and letting his voice trail with the gentle breeze blowing off the nearby river.

Parker drained his glass of wine before responding. "We're looking for some people, Patrick."

The words hung in the air. Gibson was happy to finally be getting somewhere. Parker filled his glass with wine. Patrick stared uneasily at Parker. "And why do you think I would be of any help to you?" Patrick said, his face turning from an expression of joyfulness to seriousness. The dog Niska came running out of the house barking before Sandrine led her back inside.

"Because you're the only person I know living in the French Pays Basque who is a member of a Basque choir group, a Basque gentlemen's club, a Basque dance group, and who possibly knows the kind of people we need to talk to." Parker's voice was firm and direct. Gibson was surprised at Parker's sudden change of attitude. He transformed from a fun loving drunk, spouting stories of days past and toasting memories, to someone determined to get an answer.

"What kind of people are you're talking about?"

"The kind that you're not going to want to talk about, but the kind I know you're connected with."

"And why would I help you? You work for the fucking CIA. As far as I know, your colleague here does too. I love the Basque people. They're the greatest race on Earth and I wish I were Basque. The closest I can ever come is to live here, speak Basque, and marry a Basque girl, which I'm hoping Sandrine will do me the honor of some day. I don't agree with killing people, but I agree with the goal of the Basque independence movement. There should be an independent

Basque country. This is a people that doesn't speak Spanish or French, but their own unique language—Basque. They have different customs, traditions, and an entirely different culture. Franco killed thousands of Basques in Spain during his reign and no one on the outside world said much about it. But now that the Basques are fighting for independence and a few people get killed, there is this overgeneralization that all Basques support terrorism. And you work for a faceless dirty agency that seems to have no cause except to do whatever it wants, whenever it wants, anywhere in the world. So I'm more inclined to say *va te faire foutre.*"

Gibson watched the expression on Parker's face while Patrick talked, waiting to see a nerve hit and Parker react. But to his surprise, Parker remained calm, patiently waiting for a chance to speak. "I may not agree with everything my agency has done in the past or everything it does today, but I like my job, so back the fuck off. And it's not just a few people that have been killed by ETA and associated groups, by the way. It's now getting close to nine hundred people that have been killed in the name of Basque independence. That's no insignificant number."

"What does the CIA care about ETA? Their targets are in Spain and France, not the United States."

Parker smiled slyly, not saying a word.

"When? I haven't heard anything," Patrick sputtered.

"No, and you probably won't," Gibson added from the far end of the table. Patrick flashed him an unfriendly glance, then turned back to Parker. "Have you heard of José Aldarossa Arana?" Gibson quietly added.

"I follow what the Basques are doing in the States and make trips over to meet with various societies whenever I can. So, yes, I know him and have met Arana on many occasions. It's not every day that a Basque-American gets elected to the city council of San Francisco," Patrick said, rolling his eyes away from Gibson.

Silently, Gibson cast his eyes on Parker, asking if they could trust giving more information to Patrick. Parker sensed the question and gave a slight nod of approval to continue.

Gibson took a slow drink from his water as Patrick waited, clearly growing impatient. "Mr. Arana was brutally tortured and murdered. His body was found in a San Francisco alley…" Gibson paused again, taking control of the conversation. His eyes narrowed on Patrick across the table. "We think ETA carried out the assassination."

Patrick reflected on the words for a silent, tense moment, then took a long drink of his wine, draining his glass. Speaking to the bottom of his glass he said, "That is hard to believe."

"Why's that?" Gibson asked.

"Because ETA is not made up of a group of peasant fools, as I'm sure you would like to label them. *Au contraire*, they are highly trained, educated, and aware of the political responses from their actions. They would not pick American targets now, not after everything that happened on September 11th." In an icy voice, Patrick added, "That is why it's very hard for me to believe they would do such a thing, Monsieur Gibson." He turned to Parker and said, "I'm surprised you of all people believe in this *bordel*."

Parker correctly guessed it was time for him to step between the two men's growing animosities. "Okay, hold off here, fellas."

Parker pointed at Gibson. "You take it easy for a minute over there."

To Patrick he said, "Patrick, I know it seems unlikely at first glance, but the signs are that this was carried out by at least some faction connected to ETA. I'm sorry I can't tell you any more than that, but you're going to have to just trust me on this."

"You ask me to trust you when you tell me you can't trust me with all the information you have?" Patrick asked in Basque.

Parker quickly countered in Basque. "You are my friend. This is just a very delicate situation."

Gibson didn't like the mix of languages and gave a cough of dissatisfaction. Parker gave him a sideways glance and continued in English. "You know better than anyone that I want all the best for the Basque people, but killing is not the answer. In fact, I think if those in ETA are so pissed off at not having their own country, they should not blame the Spanish or French governments, but their ancestors who did nothing for hundreds of years while conquerors overthrew their lands from the Romans to the Franco regime to the Mitterrand presidency. Apathy is not a good excuse for inaction, as far as I'm concerned."

"As far as you're concerned? And what are you really? I think you're a damn hypocrite working for an evil agency in a tyrannical government trying to take over the fucking world!" Patrick yelled, springing to his feet and slamming his palms into the table.

The sudden action made Gibson involuntarily touch the breast of his jacket. Gibson actually wanted an excuse to whip out his gun.

"Are you finished?" Parker asked calmly after taking a long gulp of his wine. His look revealed no hostility. It was one of the rare moments when Gibson regrettably admitted to being impressed. Calmly, Parker set his glass down and produced a cigarette from somewhere hidden in his jacket pocket. He lit it, inhaled and exhaled a smooth cloud of smoke, while never removing his sharp eyes from Patrick. "Is it all right for ETA to kill innocent civilians in their quest for an independent Basque homeland?" he gently asked.

Patrick's eyes narrowed on Parker. "What you and everyone else in the world must realize is that there is a war going on here. There may not be a defined front or catastrophic battles, but it's still a war. This is a war that's fought on the streets. This is a war of politics, information, industry, and culture. This is a war of this century. If people die, people die. That's what happens in war. This war is about defending a culture from annihilation, and perhaps not just about defending it from France or Spain, but from the world today."

Two even lines of smoke streamed from Parker's nostrils as he closed his eyelids to reflect on Patrick's statement. He coldly responded, "What if Sandrine was accidently killed by a car bomb?" Parker paused, but Patrick displayed no sign of emotion.

"Do you know how long the French anti-terrorist squad keeps suspects for interrogation without charging them these days? I'm sure you know that some people, even in France, have been jailed for mere collaboration with the ETA. Collaboration is a rather undefined word, don't you think?" Patrick countered.

Parker leaned slightly forward over the table as he spoke again. "I'm sure you know this, because some of your friends in ETA are now sitting in French jails in the north of France, far from here. Do you know it wouldn't be very difficult to connect you to ETA?" Parker quietly added, causing Gibson's head to snap to attention.

Patrick returned to his seat and refilled his glass with wine. He downed his full glass. "*Tu espèce de petite merde.*" Although he didn't understand what Patrick said, Gibson was sure it was not friendly.

Parker laughed at Patrick's comment and stubbed out his cigarette in the ashtray on the table. "As you said yourself, I work for an agency that does what it wants. Kill me and you'd have the entire forces of the CIA coming down on ETA, and we both know ETA would never measure up to that sort of an additional challenge. Not too many people know about this corner of Europe, and that's why not too many people are concerned with your little war here." He pulled out another cigarette and lit it. While smoke crept slowly out of his mouth, he added, "So, *va à l'enfer, mon ami.*"

Patrick stared at Parker as if he were gazing at an unpredictable person who'd had too many apératifs. "Just how is it that you think I can help you?" he finally said, now calmer. "I don't know much of what goes on. No one does. Being so secretive to its own members has always been a great advantage to ETA. You know that better than anyone. If not too many know about the details of each individual operation, not many can be used to incriminate those involved."

"Parker, why don't we just haul his ass over to the French authorities and let them beat it out of him?" Gibson suggested from the far end of the table.

The other two men turned to look uneasily at him. "Gibson, why don't you go wait by the car? I'll be there in a few minutes," Parker said, turning away.

Giving Patrick a threatening glance, Gibson reluctantly rose from the table and strode past them. The whole time, Parker's eyes remained fixed on Patrick. Gibson passed through the small yard and let himself out of the low gate to the road. When he reached the car he paced around it, feeling like a child that had been sent away from the dinner table to sit in a corner.

Twenty minutes later, Parker appeared, coming through the gate. Gibson thought it strange that for as much wine as he'd consumed, Parker didn't show the slightest stumble in his walk. Looking closely at

Parker's face, he instantly knew he'd been successful in at least some regard. It wasn't quite a smile or even a smirk. But it was a look of confidence.

* * *

The entrance was nothing more than a wooden door located in a small empty square between groups of buildings, all with closed shutters on their windows. Once inside, a vast room opened up with high ceilings and rows of chairs on two levels that overlooked what Gibson thought was an oversized enclosed racquetball court.

The room was mostly full of older men drinking red wine. Parker said little after leaving Patrick's house, only revealing they had some sort of a meeting in a few hours. They returned to their hotel for a nap, and then Parker led them back through the streets of Petit Bayonne.

Gibson's impatience grew enormously when they walked through the doorway and Parker said something in Basque to the bouncer at the door. This door guardian, who had a neck the size of an ox, nodded approval. The ox made a comment directed at Gibson that didn't sound approving in any language. Parker shook the man's huge hand and said something quickly, nodding to Gibson. The bouncer eyed Gibson unevenly as he passed by, but said nothing more. Later, Parker would tell Gibson that offering money, as a bribe, would have been an insult to the Basque man at the door. Instead, Parker had offered to take the man out to get him drunk some night.

The room was packed with bodies of men who smelled like wine, heavy tobacco, and the outdoors, all wearing black berets. It was strange to Gibson that in the middle of a city the size of Bayonne, there were men who gave off the impression of having just come from a full day's work in the fields. Looking around at the faces, he noticed they were full of joy and cheer.

Then he lost sight of Parker.

They had been threading their way through a mass of bodies and while he was enjoying the atmosphere enveloping him, Gibson fell further behind Parker and now could see him nowhere. Panic set in as for the first time he realized the faces surrounding him were not friendly toward him. They were not really unfriendly, but were quite obviously shunning him. He tried to look over the barrage of black berets in every direction, but still could not see Parker's crazy head of hair anywhere. In his suit, and without a glass of red wine in his hand or without a black beret on his head, Gibson stuck out like a Buddhist at confirmation.

The men nearest him all turned their backs to him and he recognized that they were speaking Basque to each other. He recognized Basque being spoken around him now as the language was unlike any other he'd ever heard. For some reason, hearing this language made him feel even more lost. He imagined they were talking about him.

Backs began to slowly press against him and he felt like he couldn't move. Soon the pressure of his gun against his breast became uncomfortable and he momentarily considered pulling it out.

Then he felt a hand firmly grab his shoulder from behind. Looking over his shoulder, he saw Parker's beaming face and a glass of red wine being handed to him. He took the glass, with no intention of drinking it, and let Parker direct him through the crowd. En route, Parker finished the glass he'd been holding, and looking back at Gibson's untouched one, replaced his own with Gibson's and quickly downed the other. Patrick and his ponytail suddenly approached from between a pair of ruddy faced men that were toasting life or love or both or neither.

Patrick said something in Basque to Parker and then spoke to Gibson. "Glad you could make it. Have you ever seen a pelote match?"

Gibson stared at him for a second, not knowing what to think. He noticed a group of men surrounding them, watching him in particular. Patrick appeared to have gotten over his anger, as he now looked pleased to see them. "No, I haven't. What is it exactly?"

Patrick beamed with delight at having the opportunity to explain something Basque. He spoke in English, mostly. "Oh, *mon dieu*, you don't know one of the best things of the Basque culture!" He paused to clink glasses with Parker, who promptly drained his glass of wine. "It's a game that originated in Basque antiquity and has now spread around the world in various forms. You know the game jai alai that they play in Florida?" Gibson nodded his head. "Well, that game is a form of pelote. It's one called *cesta punta*, and most of the best players in Miami are Basque and come from here." Gibson tried to display that he was impressed. "The matches that take place in here are not exactly like the ones in Miami though. Here they don't play with the basket-like thing players wear on their arms. In here they play the old fashioned way, with their hands." Patrick held up one of his hands to emphasize his point.

Surrounding them, the men seemed to be listening without actually displaying interest. All nodded in approval to each other when Patrick held up his open palm. Not one of them turned to face them though.

The spectator chairs were arranged in a style of rustic stadium seating behind a net that stretched from floor to ceiling. A lower and upper balcony of seats divided spectators. When four players stepped onto the court, the crowd of men herded to the benches. Patrick tapped him on the shoulder and led him to a seat.

As he sat down, Gibson noticed Parker walked in a different direction and sat down at the end of the row from them. He was talking with a squinty eyed man not much older than Gibson.

Patrick leaned closer to Gibson "You should actually consider yourself very fortunate to be in here with this…" he searched a moment for the word he was thinking of, "exclusive little society. You see, this is a bit of a secret pelote court and not many people know where it is. Though they might know it exists, they don't know how to get here. You're the only two who came in through the front door there. Everyone else came in through less obvious ways."

Patrick continued. "In fact, Sebastian's never even been in here," he said, discretely nodding at Parker.

"Who's he talking to over there?" Gibson asked.

"That's Eduardo Javier Munoz. He's also known as, what roughly translates as, the Igniter." Patrick leaned closer and spoke barely above a whisper. "He used to be the leader of an ETA commando unit in Madrid, back when Franco was still in power. They say he's somehow responsible for about twenty deaths attributed to ETA's history. But after Franco signed off, he quit and moved up here and began a family life. Every policeman in Spain and France knows who he is, but they can't pin a thing on him."

"Oh, a family man now. That's good. For a second there, I was getting a little worried for Parker."

Patrick laughed. "I wouldn't toss all worries out the window just yet. He's still capable of being extremely dangerous. Sebastian's a tough little shit, but I doubt he is going to enjoy his first pelote match in here."

Gibson discreetly cracked his knuckles on both hands with his thumbs. "Parker really has never been in here?"

"Being Basque is normally a requirement to even be considered to be let into this place. I'm lucky to be allowed here myself."

Raising his eyebrows in mock astonishment, Gibson said, "Then I guess I should be impressed, but I'm not. I've always believed when any one group goes so far to keep itself exclusive, the mentality is bordering on fascism."

Patrick responded in an even more hushed voice. "The Basques aren't fascists, John. If they were fascists, they would have joined to fight with Franco on the nationalist side of the Spanish Civil War. And if they were fascists, they wouldn't have been such key players in the resistance down here during World War II. Do you know they helped get a lot of American soldiers out of occupied France? No, the Basque people are very far from fascists. If you said they were communists, I might be able to agree with you, partly anyway, because they are very split over the political spectrum."

"Thanks for the lesson in Basque history and politics. I see why you and Parker get along." He paused to reflect on how he felt satisfied to get in the last word. "Can you tell me why they all seem to go by three or four names?" he asked.

Patrick shrugged his shoulders. "Sometimes their mother's maiden name or their father's first name is added to their own as kind of a family lineage."

"Odd people," Gibson said, rolling his eyes.

* * *

The small ball pounded against the indoor fronton and the noise echoed throughout the room. The crowd nodded approval. One of the players wound his arm back and hit the ball with a loud smack that made Parker's own hand tingle with pain. The ball bounced off the wall and because of the spin the pelote player put on the ball, it didn't bounce straight back, but instead, took a direction toward the far sideline of the court where the opposing team's player couldn't reach it. Immediately, the crowd of men gave big silent nods of approval for the shot.

"Patrick tells me you are looking for help finding some people," Eduardo Munoz said to Parker.

"I am," Parker admitted.

"And what makes you think I'm going to help you?" Munoz said, after a chorus of disapproval following a bad shot.

"Nothing makes me think you will, but I know that if you want to, you could help me."

Munoz turned in his seat to look Parker in the eye for a prolonged moment. "Patrick said you were different and intelligent. Maybe you are." Parker waited for him to continue. "I actually wish I could help you more than I can. I believe in the Basque Country. I believe in the Basque people. And I believe in the cause of ETA. But what I don't believe in is that civilians are targets in our war." A loud smack of a flat hand hitting the hard ball on the court made Munoz stop to check out the action before continuing. "That's why I left the organization."

"Is that the only reason?"

"No, there were other reasons. One in particular," Munoz admitted with a shrug.

"As in…" Parker raised his hands in emphasis.

"That is not important," he flatly replied and turned to watch the pelote match. "I shouldn't be talking to you, Mr. Parker, but I like Patrick and trust him when he says you are a good man. But we need to give the impression we are only here watching pelote."

Parker sensed he was losing favor and reacted quickly. "But what happened in San Francisco was done by them." He leaned and spoke quietly, but did not make the sentence a question.

Munoz kept his eyes on the ball flying around the court, but nodded his head forward. "It was and it was not," he said out the side of his mouth, still looking at the pelote match. Then he added, "You're a bright young man, I'm sure you'll figure it out."

Parker watched his face tighten. He worried he wasn't going to get much more information out of their meeting. Then, Munoz softly added, "Have you ever been to the Fête des Piments d'Espelette?"

"Yes, I have. It's one of my favorite festivals in the northern Basque Country."

"Then you know it begins tomorrow." Munoz still did not look at him and he spoke quietly, barely moving his lips. Parker had to lean closer to hear him. When Parker nodded his head, Munoz continued. "You could go there tomorrow night. You could go to the bar next to the fronton. You could tell the bartender I have arranged for you to meet *le bomb*. If you do all this, you will be led to Peio." His face had grown stern and even tighter as he spoke. Parker recognized the words were difficult for him to produce.

"And what will this *le bomb* be able to tell me?" Parker asked, watching one of the players dive to save a shot. The player missed the ball and the crowd let out a gasp.

"I imagine he will tell you nothing." Parker waited. "But you should be looking for him and once you find him you should be able to locate the others," Munoz said, after a pause.

Parker nearly fell off his chair. "How many?" he barely whispered.

"One for each province in the south." There were four Basque provinces in the south including Navarre, which any Basque patriot would consider included, even if the province was not officially labeled as such by some. Parker had his answer. Then Munoz added, almost under his breath, "But there is another who is not here."

Parker's eyes widened slightly and he had difficulty restraining himself from being too anxious. "Where is the other one?"

"There are a lot of Basque-Americans in the western states of your country," Munoz said, staring blankly at the players below.

Parker had to bite his lip to keep from smiling. "Thank you very much for your help."

"I haven't helped you. We are just sitting next to one another watching a match of pelote," Munoz barely replied, a blank expression on his face.

"Of course," Parker responded, leaning back in his chair to enjoy the rest of the match. He could feel Gibson staring at him down the row, but Parker didn't look at him. Making eye contact with Gibson would be a sure sign to anyone paying attention that something suspicious was occurring. And actually getting up and leaving before the match ended would be sacrilegious.

* * *

Spain Foils ETA Summit Attack

Spanish authorities say they have prevented a major terrorist attack before a summit of European and Latin American leaders in Madrid. The Madrid regional governor said nearly 200 kilograms of explosives, as well as detonators, automatic weapons, and false license plates were found in an apartment in the center of the city.

He also stated the cache belonged to three suspected members of the Basque Separatist Organization, ETA, two of whom were arrested. A third suspect has so far escaped arrest.

Police in Spain say they arrested six people in the Basque Country believed to be involved in the same operation. Four men and one woman were detained in Eibar, Guipuzcoa province, and another man in the nearby town of Hondarribia. The six were also wanted in connection with the murder of a Basque socialist leader.

Explosives were found at a location near the National and Supreme Courts. Another 40 kilograms were found in a stolen car.

ETA recently claimed to have detonated two car bombs to coincide with the Champions League semi final second leg between Real Madrid and Barcelona.

15

Basque Country, France

AGENT GIBSON SCANNED the crowd of reddened faces happily filling the tree-lined city square. Inside the square there was a fronton and a fountain. Some people were sitting at tables arranged to leave a dance area in front of a stage where a band was playing festive music. The music sounded cheery to him, even though he didn't understand any of the words they were singing. He correctly assumed the band was playing traditional Basque songs.

There were stands with steaming bowls and plates of food and rows of bottles of wine on the edges of the dining tables. It seemed that everywhere he looked he saw strings of small red peppers hanging around doorways and balconies, covering entire sides of houses. Next to the square were the village church and adjoining stone cemetery. In the middle of all the liveliness and joy, the cemetery was out of place, he thought.

Parker had told him they were going to the Espelette Pepper Festival. Gibson had a difficult time following Parker's description of a fête. Apparently in France there were thousands of little festivals such as this one where basically everyone came out to socialize, eat good food, and drink all day and night. Each fête was a little different in that it would be either a general fête for the city or town, or it would be like the one in Espelette, where it focused on something regionally specific. At one point, Gibson asked Parker when people in France went to work.

Shrugging his shoulders, Parker said, "It's the law in France to only have thirty-two hour work weeks and six weeks of vacation a year."

Even though Gibson was usually an all run and no fun American, he thought a thirty-two hour workweek would be nice from time to time.

From Bayonne, Parker drove them out into the countryside on a highway he said the French called an *autoroute*. After leaving the limits of Bayonne, they quickly came to a smaller city spread across the banks of the Nive River called Ustaritz. Parker mentioned that Ustaritz was at one time a much more important city to the French Pays Basque than the city was now. Gibson wasn't in the mood for a history lesson.

Ustaritz quickly passed by, only consisting of a few rows of buildings along the bank of the river on one side, and a row of houses on the other. A large complex that looked like a convent was perched on a hillside high overhead.

The land quickly opened up into series upon series of rolling hills, stretching in every direction. White stone farmhouses, with either red or green trim, dotted the landscape and Gibson noticed the men he saw working in their fields all wore black berets. When they came to the top of a rise, a line of low mountains appeared directly in front of them. Gibson looked to his right and noticed an expanse of craggy mountain ridges that were much higher, extending from one end of the horizon to the other. Parker was quick to point out that these were the Pyrenees Mountains and just on the other side was Spain.

Since leaving the limits of Bayonne, Parker hadn't lit one cigarette. He cracked his window and breathed deeply, inhaling all the rustic and vibrant scents of the Basque countryside he cherished. Out of the corner or his eye, Gibson watched how elated Parker looked as he drank in the green rolling landscape surrounding them. Gibson agreed that everything he'd seen of the place so far was beautiful, possibly even considered breathtaking. But what this place did for Sebastian Parker was beyond Gibson's understanding. It was clear that Parker lived for this place.

Before they left the hotel, Parker called Capitaine Nivelle. The Capitaine refused to speak of anything over the phone and insisted on coming to their room to discuss. Parker slammed down the phone and translated the conversation to Gibson.

Once they arrived in Espelette, Gibson easily spotted the non-uniformed men hanging around the square Nivelle had brought with him. Though they were trying to fit in, to any trained eye they were an obvious give away. This made Gibson nervous about the chances of their mission's success. And then there was Nivelle, pacing alone around the outside of the square, looking at everyone that crossed his path with unveiled suspicion.

Though it was midday, the square was already filled with people drinking and chatting. Parker insisted he go alone to find his contact and disappeared into a crowd of wine-chugging people. Gibson imagined he was seated at a bar finding out how fast he could get wasted.

In truth, Parker was seated at a bar knocking back a glass of red wine, but he was not there for pleasure. He was waiting for the right moment when he could pull the bartender aside to tell him discreetly what needed to be said. When a group of already sloppy drunk men next to him left the bar, he saw his chance. He knew he only had a small window of opportunity, so he drained his *verre* and acted quickly. Leaning over the bar, Parker said what Munoz instructed him to say.

The bartender slowly moved back and gave him a searching look. He told Parker, "I only believe you because Munoz called me earlier and told me a young man would be coming in and asking for this person. Le bomb will be in this bar in about an hour with two other guys. They will all be young, hardly old enough to be called men. The shortest of the three will be le bomb, but he will also be the most *costaud*."

Parker remembered his French slang and knew this meant le bomb would be the most muscular. "That isn't much to go on, especially since the bar will be packed all day and night with short, young, *costauds* men," Parker told the bartender.

A shrug of shoulders was all Parker received as a reply. The bartender grabbed Parker's wine glass and Parker thought the man was walking away from him until he saw him stop at the end of the bar and do something out of sight. Soon his glass was returned to him, full, with a napkin underneath it. Without another word, the bartender disappeared.

Picking up the wineglass, Parker swallowed the wine in two large gulps, then grabbed the napkin and slithered his way through the mass of bodies blocking the exit. Once outside, he looked down at the napkin he was holding in his hand. On it was written in French: "Peio, one hour."

Parker forced himself through cluttered groups of people, tables, and chairs in the direction of a wine stand. The task was made more difficult by the unpredictable movements of people around him. Most of them were red faced and rolling in red wine, resulting in arms and bodies carelessly moving about. Suddenly, a large Basque man sidestepped to keep his balance and his gigantic shoulder rammed into Parker, nearly knocking him to the ground. Parker caught his fall by extending his arms and catching the side of a vacant table with the remains of lunch left by the table's previous patrons. With both hands outstretched on the table in front of him, he found himself staring into an empty wine glass. The food left on the plates reminded him of how hungry he was.

Peppers were a precious gift from the earth, in his opinion, and every dish served during the la Fête des Piments was loaded with piles of the local red chili peppers. Someone at the table had *axoa* and he was instantly jealous of whoever had been so full to finish their plate. *Axoa* was at its absolute best during the festival in Espelette. Someone else had *poulet basquaise*, and another piperade. His stomach growled loudly as his mind pictured a menu in his head: the slightly soupy *axoa* with peppers, tomatoes, garlic and spicy sausage; *poulet basquaise* with chicken smothered in red, yellow, green peppers, tomatoes, topped with black olives and ham; the Basque omelet of piperade with peppers, tomatoes, onions heavily sautéed and topped by a generous slice of powerful and salty *jambon de Bayonne*. He was about to begin drooling over the thought of all this wonderful food. Right away he promised his stomach that after talking to Nivelle, he would get some food.

Looking around, Parker saw the large Basque man who'd run into him straighten his stance and his beret before jumping back into the highly animated conversation was having with a couple of other men who looked even fuller of wine. The man was too tipsy to realize what his inebriated body had done to Parker. Accepting this fact, Parker shrugged his shoulders and mentally excused the lack of an apology and moved on.

When he reached the wine stand, he ordered a glass of *rouge* and drained it as soon as handed to him. Immediately, he ordered another. The middle-aged, pleasant looking woman dressed in traditional Basque clothing behind the stand took the coins from his hand and gave him a questioning glance. Parker was able to ward off any concern she may have had by flashing a charming smile and telling her in Basque that her outfit looked very nice.

The band on the central stage in the square turned up the volume on their amplifiers. Speaking a little louder in order to be heard, he asked the woman if he could borrow a serving tray for a few minutes, and also the red beret that was lying on top of the box behind her.

Surprisingly, she didn't seem at all shocked by his request. On the contrary, she was more than happy to let him borrow a tray, pulling one out from behind the stand and handing it to him. He traded her a twenty euro note and asked her if she would mind filling a few glasses with wine and placing them on this tray.

She obliged and a few moments later he was making his way through the crowd with the tray held high above the tilted red beret now perched on his head. He was thankful for having worked as a waiter during graduate school because it took a degree of talent to make it all the way across the square full of enthusiastic drinkers to Capitaine Nivelle. When he finally arrived at Nivelle's table, he lowered the tray and offered a *verre*, as if Nivelle had ordered one. Though Nivelle looked irritated, he took a glass off the tray and tried a sip. After swallowing a sip, he made a sour face saying, "*C'est comme de la merde*. These Basques don't know good wine. They just drink to get *ivre*."

Feeling confrontational, Parker asked in French, "If you didn't know it was Basque, would you still think the same way?"

Surprised he would talk to him in such a matter, Nivelle cocked his head and looked at Parker, wanting to squash him like a bug.

"Monsieur Parker, do not forget you are a guest here in France, and for as much French or Basque you may know, or for all the people you think you know, you'll always be an outsider here or anywhere else in France." His words were sharp and to the point.

Parker offered his tray to a good looking couple passing by who he figured were Parisians by the way they were over dressed. When they each took a glass, the man began to pull money out of his suit pocket, but Parker stopped him by saying that the glasses were on him.

The man and woman smiled at each other. Parker overheard the woman tell her partner that she didn't think the Basque people were as cold and unwelcoming as they were portrayed to be.

Parker smiled at them in response then placed the tray down on a stone partition that was in the middle of the road to mark off the pedestrian zone of the city square. He leaned back and lit a cigarette. He knew Nivelle was waiting for his comeback, but purposefully waited a few minutes longer than necessary before responding.

"Well, Nivelle, to tell you the truth, I wouldn't want to live anywhere besides the Basque Country in France anyway. And I've always felt like an outsider, even in America. If I ever do move here, I'll be sure to let you know." Parker insulted Nivelle as much as possible, by not looking at him when he spoke, by not calling him by his title, and by speaking in English.

"Believe me, Mr. Parker, whenever you return to France, I will know." Nivelle's tone was icy, his accent thick and murky.

Parker dropped his cigarette butt to the ground and put it out with his foot. He picked up his tray, which still had a few glasses of wine on it, and lifted it over his head. "Well, Capitaine, if you still want to bust this guy, I suggest you notify your men that he's going to be at that bar right over there within an hour." He pointed to the bar where he'd talked with the bartender earlier.

"How will we know who it is? And where will you be?" Nivelle was now very interested in talking to Parker.

"I'll be in there and I'll identify him. Just have your men ready and watching me. When I walk up to a young man and place my hand on the back of his shoulder, you'll know it's him. I'll try and get him to go outside the bar alone with me so you guys can snatch him away, but I can't promise I'll be able to do that. It'd be a shame to ruin the festival by barging in there to get him though. So if nothing else, you could move in and take him quietly."

"Mr. Parker, do you really think I care if I ruin this *putain fête*?"

Parker didn't feel Nivelle's comment required a response. He turned on his heel and walked back into the crowded square, heading once again across it. This time his purpose was to find Gibson, who he imagined was by now having a hernia about him disappearing.

As he passed Gibson, Parker tapped him on his arm and began walking toward the entrance to the bar. Gibson followed behind, feeling more and more anxious with every step closer to the mass of bodies flowing out from the bar. Parker saw something that motivated him to get inside.

From the corner of his eye, Gibson noticed Nivelle's men moving casually in from all angles. Gibson also realized that where Nivelle's men looked nervous and out of place at the fun loving festival, Parker looked cool and right at home.

Gibson watched Parker grab a glass of wine off a passing waitress's tray and give her a nice kiss on her lips for payment, which seemed sufficient, as she only smiled and went about her way. Parker melted into the crowd and Gibson had trouble keeping up with him. Bodies seemed to step aside for Parker as he passed by, but seemed to move in front of Gibson.

Gibson eventually picked out Parker in the crowd and watched him move deep into the room until he was at the bar. Within a few moments, he caught up with Parker and when he did finally make it to his side, heard Parker ordering something from the bartender. Though Gibson felt a strong urge to scold Parker, he didn't for fear of blowing their cover. Also because he knew his lecturing would fall on deaf ears. Gibson merely lowered his eyes as he watched Parker down a shot of some vibrant yellow colored liquor.

As it slid down his throat, Parker half-closed his eyes in a state of pleasure, and then placed the shot glass back down on the surface of the bar. Glancing at Gibson, he smiled before quickly glancing at the entrance of the bar. He produced a cigarette from his shirt pocket and lit it.

"What the hell are we doing, Parker?" Gibson hissed, severely annoyed.

Parker peered through the smoke rising from his cigarette and leaned inward. "We're about to catch one of them," he said near Gibson's ear.

Gibson gazed uncertainly at him for a moment before saying anything. "How's that? Are we just going to sit here bucked up at the bar and he's going to come to us?"

Parker smiled at him again, in his half-drunk kind of way with his eyes wide and shining. Then his eyes narrowed and his face tightened. He let the cigarette drop from his lips to the floor and killed the ember by stepping on it. "My dear fellow, I fear you'll never understand me," Parker spoke with an exaggerated British accent and kissed Gibson on the cheek, his face now returned to a subdued state. He turned and walked up to a group of young men who looked to Gibson to be no older than boys. Gibson watched as Parker said something to make the boys laugh. Parker then put his hand on the shortest one's shoulder.

Later, Gibson figured out it had taken longer than he originally thought, but at the time he witnessed the events take place, everything seemed to be over in a matter of moments.

The whole affair was conducted differently than any law enforcement action he ever witnessed. It was conducted in Parker's own way, with Parker making up the rules as he went along. Being a direct witness, Gibson could not doubt Sebastian Parker's command over the situation.

When Parker left him standing alone at the bar, he joined the group of three young men and was instantly taken in. Gibson watched Parker pull out his box of cigarettes and offer them to the happily accepting group. Clearly, Parker was paying more attention to the short one of the group, yet he didn't neglect either of the other two.

Parker bought glasses of red wine for each of them and they toasted the ceiling. As Gibson watched, he saw Parker somehow manage to get the group moving in the direction of the bar's exit. Glancing around, Gibson noticed Nivelle's men were now inside and also moving slowly toward the exit as well. At a safe distance, Gibson watched how once outside, Nivelle's men moved in like trained attack dogs and surrounded the four young men, Parker included.

No guns were drawn and the entire event didn't disrupt the festivities of the night. The four were escorted away from the square into a lifeless alleyway where Parker was separated from the other three. The others were placed in the back of an unmarked van. Glancing at the back of the van, Gibson noticed there were two men inside with automatic rifles, sitting on stools, waiting for company. Gibson thought the entire operation was conducted smoothly and precisely. Later, Parker explained to him that Nivelle had called in the RAID group of the national police, an elite swat team, to assist with the operation.

Nivelle walked over to Parker and hurriedly spoke to him out the side of his mouth before jumping into the passenger seat of the van. Nivelle had a wide, mischievous grin plastered on his face, making his moustache turn upward even more as if, it too, were smiling. Parker stood and smoked, silently watching the van hurry off into the rolling Basque countryside.

* * *

"Sara Gamboa was found dead in her house two days ago," Gibson said as he drove. Parker was trying to find a radio station that suited him. Up to that point, he'd been ignoring Gibson, as Gibson had mainly been complaining about French hotels and French driving habits. But the mentioning of Sara Gamboa's name quickly caught his attention.

"What did you say?" he asked, eyes glued to the beams of light shooting into the darkness of the Pays Basque night surrounding them.

"I said, Sara Gamboa was found dead in her house two days ago. It took my guys a while to get out there, but they've taken over the investigation. They've got no leads so far though."

Parker dug his fingernails into the front of the glove compartment and spoke through clenched teeth. "Why didn't you tell me before?"

"Because you didn't need to know, Parker. In fact, you didn't need to know now. I'm only telling you out of courtesy. There's no way we can know for sure that her murder was linked to this case. The world is full of lunatics. Maybe someone killed her just because she was a nice piece of ass they could never touch. Who knows?"

"That's really sick, Gibson."

"Hey, kid, I've been doing this for a long time and I've seen just about everything. If that thought is so sick to you, I wouldn't recommend turning to law enforcement in your career."

Parker lit a cigarette before saying, "I wasn't planning on it." He exhaled a stream of smoke out of the cracked window. "But you can't tell me you don't see any relationship between her murder and our case."

Gibson rolled his head to crack his neck. "Parker, my job is not to speculate until I have facts. So, officially, I'd say they are not related. However, between you and I, I'd say they most certainly goddamn are."

Parker raised his hands in excitement. "Hell yeah they are! So what do we do now?"

"We do our job here. We've got people looking into the Gamboa case."

"She's already lost her identity and has become a case?" Parker exclaimed, waving his glowing cigarette in the air.

"Cool down, Parker. The best thing you can do to help her now is to solve the case here."

"Well, what if we can't solve the case here without solving it there as well?"

Gibson turned his head as he smiled so Parker wouldn't see his expression, acknowledging Parker's cleverness. "You know, Parker, sometimes you surprise me…sometimes."

"*Va te faire foutre,*" Parker said.

"I can guess what that means."

"Guess this," Parker said, holding up his middle finger at Gibson.

Laughing, Gibson said, "You really are a little shit, Parker. But tell me, did you notice anything strange about our guy back there?"

Parker quickly shot a questioning glance at Gibson. "Yeah, he wasn't much of a guy at all. More of a boy, maybe nineteen."

Gibson opened his window and breathed in the fresh evening country air. "Yeah—a boy."

***

Aurelion Irazoqui felt a deep stinging in his stomach that felt like he'd swallowed a piece of iron. The news of Peio's incarceration, *incarceration* since as far as anyone knew he had not been charged with any crime yet—normal practice of the Spanish and French police forces when dealing with Basques—spread fast. *Les flics* walked into the most crowded bar in Espelette, right in the middle of the Fête des Piments, and took him. If they could take Peio, how hard would it be for them to take him?

From the moment he stepped off the plane in Amsterdam, Aurelion felt a surge of pride he'd never felt before. In the days following, the wonderful feeling of elation only grew in heated anticipation of being with Marie-Hélène, who would love him more than ever for being brave and doing so much for the cause. Now, sitting next to her in the back room of a small apartment outside of Dax, he didn't want her to be there. He felt like crying in fear, but didn't want her to see him so weak.

Earlier, Marie-Hélène told him the news. He was scared and didn't want her to see it. She told him they would be moved to a more secure location, either somewhere deep in the region of the Landes, or in the mountains, maybe even as far as Pau, or into Spain. No one knew for sure. They wouldn't know until the transporter arrived.

The waiting was really getting to him. Aurelion had nearly smoked half of Marie-Hélène's pack of cigarettes, and he hated smoking. His left hand shook uncontrollably. Talking wouldn't help, as he knew he would only end up sounding like a baby. She would then comfort him by telling him everything would be all right.

He wasn't so sure.

Aurelion feared he might be "silenced" instead of transported. He didn't want her to have to see that. He wanted her to go and leave him to his fate. But she wouldn't leave. There were many reasons why he loved her. This was a perfect example of one of them.

When two loud knocks pounded on the door, Marie-Hélène told him to stay where he was while she answered it."

As she headed for the door, Aurelion was unable to sit still. He stood up and walked to the entrance of the front room, only leaning his head out just enough to watch. Before opening the door, Marie-Hélène asked who was there.

Satisfied with the response she received, she opened the door. A man she didn't know stepped into the room. He had long black hair pulled back into a ponytail and he was dark skinned like a Spanish Basque. The man was wearing torn jeans and a denim jacket. He only spoke enough to say that they had five minutes before leaving. And he stressed that only Aurelion was going with him."

Marie-Hélène was also apparently not to know where Aurelion was going, as the transporter refused to answer her when she asked. Aurelion cringed even more, but a firm look from Marie-Hélène told him he couldn't resist. Her look said that this was how it was when you are a member of the cause.

Aurelion threw the few things he had into his large duffel bag. Then he saw the most beautiful sight he could possibly imagine: Marie-Hélène was looking at him with both desire and concern. She walked up to him and placed her lips on his cheeks and her arms tightly around him. They stayed in this embrace for a full two minutes, as if nothing else was happening in the world. She gently pulled away and placed her pack of cigarettes in his shirt pocket.

Tears welled in his eyes, but he didn't let them fall. He told himself that now was not the time for tears. It was time to be strong.

He walked out the front door behind his transporter. Marie-Hélène stood behind at the doorway, watching him go. Aurelion wanted to look back at her one more time in case he never saw her again, but he didn't. He told himself that if he didn't look, he'd see her again.

* * *

Madrid did nothing for him. Lopé found it too Baroque in style, and he couldn't understand why so many tourists took pictures of the ugly Prada building. To him, it looked like an old factory that had survived from the early Industrial Revolution days.

He'd been there already for two days and in that time hadn't been able to sit still. They'd told him to stay away from public places, knowing that if they told him he couldn't go outside all together, he would go anyway. But he reasoned that if he was going to be stuck in Madrid, he may as well check out places for future attacks.

He walked slowly through the plaza in front of the Prada and saw spot after perfect spot for a hit. Thoughts ran quickly through his mind.

A bomb planted in a post box there. An explosive set off in a car right near the main entrance to the museum. A bomb set off right outside the section of the museum that houses some of the most famous Spanish works of art…all would be perfect. Maybe that would get the government's attention by destroying the most priceless Spanish works of art of all.

The thoughts pleased Lopé. He could imagine the Prime Minister standing at a podium the day after, insisting that the Basque bandits be stopped. Lopé laughed to himself and couldn't wait to tell his new temporary unit of his plan.

The problem was that he was still waiting to meet his new unit. Apparently, he was told, they were all reluctant to meet with him until things settled down.

News of Peio's detainment spread quickly through the communications network and Lopé had raised a glass to his fallen colleague. But he also cursed his new group for cowards. *How good could they possibly be if they get scared just because someone was picked up?*

This question bothered him deeply and almost made him wish he could conduct his own operation until he was reunited with his crew. At least give me Graciana, he thought. With just that sleek minx he could get a lot accomplished. Once she told him that she stabbed a man in a bar in Petit Bayonne even with a group of people surrounding her. Why? Because the man kept trying to grab her ass.

I miss all of them, he thought, but especially her.

As he left the plaza, Lopé began the long walk back to the apartment. He liked walking in the warm night in order to glance into the houses as he passed by, trying to catch someone's eyes so that he could possibly convey a silent message and threat. *I have come here to your city, and it will never be the same again.*

Arriving at his apartment, he opened the door to find a pleasant surprise. A group of eight people was there, five men and three women. They were all busy doing things and no one seemed to pay particular attention to his entrance, as if they knew he would walk in just at that moment.

Pausing to glance around, Lopé saw the men had field stripped some weapons and were cleaning them. The others were loading pressure cookers with homemade bombs, while the women were sorting and bagging an assortment of drugs spread across the wooden dining table. Lopé recognized the drugs they were handling: hash, ecstasy, and cocaine. Though the cocaine looked especially inviting to him, he knew the oath he took to the cause forbade him from stealing from one the organization's financing sources.

He'd been told to stay at this address once he arrived in Madrid and that his commando unit would eventually contact him. But he had no idea that meant he would enter his apartment one day and find them there. In the few days in Madrid, he'd only been in contact with one person, who told him about Peio and the delay of joining his unit.

Lopé knew this was not a moment for words. Since this was the group he would be working with in the foreseeable future, he wanted to give a strong first impression. Without saying a word, he clasped his hands behind his back like a general viewing his troop and walked across the room, taking a seat on the hard wood floor next to the men. He picked up a semi-automatic rifle lying on the floor and quickly disassembled the weapon for cleaning. No one said a word to him, but he knew everyone in the room had been watching. When finished, he set the parts of the gun aside and pulled out one of his short yellow Gauloises cigarettes.

Maybe they aren't so bad, he said to himself, as he casually glanced around the room.

* * *

The boy looked terrified. Gibson watched as Nivelle and two plain-clothes officers, if that was what they were, interrogated Peio in the concrete, windowless room. Though Peio was trying to play tough, he looked like he was about to start foaming at the mouth. Gibson had seen enough interrogations in his career to notice fear coursing through a body. In the small room the air was thick with smoke from the cigarettes.

Glad to be outside the room looking through a two-way mirror, Gibson saw Peio, at one point, motion for the open pack of cigarettes on the table in front of him. He received a backhand from one of Nivelle's men in response.

Parker warned him things were done differently in France when it came to police matters, and especially when it came to suspected terrorists. Gibson was now being shown firsthand just how different. The boy had been either hit or slapped more than four times in the hour since they'd arrived. He already had a dark eye and a bleeding lip. Nivelle made it perfectly clear to Gibson and Parker that they could be present, but that Peio was now in French custody. This seemed to be his way of telling them to stay the hell out of his business.

With a look of both anger and concern on his face, Parker stood next to Gibson observing through the two-way mirror. Gibson noticed that every time one of the three men even made a motion to touch Peio, Parker would tense and narrow his eyes. Gibson was just waiting for the moment when Parker would have enough, break into the room, and confront Nivelle. That would sure be amusing.

But two hours passed and Peio still said nothing. Even though he couldn't understand what was being said, Gibson imagined he knew the questions being asked. Parker didn't bother to translate. After the first hour, Gibson sat down. Parker remained standing the entire time, not removing his eyes from watching what happened in the other room.

One of Nivelle's men gave Peio a slap at the back of his head and the three men left the room with Peio sitting at the table alone, looking like a cornered pit bull. They entered the room where Gibson and Parker were waiting and Nivelle said something in French to Parker. Though Parker didn't say a word to him, he turned to throw a glance of confidence at Gibson. Nivelle and his men left the room.

A few minutes later, Gibson and the three Frenchmen, watched Parker walk into the room with Peio. He moved slowly, carrying a glass of water, setting it down in front of Peio. Parker moved the other chair in the room so he was sitting directly across from the young man. For the first time in hours, Peio actually looked up from the spot his eyes had fixated upon on the wooden table in front of him. Parker spoke in Basque to him and told him he should drink the water.

Gibson smiled inwardly as he noticed the expression on Nivelle's face turn to outrage at Parker giving the suspect water without his permission.

Peio looked at Parker momentarily, trying to decide who he was now dealing with. He decided to greedily gulp down the water. He drank it so quickly it made him have a coughing fit. When he could speak again, Peio thanked Parker.

For once, Gibson didn't feel so worthless. The other three men also couldn't understand the conversation occurring in the opposite room. But he could see that whatever Parker was doing so far was working. He watched Parker work his charm.

"Want a smoke?" Parker asked him, holding out his box of Chesterfield Lights.

Peio carefully took one of the cigarettes from the box and put it between his lips. Parker leaned across the table and lit it with his lighter, then lit one for himself. They smoked in silence for a few minutes.

"I apologize for my Basque not being very good," Parker said.

Peio looked at him with a small grin. "Not many Basque people even speak Basque, so you're better off than many." The two smiled.

"Are you French?" Peio asked him.

"I'm from America. I've been sent here to try and find some people who recently took a trip there. I think you can help."

"Why would I want to help you?" Peio slowly asked.

Parker took a long drag off his cigarette before replying. "Because if you help me, I can help you by getting these guys to back off and charge you with a lesser crime."

"How do you know I've committed a crime? Where's your proof?"

"Peio, you know as well as I do that if they want, they can come up with something to charge you with to hold you until they do have proof they need. That might take years, but they will find it. In the meantime, you'll be sent to a prison as far away as possible from the

Basque Homeland, and you will not be allowed to have any visitors. You will spend the rest of your life in prison. Unless you help me."

Peio stared at him without blinking. "I knew you weren't French. I just wanted to see if you would lie to me. In fact, I was told you were here and that you might be working with the French. Although I didn't know what you looked like. Otherwise, you may have had such a good time in Espelette."

Parker had to bite his tongue to keep from displaying shock. "Who told you?"

"You forget that as a people, we are very connected, especially those of us who are young."

"So, you want to spend the rest of your life in prison? How old are you? Nineteen?" Peio nodded his head affirmatively.

"We're going to catch you all. It's only a matter of time. That man you killed in San Francisco was a very well respected Basque-American. Do you really think you helped the cause by killing him? Now you could have the full force of the American government against ETA. That could end any cause here forever."

"No. You're wrong!" Peio shouted as he slammed his hands on the table. "The cause will never die until we have our own country!"

Parker looked at him calmly and coolly. "Killing people is not the answer anymore, Peio. You've been brainwashed by ETA to think it is, but if it didn't work for the IRA in Northern Ireland, it's not going to work here for ETA in Spain and France." Parker handed him another cigarette and Peio appeared to relax a little, leaning back in his chair.

"Listen, I'm not here to discuss politics with you. I'm here because I need to find the other three guys that were with you. If you give me something to work with, I'll make sure you're fairly treated. I've got the backing of the American government that I will be able to use against the French if you help me. So what do you say?" Parker asked.

Peio held his cigarette in front of his face and watched the glowing ember a moment. "You Americans have no idea what defending a culture is like. You let people of all kinds into your country. Here we have been repressed for centuries and are hanging on by a thread. Did you really think I would turn in my companions? I would rather die!"

Remaining composed, Parker leaned forward and lit another cigarette, exhaling a thin line that streamed just above Peio's right ear. "Is that all?"

Amused, Peio replied, "You shouldn't assume only men could do this work. Basque women are some of the hardest in the world."

Nivelle and his men suddenly burst open the door and Nivelle ordered Parker out of the room. Parker grabbed the end of the table and looked deeply into Peio's eyes. "How many? One? Where is she?"

Nivelle yelled at Parker to leave the room. Nivelle's men grabbed Parker and started dragging him out of the doorway.

He caught one last glance at Peio, now being barked at by Nivelle, before he was yanked from the room. Peio called to him with a wide smile on his face. "Why don't you talk to Alaitz, Sebastian?"

* * *

Five ETA Suspects Held in France

Police in France have arrested five people suspected of belonging to the Basque guerrilla group ETA.

The four men and one woman were detained in the western town of Niort. Police say they were allegedly preparing to steal another vehicle. The five, who were carrying shotguns, are reportedly Spanish nationals.

16

Basque Country, France

GRACIANA WAS SURPRISED to hear Peio had been caught. If any of them were to get caught, she figured for sure it would be Aurelion. He was the weakest of their crew. Peio was strong. She knew he would never talk to *les flics*. Nonetheless, Peio's capture scared the shit out of the leadership, and she'd been forced to leave Hendaye for Saint-Jean-de-Luz up the coast. She was placed in a "safe house," which turned out to be a room in a house owned by a French-Basque family. The family consisted of a wife, husband, and their two children, a boy and a girl. Their house was located in the heart of the old fishing village, now turned into a city, right next to the church where Louis XIV was married to Maria Theresa of Spain in the 1650s, the husband of the family told her.

Graciana's room was located near the back of the house. Outside her window was a make-shift fire escape she could use if the occasion ever called for her to suddenly leave. She hadn't been told how long she would be at this location and knew the couple she was staying with wouldn't know either.

ETA didn't work that way.

They told you what to do when they wanted you to do it. That was it. At times, the attitude of the leadership annoyed her, but she couldn't complain about her situation. Saint-Jean-de-Luz was a city that suited her well with its port in the center and its ancient winding roads. And she still had her beloved ocean. True, it was lacking the curved beach of her Hendaye, but it did have a large bay surrounded by rocks that was a great place to walk.

She even had to admit the people she was staying with were good, nice people who both cooked fantastic dinners and loved good wine. Though they were avid nationalists, they were only partially Basque through intermarriage. Both husband and wife had come from families where, sometime in the past, a Basque woman had taken a French husband. Graciana knew this had been done more due to lack of options than desire to steer away from Basque men.

For a good deal of the 20th century, countless numbers of Basque men had left the Basque country in both Spain and France seeking employment in the New World, whether it be in America or somewhere in South America. Many had become sheepherders and lived a solitary life in desolate areas of the American west or Uruguay, and they didn't return to the Basque Country until they were old and gray—far past the age of child rearing.

Every night she would have dinner with the couple. Graciana appreciated how they sat down at the table for dinner at a time anyone in Spain would be proud of: 8:00 p.m. She would usually have an aperitif with the wife and husband before dinner and listen to them talk to each other about their days while the children, who must have been somewhere around the ages of nine and ten, would play or watch television in a neighboring room. Though Graciana didn't talk much, the family was kind enough to give her space. They let her be and that worked perfectly well with her. Besides, she knew today or tomorrow she could be moved on to another location and didn't want to establish much of a connection with anyone.

Since San Francisco, her life had changed drastically. ETA members were sometimes transplanted to Mexico, Venezuela, or anywhere else and they would mistakenly think they no longer had to worry about being tracked down and caught. When they relaxed into their surroundings and tried to forget their past—that was when they were more vulnerable and caught. She knew she could never stop looking over her shoulder for as long as she lived.

* * *

They were walking through the dimly lit streets of Bayonne returning to their hotel. Both men felt the pressure of the day bearing down on them like an illness.

"What did he say to you as you were being, ah…removed from the room back there, Parker?" Gibson asked.

"Nothing," Parker replied.

Gibson knew Parker was lying, but he held off for a later time. It had been a long day.

Parker didn't look as tired as he did furious. Gibson knew whatever Peio said to him immediately bothered Parker. Ever since, Parker had been silent. Even when Nivelle came out of the room to yell at Parker, he said nothing. His young partner had not been his usual smart-ass self or snapped back with his normal quick defenses. Instead, he stood quietly and let Nivelle bark at him, while looking down the long, bare corridor.

They walked in silence. Gibson thought he sensed a touch of salt from the ocean in the air.

* * *

At 8:00 a.m. the next day, Gibson rose from bed. Looking at the time on his watch, he cursed himself for having slept so long and quickly got himself into the bathtub with a hose, as he had come to call it, to wash off. Within fifteen minutes, he was dressed and headed for the door to wake up Parker, who likely was still asleep in his room.

As Gibson reached for the door handle, he glanced downward and noticed a small piece of paper at his feet that had obviously been slid under the door. It must have been there when he woke up, but in his rush to get washed and dressed, he'd not noticed it. The note was from Parker. He read it aloud to himself:

> **"Gibson,**
>
> **There's something I have to take care of. I'll meet you at the hotel bar for an apéro at 6:00 tonight. Maybe you should go back and talk to Nivelle to see what, if anything, he was able to beat out of Peio. Then you should have a long lunch with General N. He's at least French, so he'll appreciate taking you to a good restaurant for a proper lunch. À ce soir.**
>
> **-Sebastian"**

Gibson crumpled the note in his hand and punched the wooden door inches in front of him. A sharp pain shot through his hand. "That little shit!"

He steadied himself, closed his eyes, and breathed deeply in and out through his nose. A minute later, he still felt just as angry and gave up on the breathing and punched the door again. When his hand fell back to his side he felt a small trickle of blood run down his fingers. He stuffed the crumpled note into his jacket pocket and opened the door.

* * *

He drove through Basque countryside's waves of gentle hills. A morning mist clung to the hills, giving the scene a mystical quality. Then he found himself standing before a door with a wooden sign over it that read 1653. Looking down at the worn cobblestone street of Saint-Jean-Pied-de-Port, he wondered to himself how many others had passed by this spot over the centuries. In recent times it would have been mostly tourists, stopping to take photographs of each other standing in front of the doorway.

Alaitz's mother opened the door and eyed Sebastian Parker suspiciously with her small brown eyes. He nodded graciously as she reluctantly moved to let him enter the house.

Zurina Etxegaraya recognized him immediately, and he knew she despised him from the moment Alaitz first brought him home so many years ago. He wasn't Basque, not even French-Basque, and therefore not good enough to be hanging around with her daughter. Alaitz always downplayed her mother's disapproval of him, but he'd always felt her mother's displeasure of him. As he felt it now.

She closed the door behind him just as a group of intrusive German tourists were trying to take a picture of the interior of the house. Closing the door, she turned to stare at him. She didn't say a word.

In the years since he'd last been here, she hadn't changed much. She was thick and strong, and looked older than she actually was. Her once tightly stretched face had turned into folds of small wrinkles. Parker stared back at her, meeting her gaze.

In the past, he'd spent too much time worrying about how this woman felt about him. Now he accepted that she hated him and didn't give a damn. He was there to see her daughter, who he just happened to be in love with, and there was nothing she could do to keep him from stopping him.

Neither of them said a word until Alaitz broke their silent conversation by stepping out from the kitchen to see who was at the door. She nearly dropped the long baguette she was eating when she saw him standing in the entryway to her mother's house. Her eyes went directly from him to the floor at her feet. For an awkward moment the three of them stood silently, not one knowing what to say.

Alaitz's mother finally broke the silence by pushing by her daughter. As she went into the kitchen, she muttered something to Alaitz in Basque that Parker couldn't understand. Once she was in the other room and had turned on the sink to wash vegetables, Alaitz finally lifted her eyes from the floor.

"*Mais qu'est-ce que tu fou là, toi?*" she asked him.

"*J'ai besoin de te voir,*" he answered, telling her he was there because he needed to see her.

"Are you crazy?" she replied in English.

"I wouldn't doubt it. But at least I wouldn't betray a friend."

"What are you talking about?" she asked, as she set the baguette down on a gigantic, but simple wooden table. She pulled a cigarette out of a pack on the table and lit it.

"I'm talking about you knowing more about why I'm here than you're telling me. You always knew exactly why I was here," Parker calmly stated, as he produced his own cigarette and lit it.

"You've become paranoid, you know that? Working for the government has made you scared of everything," she snapped.

"Why don't you cut out the *merde*, Alaitz?" Her eyes turned cold, but she didn't respond. Instead she stood across the little room from him and blew smoke at him in thin streams. "Peio told me to talk to you," Parker added.

Upon hearing Peio's name, her entire body tensed and the smoke from her cigarette stood still in her lungs. She moved her eyes around him, then told him hurriedly, "We need to leave."

She disappeared into the back rooms of the house and reappeared carrying a small backpack and a pair of hiking shoes. Walking up to him, she whispered in his ear. Feeling her small breasts press against his arm, he had trouble concentrating on what she was telling him. Only after following her through the house and outside the back door where her mother's car was parked it hit him that she told him they were going for a hike in the mountains.

Neither of them said a word as they drove outside the small city, on a narrow road that followed a swift creek up an incline into the rocky Pyrenees. Alaitz pulled off the side of the road on what Parker thought was more of a spot to stand when looking out over the expansive countryside instead of a parking space. On one side of the car was the gradual incline of the mountain, and on the other, a steep cliff that bordered the road without a guardrail. She tossed her cigarette out of the window and opened her door.

Alaitz was already hiking up the side of the low mountain before Parker realized by catching a glimpse of her backpack in the rearview mirror of the car. He got out of the car quickly and started after her.

It was amazing how quickly Alaitz could move in the mountains. Parker always assumed her natural agility in the mountains came from some deep Basque ancestry hidden deep inside her. For a time, he had trouble catching up with her but when he did, fell in step behind and took comfort in watching her firm legs and narrow back move in front of him. And, of course, he really liked watched her ass in front of him. Before long, he felt his thighs burning. But he figured he could easily follow Alaitz's ass anywhere.

Alaitz had received the best qualities of her heritage—the looks of a French woman with a Basque woman's attitude. Her mother was full Basque and her father, who Parker knew was deceased and Alaitz never spoke of, had been French-Basque.

They ascended up the side of the mountain at a steady pace, stopping once to drink from a bottle of water Alaitz had in her backpack. Parker liked seeing the worn backpack pressed tightly against her body. He had sent it to her as a Christmas present four years ago and it had obviously seen some use since then. Thinking about it made him smile, but just as he did, she stopped and turned around. The look on her face was one of complete seriousness and quickly diminished his happy thoughts.

Suddenly, she changed her direction from moving upward to crossing the side of the mountain. Parker followed without questioning, mostly because he knew from experience that Alaitz knew these mountains as well as any sheepherder.

He felt the sun touching him and his exposed skin began tingling. When they rounded the bend of the mountain, they came to a rock outcropping that looked to Parker like a place where a Neanderthal would have taken watch in order to survey the surroundings. Looking closer, he saw that one of the large boulders rose up and jutted out from the mountainside, forming a little cliff.

Alaitz was still ahead of him and, without hesitation, began to scale the side of the rock. Parker watched in admiration as she quickly free climbed upward. When she reached the top, about twenty feet up, she didn't look back down at him. What she did do was remove her backpack, and then her tank-top, letting them both fall to the rock at her feet. For a moment, he stood awestruck looking at the smooth skin of her upper back, but he was then on the wall using his hands and feet to scale the rock as fast as he could.

When he reached the top, he saw that she had walked out to the end of it. She was lightly teetering over the edge and for a moment Parker thought she would jump. He called her name and as she turned to look at him, her hair fell in wispy strands on her bare shoulders and its ends landed softly on her exposed breasts. His heart skipped a beat. She looked at him in a way she never had before. Her eyes told him that she had always felt exactly the same way about him as he had about her. With a few graceful movements of her hands and hips, she eased out of her shorts and then was standing before him in only her hiking shoes.

Parker could barely breathe and wasn't sure what he was supposed to do, so he did nothing, waiting for her move. She appeared to move in slow motion as she glided up to him and pressed her body against his, placing her lips on his in a slow, deep kiss.

Sebastian Parker thought to himself that if he died right at that moment, he would die a happy man.

Keeping her eyes closed, Alaitz lifted off his shirt and began to brush her soft lips behind his ear. She undid his pants and pulled them down as she began to cover his collarbone in wet kisses. She ran her fingertips slowly down his bare back and raised her lips to meet his in another deep embrace. Then she eased him down onto the rock and straddled him with her legs. Her eyes had been closed since she had first approached him and they remained shut, only opening to look into his as she grabbed him and guided him into her.

* * *

Already 6:30 p.m. and Parker wasn't in sight. Gibson felt the urge to rip off his watch and smash it against the wall. This time Parker had gone too far. He'd have to try not to break the punk's nose as soon as he saw him.

For forty-five minutes, Gibson had sat in the hotel's bar impatiently waiting for Parker. Through hand signals, he ordered a draft beer by pointing to a glass of unfinished beer sitting on the bar counter. But he hadn't touched the *pression* in front of him.

Ten minutes later Parker sauntered in, looking carefree and relaxed. He walked up to Gibson sitting on a stool at the bar. "That beer won't drink itself."

Gibson stared hard at him, trying to convey his anger through a look. His plan didn't appear to work though, because Parker plopped on the stool next to him, lit a cigarette, and ordered something from the bartender.

"The way I figure it, you drink enough for both us," Gibson complained. Parker poured water from a small carafe into a glass that had been partly filled by the bartender with a milky colored liquor.

"Well, as they say, when in Rome…" Parker lifted his glass in salute and drank half the contents of the glass in one swallow.

"Parker, what's that shit you're drinking now?" Gibson demanded.

"Ah, this is pastis. There's nothing quite like a nice pastis on a warm day." Parker took a long drag on his cigarette. "This is the Frenchmen's way of getting around the outlawing of absinthe back in the early 1900s. It's pretty much the same taste as absinthe, just without the opium."

"That's great. Doesn't change the fact that I'm really tempted to take you out behind this place and beat the hell out of you for the stunt you pulled today. And then you couldn't even get here on time."

"We're in southern France. No one is ever on time down here," Parker said casually, gulping down some more of his pastis.

"How did anyone ever hire you again?" Gibson asked.

Parker didn't answer right away, but turned around on his stool to check out the room. There were only a few scattered groups around the bar and no one looked as if they were watching them. "I don't know, honestly. But even though it's not part of my job description, unlike you, I can fit in while I'm in a place like this."

Leaning closer to him Gibson asked, barely above a whisper, "Why are you looking around like that?"

Parker didn't respond. Gibson tapped him on the arm. "Sorry, it's nothing," Parker said.

"What did you do today?" Gibson thought he noticed Parker blush after he asked the question.

"Conducting international relations."

Gibson decided to leave the point alone for the moment, but made a mental note to revisit later. "Well, Capitaine Nivelle was glad to see me today."

Parker laughed. "I'll bet he was. There's probably a better chance of us getting information from him if I'm not with you. Find out anything?"

"I asked to see the kid, but Nivelle said he's already been moved to an undisclosed location. What's that all about?"

"They tend to do that with Basque prisoners here. They move them all over the country without notifying anyone of the move until months later. Even inquiring families of those incarcerated. They used to send them to their foreign territories, like Algeria or far flung territories around the world. Did Nivelle say they were able to get anything out of Peio before they shipped him off?" Parker asked, taking a drink of his pastis.

"I got the feeling they really roughed him up and out of that came mention of a city in the Spanish Basque Country. I don't remember exactly, but it sounded like your name."

"San Sebastian."

"That's it," Gibson confirmed. Nivelle told me Peio said some taunting gibberish about the *wolf in San Sebastian* being too smart for them. Does that mean anything to you?"

"Not right now, but it may eventually. We need to get out of here so I can call Patrick. I'll have him arrange a meeting for us in San Sebastian tomorrow." Parker quickly drained the rest of his glass. "I told you, you would get more out of him without me." Parker stubbed out his cigarette in an ashtray on the counter and produced another. He lit it, exhaled deeply with his eyes closed, and added nothing more.

"Maybe, but that doesn't change the fact that from now on you let me know what's going on before you do something," Gibson ordered, as he stood up as well. "And, by the way, what were you really up to today? And what the hell did Peio say to you last night?"

Parker looked away and took a long pull off his cigarette. "Leave it alone."

With speculation running through his mind, Gibson watched Parker walk out of the bar and into the street.

* * *

The constant ringing of the phone forced him to open his eyes and lean over to pick up the receiver. He managed to get out a scratchy *bonjour* before Gibson's voice told him to get dressed immediately and meet him in the lobby. Looking at his watch on the night stand next to the bed, Parker saw it was far earlier than they had arranged to set out for San Sebastian. He'd spent most of the night in his room with cigarettes and a bottle of cognac and thoughts of Alaitz that wouldn't leave his head. An extra hour of sleep would be so nice, he thought, but Gibson was clearly not going to give up.

With extreme effort and concentration, Parker dragged himself out of bed and pulled on his clothes. He briefly thought of how nice a shower would be, but knew it would take too long. Even though he was still half asleep, he sensed from Gibson's voice that something serious was happening.

When Parker opened the door from the stairwell and walked into the small lobby of the inn, he immediately picked up from one glance that Gibson was both alert and anxious. Gibson's entire demeanor was all business. Parker imagined Gibson had the safety on his gun switched off.

As soon as Gibson noticed him, he silently motioned for them to go outside. Gibson had the keys to their rented Peugot in his hand. Parker's stomach dropped at the thought of riding in a car while he was still dealing with the bottle of cognac that he had put a respectable dent in only a few hours earlier. As he led the way to the car parked on the street, Gibson didn't even turn around. It annoyed Parker that Gibson didn't have the mercy in him to slow his pace down a little. Every step felt as if Parker was walking through wet cement.

Not until they were seated in the car, with Gibson behind the wheel, did he turn to look at Parker. Parker's eyes had red lines shooting out from his irises and there were bags underneath them. Gibson realized from, the state of his bed head, that Parker had not bothered even looking in the mirror before leaving his room. Although he was upset with Parker for being in such a state, part of him respected that he'd left without uttering one complaint. Parker whipped out a cigarette and lit it.

"You're going to age yourself before your time if you don't watch it, Sebastian." Gibson said, turning the keys in the ignition.

"Hopefully," Parker replied through a breath of smoke. "We aren't meeting the guy until lunch, which is 2:00 p.m. in Spain. So would you mind telling me why we're leaving this fucking early?"

Gibson waved his hands in front of his face and opened the window on his side of the car. "We're leaving this early because Nivelle called me this morning to invite us to see something they've found in the mountains. Or, I guess I should say, to see *someone* they've found. He seems to think it could be related to our case."

"Ah, how sweet of him to think of us."

"All right, listen, Parker. When we're out there you need to behave. This is my investigation and we need Nivelle's help, so you're going to keep your damn smart mouth shut! Understand?"

"So, you're saying that I can't tell Nivelle to get fucked?" Gibson felt an immediate flash of anger, but it was quickly dispelled by the sound of Parker laughing at his own joke. "Do you have any idea where we are supposed to go, anyway?" Parker added.

"He said it's the first road off in Roland's Pass," he answered as he pulled out a piece of paper from his pants pocket and spelled out the name, I…t…x…a…s…s…o…u. Supposedly a farmer found the body early this morning, dumped on the side of the road sometime last night."

"Itxassou," Parker said quietly. "Too bad we weren't here a few months ago."

"Why's that?" Gibson asked with a quick look at his young partner.

"Because, Itxassou has a great cherry festival every year."

"Does any place here not have some sort of a damned festival?" Gibson asked.

"Don't you think it's better than going to a cheesy 4-H Fair every summer?" Parker commented, then took a long drag from his smoke. "Anyway, I can see why Nivelle called you. Dumping a body off the side of a small country road is a very typical tactic used by the ETA, but I can't imagine how this could be related to our case. I guess we'll see."

"I guess so. Now you want to tell me how to get out of here?"

Parker rolled down his window and flicked out his finished cigarette. "Just pull out of here and take a left at that large street up there. It will take us to the highway that leads out into the countryside. In the Basque Country, the countryside is never far away."

* * *

Parker and Gibson looked down on the beaten body at their feet. Capitaine Nivelle had one of his men meet them at the road and then walk them to where the body had been dragged and dumped. It was the body of a young man, probably no older than eighteen, Gibson figured. It had been left in a stand of trees about fifty feet off the side of the road. Looking around at the setting, Gibson assessed the area.

It was a small forested area on the side of a brilliant green hillside with a wide view of an open valley filled with farmhouses. How nice it would be to not be in the presence of a dead and mutilated body, he thought. He noted the face had been severely bruised, and it was obvious from the blood on the clothes that he'd been cut with some sort of an object in numerous places before the fatal slice across his throat.

Once again, being in the presence of death proved too much for Parker. Soon after the young officer led them to the body and the entourage surrounding it, Parker was darting for the bushes to vomit behind a fallen tree. His retching appeared to bother the entire group surrounding the body, as they all grimaced with each gag they heard Parker make, but it aggravated Nivelle most of all. He judgmentally stood over the body with a pad of paper and pen, and had not looked up to see them approach. Gibson observed, however, how each time Parker produced an awful noise that disrupted the quietness surrounding them that Nivelle would mutter something through his clenched teeth. After a few minutes, Parker, walking a bit wobbly, made his way back to the group.

He didn't give anyone the satisfaction of ridiculing him with their annoyed looks. Instead, Parker walked in front of the entire group and stood with his eyes focused on the body sprawled on the hillside. It was then that Gibson noticed something different about him. He hadn't just been sick over the sight of the dead body before them. There was something else. All the French police officers around them sensed the tension rolling off Parker, just as Gibson did, and they all took a step backward.

Gibson watched Parker closely. Parker may not have been considered an apparent threat to anyone with a quick look at him, but once one looked closer, it was impossible to not notice the wildness and unpredictability in his eyes. It was as if, at times, he saw things no one else could. And maybe he could, Gibson thought.

Over his shoulder, Parker said something in French in the direction of Nivelle, who responded with a spatter of words. Parker added something that made everyone in the group look at him in shock, even Nivelle. Gibson correctly guessed that Parker said a name—Parker named the dead body on the green hillside in front of them.

Nivelle quickly said something, but Parker only stared at him with piercing eyes and then walked away. Yelling the entire time, Nivelle hopped to his feet to follow after. When he caught up with Parker, he reached out and grabbed his shoulder. Parker reacted by swinging around with a raised fist, ready to smash it against Nivelle's face. That's exactly what would have happened had Gibson not had the instinct to beat Nivelle to Parker and grab him from behind as soon as he turned to introduce his fist to Nivelle's face.

Pointing at Nivelle, telling him without words to stay back, Gibson dragged Parker away. Though Nivelle snarled something unpleasant, he turned away and began walking back to the body.

Parker shook himself free of Gibson's hold and then stomped around in the tall grass, shaking his head and shoulders. Gradually, Parker was able to calm himself down and slumped down on the ground and lit a cigarette.

Cautiously, Gibson approached and sat beside him. Parker was silent as he looked off at the wide green valley below them. The morning sun gracefully fell on their shoulders in a soft glow. "Did you know him?" Gibson asked.

Parker rolled his head and exhaled deeply through his nose before he replied. "I knew him years ago, when he was just a little boy." He took another drag on his cigarette. "Now he's a young man. And now he's dead."

Trying to study the expression on Parker's face, Gibson asked, "How did you know him?"

"He was the younger brother of one of my good friends while I was in lycée here."

"How is his death your fault?"

"It's not," Parker quickly responded. "It's France's fault. It's Spain's fault. It's ETA's fault. It's Haika's fault for all I know."

"What's Haika again?" Gibson asked, but Parker was too preoccupied with his own thoughts to hear him. He was staring off into the Basque Country as if looking at the landscape for the first time, or the last time.

"This shit needs to end before the poison from both sides, and within, takes over this wonderful land," Parker remarked.

"So how do we beat this?"

Parker's look bored into Gibson's eyes. His face had gone from a look of sheer anger toward Nivelle into one of stone. "We don't. The Basque spirit for independence goes back to the time of the Romans, and probably earlier, and it took the cruelty of that bastard Franco to relinquish it from their combined psyche. What we are doing is only touching the surface. We can only catch a few who went too far, but I'm not even sure about that anymore."

Confused, Gibson stared at him a moment. "What the hell do you mean, Parker? Look at how far we've come so far."

"We've been lucky. If the majority of the Basque people didn't want these people identified and caught, they wouldn't be. For centuries the Basques have been hiding from trouble in their mountains and no one ever finds them when they want to protect their own." He nodded to the rocky outcroppings strung along the line of low mountains surrounding them like an extended fortress. "And besides, I have a strong feeling that our work in the States is not finished either."

"What do you mean by that?"

Parker ground his cigarette butt into a rock. "Never mind, let's just try and finish what we came over here to do first. I have a good idea where to find our next lead," he said with an absent glance behind him toward the tortured body of the young man on the side of the mountain.

* * *

A group of older men sat at a table in the corner of the small bar. They all had thick glasses of wine in front of them. Dressed in plain clothes, on their heads they each wore a black beret. Gibson thought the men had given each other a look of disgust as he and Parker entered through the doorway, but he couldn't say for sure. As far as he could see, Parker didn't seem to be noticing anything aside from what he called the "young red wine" he was forcing into his body. After descending from the low mountains into the rolling countryside surrounding the small village of Itxassou, Parker drove them onto a small country road that Gibson recalled was not the road that would lead them back onto the autoroute.

When he asked where they were going, Parker merely responded they were going for a drive. Realizing how upset Parker still was after the encounter with Nivelle, he avoided questioning his motives.

They drove on a small winding road through the hills, occasionally passing a farmhouse and cultivated fields. Very few cars passed them coming from the opposite direction. When they did, each car slowed its speed and moved over as far to the edge of the road as possible, in order to safely pass each other.

Coming over a line of green hills speckled with patches of trees, orange tiled roofs of a town presented itself. With a vantage point above the town, one could see its entire layout. It was situated on the convergence of hills in all directions, and the small streets looked like they started in the center of the town and ran out in steadily rising inclinations. Gibson noted the perfection of the place, with a church at the center of the town and its adjoining cemetery, a fronton, and a quaint central square lined with plane trees. The few buildings and houses that made up the village were either directly off the square or along one of the roads that disappeared into the surrounding countryside.

Around the village, the hills were larger than those they had driven through. In all directions there were large green or light brown hills. Directly behind the town, a long line of the higher mountains crossed the horizon and one jagged mountain in particular seemed close enough to touch.

"This mountain is named La Rhune. For the Basques it is regarded as a mystical and sacred place," Parker explained.

They were entering the village of Sare, and one would imagine it looked similar to how it did during the Middle Ages. The hills and mountains surrounding the town gave the impression of being an isolated *endroit*, a place cut off from the outside world and not showing any signs of wanting to modernize. There was a sign on the side of the road before they entered the village. Parker read it in French and then translated into English. The sign said: "The town of Sare is regarded as one of the most beautiful villages in the country of France." Gibson hadn't seen much of France, but he was sure he agreed with the sign.

Inside the bar, they sat at a table near the window with a view of the central square and the mountains looming in the distance behind a line of terraced houses. Parker had already drunk two glasses of wine before the barman brought them over a pair of sandwiches—baguettes with sliced ham and butter. Gibson was amazed at how good the sandwich tasted. The bread was crusty on its outside, yet soft inside. The ham was a deep, reddish color. Real butter was used and perfectly complemented the salty ham and bread. He drank a French beer that Parker recommended and looked out at the old women sitting on benches in the shade of the plane trees or standing on the edge of their green or red painted balconies trimming their flowers or beating the dust out of rugs. A group of young boys played pelote at the fronton.

From Sare, Parker drove them west along the edge of the mountains until they came to a large autoroute that snaked along the Côte Basque. They headed north along the coast. Gibson stared out at the rocky coastline that would occasionally break to reveal a stretch of beach touched by small waves from the ocean. At one point, he noticed a large estate set far from the road that looked like a castle. It was surrounded by green fields, bordered by trees and the wide ocean. Parker hadn't said a word since they left Sare, and Gibson hoped they would find the next lead Parker had mentioned earlier.

Before they left the bar in Sare, Parker made a phone call to his friend Patrick. He spoke entirely in French on the phone and didn't bother translating the conversation to Gibson after he hung up. Gibson correctly assumed their meeting in San Sebastian had been canceled.

At the first exit for Biarritz, Parker turned off the highway. Passing through the *centre ville* reminded Gibson of being in a Southern California beach town: surf shops with signs above their doors in English; palm tree lined streets; large obtrusive 60s and 70s architecture looking buildings filled with seasonal condominium dwellers; men in wetsuits carrying surfboards; and, gorgeous, tanned women walking around in string bikinis. When Parker parallel parked on the side of a road, he rammed into both the car behind and in front of the spot. His only acknowledgment was a shrug of his shoulders.

They walked down a wide esplanade that followed a crescent beach. On one side was a picturesque lighthouse, on the other a string of large rocks jutting from the ocean floor, leading to a tiny island at the end. A small bridge connected the rocks and Gibson thought he saw some sort of object on the furthest point. With the two peninsulas reaching into the blue abyss of the ocean, the city of Biarritz was structured along the wide cove their arms created.

There were a few rocks not far out from the beach where the ocean's small waves crashed and created a light mist of vapor. As it was the weekend and warm, the beach was full with people. Many of the women, he noticed, had removed their tops. Women were walking along the beach wearing beach wraps around their waists and they passed groups of dark, gold necklace wearing, Italian looking guys who didn't conceal their stares at their bared breasts. Small children screamed with excitement as they tried to outrun the waves lightly crashing on the shore. Groups of surfers sat on their boards in the water, waiting for their waves to come and every once in a while one or two would get up on a wave. There were two or three different ice cream stands, and people were sitting along a walkway just off the beach. People sipped cocktails outside cafés fully dressed, wearing sunglasses, and trying to look important.

As they continued walking northward along the beach, Parker and Gibson arrived in front of a large brick colored hotel at the far end. It looked regal and sophisticated. Parker explained that Napoleon III used to spend his holiday in this hotel, called the Grand Palais, and now princes of England and the Middle East stayed there often.

Looking up, Gibson saw a sign and was able to decipher from it that the beach they were walking along was named the Grand Plage. If nothing else, he did agree that it was a very grand place.

"So where are we going, Parker?" he asked, as they passed an elderly woman wearing a wide-brimmed hat and walking a poodle with bows in its hair.

"We're going to find one of my old friends, Etienne. Any self-respecting surfer from this area wouldn't be caught dead at this beach, but this guy is more interested in the tourist girls seeing him as a surfer than he is in actually surfing. I know we'll find him here."

"Sounds noble," Gibson remarked.

"He's about to find out his brother was killed. I don't expect anything noble to come out of it," Parker curtly replied.

"I don't know what the hell that's supposed to mean, Parker, but you've been in a weird-as-hell mood all day, so I'm not going to try and figure it out. All I know is that we're running out of time here and we don't have much going so far."

Parker stopped walking and turned to stare at Gibson. "Then why don't you fucking send me home and bring over some of your friends?"

Gibson looked out at the dark blue ocean before responding. "All right, I'm sorry. I know you're trying your best," he said with his eyes locked on the expanse of ocean in front of him.

At the edge of the pavement and the beach, Parker took off his shoes and socks and went barefoot. Parker was wearing a pair of jeans and loose, white button-up shirt. It looked natural for him to be barefoot. With his mildly unruly, sun-bleached hair and a bit of tan, he almost looked like a surfer anyway, Gibson thought.

"Wait for me here," Parker said. He started off weaving through bodies sprawled on the sand. Gibson moved back into the shade of a restaurant's outdoor patio. He was wearing a dark suit and the sun was pounding down on him. He watched as Parker made his way to where a group of young people had claimed their own territory. Seconds later, he was seated next to them. Gibson watched Parker accept a pass of what looked like a joint. *God dammit, Parker.*

Gibson grew agitated as he waited. Parker was leaning back on the sand and talking with a girl sitting on the blanket next to him. He seemed to fit in perfectly among the group of young people, and it reminded Gibson of Parker's youth. Just as he was about to give in to impatience and begin trekking across the beach, Parker got up from the blanket, rolled his jeans up his leg, and strolled to edge of the ocean. He walked out in the water until he was ankle deep in the water.

For a moment, he stood with his arms outstretched, letting the small waves touch his body while staring out into the vast abyss of the ocean. The sun's heavy rays appeared to focus directly on his white shirt and his image could almost be described as glowing. After a few minutes, a surfer who had been out a ways in the ocean, sitting on his surfboard looking inland, swam in on top of his board to meet Parker. The two shook hands and then Parker placed his arm around the wetsuited surfer and walked him onto the beach, to a point on the edge where there were only large boulders strewn on the stand and no beachgoers. Gibson watched them until they disappeared behind a thin cliff that extended out a ways.

Ten minutes passed with no sign of them. Ten minutes turned into twenty. Gibson was beginning to get nervous. He was relieved when he saw Parker emerge from behind the wall of rock. He was alone.

Passing the group lounging on the blanket, Parker briefly said something, and continued walking to Gibson. When he reached the edge of beach and pavement, he didn't stop to put back on his shoes, choosing instead to walk on the scorching rock with his bare feet. His jeans were wet. He held out his hand when he reached Gibson requesting the car keys.

As he opened the door to the driver's side of the car, he looked over the top at Gibson. "This truly is a sick world. Because of a murdered younger brother, we now have what we need to find the next one." Without saying another word, he got into the car and started the engine.

"Yes, it is, yet we seem to love it," Gibson responded, getting into the passenger side of the car. A gentle breeze blew into the car as he lowered the window.

* * *

"I've never had to break the news to someone that one of their family members was killed," Parker uttered into the foamy top of the glass of beer sitting on the table in front of him.

Before responding, Gibson looked at him and gauged the level of hurt on Sebastian Parker's face. The hurt went deep. "I'll admit, it's not an admirable job for anyone." He paused a moment to look away, then turned back. "You did the right thing though. Just think how he would have felt if it had been one of Nivelle's guys who told him?"

Parker snapped his head around, shooting Gibson a menacing look. "All I'm saying is that it's better to hear tough news from someone you care about than from a stranger."

"I just told him his brother was brutally murdered in order to get information from him!" Parker exclaimed, causing the other clientele of the bar to turn their heads.

"Parker, keep your damn voice down."

"These *papis* don't speak English!" Parker snapped, turning around to glare at the table of aged men sitting at a table behind them. The men merely shrugged their shoulders and returned to their card game. He added, now in a lower tone, "I'm not like you, Gibson. I can't do this and I don't want to do this. It must take a special sick breed of person to do this sort of work and I'm not it."

"Sebastian, you need to calm yourself. You did your job and that's all," Gibson said. "So tell me why this surfer guy that lost his brother would tell you anything?"

Again, Parker spoke into his glass of beer instead of speaking directly to Gibson. "Because he hates ETA, always has. He was one of the most rationally minded Basques I met when I lived here and, at that time, he was only sixteen. His family is one of the largest, most influential, and best connected in the French Pays Basque. He relentlessly tried to dissuade his brother from having any involvement with ETA or Haika, but it was a wasted effort in the end. I knew he would tell me where we might find these people."

"You've never really explained Haika."

Parker pounded the rest of the glass of beer in front of him. "Basically the youth wing of ETA. They recruit kids as young as eleven and twelve and start indoctrinating them to eventually graduate into the organization." He pounded the full glass of beer on the bar in front of Gibson. "All right, let's order a terrible pizza, pick up some good Navarre rosé wine, and watch some shitty French television show in one of our rooms. I need a break from all this for a little while."

Gibson eyed him curiously.

Parker pulled out his box of cigarettes and put a cigarette between his lips. "Don't worry, I'm fine. I just needed to vent for a moment."

* * *

Former ETA chief jailed for murder

A Spanish court has sentenced a leading member of the Basque separatist movement, ETA, to 28 years in jail for murdering a policeman in the city of Bilbao

The man accused, known as "Potato," was arrested in France in 1996 and recently extradited to Spain. He has also been on trial for kidnapping a Spanish businessman. A verdict on that charge is also expected. His conviction came hours after police in France discovered a large cache of weapons in a holiday home believed to belong to ETA in southwestern France.

The man accused has been serving a 14-year prison sentence in Paris for running ETA's operations in France.

17

Basque Country, France

SHE LOVED BREAKING the rules. From the moment she returned to the Basque Country, they tried enforcing rules on her. Men tried to rule her, and Graciana reflected on how men tried to rule women throughout the world. Whatever she did, she would be cautious. But she definitely was going to do whatever the hell she wanted.

Graciana was moved to a new location in the small country village of Saint-Pée-Sur-Nivelle, commonly referred to as Saint-Pée. She was placed in a small apartment above the town's only boulangerie. She enjoyed waking up each morning to the smell of freshly baked baguettes and *pain de campagne.* While walking through the town's streets she would nibble on a thin, warm baguette.

But she missed the ocean.

Sometimes she believed she could smell its salty fragrance greeting her through an open window to the west. Saint-Pée was pretty, but there was nothing there for her. She could go by herself to a café in a larger place such as Saint-Jean-de-Luz, or Biarritz, or Bayonne and sit at a bar by herself and go unnoticed. But in a tiny place like Saint-Pée, that was impossible. She tried one time and felt as if all eyes were on her. It didn't matter that she was an attractive woman, in any situation she would be a woman by herself in a room full of men.

To have something to do, she began to spend time writing poetry, something she liked to do, but had never told anyone about. Yet this was not enough to preoccupy her mind. She was going crazy and had to get out.

She was never exactly sure who was watching her movements, but she knew she was being monitored. ETA was divided and suspicious of its own members and no one knew who they could ever trust. She'd been told that it'd always been that way in the organization, but only recently had it grown to such a level of internal suspicion.

The numerous divided factions were always competing against each other and acting under different motives. The more she learned about this organization she'd joined, the less sense it made to her. She wished she could have been a part of the movement back in the 70s when there was only one cause or reason—independence for the Basque Country. Nowadays, there was a lot of disorganization.

Separated groups competed for control with little taste for real action. There were about ten different causes falling under one headline. It made her sick when she thought about it.

She managed to carefully contact a friend in Bayonne. He informed her of an upcoming Haika gathering that was going to be held in a supporter's field outside of Cambo-les-Bains. The event was a Basque music festival, but she knew the real purpose behind the event would be to recruit new members and to get everyone together to strategize about future activities. Although she knew very well that ETA would have some of their younger members present at the event to spout their rhetoric to anyone willing to listen. She decided she would go. After all, how could they really expect her to stay in one small little town in the countryside? Graciana knew she would be seen and reported, but she didn't care. No one would run her life.

On the day of the event, someone picked her up on the far side of the small village and she was driven to the outskirts of Cambo. The young man driving the car passed her a joint rolled with tobacco. They smoked the joint, passing back and forth, as they drove across the rolling green countryside. He didn't speak to her and she respected him for his silence.

Leaning back in her seat, she felt the air pound against her from the open window. So nice to be actually doing something, she thought.

* * *

Gibson was livid. Parker insisted the go off alone again, and Gibson hated the idea. Not only did he not like that he was not in control of the situation, he reluctantly admitted to himself that he didn't like not being able to watch over Parker. He was so young and defenseless. Gibson knew that Parker was completely knowledgeable of the extent of the fierceness ETA was capable of, but he seriously doubted Parker truly appreciated the closeness of the threat. Parker was a desk jockey, no matter how one looked at it, and he'd never been face to face with a clear threat. One could study a terrorist organization from an office all they wanted, but it wasn't until you got out into the real world and dealt with such organizations that you saw, firsthand, how dangerous they could be. Something about the kid was growing on Gibson and he hated to admit, but he was concerned for Sebastian Parker.

After their return from Biarritz the night before, Capitaine Nivelle called Gibson's cell phone to tell him they had a lead on a terrorist training camp somewhere north. Gibson relayed the conversation to Parker, who said he thought it would be educational for Gibson to accompany Nivelle and his men to raid the site the following day as Nivelle suggested.

When Gibson asked why, Parker said he didn't need to be present as well, and then changed the subject. He described to Gibson that the raid with Nivelle would be in the next region north, known as the Landes. Despite Gibson's barrage of questions on where he would be, Parker didn't capitulate. Infuriated, Gibson had no choice but to accept Parker's decision since he knew wherever he was going would be a direct result of the information he obtained from the dead boy's surfer brother. Instead of continuing to argue with Parker, Gibson opted to put faith in the kid and hope that he didn't get himself killed.

* * *

The police car came to a screeching stop in front of the hotel. Nivelle was in the passenger seat. One of his men drove the vehicle. With a brisk wave of his hand, Nivelle motioned for Gibson to get into the back seat of the vehicle. As soon as Gibson closed the door, the driver floored the car through the narrow streets of Petit Bayonne.

Gibson noticed how the man savagely ground the ignition before shifting gears just as Parker had.

After they crossed a large, red, newish bridge across the river, Nivelle turned in his seat to scan the backward with his squinty eyes. Gibson waited respectfully for Nivelle's reaction at figuring out that Parker hadn't joined the excursion. However, no change in Nivelle's facial expression indicated one way or another as to how he felt in only seeing Gibson. He merely twitched his thin moustache at Gibson and turned back around.

The further they drove north from Bayonne, the flatter the land became. Soon there was nearly no deviation in the landscape, just flat fields bordered by stretches of thickly wooded areas. The trees were thin pines, straight, and tall. Different types of bright green ferns grew at their base. Styles of the houses changed as well. The whitewashed houses with green or red trimmings were gone. Now he saw houses with more brown color to them and exposed wood, and they were wider than houses in the Basque Country he'd seen. The overall effect of the landscape was not as drastic and colorful as the land to the south, but it did have its own character, he thought.

"Where are we going?" Gibson asked.

"A little to the north of the city of Tyrosse, outside a small town named Tosse. There are a few lakes up there and a hunting cabins. Otherwise, there are only fields and the forest, a perfect place for a guerilla training camp." Nivelle responded, without turning around.

"Do you really think we will find anyone out there?"

Nivelle cranked his thin neck and glared at Gibson. "*Mais, bien sûr,* we will. It was not some worthless Basque who gave us this information, but a good Frenchman. We will find them, arrest them, and make them tell us where we can find the others of this little group of so-called commandos."

Feeling scolded, Gibson didn't want to antagonize Nivelle further. He sat back in his seat and turned his eyes to look out of the window at the passing countryside. "Where is your little friend today? Too much *vin* last night?" Nivelle added with a sharp tone.

"No. Parker had a lead he felt he needed to go alone to investigate. He was gone before you picked me up, and he specifically suggested I come along with you for my educational enhancement, whatever the hell that means." Gibson quickly retorted.

"Ah, well, your friend is far too taken with these people, I think. He would do better to join our side," Nivelle commented.

Something inside Gibson made him feel he needed to speak up for Sebastian Parker, even if he did still have some lingering doubts about him himself. "He's not my friend, he's my partner. And I seem to remember it being Parker that found us the first one. So, I think he deserves a little faith." Nivelle didn't say anything, but Gibson watched as the muscles in his neck and shoulders tensed as if a current of anger rushed through his body.

An uncomfortable silence endured for the remainder of the drive.

* * *

Parker met Alaitz on a street corner near the hotel in Petit Bayonne. They said *bonjour* and kissed each others' cheeks three times, opposed to the more standard practice in France of two cheek kisses. He got in her car and they said nothing more as Alaitz drove. It was going to be a quiet ride, Parker figured. Reaching over, Alaitz turned up the radio's volume until it was blaringly loud as she drove into the green rolling countryside as if she were a racecar driver.

When they passed by Ustaritz, Parker tried to start a conversation with her by turning down the radio. "I read somewhere that in the past, Ustaritz, for some time, was the capital of the Labourd region of the Pays Basque," he mentioned.

In response, Alaitz looked at him for a brief moment and smiled, but her eyes didn't match her smile. They were hard. Parker saw happiness in her smile and fear in her eyes. Lighting a cigarette, she turned the radio knob back.

She was uncomfortable bringing Sebastian with her to the gathering. It bothered her how he found out about it in the first place, as it was really a Haika gathering being disguised as something else. But she had always known him to be bright and capable. Maybe too much for his own good.

One had to be Basque to be well connected in the Basque Country. Even being part Basque wasn't always sufficient, but somehow

Sebastian always managed to amaze her. He insisted she take him. She reluctantly agreed, but only when he offered to not hang around her once they got there and to find his own way back to Bayonne. She was already regretting her decision.

They never discussed what Sebastian did for his job, but she knew very well that he worked for the CIA. He was going to get himself into *la merde* someday, with or without her, she thought. But at least when he was with her, she could try to help keep him away from danger.

And even though she told him once they arrived at the gathering they would have to go their own ways, she was planning to keep an eye on him. Though smart, charming, and lucky, he could easily get himself hurt or worse. Even for all he knew and would ever know of the Basque people, he would always be regarded as an outsider. If she could prevent him from being hurt she would. But she worried that the deeper Sebastian delved into what was going on, the farther he moved from her protection.

Looking at him now, she saw him gazing out the window at the passing farmhouses and the rising hills that eventually turned into the mountains to the south. She knew he loved this land more than most. Her deepest hope was that he was not ready to die for this land he loved so much.

Finally, Alaitz pulled off the highway onto a narrow paved road that led over a large hill. Once over the hill, she turned onto a one lane dirt road that cut through a group of trees and crossed a small, meandering creek. Soon the trees cleared, opening onto a wide field situated in a valley surrounded by gently sloping hills. There was a stage on one end of the field and cars parked at the other end. In between the stage and parking area was a large congregation of young people.

Alaitz parked the car and as agreed, Parker was out the door, going off on his own before she had a chance to say anything. She watched him inconspicuously merge into the mass of bodies and soon lost sight of him. He may fit in well, but if anyone found out who he really was, he would be lucky to leave the rally in one piece. She said a prayer for him in Basque and opened the car door.

* * *

Etienne told Parker who to look for—a strikingly beautiful, tall, blonde girl named Graciana. Etienne said he'd known her well in the past. They had endured many heated disputes over the struggle for Basque independence, and while Etienne was really primarily concerned with getting into her pants, Graciana had him jumped in an alley in Petit Bayonne by her Haika friends at the time after he told her he thought ETA was nothing but a bunch of cowards. If anyone knew where to find those involved with a hit, it would be her. But he warned Parker that this Graciana was sharp and cunning, and that it would be dangerous to approach her directly.

Knowing the historic strength of Basque women, Parker didn't try to deny the level of danger into which he was putting himself. ETA was sure to have a huge presence at the rally and have a dual purpose. One would be to try and encourage new supporters for the cause. The second would be to keep an eye on the young leaders of Haika and bring them over into the full ranks of ETA when it was judged they were ready for more serious action.

However, even recognizing the danger he was getting into, all Parker could think of as he worked his way through the herd of bodies was that most Basques are not blond haired nor tall, but dark haired and shorter in general. He'd be surprised if she didn't have the strong chin and pointy nose that were also textbook characteristics of the Basques.

There was a group onstage playing some sort of hard rock and singing in Basque about independence for the Basque provinces.

It took Parker nearly a half hour of wandering around the gathering before he found her. One glance told him he was not mistaken. She was sitting alone under a tree next to the stage, smoking a cigarette, a bottle of wine next to her. Just as Etienne had described, she was tall with blonde hair and quite stunningly beautiful.

Not wasting any time, Parker bought a bottle of rosé wine from a man selling bottles from the back of a car and approached her. She didn't acknowledge him standing in front of her until he said *kaixo* in Basque and then, switching to French, asked if he could sit with her. Graciana turned from watching the band playing on stage to give him a once over sneer that matched the scorching look in her eyes. She returned her attention to watching the stage and didn't grace him with a response.

Ignoring her attitude, Parker sat down next to her anyway and held out his opened bottle of wine to her. He noticed her look at him from the side of her eye. She silently held out her cup for him to fill. He then filled his own cup—the guy he bought the bottle from had given him one—and she held up her glass to meet his *topa.*

Without exchanging words, they both silently drained their glasses in one gulp then pulled out cigarettes from their respective boxes. She produced a blue box of matches from the small purse lying next to her. Parker offered his lighter, which she accepted by leaning over to light her cigarette. Casually, she threw the box of matches back into her small bag.

They smoked in silence until she finally looked at him and announced in French, "You're not Basque."

"No. I'm not Basque. How did you know?"

"Aside from the way you look, a Basque guy who would go out of his way to try and hit on me would have been trying to talk to me this entire time. You, on the other hand, have just sat there."

"Would you rather I talked?"

Graciana stared him up and down for an extended moment and exhaled a stream of smoke. "No. I'm talking to you now only because you didn't bother me." She didn't smile at him, but she was no longer scowling either.

"You know, you don't really have Basque features either," Parker commented.

"That's true. I inherited my looks from my mother's side of the family who married a Basque man. But my heart has always been purely Basque," Graciana replied.

Parker refilled their cups. "I've never seen this band before. Are they from Bayonne?"

"They're from Donostia. They don't speak French, but they're a good group of guys." She lit another cigarette from the dying one between her fingers. "You speak French very well, but I don't think you're French either. You still have an accent," she added, looking him straight in the eyes.

Parker exhaled a cloud of smoke and stubbed the cigarette butt into the ground. "I don't think anyone who is not raised speaking French will ever speak it perfectly. We, unfortunately, are always cursed with a touch of an accent," he replied.

"Ah, but accents are not all bad. The way you speak is kind of cute actually. So what are you and what are you doing here?"

"I'm an American with Basque roots. My family went to the American west at the turn of the last century," he lied. "I was raised by my parents to have very nationalist feelings for the Basque independence movement. I'm what we Basques call an *arbetzale*. I've lived in the Basque Country at different times in my life, and now I'm trying to learn how I can support the movement from the States." She concentrated on every word and movement he made. He realized he was being thoroughly studied.

"There are groups in the United States that you can join without coming here," she coldly replied.

"Yes, there are groups over there, but they're too tame for me. All they want to do is talk about Basque independence and create websites. I don't see how that's going to help the Basque Country." Quickly, he added after downing his wine, "This is where it has to begin. I know a lot of Basque-Americans who are young like we are who want to do more. I know there are a few groups over there with direct connections to people here, and I think this is the way it must work if we are ever to make a difference."

For a few moments, Graciana reflected on what he'd said. "You may be more right than you know." She held out her long, thin hand to him. "My name is Graciana."

He lightly shook her hand. "I'm Sebastian Parker."

"That's not a very Basque family name, Sebastian," she remarked.

"I know. My grandfather was a weak man and decided to change his name because he was ashamed of being labeled a sheepherder. He changed it when he arrived at Ellis Island and it's been that way ever since. My father had to learn about his heritage through books and talking with other Basques who had come to America."

Graciana responded with passion in her voice and a new light in her eyes. "Ancestry is very important to us Basques. I think it is a great injustice to you, Sebastian, that you must live your life being ashamed of your grandfather."

Parker lit a cigarette and exhaled languidly, looking off at the lines of rising hills. "Yes, it is a shame, so let's not speak of it anymore," he forcibly said, trying to look upset and disappointed at the same time. He didn't look at her, keeping his stare focused on the horizon, but he could feel her watching his profile.

He hoped he'd been convincing, and knew he had passed at least an initial test when she said, "You really must be Basque, even though you don't have any Basque features. Not many others would be so disgusted to speak of a relative's actions. From the look on your face just now, I can see that you despise him for this. The Basques are maybe the most unforgiving people in the world. Even in death we do not forgive."

She reached over him to grab the bottle of rosé. As her slim body crossed his midsection, she gently leaned against him. Her scent was a mix of perfume, tobacco and something else he couldn't describe that made him think of wildness. Then he felt her hand fall on his as she adjusted to keep her balance. Reseating herself, Graciana smiled at him.

Refilling his cup, then her own, Graciana tilted what remained of the bottle into her lipstick lined mouth. She lightly touched her lips around the mouth of the bottle, leaving a faint trace of color on the bottle she handed back to Parker.

"After World War II, many Frenchmen and Frenchwomen had a relative to be ashamed of for some reason or another. But the French forgive much easier than we Basques," she commented, while lighting a new cigarette.

* * *

From a distance, she stood watching. She had mingled into the crowd of jeering music listeners for a while in order to go unnoticed, but she could see Sebastian sitting with Graciana perfectly well. And there was no doubting that it was indeed Graciana.

Alaitz watched them drinking, smoking, and talking together. Then she watched Graciana purposefully fall into his lap as she was reaching across him for the bottle of wine. It made her fists clench. Everything about the woman was so sexy and graceful. Alaitz hated her.

On previous occasions, she'd run into Graciana and knew her well enough to know Sebastian was in trouble sitting next to her. Graciana was the type who got off on making guys fall for her and then using them at her will for whatever she wanted. Every guy taken in by her charms didn't realize she actually had no interest in men and was a lesbian. She hoped Sebastian knew what he was doing. If she had known it was Graciana he'd come to find, she would never have agreed to bring him.

Alaitz weaved her way through the crowd until she was standing just on the edge of the field in front of the little hill where Sebastian and Graciana were sitting. Though she was still out of sight to them, she was close enough to see everything.

* * *

Capitaine Nivelle motioned for his men to walk slowly as they moved through the forest. The trees created a canopy overhead, making the light dim below. Agent Gibson treaded through the bright green ferns alongside Nivelle and the policeman who had driven the car. Nivelle looked completely calm and confident, while the young driver looked scared shitless.

Gibson crept through the forest at the same slow pace Nivelle was keeping with his .45 in hand. Birds were chirping in the trees and the sun shone in brilliant rays through the gaps in the ceiling of branches overhead. When a clearing came in sight in the distance, Nivelle halted his step and drew his pistol. The young driver hesitantly followed suit. Now at full alert, Nivelle burst through the underbrush at a full charge into the clearing. Gibson and the driver followed his lead, but when they came onto the clearing in the forest, they found nothing except a line of burnt-out vehicles, piles of gun shells at their feet, and a mound of dirt. Nivelle confidently stood, revolver in hand, as if he had just taken Fort Douamont back from the Germans. A group of six other gendarmes then appeared from the opposite side of the clearing. The only sounds were from the unseen birds and the gentle breeze blowing through the trees.

Surveying the scene, Nivelle raised his hands in triumph.

"What are you so happy about?" Gibson asked.

Nivelle looked at him as if he had been asked an ignorant question. "Are you mad? This is a great accomplishment. We have discovered and ended any future use of this ETA training site!"

Gibson shook his head in disbelief. "You mean to say that you feel this little mission was a success because we found an abandoned training site?" Nivelle's unchanged confident look was all he needed for an answer. At that moment, Gibson realized how insightful his Parker had been.

He walked to one of the burned vehicles and, pointing to it, said, "Do you see this car, Nivelle? From the rust on the charred metal, this car was bombed quite a long time ago." Seeing no change of expression on Nivelle's face, he continued. "This place has not been used for a long time. Just look." He walked toward Nivelle and stopped to pick up a bullet cartridge from the ground. "These bullet casings are halfway buried into the earth."

"And? What is your point, Agent Gibson?" Nivelle asked, straight faced.

Taking a deep breath, Gibson calmed himself down before responding. "My point is… this was a waste of time," he said with effort.

Nivelle walked over to him and took the bullet casing from his hand. "You Americans are all so cowboy and action oriented. It must always be blood and guts for you to see progress. I think you all watch too many of your own Hollywood films *de merde*. But here in France, this will be held as a victory for the government and a defeat for the terrorists," he said directly to Gibson's face. Nivelle passed by Gibson and walked to the line of burnt vehicles.

Gibson thought of Parker, and as soon as he did, he felt an unexplainable tenseness. Something was wrong. "I think you should take me back to the hotel," he called to Nivelle.

Nivelle, now crouched next to one of the vehicle carcasses, looked up at him with piercing eyes. "*Mais, quoi*? Take you all the way back to Bayonne when we just have arrived?" he coldly asked.

Gibson responded firmly, "I think Parker is in trouble, and if he needs me, I will be closer to him there."

"*Non. C'est pas possible.* He went off on his own so he can make do on his own."

Gibson felt an urge to reach for his now holstered gun, but held his hand back from grabbing it. "As far as I know, your superiors ordered you to assist me in any way possible. You've got more than enough men here to do an investigation of the area, especially since I don't see what you're expecting to find out here anyway." It was hard for him to control the level of rage he felt growing inside him.

Nivelle stared at him for a moment without blinking. He then motioned to one of the gendarmes standing next to him and told him in French to take Gibson back to his hotel. The officer began walking through the woods in the opposite direction from where they had approached. Gibson followed.

* * *

If she were attracted to men, she would be attracted to him. He wasn't too aggressive or too testosterone-laced. Instead, he was confident and sensitive. She liked the mix in him and for a brief moment considered letting a guy have a chance. But as soon as she considered this, she felt disgusted at the thought and decided she was going to play with him just to get back at men in general. Though he might be nice, he was still a guy, and that meant all he really wanted was to get between her legs.

Slowly, she ran a hand down her jean covered leg, tossed her hair back and rolled her neck to face him with half-closed eyes and slightly parted lips. When she smiled at him, she was surprised to find him making no attempt to move closer to her. He didn't try to place his hand on her thigh. He didn't tell her how beautiful she was. He just sat there, looked at her a moment, then looked off at the mountains in the distance.

"Are you a homosexual or something?" she asked him directly in French.

"No. It's just that I already have a girl and I don't need another," Parker replied.

Graciana thought over his words. "Is she more beautiful or sexy than me?" she wanted to know.

Parker moved his eyes languidly from her black shoes, up her narrow legs tightly clad in dark jeans, past her slight hips, and over her small waist. He could see a line of tanned stomach at the bottom of the black short-sleeved shirt that encased her breasts. He looked into her eyes . "To me, she is more beautiful in reality than anyone. But I'm sure any other guy would think you are the sexiest woman in all of the Basque Country."

Looking into his eyes, she saw them soften as he stared into hers, and she noted the sincerity of his voice. It made her look away. For a few seconds, she felt horribly vulnerable.

She was still looking off into empty space when she reluctantly admitted, "I didn't think there were actually men like you." He handed her a cigarette, which she freely took. "She's very lucky to have someone like you," she added.

Parker lit a cigarette for himself. "To tell you the truth, I don't think she really wants me." He inhaled and held the smoke in his lungs until it hurt before releasing from his body.

"What? Why wouldn't she want someone like you? You're good looking. You're smart. You're nice. And you seem to be a good person. All of these things are hard to find."

"I don't know. I've never claimed to be able to understand women and I never will. I guess it's just that some people who have something great in front of them don't know how to accept what they could have."

Parker was beginning to feel uncomfortable and wanted to try and change the subject. He could only act a part so long before personal issues became too real. "Actually, it's kind of like those of Basque descent who don't want independence for the Basque Country." He added, after a short pause. "I don't know what the hell those people are thinking either."

"Ah, yes. But the time is nearly upon us when those people will no longer be able to deny our strength."

"What do you mean?" he asked, doing his best to hold back from revealing the relief on his face at the new topic.

"I mean something has been done in your country that will soon be claimed by us. Then the world will see how powerful we are," Graciana said defiantly.

"This is my country, right here. I may have been born there and I may live there now, but my home will always be here in the Basque Country." As the words quickly and involuntarily escaped from his mouth, Parker was not able to determine whether or not he was lying or admitting the truth. "What's happened?" he abruptly asked.

She looked at him with her eyes boring into his skull. "A man has been killed. Someone who will not go unnoticed."

Parker didn't dare breathe as she spoke, and he hoped his eyes did not reveal his thoughts. She was unwavering in her gaze, and he began to feel uncomfortable sitting next to her. Her eyes seemed to harden as she spoke. He tried to make himself sound confident. "I didn't think ETA conducted activities outside of Spain and France?"

Graciana didn't flinch. She didn't blink. She smiled and shook her head. "ETA hasn't. IK hasn't. But now another group has taught these ancients how to conduct this war in this new age."

He sat spellbound, not yet believing what he was hearing. "But the only other group then is…" he stuttered in disbelief.

"Yes. Haika," she said as she blew a fine stream of smoke past his ear.

"But Haika is a youth organization. The oldest member could be no more than eighteen, because ETA or IK would have already recruited him or her by that time. How could they possibly pull off such a thing?"

She cast him a seductive look. "You don't think that younger people can be dangerous?" she spoke slowly. Then she asked, "How old do you think I am?"

Parker had to mentally slap himself out of her spell as he replied. "I would guess you are no younger than twenty-two."

Graciana's eyes smiled at him and her mouth puckered into a sort of kiss as she winked at him. "I'm eighteen."

* * *

Gibson was standing outside his room when Parker returned to the hotel. Parker nodded to him, but said nothing. He opened the door and let Gibson in, who immediately began to nervously pace the length of the small room. First thing, Parker went straight to a bottle of Izarra on the nightstand next to the bed and poured himself a glass of the potent green liquor and lit a cigarette. He then propped himself on the bed with his back against the wall.

Gibson watched him as he paced the room, waiting for Parker to speak. When he realized he was going to have to initiate the conversation, he asked, "So what happened?"

"Well, let's see. Last night a car bomb exploded in the center of San Sebastian's business district, right outside a major Spanish bank. Some kids threw Molotov cocktails at the storefront of a realty office in Ustaritz, and a prominent Spanish politician in Madrid apparently received a very graphic death threat on his family. But you'll see none of this in the papers and it won't be covered in the news because there isn't a war going on over here. All these things are just blown off as minor events, even though these *minor* events have been going on pretty much nonstop for over thirty years now."

"That's all great, Parker, but why don't you quit being a pain in the ass with your preaching and tell me what I really want to hear?"

Looking into the emerald green of his drink, Parker said, "ETA didn't do it—not really anyway."

"What does that mean?"

"It means that this civil conflict has taken a new turn. The surfer guy on the beach, Etienne, told me that his younger brother, Aurelion, had lately fallen out of contact with the rest of his family and no one really knew where he was or what he was doing. Recently, Etienne tried to get in touch with him and was told by Aurelion's girlfriend that he'd gone somewhere and would not be returning for a week or so. When Etienne inquired further, the girlfriend suspiciously would say no more. I didn't really think anything of this at first, but after my encounter earlier today, I can't deny the significance."

Parker took a large gulp of Izarra and stubbed out his cigarette in an ashtray he had placed next to him on the windowsill. Gibson stopped pacing and sat down in the simple wooden chair by the door, intently waiting for Parker to continue.

"Didn't you think it was odd how young Peio looked? I myself was a bit shocked to have received help so easily from a senior member of ETA. I also thought it was very odd that Aurelion was killed, who, by the way, I believe we can without doubt now say was a member of the group we are after. So now, all of these things are beginning to make sense." Parker paused to look up from his now empty glass at Gibson. Gibson's face was blank.

"Well, I'm still lost. What are you getting at, Parker?" Gibson asked, shaking his head.

"The hit on José Aldarossa Arana was carried out by a bunch of kids, probably not one of them older than eighteen. My guess is that the majority of the various factions within ETA didn't approve it and these young people mostly did it on their own. There are obviously some who have grown tired of merely burning storefronts and painting walls. A new form of ETA did this. A group representing a new generation of Basque extremists. *Haika did this.*"

Gibson's jaw dropped in astonishment. "You mean to tell me that a group of kids carried out an international terrorist hit?"

Parker looked Gibson straight in the eyes. "Never underestimate the power of youth, especially when a cause is involved. But I don't think they did it on their own. I think, like I always have, that they had help from the States. I imagine this help was much more than just a ride out of San Francisco. This group we're after was financed by someone over there. When we're done here, you'll have more people to go after back in the States. I promise."

"That'll come later. We still have two people to get here," Gibson confidently said.

"Yeah, we caught one and we found the other face down on the side of a mountain," Parker, absent-mindedly, muttered.

Gibson stood up, excited. "This is progress, though, Parker. I need to let DC know we're getting somewhere before they either pull us out of here or send more people." He grinned widely, but the grin changed to an expression of concern as he saw the distant expression on Parker's face. "What's wrong? You don't think this is good news?"

"I think it's unfortunate, Gibson. Young people here should be learning Basque and studying law and politics so that they can one day negotiate more autonomy for the Basque Country without guns." He filled his glass half-full once again with green Izarra.

"Sebastian, you've got to keep yourself apart from this. This isn't your home. This isn't your conflict."

"Are you sure?" Parker asked, unconvinced.

"Yes, I am." Gibson began to pace the room again. "But tell me—why would they kill one of their own people?"

"I think it's safe to assume that Aurelion was murdered by ETA and not Haika. ETA is like the IRA of old. It has various factions within it and none of them seem to agree very often on how they should conduct themselves in the fight for independence. It could be that our group pissed off some key members of the organization and so they wanted to make an example of what happens when rouge groups go astray. Or he could have been killed because they don't want us to catch any more of this group and clearly identify the link between Haika and ETA. Who the hell knows?"

"But if we catch them they could get more publicity out of the hit, couldn't they? And wouldn't that be what they want?" Gibson asked.

"Maybe not. As I said before, the different factions within ETA rarely agree with each other. It could be that one faction doesn't want the murder blamed on ETA and they ordered Aurelion and the rest to be killed because they fear the U.S. will retaliate by helping Spain and France crush the struggle in the Basque Country. And maybe this same faction decided that only he should be knocked off to set an example to other young radical groups, telling them to not stray off on their own. Or yet, maybe he was picked out in particular because they thought he was the one most likely to be caught. I imagine we'll know which theory is true soon enough."

Parker's voice had gradually risen in volume. He broke to light another cigarette before continuing. "It's all a big fucking mess. The most crazy thing is, this goes back much further than, say, the boundary conflicts in Africa we see today that are direct results of the mapping by European imperialist powers merely a century ago. This conflict goes back to the time of the Romans."

Gibson stood and stared at the floor. "Complaining doesn't do any good."

Parker sneered at him with fire in his eyes. "Yeah, well I guess that's what those kids were thinking when they tortured and murdered that innocent man in San Francisco."

"All right, all right. I don't want to piss you off anymore, Parker," Gibson said, attempting to relieve the rising tension in the room. "Maybe it will cheer you up a bit to know you were right on about Nivelle's little excursion into the forest," he added with a slight smile.

Parker blew out a puff of smoke from a widening smile. "So, did you find a nice blown out car and a few empty shell casings?"

Gibson didn't hesitate to respond truthfully. "That's exactly all we found."

"Just wait until we see the paper tomorrow morning. I would bet you a hundred dollars that's not all they found."

"What do you mean?"

"You'll see," Parker winked at him. "But while we're reading the paper we can also mosey on down to Nivelle's office at the local gendarmerie and ask him to accompany us to Saint-Pée, where we will find another member of our four." Parker smiled contently at Gibson, his eyebrows suspiciously rising.

Gibson watched the young man before him adjust himself awkwardly. He had a mixed look of confidence and embarrassment. "How would you know that?" he asked.

It was clear to Gibson that Parker had to think about his response before speaking. "Because she told me that's where she's been staying."

"Who's she?"

"Graciana is her name." Parker rolled the *r* in her name, as any French speaker would do.

A puzzled look crossed Gibson's face. "And why would, Graciana," attempting, but valiantly failing, to roll the *r*, "tell you that?"

Parker languidly blew a stream of smoke between the fingers of his outstretched hand. "Honestly, I think she talked to me because I was nice to her. And because I wasn't trying to get in her pants."

"She talked to you and told you her secrets because you were nice to her?" Gibson exclaimed. "I haven't met any women who would do such a thing," he said, imploringly.

"Maybe you haven't met enough of them, or maybe just not the right women," Parker calmly replied.

As he watched, Parker saw Gibson's expression turn mildly violent. "Maybe that's the case, but it may also be that they like to screw over men!" Gibson abruptly stood up. He walked to the window to peer through the curtains and stare into the nothingness of the empty street below.

Parker stared inquisitively at the grown man in front of him who sounded like a young man who'd been rejected too many times at the bars. "They may well all be that way, and I can't say that my experiences with them have amounted to me thinking any differently, most of the time. But I still like to think that some of them are different. I'm sure you're dying to say that's just naïve of me, but I like to hold on to some speck of hope, as unattainable as it may seem," Parker admitted, gazing dreamingly into the light of the bedside lamp.

Then Parker jerked his head away from the daydream. "But regardless, I chatted with one of the four we are here to catch, and I know where she is, so let's go and get her tomorrow morning. I know she's not returning there until then."

Gibson turned and incredulously stared at him.

"Well, I couldn't have just gone and arrested her by myself in the middle of an ETA-sponsored rally now, could I?" He paused to gauge Gibson's emotionless reaction. "What's made you so damn bitter, anyway?" he added.

Gibson looked away from him into a blank corner of the room. "You kind of lose faith in women when the one you married leaves you," he slowly articulated.

"Gibson, I'm sorry. I didn't know," Parker replied.

Shaking off the sadness, guilt, and loss that he always felt on the rare occasion she returned to his thoughts, Gibson said, "Don't worry about it. Just take my advice and be careful with your heart. It can fool you, and the price is more than you could possibly imagine."

Stubbing out his cigarette, Parker silently offered his glass of Izarra to him. Gibson took it and downed the vibrantly colored liquor in one drink.

* * *

Venezuela arrests suspected ETA activist

Police in Venezuela have arrested a suspected member of the Spanish Basque separatist movement, ETA.

The man arrested in the city of Maracay, to the west Caracas, is wanted in Spain on terrorist charges. He is being held in a Caracas jail, pending extradition proceedings.

Spain has repeatedly called on Venezuela to extradite a number of suspected ETA activists who, it says, are living there.

18

Basque Country, France

CAPITAINE NIVELLE CALLED up more of a force than he had for Peio. He didn't bother to have his men try to be conspicuous. They wore their uniforms and drove marked gendarme vehicles. The small picturesque town of Saint-Pée was surrounded. Every road heading out of the town was blocked.

Beforehand, Nivelle sent someone to scout out the town, searching for a young blonde woman. She was quickly spotted. A pretty, thin, young woman could not go unnoticed in a place like Saint-Pée, where aside from the tourists staying in bed and breakfasts surrounding the town, most of the female residents were older women shuffling to and from the boulangerie. This one was noticed entering the bakery as well, only she did not reemerge from the storefront.

The police parked behind the building on the edge of a green field that extended up the slope of a hill. Silently, Nivelle motioned for Gibson and Parker to stay behind him as he directed his men to surround the building. Leading the way, Nivelle approached the external staircase on the side of the building with his gun drawn. Two of his men following stood on either side of the door at the stop of the stairs, while another broke in the door with a ramming device. Immediately, Nivelle and the other two policemen flew up the stairs to the door at the top. One of the men accompanying Nivelle promptly kicked the door open.

Gibson and Parker were told by a gendarme at the foot of the stairs to stay, as he held out his arm, blocking their way. Ignoring him, Gibson pushed the arm aside. Followed closely by Parker, they quickly strode up the staircase. The two gendarmes were standing confounded in the middle of the room and Nivelle was picking something up from the windowsill. Aside from a mattress in one corner, the place was empty. Parker didn't try to conceal the small smile on his face.

For the remainder of the morning, Nivelle's men interrogated nearly the entire town, coming up with nothing. While they did, Parker sat with Gibson at a café.

A group of older men were in the café at the outbreak of the commotion of police vehicles filling the square. The men remained where they were, with hardly a glance out the front windows.

"So where do you think she is?" Gibson asked Parker.

"Who knows? Not very far from here, but far enough that finding her is going to be very difficult. Somehow they were able to smuggle her out of here right under Nivelle's pointy nose."

"That's not very encouraging, Parker."

Gazing off at the jagged line of La Rhune, looming above them like a sentry guarding the border into Spain, Parker said, as if speaking to the mountain itself, "My cover's blown."

"Whoever Nivelle had snooping around here earlier today could have tipped them off, not you," Gibson offered, trying to shift blame.

"No, I don't think so. Someone must have tipped them off about me after seeing me talking to her at the rally."

"Then why didn't they stop you then, if they knew who you were?"

Parker didn't answer him. Instead, he finished his coffee and lit a cigarette. "Why are you so sure your cover is blown?" insisted Gibson.

"Because that room must have been cleared out very quickly as nothing was left for us to find except the small thing on the windowsill."

"You mean the blue box of matches?" Gibson asked in surprise.

Parker turned his lighter in the faint sunlight that pierced through a partly overcast sky before he replied. "Exactly. A blue box of matches that she knows I saw in her purse."

* * *

In vain, Parker tried to reach Alaitz. He called her cell phone number at least ten times before finally leaving a message. He told her that he needed to meet her that night at the Euskaldun. He said he would be there early and he expected her to be there. He added that it was very important that they talk and it could not wait.

Later, Gibson and Parker had a simple, but hearty, meal in the hotel's restaurant. The meal consisted of pumpkin soup, roasted lamb, au gratin potatoes and cherries seeped in red wine for dessert. Afterward, Gibson said he needed to make a report, but that he didn't trust the phone lines in the rooms, or the pay phones on the street, or even his cell phone. He was going to walk to Nivelle's office to make the call.

Parker, seeing a golden opportunity to ditch Gibson, feigned a sore stomach, and feigned it well. He claimed he was going to go to his room.

As Gibson left the building through the front entrance, Parker slowly crept up the stairwell next to the small restaurant that led to their rooms. Gibson told Parker he would stop by after he returned from making his call to fill him in on the conversation with the States, and whatever he could find out from Nivelle.

Sebastian Parker had other plans.

Once reaching his room, Parker waited long enough to smoke a cigarette, giving Gibson time to get down the road. Then he darted down the stairs and out the door, headed for the Euskaldun at a brisk pace.

For perhaps the first time, Gibson felt the charm of the place surrounding him as he walked along the narrow cobblestone streets of Petit Bayonne. The roads wound in between the lines of old buildings and were lined by thin sidewalks not wide enough for two people to walk past each other without one having to step into the street. He noticed the three-story buildings opened up to reveal the gentle river crossed by a few small stone bridges, and on the other bank was a line of crooked row houses with storefronts at their bases and the spires of the cathedral looming behind.

While crossing one of the bridges, he stopped to gaze at the expanse of mountains outlining the horizon to the south. The sun had long since gone down, but its light still made the sky and scattered clouds glow pink, orange and purple, highlighting the stretch of peaks in the distance by the contrast of dark land and light sky. Just as it passed the reach of the city and disappeared into the countryside, the river made a turn. Gibson had not seen many places that reminded him of mystical locations described in books and shown in movies, but this place came as close as any. He continued on his way to the gendarme station feeling refreshed, with lightness in his step.

Parker, on the other hand, was feeling his legs getting heavier and heavier the closer he got to the bar where hopefully he would soon meet Alaitz. He intended meeting the one girl he loved, and would always love more than any other—the girl he was positive had betrayed him.

When he arrived at the bar, he found it unusually empty, except for a few men hunkered over their drinks at a table in the far corner of the room. He sat himself at the bar and ordered a Patxaran. He waited.

Just as he was finishing his second drink, she boldly walked up to him. Without a word, he grabbed her hand and led her outside into the night. As he led her through the streets, still gripping her hand, she repeatedly asked what was going on, but he didn't answer. He led them behind the old Basque church, past the chateau and its crumbling ramparts. They followed a rising street that led out from Bayonne to Saint-Pierre-d'Irube.

After about ten minutes, he stopped and pointed to a bench facing the city. From this vantage point they could see all the lights of the city below surrounding the low valley which the meeting of the two rivers created. The lighted, all-seeing spires of the cathedral towered over the area. As they sat down on the bench, Parker lit two cigarettes, handing one to her.

"This is romantic and all, Sebastian, but if you wanted to get me turned on, you could have just taken me out to dinner you know," she said to him in French. She brushed his arm as she spoke, trying to break his icy mood with a little flirtation.

Parker's eyes were fixed on the illuminated spires of the cathedral as if they were going to tell him something she or anyone else could not. He exhaled deeply, his eyes closed. "Do you know, Alaitz, that if you wanted to put a death warrant on me you could have just told me to leave instead of selling me to ETA," he said in English, his voice barely above a whisper.

Alaitz shook her head in disbelief, making strands of her hair fall from their resting place behind her ears. "What?" she exclaimed, now speaking in English as well.

Parker stared at her, his eyes piercing through the darkness. "Don't lie to me. You told them and they moved her. Do you really want to be involved with an organization that mercilessly kills people, Alaitz?"

"I don't know what you are talking about, Sebastian." She looked away from him into the darkness.

"You're going to tell me that you didn't see me talking to Graciana yesterday? You're going to tell me that you're no longer involved with those people?" His voice rose as he spoke and he could feel his pulse racing.

Alaitz lifted her hand up in protest. "*Tais-toi, mon dieu*! Just because you don't hear people speaking English here doesn't mean they don't understand."

Parker tried to control his breathing and lower his temper. He continued in a much calmer and deliberate tone. "Yes, I know that, Alaitz. I did live here for a couple of years, if you'll remember. But we aren't talking about that. What we're talking about is you answering my questions."

She grabbed ahold of his arm and squeezed it tightly. Even in the darkness, he could see the anger on her face. "You want answers to your questions? Well here they are. Yes, I did see you flirting with that *salope*. No, I did not say anything to anyone. And, no, I am not involved with those bastards anymore. But since you don't believe me, I'm going to go home now and you either can sit here with your *putain* accusations or walk with me back to my car!" She threw her hardly touched cigarette into the street behind them.

Parker was too upset to recognize the emphasis she'd put on his involvement with Graciana. She was jealous.

"Then why do you still know so much? And how did they know enough to move her just as we were moving in to get her?"

"Sebastian, sometimes I hold you above all of the other dumb-ass guys of the world, but sometimes I wonder if I don't give you too much credit. I know so much because I live in the Pays Basque, I'm young, I'm intelligent, I know a lot of people, my family's has always been involved in the movement, and most of all, because I want independence from these two ancient imperialists for the land of my ancestors. No, I don't think killing innocent people is the answer for independence and that's why I got out of it. And as far as she is concerned, I would have gladly helped you catch that bitch if you had told me what you were up to. I'm actually disappointed to hear you didn't catch her."

"Do you know where she's been moved?" he quickly asked.

Alaitz turned away from him. Staring into the darkness with her back turned to him she replied, "No."

"Why are you disappointed we didn't catch her?"

Alaitz let go of his arm. "It's because of people like her that I got out of all that craziness. And, by the way, she's a lesbian, if you didn't figure that out while hitting on her."

"I knew that," he quickly responded, straightening himself on the bench and looking away from her. "And I didn't hit on her, just talked to her," he clarified.

Both tried to check out the other while at the same time trying not to make it noticeable. But neither missed the smile creeping across the other's face. They turned to look at one another and burst into laughter, not caring how loud they were. When the laughter subsided there were tears bunched in the corners of Alaitz's eyes. She reached for his neck and pulled him against her, burying her head into his shoulder.

"Oh Sebastian, I think you should leave this place now and never come back. You are in great danger. You are in danger with the people here, with the land, and with me," she said in a sad voice that was muffled by his shirt.

He pulled her head away from him and lifted her chin gently with his fingertips. "If I leave and never come back, I would never again see all that matters to me in this world. Why do you think I accepted this assignment in the first place?"

She pressed her now wet face against his hand. "You're such a fool, Sebastian. You're going to get yourself killed."

"Everyone needs a cause in their lives. At least I'll die for a good reason," he said, smiling confidently.

She didn't return his smile. Instead, a flood of tears escaped down her face as she returned to pressing her face against him, just to feel close to him for a short time. In her mind, she tried to imagine the two of them living in a farmhouse in the countryside, raising a family. *Maybe someday.*

He put his arms around her, making her feel secure and safe and loved for a brief moment. However, sitting with him felt too much like a dream that she didn't believe would ever come true. Alaitz never cried so much.

* * *

Gibson pounded on Parker's door until he was convinced the room was empty. Instead of opening the next door down the hallway, the door to his own room, he sat down on the floor next to Parker's door, pulled his gun out from under his jacket, and laid it under his leg. He would wait.

About an hour later, Parker came strolling down the hallway, grinning from ear to ear. So engrossed in his happy thoughts, he didn't notice Gibson sitting on the floor next to his door. In fact, Gibson didn't think Parker was noticing anything. He walked as if strolling on clouds and his eyes were rolled upwards. Gibson had seen him in this state more than once. Though he didn't exactly look intoxicated, something about him definitely was strange.

Gibson's instinct was that Parker was on some sort of drugs. "Parker! You said you were sick and that you were going to stay here. Now you're sneaking out to take drugs?" Gibson stood up while he spoke. He grabbed Parker by the shoulders and shook him. Parker stood still and didn't resist, still keeping a silly grin on his face.

Shaking him, Gibson added, "That's it. I've dealt with having a drunk as my partner on this investigation long enough and now turns out you're a goddamn druggie as well! I'm going to call the States and tell them I'm sending you back. You're no better than the punks we're here to find." Abruptly, Gibson pivoted and began walking toward the stairwell.

Parker had to wake himself from what felt like a trance. "Wait!" he called out. Gibson stopped. Parker opened the door to his room. "Care to come in?"

Gibson reluctantly obliged. Once inside, Parker explained to Gibson what he'd been doing, of course leaving out the extent of his feelings for Alaitz, and forced Gibson to give him a quick intoxication test to prove he wasn't under the influence of anything.

Somewhat mollified, Gibson asked Parker why he looked so wasted.

In response, Parker conveniently changed the subject. "How was your encounter with Nivelle?"

"He didn't have anything, not really anyway. All he said was that one of his undercover men somewhere overheard something about a larger city in a place called *Soul* being important, and maybe they heard mention of a girl involved. His man doesn't understand Basque very well, even though he is one, and he didn't think the information was significant."

Parker's interest was peaked when he heard Gibson slowly pronounce the easternmost French Basque province. "Nivelle's a *con*. He doesn't realize what that means. They may have moved her from Labourd to Soule, thinking the French authorities would not think of this move. Normally, after a failed raid like today, they would move someone either to a crowded area like Paris or to a safe house around Pau or in Brittany." He paused to light a cigarette. "This could be a good break. I think I just may know someone who can help us."

* * *

"Which one is he?" Gibson asked impatiently. A group of young men were playing in a rugby match in front of them. The field was situated at the base of a section of crumbling former ramparts that used to surround the city of Bayonne in medieval times.

Parker just smiled. "Patience is a virtue, John Gibson."

"Yeah, well, not when we're running out of time," Gibson said, shifting his weight to one leg. "Why don't you call out to him and get him to come over here?"

Parker's expression turned serious. "Gibson, we're running out of time here faster than you think. I'm almost positive our cover as tourists is blown. If that's indeed the case, no one will even talk to me in public, and maybe not even in private. We have to be extra careful now or we'll get someone else or ourselves killed. I just want him to see me. He'll know where to meet me after."

"How will he know?"

"Because it's a place we used to always meet." As he spoke, his chin slightly raised in recognition of someone in front of them. "All right, he's seen me. Let's go. When the match is finished, he'll come meet us."

"I don't think they would kill us, Parker," Gibson said, defiantly, as they walked away from the field.

Parker continued a few steps before commenting, "We can't predict what will happen in life. I'm sure when you married your wife, you didn't think she would one day leave you."

Gibson felt an overriding urge to strangle Parker. He calmed himself instead. "Is that your philosophy on life? So what are we supposed to do? Go through life being constantly afraid to do anything?"

"No. That's not what we're supposed to do, Gibson. I don't really know what we are *supposed* to do, and I don't think anyone does. But I think we shouldn't be scared. We should always be mindful of what we are doing."

"Thanks, junior Yoda."

"Whatever, grandpa," Parker said as he lit a cigarette. "And by the way, you should give much more credit to who we're dealing with here. I've been studying and following the Basque separatist movement since I was old enough to define the word movement. This is no joke here. They are for real. More people know more about other independence movements around the globe, like in Sri Lanka or Quebec, than they do about the Basque conflict."

Gibson was pleased to hear that, despite his earlier worries, was in fact not taking the situation lightly and recognized their potential dangerous situation.

Parker blew out a hurried puff of smoke before he continued. "I can assure you that living here is nothing like you've ever been able to imagine. Up until the last few years, people in the States didn't understand the possibility of a terrorist attack as most of the world lives with every day. And it may feel peaceful to you here, but I promise you it's not. How about I tell you a little story while we walk about what life can be like here?"

* * *

The adjustment going from the United States to southern France was not as easy as he thought it would be. Of course, the language factor was considerable. It made him laugh to think how some Americans thought they spoke a foreign language after a few years of high school classes. Being a solid student for three years of high school French classes in the States amounted to him being able to say I am tired, in French, when he first stepped off a plane onto French soil. Even then, he pronounced the words with a horrendous accent.

Some days were more frustrating than others, and some days he felt like he would never be able to learn the language. Then, months later, he woke up one glorious day and found something had changed.

He automatically said good morning in French to his host mother before stepping out the door and walking to the bus stop. As he passed street signs and storefronts, he realized he was able to read them all without a second thought. Also, on the bus ride to the center of Bayonne, he overheard various random conversations around him and realized he understood what was being said. When arriving at the lycée, he automatically said *salut, ça va* to others. He listened to the teacher's lecture and took notes. That evening he talked freely with his host family about current events at the dinner table.

In bed that night, just as he closed his eyes, suddenly he realized something else. Not only had he spoken only French that day, but he had also thought only in French the entire day.

But there was something else that bothered him. He didn't think of it as being homesick, because he had never liked where he'd grown up and had always felt out of place. Instead, he decided that what he was feeling was more disturbing in his soul due to the fact that being in France, he felt more lost than ever. Though the world had opened its wide arms to him, he felt now blindfolded.

Day after day slowly passed. Gradually, he began to accept the fact he might never know his place in the world.

One particular day, as he was walking from the bus stop to the lycée for class, he thought the sooty spires of Bayonne's cathedral smiled at him. They seemed to be telling him to listen. Considering all they had seen over the centuries from their towering pinnacle, Parker did try to listen. It was at that moment he told himself he could learn more sitting on a park bench than in a classroom.

It was fall and the air was chilled and thick with the scent of decay. A slight, warming breeze blew from the south and fallen leaves casually blew by him. He sat on a wooden bench that was on a walkway at the edge of a small open field that abruptly ended at the edge of a crumbling rampart, part of the of the city's former fortifications. Above the rampart there was an uneven line of row houses that appeared as if they had not been painted in the last fifty years. Behind and above the line of rooftops, loomed the spires of the cathedral. He stared at them and as he did, a rush of emotions overcame him that he couldn't begin to describe. It made him consider taking out a pad of paper from his backpack and attempt to record the wavering streams of thought racing through him, but he realized he couldn't begin to put his description down in words. There was too much for him to record on paper. The passing traffic on the busy street behind him ceased to exist, and so did everything else. All that existed was just this place with him in it.

A loud explosion woke him from his trance-like thoughts. Looking around, he realized that for quite some time he had been absently staring at a half-green and half-brown leaf that had landed on a tuft of grass in front of him. Then he realized a thick cloud of smoke was rising from somewhere within the business district of the *centre ville*.

Immediately, he got up from the bench and moved in the direction of the dark smoke.

As he grew closer, he smelled the strong scent of the smoke. Other people were walking down the boulevard casually, away from whatever he was moving toward and policemen were present everywhere, machine guns in hand. Later, he would think that perhaps it hadn't been such a good idea to get close to the scene as the police could have been randomly grabbing people at gunpoint to ask for identification, and he didn't have his passport.

Just as he passed the Galeries Lafayette store, he saw the source of the smoke. It was a local branch office of the English bank, Barclays. The area had been quickly cordoned off to prevent people from getting too close to the flaming building, but Parker could see that the front of the small office had been blown out. Glass and debris covered the sidewalk and street in front of the bank. Clouds of smoke poured from the building. Firemen were already busy at work spraying streams of water through the blown out windows.

He was surprised to find that aside from a few other onlookers, not many people were taking much interest in the scene. Whereas Parker wished he had his camera, others walked by and merely shook their heads slightly, as if the event was of little importance. Even the police presence seemed to be only there for show, as he noticed they didn't appear to be looking very closely at anyone passing by. The entire situation was bizarre, and he walked away feeling both disturbed and confused.

Parker did his best to bring up the event with his host parents, but as far as he could tell, they didn't know anything about the bombing. He watched the regional news on television that night expecting to see a report on the incident, but there were none.

The next day, he picked up a Sud-Ouest Newspaper and was only able to find a small article on one of the back pages of the Pays Basque regional section. The article reported that ETA laid claim to the bank bombing. Evidently, the bank had been targeted for the symbolic purpose of ETA's stance against foreigners, such as the English, taking over industry and housing in the Basque Country. Someone claiming to be in the organization phoned the police an hour before the bomb was set to go off so they would have time to evacuate the area. To Parker, that answered why the area had so quickly been cleared and covered with both police and firemen.

The next morning when he inquired, as much as he was able to in a strange mix of French and English, into the event with those in his class, he only received muted and uncaring responses. Sensing his tortured confusion, a girl in his class took pity on him. She explained, in near flawless English, that ETA and its other linked groups carried out small attacks such as the one the day before on a regular basis on both sides of the border. It had become so commonplace that these attacks were hardly viewed as big news to anyone. Sometimes it was an incident as little as burning trash bins in the alleyways of San Sebastian. Sometimes the bombing of a business in Bayonne. Sometimes the defacing of a tourism sign. Sometimes more. The attacks were just a normal, near daily occurrence of living in the Basque Country.

Although the incident was quickly forgotten, the bank's storefront was quickly boarded-up and the office was moved across the street, Parker was never able to forget that day he was introduced to a different world than the one he'd always known.

* * *

"So that's my example on how cultural differences can be more drastic than we can ever imagine from within our safe and isolated nation's borders, and how crazy this place can be," Parker said at the conclusion of his story. "The level of violence and ETA presence may never have been as prevalent here on the French side of the border, but it's always present."

"Parker, what the hell do you think I do for a living? I know quite a bit about cultural differences."

"But you don't seem to know shit about this place. The omnipresent governments of Spain and France have contained all this from its start more effectively than the United States is able to cover a military blunder."

Parker's comment made Gibson's muscles tense. "Why don't you quit your job working for the government since you seem to despise it so much, and then move here and join them, Parker? You seem to love them and their cause so damned much. In fact, I still question what the hell you're doing here."

The quickness of Parker's reaction caught Gibson by surprise. It was similar to his reaction when Parker had sprung on Nivelle. But this time it was not Nivelle, but Gibson, who suddenly found himself pinned by Parker, as the younger man got in his face.

"If you want to accuse me of something then fucking do it! If not, then shut the hell up and follow me. I'll deliver you the rest of these people," Parker icily said.

Gibson was tempted to bring up Parker's earlier comment on the possibility of ETA wanting the group they were after to be caught, but decided to keep it to himself. He was also tempted to physically knock the hell out of the cocky little shit, but also decided against it. Instead, he waited for Parker to back off. Parker let go of him and walked away.

* * *

"My old friend, Michel Michelena, is someone who would be glad to help us. His family is Basque by name, but his great-grandfather married a French woman, and they long ago shuddered off any connection to the Basques. In fact, they don't like them at all," Parker said as he finished the last of his coffee. He and Gibson were seated at an outdoor table of a café, with their tempers cooled. The café was perfectly situated so that when sitting outside, one could see a profile of the cathedral at one end of the narrow pedestrian cobblestone street and at the other, the broad front of the hotel de ville.

Gibson looked around suspiciously, before saying, "Parker, aren't you worried about talking about this in a public place?"

Before replying, Parker lit a cigarette and looked at Gibson. He didn't hold any bad will toward the man, but felt no regret either. "For one, we're not in Petit Bayonne over here, so ETA sympathies are drastically reduced. For another, people stick to their own business much more on this side of the river. So, no, I'm not overly concerned."

Looking confused, Gibson asked, "Can you tell me why it seems as if there are so many people over here who don't like this group, yet somehow they manage to always stay on their feet?"

Parker blew out a line of smoke. "There are enough who do support them, indirectly, and who keep them afloat. And there probably always will be, as long as tension remains in the Basque provinces on both sides of the border."

Gibson wasn't sure he completely understood, but he had more questions. "But what happened to Patrick? I thought he was your key connection?"

"Patrick helped us, and he may be able to help us again. He owes me a string of favors in life after I knocked sense into him once upon a time when he was cheating on Sandrine. But due to the fact that our target has drastically changed with new developments in the last few days, I don't know how much he will be able to help us anymore," Parker answered.

"But how is Michel," he pronounced it the French way like *Michelle* in English after hearing Parker say it this way, "going to be able to help us?"

"You'll see," Parker said. His eyes were diverted and he rose in his chair to call out to a strapping young man walking up to the café. "Michel! *Comment ça va, mon vieux*?"

The young man approached Parker and they gripped hands in a firm handshake followed by a strong one arm hug. "*Bien, bien. Et toi*?"

"*Ah, pas mal, pas mal du tout. Je suis là, donc tu sais bien que je suis heureux*," Parker answered, explaining he was doing well and pleased to be back in the Basque Country. He turned to face Gibson and presented him as an old family friend. "*Je te présente*, John Gibson."

Michel extended a hand to Gibson, who rose to shake and then sat back down in his chair.

Parker continued speaking in French to Michel and their thin waitress appeared. Gibson correctly guessed Parker ordered drinks, because the waitress returned with a tray of three bottles of beer and three glasses. Michel and Parker smiled at each other as they filled their glasses and toasted, saying, *santé*.

The bottle of Kronenberg and the glass in front of Gibson remained untouched. After a few drinks of beer and standard pleasantries, Parker turned to business. He spoke in English for Gibson's sanity. "Michel, we need your help finding someone who I think is hiding out in Mauléon." Parker referred to the largest city in the province of Soule in the French Basque Country by the shortened name from the official full name of Mauléon-Licharre.

"Ah, who are you fucking with this time, Sebastian? Has Alaitz moved without telling you?" Michel replied, in perfect English, without much of a traceable accent. He playfully hit Parker in the shoulder and laughed at his joke.

"ETA," Parker said quickly and quietly. He made a point to pronounce the infamous three letters individually instead of the pronunciation Gibson heard used most of the time.

Michel's face turned hard. "Now that's a challenge worth a comparison to Alaitz, *mon ami*. Who are you looking for?"

"Tall, thin, blonde hair, strikingly sexy—her name is Graciana," Parker said, contemplatively.

"Graciana, huh?" Michel thought for a moment, and Gibson thought he saw the enlarged muscles of his neck tighten. "No. I don't know any Gracianas in Mauléon by that description. And as you know, I am acquainted with one or two people in Mauléon."

"Yes, I know you're connected there and that's exactly why I'm asking for your help. She wouldn't have been there long, very recently moved there. And they'll try to keep her out of sight, hidden."

Michel gazed intently at him. "How am I supposed to be able to find her then? Mauléon is small compared to most cities, but as you know, it's not just a village."

"Because I said they will *try* to keep her out sight. I have a feeling though that she will not stay out of sight for long." Parker paused to take a long drink of his glass of beer. "Besides, a girl like that will not go unnoticed compared to the country girls of Mauléon, no matter how much she tones herself down." He returned a punch to Michel's shoulder.

"You've met her?" Michel asked.

Parker nodded affirmatively. Michel shook his head. He turned to Gibson. "And they say we Frenchmen are the ones who are dangerous with *les filles*." He rose his glass in a toast. Gibson raised his empty glass to meet the other two. Parker and Michel polished off their glasses and, without looking at Gibson, Parker grabbed his beer and poured into Michel's glass and his own.

"And what about Alaitz?" Michel added.

"*Laisse tomber*," Parker said in response, telling him to drop the subject. He turned his back on the two of them and looked upward at the spires of the cathedral.

* * *

"Nivelle left a message at the front desk. He wants us to go over to his office and compare notes," Gibson said. He was seated next to Parker at their hotel's small bar.

Parker took a long drink from the glass of beer in front of him. "Why don't you tell Nivelle *va te faire foutre*," he replied, pronouncing the French expression slowly.

Gibson tried to reproduce the French words with little success. "What's that mean again?"

"It means, *go do yourself*, in a very explicit way."

"I'm sure that will go over well, Parker." Gibson scowled at him as a father would at a son for cursing. "As much as you may not like it, we do have to work with this guy."

Parker returned the scowl. "Fine, but diplomacy sucks." He finished off his beer. "Tell that asshole to meet us at L'Auberge des Pyrenees in Archanges for dinner in an hour. We've been seen walking into that damn gendarmerie enough."

"But won't people recognize him just as much in a restaurant as anywhere else?"

"Maybe not. Don't forget that this guy isn't normally stationed here, not in the last decade or so, anyway. He's from an office in Paris. I imagine he's regarded as France's finest, and that's why he was sent down here to watch us. People in the countryside here don't pay such close attention to current events, and there's a good chance no one will recognize him. And one thing for sure is that ETA's minions will not be looking for him, or us, in a sleepy countryside restaurant." He lit a cigarette and blew the smoke past Gibson's shoulder.

Gibson looked at him intently. "You're smarter than you look, Parker, but that's a nasty habit you've got there."

"*Va te faire foutre*," Parker said, smiling.

* * *

Graciana felt her body pound against the hard floor before she fully felt the pain of the man's hand backslapping her cheek. Rising defiantly, she faced the broad face with a long scar running along one cheek, shadowed by a black beret staring down at her. The stout man with the scar hit her again and, once again, she fell to the floor. When she rose, a stream of blood seeped from her nose. Instead of wiping it away, she let the blood run down her face and drip from her chin. Still defiant, she blew a kiss to the man standing in front of her. He responded by hitting her again, this time fully punching her in the mouth.

He'd been sent to the apartment in Mauléon to punish her after she was spotted at the Haika gathering. They moved her from Saint-Pée to Mauléon. No one said anything to her about the incident. But now she was hearing their disapproval.

She didn't bounce back up after another forceful punch. She had to lean on her side to spit out a puddle of blood. It felt as if a few teeth should have been included in the small pool on the floor. Coughing, she spat a last bit of blood from her mouth before once again rising to meet whatever was coming next.

This time she winked at him, to the best of her ability. Now it was his turn to smile. As he smiled, he rammed his fist into her stomach and she felt as if her insides were knocked out through her back. Doubling over in pain, she fell to her knees on the floor. The man with the scar approached her again.

In an instant, she pulled the small blade she had tucked in her jeans against her lower back and had it jammed against the base of his neck, right on his artery. The man slowly moved away from her and silently left the room.

Then she was alone.

Her body crumbled and she fell to the floor. After lying motionless for a few moments, she pulled herself across the dirty wooden floor to a small table in the corner of the room. Reaching up, she grabbed a box of cigarettes and a lighter on the table and carefully lit a cigarette.

Blood dripped from her nose and it hurt to exhale smoke through her nostrils. When she took the cigarette away from her mouth, the end was covered in red. Halfway propped against the wall, she sat on the floor smoking, ignoring the bleeding.

* * *

France Makes ETA Arrest

French anti-terrorism police have arrested a suspected senior member of the Basque separatist group, ETA, wanted by Spain for more than 15 years.

The man is accused of a series of bomb attacks in Spain in the 1970s and 1980s in which a number of police officers died.

The suspect was arrested at the home of a couple in Ciboure, near Saint-Jean-de-Luz, in France's Pyrenees-Atlantiques region. The man and woman, both teachers, were also detained.

French police said the suspect, an alleged explosives expert, would be taken to Paris for questioning, then extradited to Spain.

The Spanish Interior Minister told a news conference that ETA had recently recalled the man from hiding, somewhere in Latin America, most likely in Uruguay. "We are forcing them to recall people with a long history in ETA. We can see that the last cells have been made up of very young or very old people," he said.

It was the twelfth arrest of a suspected ETA member in France this year. Spain says it has arrested 58 people with suspected ETA links this year and dismantled six alleged terrorist cells and a civilian support group.

19

Basque Country, France

THE AIR HAD TURNED COOLER and there was not a cloud in the evening sky. They had been driving for about twenty minutes and were now deep into the dark countryside. Unlike during the day when the rolling hills of the Basque Country looked invitingly charming, at night they looked ominous and distrustful to Gibson.

"Do you think your friend is going to be able to find her?" Gibson asked, as Parker sped the car down the narrow two lane road.

"He might and then again, he might not," Parker said, shrugging his shoulders. "I just figured it was worth a shot because I trust him and because, after our mishap in our first attempt to get her, I think it goes without saying that we'd be damn lucky to get that close to her again," he added.

Gibson felt Parker's uneasiness growing the closer they came to their meeting with Capitaine Nivelle. "He's not that bad, you know. He's just doing his job," Gibson offered.

Parker glared at Gibson in the passenger seat. After turning back to see the road, he pulled out and lit a cigarette. "He's a glorified fascist."

Gibson decided to leave Parker and his mood alone. After ten more minutes of driving down tiny country roads, Parker turned off onto a small lane that led behind a convergence of hills to a large, brightly-lit farmhouse. Cautiously, Gibson stepped out of the car. Before closing the door, he looked around. Except for the farmhouse, there were no lights in any direction. The shadows of hills behind the building told him they were on the edge of a wide valley. The place must have a great view in the daytime, he thought.

Closing his door, Parker looked at Gibson over the top of the car. "I can imagine what you're thinking. And, yes, it's a spectacular view. Not only is there a sea of hills surrounding this place, but on a clear day you can see the highest peaks of the Pyrenees south of Pau over that way." He pointed in a direction off in the distance. "But the view now isn't bad either," he commented, pointing upward.

Looking up, Gibson noticed the brilliant display of stars. They seemed so bright one could reach up and touch them. "Not so bad, huh?" Parker asked, as he began walking to the building.

"I've only seen stars like this in remote places in the U.S." Gibson commented. He briskly walked to catch up with Parker.

"I'm telling you, this is a special place and I'm just happy not too many Americans know about it. If that were the case, they would probably just rape it like they have the Côte D'Azur," Parker said, holding open the door to the restaurant.

"Don't you mean *we* would rape it, Parker?" Gibson asked, receiving no response.

As he stepped into the converted house, he was struck by an intense wave of rich aromas. Filling the air was a blend of cooking meat and thick wine sauces overwhelming his nostrils. He was instantly hungry. Essentially, the restaurant was a wide open room with high ceilings and large stone fireplaces on both sides. There was a pair of sizeable windows at the back. The walls were painted white and had sparse adornments. Tables were scattered throughout the room, nearly all full, and despite the plainness of the place, Gibson found it cozy and comfortable.

But it was not inviting.

As they entered the restaurant, every eye turned on them for a brief glance. The looks were not hostile, they just were not friendly. Gibson was getting used to this look the more time he spent in the Basque Country. He began referring to it as the *Basque look*. Recognizing that they were foreigners, the eyes quickly turned away and the groups sitting near the front of the room, where they were standing, switched languages from French to Basque.

A large, stout woman emerged from a doorway at the back of the room. After unloading a tray of steaming plates she was carrying, she approached and asked in French if she could help them. Parker responded, in Basque, that he'd called earlier to reserve a table for three. The woman's round face went from revealing no particular emotion to lighting up with a broad smile after she heard Parker speaking Basque. Turning, she led them to a table in front of a back window and quickly brought a carafe of red wine and three wine glasses to their table. When she skirted away between the tables, Gibson glanced around and realized she was the only hostess or waitress for the entire restaurant of some twenty tables.

Gibson watched Parker pour himself a glass of wine from the carafe. "Did you even ask for that?" When he spoke, those sitting at tables closest to them peered over at them, then returned to their own conversations.

"Nope. This place is pretty old school Basque. There's one wine, red Irouleguy in a carafe, and there's one fixed menu with hearty Basque food. The menu is different every night, often based on season."

"But what if there were some sort of seafood or fish on the menu some night? Aren't you supposed to only drink white wine with fish?" Gibson asked.

"Ah, yes, so the gastronomically inclined French say. But a lot of Basques see the French as many Americans do—snotty. My general impression of the Basque people has always been that they don't try and hide their desire to drink by covering it with an elated appreciation of wine," Parker explained. He toasted himself and took a long drink from what was not a delicate wine glass, but rather a short, thick-bottomed glass.

"I think people like the French, Basques, Spanish and you just get a little buzz from your wine and then everything you eat tastes good."

Parker looked at him as he finished the rest of his glass. Pouring himself another glass, he said, "That's certainly about the most stereotypical American view you've yet expressed in words. By the way, would you like a glass?"

Shaking his head, Gibson said, "I'll have a glass once we have food in front of us. But you'd better take it easy. I don't want you going off on our old buddy once he gets here."

Lighting a cigarette, Parker blew out a line of smoke that curled upwards. "I would only agree to meet with that *putain* jackass if two things were involved—great wine and food."

Gibson shook his head. "I guess they haven't banned smoking in restaurants yet in France?" he asked.

"Actually, they have in many places, just apparently not here. Or maybe they did ban smoking to appease some annoying civil servant, and just don't actually care," Parker replied through a breath of smoke.

* * *

Nivelle heavily made his way into the restaurant thirty minutes later. Once again, all eyes in the wide room turned to judge the figure standing in the doorway. And once again, every eye turned away without noticeable comment. Parker noticed every table conversation around them immediately switched to Basque once Nivelle was seen. These tables had gradually converted back to French after he and Gibson were initially seated.

Spotting them, Nivelle carefully maneuvered himself between the tables to them. Not one diner he passed made an effort to move their chair forward to ease his passing. Gibson rose to shake the man's hand as he approached their table, while Parker remained seated. Nivelle looked down at him, muttering something to himself as he sat down at the table.

"What makes you think this was a great place for us to meet?" Nivelle asked Parker in French.

Parker grabbed his glass and raised it to Nivelle, quickly downing the wine. He spoke in English. "I don't think it's a great place for us to meet, but I also don't think anywhere at this point would be very safe for us to meet. I imagine we are safer here than we would be at the Quick or McDonald's in Bayonne."

Parker looked hard at Nivelle and grabbed a Chesterfield Light from his box on the table. Lighting the cigarette, he added, "And I would recommend you impress Gibson here by speaking English tonight. I know that like most French people you can, but just don't out of commonly accepted principle of disgust with American culture invading your country. And besides, it's a relatively safe language for us to use here."

Knowing Parker was correct, Nivelle sneered, but refused to acknowledge Parker's foresight. However, in English he asked, "What can you tell me?"

Suddenly, the waitress set three steaming large bowls of *axoa* in front of them. She was gone before they even had time to register she'd been there. Nivelle prodded at the bowl of murky colored, non-ascetically pleasing mashed veal stew with his spoon.

"You French are too concerned with food's presentation. You should give all that a rest from time to time and just appreciate food for its taste," Parker commented.

Reluctantly, Nivelle tried the soupy substance, but quickly dropped his spoon next to his bowl after tasting it, indicating with a scowl that he would be trying no more. Parker smiled at him as he finished his own bowl and then took Nivelle's, finishing it off as well. Gibson, trying to be as diplomatic as possible, ate all his *axoa* without saying a word to the other two. Although he thought Nivelle was crazy to have given up such a delicious dish.

Once there was not one speck of *axoa* left on their table, and the plates had been almost simultaneously cleared, they began to discuss the current status of the case.

"We have one of them, one of them is dead, and every policeman and gendarme in France has the description of that little *salope*. I think we shall soon find her. And you, what do you think about the other one?" Nivelle asked, staring pointedly at Parker.

Parker noticed how uncomfortable Nivelle looked, forced to speak English. He fought off the urge to laugh by balling his fists under the table. "To be honest, I think she will be the hardest to find. I don't think you will ever find her unless she screws up somehow," he managed to say without laughing. He sipped the glass of green Izarra the ever moving waitress had put down in front of him almost instantly after he had asked her for one.

"Screws up?" Nivelle inquired with a confused look on his face.

"*Se foutre dans la merde*," Parker translated.

"Ah, and please tell me why you say this?" Nivelle asked.

"Because I think she's the most dangerous one of them. She could disguise herself and present as a law-abiding waitress in Bayonne and no one would ever know any better." Parker downed the rest of the green liquor and felt its slow burn down his throat.

"You sound as if you are, how do you say, *infatuated*, with her." Nivelle pronounced the word slowly. Gibson felt himself stiffen in preparation of having to stop Parker from lunging across the table.

Instead, Parker only laughed and motioned to the waitress for another glass of Izarra. "No, I think the better word would be *impressed.* She did make us look like fools back there."

"We shall see who's laughing when I catch her," Nivelle said, malignantly.

Inwardly, Parker felt a tinge of fear for Graciana at the thought of Nivelle having his way with her behind a closed door. He quickly hid the feeling away.

Parker stared directly into Nivelle's dark, narrow eyes. "Have you figured out yet that we're not really after ETA?"

Nivelle shrugged his shoulders and made a face as if to say he didn't care. "What difference does it make?" he said, as he took a swallow of wine.

"The difference it makes is that I'm not sure we can blame ETA for this, and neither should any press release that you send out," Parker confrontationally replied.

"You think you are so smart, Monsieur Parker," Nivelle said, tapping the rim of his wine glass with his fingers. "Of course, I've realized we are after a group of adolescents and that they are most likely members of Haika. But if you will remember, both the French and Spanish governments outlawed Haika a few years ago because of its links to ETA. Therefore, we view them as one and the same. It makes no difference how old a terrorist is—they are still a terrorist and should be dealt with like a terrorist.

"Your State Department must view this the same way, otherwise you would not still be here," Nivelle taunted.

Parker clenched his jaw, but said nothing, much to the disappointment of Nivelle who was trying to lead him into a return comment he could use against him.

Wanting to ease the mounting tension at the table, Gibson spoke up. He also wanted to change the subject as he had not actually told DC of the indirect connection to ETA. He didn't want to be taken off the case for some political nonsense over terminology. "There's still another one, though."

"Yes, but I think they have kept him somewhere in Spain in order to keep them separated as much as possible," Parker said, after taking a deep breath to calm himself.

Shaking his head in agreement, Nivelle said, "Sometimes you are too much of a sentimentalist, Monsieur Parker. But you do have your moments when you show some intelligence." Then, turning directly to Gibson, he said, "I have notified the authorities in Spain. They are on the search and questioning people as we speak. Apparently, we have a lead in Madrid. I will be going there tomorrow. Would you two wish to accompany me?"

Gibson was about to respond affirmatively, but Parker interrupted him. "Thank you for the offer, but I think we would be better serving our case if Gibson and I follow up with my lead in San Sebastian." He could feel Gibson staring at him reproachfully, but didn't look at him. Parker was positive this was the right decision.

Nodding his head, Nivelle said, "As you wish. I have your mobile number and you have mine, so please call me if you are able to discover anything on your little trip. I will do the same."

Nivelle began to stand up from his chair, then remembered something and sat back down. He lifted a single finger as if to request their full attention. "There is one more thing I should mention to you both. Knowing that this operation may have indeed been carried out by mere teenagers, one has to suspect they had even more support than what they may have received from ETA cells here." He paused and, with his gaze fixated on the center of the table, continued, "I think you will have work to do once you return to your country."

Gibson shot a glance at Parker and responded. "Yes, we are aware of this, and I have notified our superiors of this possibility."

With a nod of his head, Nivelle rose and left, cutting through the room like a knife. They watched him leave the restaurant before speaking again.

"Do I have permission to punch him in his arrogant face when we're done?" Parker asked.

"I think I'll be driving back to the hotel, Parker," Gibson said, doing his best to conceal a small grin.

Parker tossed him the car keys and shrugged in capitulation. "*Comme tu veux, mon vieux.*"

* * *

Lopé sat in a chair and glared at the two large men standing in front of him. They were representative of the wing of the organization in charge of dealing with the troubles that arose among members. All these people were the same, Lopé thought, with expressionless eyes and zero personality. Their orders were given from those at the top, and they did exactly what they were told. It could be argued that it was due to their threatening brutality that ETA had remained such a tight organization for so long. They did their work well.

He wouldn't have been surprised if he found out they were the ones who had killed Aurelion. Even though he knew he would get nowhere arguing with them, he refused to give in without a fight. "So why do I have to leave Madrid?" he spat out in Spanish.

"Because those are your orders," replied a brusque voice in Basque. Lopé couldn't tell which man had spoken. They both stood before him as if inseparable.

"But why must I leave here? I will be in just as much danger in Bilbao or Malaga or Barcelona."

"There are Americans looking for you," said one.

"And we can't let them catch you," the other said, as he touched something hard pressed against his chest under his jacket.

"Americans! You are scared of Americans? They can't find who they are looking for in their own fucking country!" Lopé quickly responded.

"Maybe so, but they caught Peio. They say one of them is different."

"So why don't you find and kill that one? That would take care of our problems."

"We can't kill an American. Not now. That would create a perfect excuse for the Spanish and French governments to move into our lands with all their force, because they would have the backing of the Americans."

Lopé looked at the thick figure that had spoken with astonishment. "Wow! I didn't know you could talk that much," he sarcastically said. He lit a Gauloise.

"Stupid punk kids like you need a good kick in the ass every once in a while. You could ruin over thirty years of work and you don't even recognize it," one of the hefty men told him.

"Where are you sending me, then?" demanded Lopé

"You're being sent to a safe house in Paris. Now gather your things. You're to leave immediately. We have word that someone has leaked information on your presence in Spain," one of them replied.

"Well I hope you've taken care of that person."

"He will be dealt with, in time."

"I hate Paris," Lopé said, as he moved to the bedroom to gather the few articles of clothing he had with him. Then he turned to glare at the two men with snarling suspicion. "You sure you're not just taking me for a ride into the mountains?"

"We would love nothing more, Lopé," one of them said, sizing him up.

"However, someone at the top likes you for some reason and we're not even allowed to rough you up a little, unfortunately," the other replied contemptuously.

Lopé smiled at the two big ugly men. His incisors revealed themselves, making him look like a wolf. "Good. Then I can tell you both to go to hell."

One of the men opened the door and pushed Lopé through it into a cascade of sunlight.

* * *

Donostia. San Sebastian. However one called it, Gibson couldn't get over the absolute beauty of the city's location. With the nearly enclosed harbor and the Pyrenees shooting up behind it, the city reminded him of a fortress. As they exited the highway into the city, Parker told him that in centuries past, the residents were able to fight off invading pirates from the ocean due to the city's geographic layout.

As they turned onto a street that followed along the half-moon beach lining the harbor, Gibson spotted the remains of a castle high above on a cliff overlooking the entrance to the city. Couples walked along the edge of the calm surf hitting the lightly colored, sandy beach. People of all ages lined the sidewalk set between the beach and the street. Some were skateboarding, some were comfortably flirting, and some were just walking to be seen.

Even though they had driven a little over a half hour from the time they met up with Patrick in a parking lot in Anglet, everything looked different as soon as they crossed over the French-Spanish border. Even though he knew the borders had been opened between the two countries years earlier, as in much of the rest of Europe, Gibson was still surprised to just pass through the border as if driving from state to state in the U.S.

Across the border, the signs were primarily in Basque, then in Spanish, whereas they had been in French and then Basque in the French Basque country. But everything about this city seemed different. Older. Even the air seemed older and more polluted than north across the border.

While passing by a border town on the Spanish side named Fonterrabi, Parker pointed out a small castle on a slight rise at the edge of the downtown area of the city. He told Gibson that Ernest Hemingway often kept a room in the now converted hotel.

Gibson was not impressed. Hemingway may have been a great author, but he was also too much of a dreamer in Gibson's opinion. He remembered having to read *For Whom the Bell Tolls* for a high school English class and he remembered thinking Hemingway had been much too sympathetic for a bunch of communists. A spade of worry ran through him as he realized that some things about Sebastian Parker reminded him of how he felt about Hemingway.

Patrick turned off the street following the beach into the inner city. The architecture of the buildings was more Baroque than it had been across the border. Gibson also noticed the buildings had a darker appearance, due to an outer layer of grayish soot coating them from sidewalk to roof.

Parking the car, all three of them got out of the vehicle. Gibson gauged his surroundings. It appeared to him as a typical modern European city. Parker muttered to Gibson that soon they would be walking into the pedestrian, old quarter of the city where he would undoubtedly notice a change.

Gibson didn't fully comprehend what Parker said to him until they crossed a busy street and stepped into what could have been considered a different city.

The streets and sidewalks became narrower. Looking up, Gibson noticed the sunlight couldn't penetrate through the rows of low balcony-lined buildings. As it was a pedestrian area, they walked in the middle of the worn cobblestone street. It made Gibson feel uneasily vulnerable. He sensed eyes were watching them from covered windows. Few people were on the streets and when they did come across any, eyes and faces were averted. Shopkeepers turned away from them as they passed by their storefronts.

Perhaps the most remarkable difference was that, whereas before they had been in a Spanish Basque city, now they found themselves in a strictly Basque city. The only language to be heard was Basque, and most of the storefronts were written in the ancient language as well. Then, there were the flags. So many Basque flags were flying from the balconies that, looking up at times, one could only see a blur of the Basque colors: red, green and white.

Gibson also noticed not only was graffiti everywhere on the walls of buildings, including the letters ETA above the image of a snake curling around an axe, but there were even posters hanging along the street wherever possible that spelled out the three infamous letters.

Parker casually admitted to him that they were walking into what was considered the most hostile area of the entire Basque Country.

As they rounded an exceptionally narrow bend in the road, a space opened up in front of them, wide enough for the sun to sneak in and bake the stones paving the square. Gibson was glad to see life did in fact exist in this place. Cafés followed the edge of the square with shaded tables outside each. Most of the tables were full with lunch diners or people having a drink and it was difficult for Gibson to spot someone not smoking. Children played soccer in the center of the square. One curly haired young boy purposefully kicked the ball toward a table occupied by two nicely dressed, elegant women engrossed in animated conversation. The boy ran over to the table and profusely apologized to the women, while the other boys laughed at him. The ladies barely noticed him and resumed their conversation.

After passing by a large, darkened cathedral at the end of the square, the three men turned into what looked more like an alley than a street. Here, the walls of the buildings were so close on either side that Gibson felt an overbearing sense of claustrophobia. He noticed they were moving into an even more secluded section of the city as their steps echoed down the nearly deserted street, and he was happy to soon reach their destination.

But it wasn't much of a destination. One couldn't quite call it a bar, as there was no actual bar. The walls were bare and even if it had been full, Gibson had the impression it would still feel cold inside. A few scattered tables filled the small, smoky room that had only one small window open to the street. Two of the tables at the rear of the room were occupied by a group of older men in black berets playing cards, smoking, and drinking. The card players didn't even bother looking at them. At the front of the room the tables were empty.

They sat down at one of the empty tables. Both Parker and Patrick sat nonchalantly, and it bothered Gibson that he couldn't be as relaxed. They both smoked while he sat impatiently tapping his fingers against his leg. Ten minutes later, a man appeared from the doorway carrying a bottle of unlabeled red wine and three glasses. Without saying anything, he placed the bottle and glasses on their table, then walked away.

Parker and Patrick promptly helped themselves to the bottle, but Gibson refused by placing his hand over the glass in front of him. Parker leaned over to him and said in a voice barely above a whisper, "Do I need to remind you where we are and that you would obviously be viewed as suspect if you refuse the wine?" Parker winked at him, making Gibson want to smack him. Instead, he let his glass be filled and took a sip of the wine.

Since the bottle was unlabeled, he envisioned the wine being as potent as motor oil, but surprisingly, he tasted a wine full of exploding flavors. Seeing the shocked look on his face, Parker told him that the wine was likely from the private stock of a nearby vineyard.

With growing impatience, Gibson sat and watched Patrick and Parker polish of the bottle. Occasionally, he would look back at the few crammed tables at the rear of the room, but it didn't appear as though anyone was paying them any attention.

When they were finished with the wine, Parker and Patrick rose, leaving a few euros on the table. Parker nodded at Gibson, letting him know it was time to leave. Dumbfounded, Gibson silently followed the two out the doors and back into the dim, narrow street. With no explanation, they walked in front of him, leading back the way they had come. Not wanting to announce his apparent inability to keep up with what was happening, he said nothing as he followed behind. He did notice though they were walking a little more swaggeringly than before they had gone in the bar.

To his surprise, once they returned to the open square, they turned to the cathedral's entrance. Gibson grabbed Parker's arm, bringing him to a halt, and Patrick stopped to stare at Gibson like he was an idiot. "Why are we going into the cathedral?

Patrick stared at him, clearly annoyed. Parker smiled at him, clearly amused. "We are going into the cathedral because someone is going to meet us inside. He was back there in the bar, and all we did was let him know we are here to meet with him. Okay?" Parker talked like he was admitting some forlorn secret to a child and it pissed Gibson off all the more. Yet, he said nothing and let go of Parker's arm.

As they passed through the heavy, wooden doors of the cathedral, day instantly went to dusk, and they were swallowed by the shadows within. The darkness swiftly subsided, and Gibson quickly noted the differences between the interior of this cathedral and the cathedral in Bayonne. Though the décor was similarly gothic, this cathedral felt more Catholic to him. Crosses lined the walls as in Bayonne, yet here the center focus of the cathedral was the giant, glinting gold wall of the saints adorning the front. The gold cast off such a bright glow that he was surprised he had sensed darkness when first entering the cathedral.

Parker and Patrick made their way into a small antechamber and sat at the rear of a line of benches. Gibson sat down next to Parker, who quickly got up and sat on the far side of him. Only an old woman, wearing a shawl over her head, shared the room with them. She was in the first row of benches with her head bent in prayer. After a few silent moments, she rose and lit a candle beneath the feet of a statue of Jesus in front of her. She slowly shuffled off into the vastness of the quiet cathedral.

They sat. Silent. Waiting.

Gibson looked over Parker's shoulder one moment and saw nothing. The next moment he looked, there was an older man sitting directly behind Parker, leaning forward, with hands held together on his knees. Gibson didn't know how the old man had snuck behind them so easily without him noticing, but from one quick glimpse, he knew it was the same man Parker had met with at the pelote match in Bayonne.

"I don't trust this man. Why is he here?" Eduardo Javier Munoz whispered in French, speaking into his hands.

"I trust him. But just keep speaking in French then, because he doesn't know a word of it," Parker replied in a quiet voice, with his hands clenched at his chest and his head looking upward.

"I don't believe you. Even the American government wouldn't be so stupid as to send someone here who did not at least speak some French." Again, Munoz spoke into his hands, yet this time with nervousness apparent in his voice.

"Watch this, then." Parker straightened his neck and turned to Gibson, who was trying not to look completely lost. "Gibson, *tu manges la merde des chiens.*" Both Munoz and Patrick had to suppress a chuckle at Parker's comment to Gibson that he ate dog shit while Gibson continued to look helplessly lost in the whole situation. "*Voyez?*"

"*D'accord. D'accord.*" Munoz managed to blurt out that the point was proven through his clenched teeth that held back laughter at both Parker's comment and Gibson's clueless expression. "I can't help you find the girl. She broke off on her own and no one knows where she is. Right now, she's in as much danger from you all as she is from the other side."

Parker had to bite his lower lip to keep from showing the small smile he felt growing as he heard Munoz talk of Graciana. "But there's another," he said, once again tilting his head to look heaven bound.

"Yes, there is another, and I would like nothing more for you to catch the bastard," Munoz menacingly replied.

"Why?" Parker asked, a little surprised.

Munoz reflected on the seemingly simple question for a few minutes. "Because, the last thing we need now is for radicals like him to spring up and inspire others to follow in his footsteps. We've tried this approach. I know, better than anyone. Many lives were lost, precisely because what he represents is not how we will achieve anything".

"But you were like him at one time," Parker said instinctively.

Even though Gibson couldn't follow the conversation, he understood the boldness of Parker's statement by the sudden turn of Patrick's head and the look of astonishment on his face as he glanced at Parker with unconcealed, utter reproach.

Parker knew he'd committed a faux pas, yet he didn't try to cover his ass by quickly responding with a soothing comeback. Instead, he continued looking upward, eyes wide open, waiting.

Gibson wanted so much to turn and see the look on Munoz's face. He was sure Parker had just knocked the old terrorist off his feet. The thought made Gibson proud of Parker. Now it was his turn to fight off a grin.

There was complete silence in the cathedral until someone bumped into one of the wooden benches causing a screeching echo throughout the interior.

Munoz eventually responded, in a frail voice that revealed his years, even if one didn't understand the language he was speaking. "Yes, I was like Lopé, but times are different now. Most all of us now know that his way is not going to get us anywhere. In the 60s and 70s, violence was all we knew. We had two dictators to deal with. The one that was in Spain is well known. The one that was in France is not. They were both terrible tyrants for the Basque people though."

Parker wasted no time. He'd heard a name. "I understand." He purposefully paused, then asked, "And where would we find this Lopé?"

"In Paris. He was just moved there. I don't have an exact address to give you, nor do I know anyone who can help you there. The ones in Paris are perhaps the most radical of us all. Our operations in Spain and France have been run from there for years. Everyone always looks to Madrid, San Sebastian, Barcelona or Bayonne for the leaders, when most of the time they have been in Paris."

Sighing, Parker asked, "So what can you do to help us?"

"I have written down the addresses of the most recent safe houses I could find in the city. He won't be in one of these places, but the strategy has always been to move people a couple of houses away from the previous spot. So wherever he is won't be far from one of these places. One would think the French would have caught onto this long ago, but it doesn't seem they have." Munoz breathed deeply. "The French!" he venomously added as he handed Parker a sheet of paper.

Parker glanced at the scribbled addresses. "Ah, Montmartre," he commented.

"Yes. It seems to be a good place to remain anonymous in Paris. It's been that way for decades," Munoz absently offered.

Lowering his head, Parker stared into the eyes of the wooden Jesus Christ on display in front of them. He sat that way, motionless, barely breathing, until he uttered, "I know. I once lived there for a time."

By the time the words crossed his lips, there was no one left sitting on the bench behind them. In fact, they could see no one else in the cathedral beside themselves. Gibson felt like asking for a translation of the conversation, but it was too quiet to speak.

An eerie stillness crept slowly through them as they listened to the echo of their footsteps bouncing off the stone walls of the interior as they walked out into the now overcast gloomy day. Not one of them said a word until they were back in Patrick's car driving north on the highway, knowing they would soon be heading back to the land of revolutions and wine—back to France.

* * *

"What now?" Gibson finally asked.

Lighting a cigarette before answering, Parker said, "When we get back to the hotel, you should get a hold of Nivelle and tell him all that happened today, but leave out Patrick's and Munoz's names. Those are things he doesn't need to know and besides, it will seriously bother him not knowing. I suppose we should head to Paris tomorrow morning," he added, with obvious discomfort.

Gibson looked at him, astonished. "But, Parker, I thought you hated Nivelle, and now you want to go up to Paris to help him? And besides, we don't even have a full name yet."

Parker replied with an unhidden scowl, "I do detest the *connard*, but I also want to catch the other *connards* and right now we know one of them is in Paris. I don't need Nivelle down here, but Paris is a different world. Actually, it's a different world from all the rest of France." Parker paused to puff on his cigarette before adding, "Come to think of it, it's a different world from most places. And I also think this guy may be able to give us a lead on our mystery individual back in the States."

Giving him a questioning look, Gibson exclaimed with fake surprise, "Wow, I would have thought issues in the States wouldn't be good enough to concern you."

Parker turned in his seat to fully glare at Gibson. "Gibson, sometimes I really want to punch you. As far as the name, I have all I need to figure it out. You're just going to have to trust me to go out by myself tonight to fill in the blanks. There is someone who will be able to tell me what we need to know."

Gibson wanted to respond that he knew the feeling all too well, but held back.

"But you want to go there with Nivelle?" Gibson asked after they had been on the road awhile and could see the towering gothic spires of the Sainte-Marie Cathedral of Bayonne approaching.

Parker halfway glanced at Gibson. "Of course I don't want to go there because of Nivelle, but Paris is his territory and I don't know many people that are still there. And to be perfectly honest, I doubt I can do much good there without him. In Paris, he will have his full strength of support available."

Growing annoyed by not receiving a straight answer, Gibson asked, "Then why would we ever go to Paris? I thought you told me before we came here that this *Piece Basque* was your favorite part of France."

"We'll go because Paris in the springtime is not to be missed," Parker said, through a smile. Then he began singing. "I love Paris in the spring time. I love Paris in the fall…"

Gibson cut him off with a loud yell, "Parker!"

"Oh, you remind me of a *vielle* sometimes," Parker retorted. Patrick laughed. Thinking to ask what a *vielle* was, Gibson decided he'd been embarrassed enough for the moment. Instead, he bore his eyes into the side of Parker's skull, waiting for a real response.

"We need to be there when Nivelle catches this one. If we want to find Graciana, I think this is the way to do it. And the *Pays Basque*," he said, putting extra emphasis on the proper pronunciation even though he was impressed Gibson even made an attempt at the French words, "is the best part of France by far, but I still love Paris as well."

They came to a roundabout and Parker accelerated into the curve, making Gibson grab onto his seat as the car went around the circle and turned off abruptly onto another road.

After composing himself, Gibson asked, "What makes you so sure Nivelle will catch this one in Paris?"

Parker tossed his cigarette butt out the cracked window before replying. "Because I think the one in Paris is the leader of our little group. I also think that ETA, and its subsidiary IK, are both very divided organizations with so many inner factions that they're constantly fighting among themselves. I know this is the case with a lot of organizations, but I tell you, if ETA were not so unstable on account of its own inner struggles, I doubt there would be anything known as the Basque Conflict today, as the conflict would be resolved. By the way, it's regarded as Europe's oldest war."

"Why would it be resolved?" Gibson asked.

A red light forced Parker to stop the car. He lit another cigarette, then explained. "Because it's quite possible that if they hadn't been so divided after Franco's death, they would have whipped Spain's ass into granting them independence. After that, there would have been no way for the French to not grant the French Basque Country at least some form of high level autonomy."

In the back seat of the car, Patrick nodded approval of Parker's predictions.

"Hold on, though, Parker. Your theories are very interesting, as always," he said mockingly, "but what does all this have to do with us going to Paris?"

"I don't think I'll be able to find Graciana without a lot of luck and some help. I've pretty much used up all the contacts I have down here. There's a chance, even if just a small one, that we may get lucky in that some group who wants this person caught in Paris will get a hold of him first."

Gibson felt relieved to finally understand where Parker was leading. "So, you think it's possible someone or some faction may have gotten to this guy who wants him to go down?"

Parker shrugged his shoulders as he took a turn onto a narrow road lined with parked cars.

Gibson thought about asking why not just kill him like they did the last guy? Before he did though, he answered his own question. Considering the various factions within the organization, having someone moved to a location where they knew the person would be caught, could be used as a double-edged sword. "But why Paris?"

"Even though I'm sure Munoz is right that a lot of ETA operatives are in and out of Paris all the time, if you look at the headlines over the years, a ton of its top members have been arrested in Paris." Parker blew a line of smoke. "Why exactly Paris, though, I honestly don't know. But, at the same time, if you recall history, Paris is a city where they guillotined their own king once upon a time."

"The French!" Gibson shook his head as he unknowingly reflected Munoz's words from earlier in the day.

"And Nivelle is going to know exactly who to look for after tonight. Go ahead and tell him the name we were told, Lopé, but this could be some sort of a nickname, and I'll soon find out the full name of our mystery guy," Parker added.

Gibson didn't approve. "I don't like the idea of you going off on your own again. I know you think this is all a game, but you're going to get yourself killed. ETA is as brutal as any organization I've come up against, and I think you're treading a thin line here."

"Don't worry. I'll be fine." Then noticing Gibson's grave expression, Parker lightly punched him in the shoulder. "I love Paris in the spring time…" Parker sang as they drove across the Nive River into Petit Bayonne.

* * *

Lights from the shops and restaurants near the small inlet revealed the brilliantly painted colors of fishing boats waiting for their skippers to steer them into the turbulent Atlantic. The boats swayed and bobbed gently in the water. Watching the water bounce against the hull of a small vessel in front of him, Parker fell into a reverie on what it would be like to have the life of a fisherman. At least then everything would be so much more simple and defined.

Alaitz would be meeting him any minute and when he thought of her, he thought of the impeding ocean out beyond the fortified banks of the harbor protecting Saint-Jean-de-Luz. The ocean was so impenetrable and dark and full of secrets. Thoughts of seeing her made him feel elated and ill at the same time. He heard soft footsteps approaching from behind. He didn't have to turn around—he knew it was Alaitz.

"Why are we here, Sebastian?" came a softly English-accented voice into the chilled, salty air.

"Yes, why are we are here, Alaitz?" he responded, without turning to face her.

The footsteps came closer. "Don't play games, *mon amour*. You know this could be dangerous for both of us."

Parker had only heard two words and the rest fell empty into the night. "*Mon amour*?" he repeated.

He turned around to face her and found her directly behind him. His body was inches from hers and he could smell her sweet perfume that he knew so well. Closing his eyes he asked, "When did I become that?"

Alaitz leaned into him and pressed her lips to his, finding his unresponsive and cold. She pulled away and sighed, turning her head, telling him how he'd always been a fool. "*Tu es con, Sebastian. Tu étais toujours.*"

Hearing her words made Parker's heart skip a beat. He felt a tingling in his chest and his legs felt numb. He grabbed her and held her against him as tightly as he could. It felt as if he was holding his world together by holding on to her. His hands pressed against her small back, her gentle hair touched his face. She breathed softly on his shoulder. He felt his body begin shaking and tears building in his eyes.

"I'm sorry," she whispered.

* * *

ETA Claims San Sebastian Bombing

The Basque separatist guerilla group, ETA, says it was responsible for the killing of a policeman in a northern Spanish province. In a statement, the group said it planted the bomb that exploded outside the city of San Sebastian as police tried to take down a pro-ETA flag.

The attack prompted protests from tens of thousands of people in the northern city of Pamplona.

ETA also said it considered Spain's governing right-wing party and the socialist opposition to be military targets because of their efforts to ban the pro-independence Basque party, Batasuna-alleged to be ETA's political wing.

A new law, which seeks to ban political groups backing extremist violence, won overwhelming support recently in the Spanish parliament.

20

Paris, France

THOUGH KNOWN as the City of Lights, or even the City of Love, Gibson renamed it the City of Dog Shit. Everywhere he stepped along the narrow sidewalks, he felt he needed to look down to make sure he wasn't stepping into a present left by some snooty Parisian poodle. The people walking along the streets of Paris didn't make the situation any easier. From his life in DC, he was familiar with people running into each other because they were in too big a hurry to get somewhere. Here in Paris, no one seemed to be in a hurry; they just didn't care if they got in your way.

It was maddening how Parker could glide so easily along, without noticeably looking down to see where he was stepping, or having a single incident of running into someone coming either from the opposite direction or someone walking at the pace of a boiled turtle in front of them. In under an hour, Gibson had stepped in two piles of dog crap and been scoffed at numerous times by passersby he kept running into despite his efforts to avoid them.

Everything about Sebastian Parker made him insanely upset at times.

After passing through a group of people with the ease of running water, Parker spun on his heels and smiled at Gibson's ill-fated attempts to avoid a collision. Since their arrival in Paris that morning, Gibson noticed something different about Parker. It wasn't that Parker seemed happier, as he was definitely happy in the Basque Country, most of the time. But something was different about him—almost as if being in the city kick-started something hidden within him that gave a spring to his step and a slyness to his smile. Clearly, Paris fit him and he fit Paris.

Parker kept walking. Gibson thought he would never stop. Parker told him they were going to go for a quick walk to clear their heads. He wanted a little time before contacting Nivelle after their short flight from Biarritz to Paris and an expensive cab ride from the airport to their hotel. But it was no short walk. Gibson's legs were beginning to feel as if they were going to fall off.

Thankfully, Parker stopped on a little pedestrian bridge crossing a narrow canal cutting straight through the low city buildings. Glancing up, Gibson noticed a sign by the side of the bridge that read Canal Saint-Martin. Green trees lined the banks of the canal, overshadowing walkways on both sides. Standing in the sunlight, Parker gazed down the canal, lost in deep thought. A young looking, handsome couple stood next to them, hand in hand, looking out but mostly stealing glances of each other.

A low boat crammed with people approached them on the canal. A contingent of small boys lined the upper deck. The boys pointed to the couple and waved. Seeing them, the couple smiled and waved back, not wanting to let the aspiring young romantic Frenchmen down. Then they looked deeply into one another's eyes, smiled, and embraced in a long, slow kiss. The two seemed to become one as they held each other, breathing as one. Having done this just as the boat was passing beneath the bridge, the boys ripped into applause as they watched the couple and dreamed of future sweethearts. By the time the boat had passed to the other side of the bridge, the boys all ran to the rear of the boat to wave at the couple who waved back.

Despite the years of hardness that had grown around his heart, the touching scene, which could have been in a movie, made Gibson smile. He lightly elbowed Parker standing next to him, as he would to an old friend to nod approval of those young and in love.

But Parker did not return the nod. Instead, paleness had overcome his handsome face. He looked as if on the verge of being sick over the side of the bridge's rail.

Parker fiercely glared at the disappearing waving boys and then turned to shoot a spiteful glance at the young couple. But they were gone. It was as if they had vanished into thin air.

Confused as ever, Gibson motioned for Parker to have a cigarette. Parker shook his head, turned, and continued walking across the bridge.

They walked without speaking underneath a continuous line of rooftops and characterless buildings. Puzzled at Parker's mood, which did not improve, Gibson noticed pronounced creases on the younger man's forehead.

After crossing the bridge, Parker slowed his pace a little, looking down but seeing nothing. He was thinking of something and it was preoccupying him so much he actually stumbled every once in a while on a crack in the sidewalk. Something Gibson had not seen him do all day.

Gibson wondered what dark thoughts were consuming the younger man so much that he wasn't even bothering to pull out his cigarettes and smoke his way through them. He tried not to see Parker's sour face next to him, but it was hard not to notice. Normally, Parker was full of life, unless he was hung over, and even then, mostly, still animated. Whatever was going through his head seemed to be slowly dragging him downward. Gibson tried to think of the right thing to say, but couldn't. He knew that pain walked better in silence.

* * *

They walked hand in hand from the docks into the heart of the city of Saint-Jean-de-Luz. It was a Friday night and downtown was crowded with locals and tourists. Everyone was jovial, drinking his or her aperitif or having dinner in open patio seating along the cobblestone *zone piétonne*. The air was fresh, with a touch of the ocean's saltiness.

In between cigarettes, Parker breathed in the air and smelled both the vastness of the ocean and the ruggedness of the mountains. He could also lean slightly and catch an intoxicating scent of Alaitz walking next to him. Dreams don't smell this nice, he thought. For a moment, he was good with the world and everything was perfect.

"Let's have paella," Alaitz suggested.

"Great idea," he replied.

Soon, they sat down at a table in a fenced off area of the street that served as a patio in front of a small restaurant. Moments later, a young woman came out of the restaurant to take their order. They ordered paella, rosé wine, and pastis as an aperitif. The waitress nodded approval and quickly returned with a carafe of water and two glasses partly filled with ice cubes and the caramel-colored liquor.

Alaitz and Parker poured the water into their glasses and watched the caramel color mix with the water and turn into a clear, milky cocktail. They said *eskerriska*, touched glasses, took a drink and lit a cigarette. Parker looked over at Alaitz and smiled. She met his gaze and for a few minutes, said nothing as she stared into his eyes. Those sitting at tables around them, and the passing people on the street, were witnessing the magic of love.

As if the moment was so good that it was uncomfortable, Alaitz asked in English, "Why did you want to see me tonight? I know there must be something."

Parker had to shake off the beautiful dreams dancing through his head as he was snapped back to reality. He took a long drag on his cigarette before replying. "Alaitz, there is something I need to ask you, but that's not the only reason why I wanted to see you tonight."

"Are you leaving?" she asked, looking away.

"No. Not yet." He paused to take another pull on his cigarette. "But I am going to have to go to Paris for a few days, and how long I will be there depends on you." As he spoke, he turned away from her to look off down the street.

She aimed a stream of smoke straight into his face. "I knew it!" she exclaimed.

"What I'm doing is important, Alaitz. Not just for me or you or the Basques or the U.S., but for everyone."

"You're such a *con*!" She took a deep breath. "Why do you pretend like you care about me when all you want from me is information?" She rammed her cigarette into her drink, forced her chair back, and rose from the table.

Parker sat motionless for a second, watching her in surprise. She stood in front of him, proud and determined. No one would ever be allowed too close to her. He loved her.

Then she began to walk away and when she did, he moved faster. Catching Alaitz by the arm, he spun her body into his. Moving her hair from her face with his fingertips, he looked deeply into her eyes. A menacing scowl remained on Alaitz's face, but she didn't fight to free herself. Bringing his lips down to hers, they were met with an equal amount of passion. They stood, kissing in the middle of the restaurant's patio with every eye in the vicinity on them. They easily could have forgotten where they were if not for the sound of applause that woke them from their embrace. Now, held in the arms of one another, they turned and blushed, finding everyone clapping and smiling at them.

Older couples looked at them and reminisced on earlier times. Young couples saw them and wished their relationship still held such passion. Those who were single watched them and dreamed of days to come. Thoroughly embarrassed, they gave a slight wave and returned to their table.

They then enjoyed a nice dinner together, filled with conversation, flirting, laughter, and smiles. But Parker's heart sank deeper and deeper with every passing minute, sensing he would never be able to have her. She was not made for the life he could offer.

Despite the depressing realization, by the end of the evening he had the name. Alaitz had met him years before when she was a member of an organization devoted to human rights for Basque political prisoners. She had never liked him and, knowing his fierce determination, was not surprised to hear he was involved in such an ordeal. She told him that Jean-Marie Uhaldes frequently went by the name Lopé.

* * *

A wide boulevard created an opening, and the great white dome of Sacré Coeur loomed above them. Its majesty and brilliance overcame Gibson, and he had to stop for a moment to take in the marvelous spectacle. Amazingly, it had seemed to appear from nowhere. Sunlight bounced off the cathedral, causing its white color to be nearly blinding. He could see it was set on a hill, rising above the surrounding area, giving it an even more celestial appearance. The sight of it even brightened Parker's spirits, as he raised his eyes to look and kept them raised.

As they walked closer to the cathedral, a change in architecture of the buildings they passed was apparent. The buildings, houses, and shops grew more colorful and detailed. Large clumps of vines hung around doorways and outlined windows. Streetlamps looked as if they had been restored from a century ago. People were lively, and Gibson felt an insurgence growing inside him. He no longer cared that his legs were aching from all the walking, or that he really thought they should be getting in touch with Capitaine Nivelle.

He was taking in the sights and sounds of Paris and he felt great. This feeling strengthened as they walked closer to the white cathedral. After climbing a steep flight of stone steps that wound themselves behind a row of buildings, they found themselves standing at the base of a hill with the cathedral of Sacré Coeur towering in front of them. Gibson calculated the hike of wide stairs leading up to the cathedral and instantly felt all the lightness he felt just minutes before drain away. It was practically climbing a small mountain to get to the top! Without second thought, Parker walked on.

"Whoa, Parker. Couldn't we just take this trolley thing?" Gibson pointed at the rail car that went up the side of the hill.

Parker shrugged his shoulders, still slightly scowling. "Sure," he said. He turned again and began climbing up the stairs. "If you're an old woman," he added, with his back turned.

"Son of a bitch!" Gibson said under his breath, following Parker up the stairway.

With his head down, Gibson walked up the steps in a straight line. Parker weaved up the stairway between clumps of people just as he had done along the streets of the city. Gibson found strength to move onward and upward in his constant cursing of Parker for somehow not suffering from the pack of cigarettes a day he smoked.

Once they reached the top of the stairs at the base of the cathedral, Gibson stopped cursing. Parker stopped to turn and take in the view. Gibson followed his lead. When he did, what he saw was best described along the lines of awe-inspiring. The entire city of Paris spread itself out like a carpet lining a floor beneath them. Off in the distance, he saw the peak of the Eiffel Tower, and despite Parker's ranting that it was merely a tourist symbol, Gibson felt deeply moved. Rarely had cities impressed him, but something about Paris stirred his soul.

Before long, Parker sighed and began to walk around the side of the cathedral. Gibson wanted to say that he wasn't ready to leave the view yet. After internal debate, however, he decided he didn't want to admit to Parker that, so far, he was enjoying himself in Paris. He followed the sauntering Parker, quickening his pace and catching up to him.

They walked on a cobblestone street into an area that resembled a village in the French countryside. The houses were more rustic and less urbanized, with thick vines mounting their walls and vegetable gardens sprouting on their porches. Wide trees were interlaced between houses, helping to cut off any views of the gigantic surrounding city. Looking backward, Gibson was struck by the awesome presence of Sacré Coeur's white dome standing guard above.

Turning a sharp corner, they stepped into a small square filled with artists sitting in front of pedestals with finished paintings surrounding them. They were either painting tourists posing for them, the dome of the cathedral, or other painters painting in the square. The air in the square was festive and inviting, and Parker told him they had just stepped into la Place du Terte.

"Did you see someone or something back there at the bridge that bothered you?" Gibson asked, as Parker finally stopped walking.

Parker faced him. He twitched slightly as he responded to Gibson's question. "Yeah. I did see something that bothered me," he said, as he lit a cigarette.

Though Gibson felt that perhaps he should back down, he decided to follow the contrary approach. "Was it related to the case?"

Looking annoyed, Parker responded tersely, "No."

"The past is the past, Sebastian. You've got to let it go," Gibson replied, delving deeper.

Parker stepped closer and Gibson could see his eyes alight with fire. "But what if you know something in the past was the best thing you'll ever have and that nothing will ever be that good? What then?"

Gibson wanted to calm Parker down, as he sensed he was on the verge of doing something crazy. "That's not the way to look at life. You're young and have your whole life ahead of you. You never know how long you're going to be around, but don't you think that while you're here, you should make the most of it?"

"You're one to talk. How many women have you dated since your wife left you?" Parker asked, stepping back a few steps into the cloud of smoke he just exhaled.

"We're not talking about me here." Gibson felt his fists clinch. He took a deep breath. "Why drown yourself in memories when you can make new ones?"

Parker slowly walked away. While he did, Gibson heard him say, "I don't want new ones."

* * *

Capitaine Nivelle peered through a pair of binoculars pointed at the entrance of an apartment building across the street. Parker called him before leaving Biarritz's airport to give him the name of their target. Within hours, Nivelle's men had pinpointed a location.

The name was all they needed. Both the gendarmes and the anti-terrorism unit had been watching Lopé for years. He was suspected of having committed numerous crimes: firebombing an English pub, derailing a line of TGV track, and breaking a storefront window of a realty office that specialized in holiday rentals to Brits, amongst other accusations.

Nothing had ever been pinned on him, however, and Nivelle and others were elated at the prospect of finally having a legitimate reason to bust Lopé. From the looks on the faces of Nivelle's squad, Parker thought there was no way Lopé would be apprehended quietly. The wolves smelled blood and were ready to strike. Lopé was twenty-two, not much younger than him. Parker almost felt sorry for him.

There was a florist with a stand of fresh flowers on one side of the doorway and a rundown looking bar on the other. Nivelle had a man disguised as a homeless person propped against a stairwell two doors down. Parker laughed under his breath noticing that Nivelle's pointy nose made a perfect perch for the binoculars.

They spent the entire late afternoon and evening on the stakeout with Nivelle and his crew. Parker was bored out of his mind and repeatedly commented that it was nearing dinner time.

On the other hand, Gibson moved freely about the small room. He examined the weapons laid out on the bed and the surveillance equipment set up in the room. It was the most at ease Parker had seen Gibson since their arrival in France.

Parker lifted his head slightly, so he could look across to the site where Nivelle promised they would spot their man. He saw that the old man selling flowers was now packing them and his stall into a beat up Citroën van and closing shop for the day. The day had turned overcast as it moved into late afternoon. Dusk was beginning to creep its dangling tentacles throughout the city. The sky above Paris had turned a light purple hue.

Day turned into night, and still no sign of Lopé. At one point, Parker asked if he could step outside for a few minutes.

Nivelle adamantly refused, saying Parker could be recognized and foil the trap. Gibson quickly looked away, obviously agreeing with Nivelle.

Hours passed, and both Nivelle and Gibson remained at the window. They stared at the doorway across the street as if their life depended on it. During a moment when the group of Frenchmen was busy discussing their favorite attributes of the female body, Parker slipped behind them and out the door. He was down the stairs and out on the street before anyone noticed him missing.

For as much as he didn't like shopping at large grocery stores, especially in the heart of Paris, Parker knew if he was going to find what he was looking for he would have to find one. The smaller shops where he could find what he was looking for would all be closed by now. He was craving a fresh baguette, brebi cheese, saucisson, and Irouleguy.

Since it was now nearly 10:00 p.m., Parker accepted he would not have much luck coming up with a fresh baguette. He knew that even this country, so famous for its bread, had its limits. Regardless, he'd be able to find a baguette that would still be better than most he could find in the States. As he walked, he also came to terms with the fact that finding Irouleguy, or any Basque wine for that matter, was going to be a miracle.

After walking a few blocks in the damp night air, he found a Monoprix. Entering, he couldn't help but be astounded by how similar larger French grocery stores had grown to the monstrosities in America. He considered all the quaint French boulangeries, epiceries, poissoneries and charcuteries—places that made France so special. The dark thought crossed his mind that soon the French would have their own Super Walmarts and would never have any need for the smaller specialty stores.

As he proceeded down the spacious aisles, he found a decent baguette in the bakery section and good saucisson, but had to settle for a nice bottle of Bordeaux red. There was a line of cheeses bordering the wine section of the store and he started moving along looking for the mountain sheep cheese. He moved down the line with baguette, saucisson and bottle in one arm while his outstretched hand passed by the extending arrangement of cheeses. Soon he found what he was looking for—brebi. Just as he was reaching for a small wheel of it, his hand ran into another hand with long narrow, fingers.

Startled, Parker pulled his hand back and automatically said *pardon* before looking into the face of the person with the long fingers. He found a young inquisitive face staring at him.

Lopé had shaved his little moustache, trimmed and bleached his hair. Parker thought he looked younger now than he did in the photo Nivelle showed him earlier in the stakeout room. Despite what he'd done to change his appearance, Parker recognized Lopé's face without a second thought. Nothing could be done quickly to change those piercing eyes watching him from behind that long nose. Both of them stood looking at each other for an extended moment.

"There's a shop down the street that has all sorts of Basque items," Lopé said in French.

Parker reached over and grabbed a brebi wheel from the rack. "But it's closed now," he replied in French, acting annoyed.

Lopé laughed and Parker thought it sounded a little like a hyena. "Yes, it is. These Parisians don't understand the good life. In our region, one would only have to walk to the nearest café to find the owner of the store and ask him to let you get something from him." Lopé grabbed his own wheel of cheese. Parker noticed he had picked up the same items as him: a bottle of red wine, saucisson, baguette and brebi.

Looking down at what he was carrying, Parker then nodded at Lopé. "Looks like we at least know how to find good food in this city."

Lopé smiled. "I knew you had to be from the Pays Basque. There are some good places to find a decent meal in this city."

Parker mocked surprise, "Oh, really?"

"There's a great Basque restaurant called La Rhune in the Latin Quarter. Believe me, when you live close by, you can open your windows and smell great Basque cooking all afternoon rising from the kitchen."

While living in Paris, Parker had eaten at the restaurant Lopé spoke of many times. It was in the heart of the Latin Quarter, surrounded by other superb, yet affordable mostly ethnic restaurants. Once again, he mocked surprise. "I'll have to try it sometime. French food can be great, but Basque food is always excellent."

"And you are Basque?" Lopé asked him in Basque.

It was Parker's turn to smile. "No, I'm not," he responded in French. "I just understand a little of the language.

Shrugging, Lopé returned to French. "Some of the best of us are not completely pure in the bloodline. They have been trying to breed us out for centuries. It's more subtle than using guns, but more effective."

Parker shook his head in agreement. As he did, Lopé noticed something. Parker didn't know what it was, but whatever it was, it suddenly ended the conversation.

"I hope to see you around again sometime, *mon ami*," Lopé said and quickly darted away to the checkout lines at the opposite side of the building. Holding cheese, wine, sausage, and bread in his arms, Parker tried to figure out what had spooked Lopé. Looking down at his clothes, he thought with his slim fitting jeans, zippered front sweater, and square toed shoes, he looked like any other European.

He began to walk down the aisle, thinking that perhaps Lopé had noticed some change in his facial expression. He'd just dismissed that thought when, out of the corner of his eye, he saw exactly what Lopé had seen. Capitaine Nivelle, holding himself high and staring into the crowds, had walked through the doorway.

As Parker made his way to a checkout line, Nivelle noticed him. He felt his cold stare fall on him.

Parker looked behind him to the other side of the store. Lopé was gone.

* * *

Parker handed his feast in a plastic bag to a homeless man huddled in the corner of a building. He'd lost his appetite and needed time to think through the situation. He wanted to walk. But he had trouble trying to think of the situation with Lopé and Nivelle as Alaitz kept dominating his thoughts.

After an hour of aimlessly walking, he was standing on the Pont des Arts across the Seine. He'd been on this stylish pedestrian bridge many times before, quite a few of those times with Alaitz. At one time it had been his favorite spot in Paris. He remembered a scene from a movie where a couple met and kissed on the bridge after confessing their undying love for each other. He felt like he'd been in that movie.

While walking through the faceless night, he suddenly felt an unnerving discomfort, as if eyes were watching him. Instinctively, he looked up from the dark pavement and felt hundreds of eyes pounding down on him. The eyes came from faces carved into stone centuries ago and time had done nothing to diminish their fierceness, except darken their complexion. The eyes of Notre Dame stared down at him.

They had seen centuries pass. They had seen everything, and he was nothing compared to what they could tell him if he listened close enough. But right now he wasn't listening. Parker had never listened to any other voice than his own. If I'm lost, let me be lost, he said to them.

The bell towers loomed above in their impressive omnipresence. They made him feel small standing in front of the great cathedral. Turning his back on the cathedral, he strode across a bridge into the Latin Quarter.

He found a payphone and dialed Gibson's mobile phone number. After numerous rings, when Parker was sure Gibson was fumbling clumsily with his phone trying to figure out how to push the talk button, Gibson answered. "Hi, it's me," Parker said.

"Parker! Where the hell are you? Nivelle says you walked off from him."

"He's right. I could have had him, but by Nivelle showing his damn face messed the whole thing up," Parker replied, wanting to bang the phone against the glass of the phone booth.

"Could have had who, Parker?" Gibson asked.

"Could have had Lopé! I ran into him in the supermarket. I was fucking talking to him before Nivelle came along and scared him off."

There was a dead pause on the line as Gibson carefully considered his response. "There's no way he, or you for that matter, could have guessed you would run into that guy while picking up some wine or whatever the hell you were doing, Parker."

"Yes, agreed. But if Nivelle hadn't been spying on me and following me in the first place, we would be much better off."

Gibson paused before he spoke again. Parker imagined Nivelle was right next to him, overhearing everything. "It doesn't matter now. Where the hell are you?"

"I'm away from you bastards. I don't want Nivelle's cronies watching me for one night."

"Parker, this is insane. I'm going to have to report you for this," Gibson reluctantly said.

Quickly, Parker responded. "Then fucking report me! And tell that piece of donkey shit Nivelle that if he wants to catch this guy, have his men get set up in the Latin Quarter and tell him specifically to stay away. They all know his face better than the faces of their own fathers."

"And where will you be?" Gibson asked with concern in his tone.

"Don't worry about me," Parker said in anger, lighting a cigarette. But something told him he was being too harsh. "Meet me tomorrow for lunch at the Egyptian restaurant on the corner of Boulevard Saint-Germaine and Rue Saint-Jacques. I know Nivelle will have his men follow you, so at least tell them to be ready to move when I say so."

Gibson laughed uncomfortably. "My God, Parker. You sound like you're taking control of this situation."

"It's *Mon Dieu* in French, and yes, I am. But since Nivelle stepped in my dinner tonight, first we're going to have a nice lunch tomorrow," Parker replied, as he slammed down the phone.

* * *

The curly haired Frenchman sitting with a delicately thin woman next to him was trying to remain civil in the restaurant setting, even though Parker felt anger emanating from him. As he was sitting quite close to them, Parker could overhear their conversation whether he wanted to or not.

The man was accusing his wife of being cold to him and not giving him enough attention. Pursing her lips, the woman only stared at him with dead eyes as he complained. He was trying to keep his voice down, but doing a very bad job of it. Even though everyone in the crowded restaurant would occasionally look their way when the man uttered an outburst, she showed no signs of being embarrassed. The man was obviously too worked up to care about any embarrassment.

Out of the corner of his eye, Parker watched the woman calmly move her straight hair from her face to tuck it behind her ears. She looked at her husband as if he were not really sitting across from her. Just as their main courses were arriving, the woman stood without a word and walked out of the restaurant.

The man sat for a few moments, contemplating his next move and Parker felt an overwhelming urge to tell him to forget about her. Apparently coming to a decision, the man threw some euros on the table and stood up to leave. As he moved past, Parker caught his arm and handed him the drink in front of him he had not yet touched. When the man looked at him, Parker saw pain and agony in his eyes. The man knocked back the glass of white wine in one gulp, then placed the glass on the table. Without a word, he patted Parker on the shoulder and then hurried from the restaurant.

Minutes later, Gibson entered the narrow, single room restaurant and sat down at Parker's table. "Well, Monsieur Trouble, how are things with you?"

"*Fous-moi la paix*," Parker curtly responded.

"You know, one of these days I might be able to understand you when you talk like that. Then I'll probably have to sock you."

"When that day comes, I'll start speaking Basque to you," Parker replied, motioning to the waiter for another glass of wine.

Parker's comment produced a dry chuckle from Gibson. "That would be just like you, wouldn't it?" Gibson glanced at the menu on the table in front of him.

"You never returned to the hotel last night. Where the hell did you sleep?" Gibson asked.

"I crashed at an old friend's place," Parker explained.

"You are resourceful, Sebastian Parker, I'll give you that. So, unless this place has the best food in Paris, I imagine you had me meet you here because you wanted Nivelle's men to be in the area?"

"That's right," Parker replied.

"You're telling me that on your own, you've been able to track someone down that they couldn't?"

Looking annoyed, Parker replied, "Looks that way."

"And how did you do that?" Gibson asked, with a slight trace of suspicion that did not go unnoticed by Parker.

Parker stared hard at him for a few moments before responding. He didn't want to start an argument. "*Par hasard, mon vieux. Par hasard.*" Gibson stared at him dumbly. When he began to swirl his hand asking for an explanation, Parker added, "By chance."

A waiter placed a new glass of white wine in front of Parker. When the waiter asked what they would like to order, Parker ordered from the fixed menu for them: hummus and flatbread, stuffed peppers, and a baklava dessert.

"So where is he?" Gibson asked impatiently.

"Close, Gibson. But first, let's enjoy this lunch and then we'll get to work. It makes me happy to think of Nivelle's men wandering around out there not knowing what's going on." Parker took a long drink from his glass of wine. "I wish I could pee on Nivelle's foot."

The two of them laughed and enjoyed a nice lunch in Paris together, without speaking one more word about the case.

* * *

She spread her legs slightly to allow the cool breeze blowing in from the ocean to creep up and kiss her upper thighs tenderly. She was wearing a light skirt that she had hiked up to her knees. Graciana was more than content to bask in the sun and drink a beer along the pale yellow beach of Cap Breton. The sun made her feel warm.

Idly, she watched the lines of surfers straddling their boards, bobbing in the distance, waiting for their wave. To the south in Biarritz, she knew they would be looking for her.

While looking in the direction of Biarritz, the remains of a German blockhouse from World War II caught her gaze. Since the days of its construction by the Nazis during the occupation, the beach had noticeably eroded. Now, after all this time, it looked out of place to see the remains of a once fortified location falling apart in the shallow shore of the ocean. With time, everything falls apart, she thought.

It also made her reflect on her escape from her guards. They had sworn to her that they were only taking her to keep her safe, but she didn't trust the look in their eyes. With only Lopé left of their original group, she knew the word *safe* no longer applied. She would either be killed or turned in to the police, she was sure.

Of course, her capture, if to occur, would be blamed on an anonymous tip, but she knew that tip would come from one of their own under strict orders to do so with the intention of withdrawing attention away from the organization as a whole.

"Fuck them!" she said to herself.

When she thought of how easily she had fooled her captors she smiled so widely it touched her newly cut hair gently curling around her face.

After being whisked away from the apartment in Mauléon after a tip that she'd been spotted, she was transported to the city of Pau for a night, then back to Biarritz.

She'd spent part of her childhood in Mauléon, but it had been when she was very young and didn't remember much of the place. She was glad to be moved. But as she was moved around, she often wondered if she were on her way to meet her death.

In her reflections, she sometimes thought of the box of matches she left behind in the apartment in Saint-Pée. She hoped he found them, so he would know she'd been on to him from the beginning. Just because he knew a little Basque history and another language or two hadn't made him much better than any other stupid man. They were pretty much all the same.

When the transporter car stopped at a small house on the outskirts of Biarritz, she hadn't known where she was at first, but figured it out after noticing a large forest of pine trees lined with sand, and a distinct smell of ocean in the air. The houses in the area were all one story and holiday resort looking. She noticed a clearing between the forest and the houses, and correctly guessed it to be a golf course. Immediately, she knew it could only be one place—the Chiberta area of Anglet bordering Biarritz.

As she came to this realization, one of the men slapped the back of her head and told her to move forward. When she turned to face him, she instantly recalled where she'd seen him before. He had the same exact scar on his face as the man who had beat her in the apartment in Saint-Pée.

She hadn't recognized his face when they came for her in Mauléon, mostly because it had been dark and they literally nabbed her off the street as she was having an evening stroll and a cigarette. But the scar on his face pulsated with each heartbeat and had a deep red tint. There was no mistake it was the same *mec.*

Her immediate reaction was to slap him back, but the other one grabbed her arm before she could follow through. The man with the scar smiled then laughed at her sinisterly. He ran his dark eyes down her body. Correctly reading his thoughts, she immediately knew she was about to be raped.

She spit in the bastard's ugly face. He responded by slapping her harshly then roughly grabbed her and forced her into the house.

Graciana didn't fought back. The man with the scar threw her down on the barren floor of the house and tore at her clothing, until he her pants were down and her panties pulled aside. He forcefully entered her while the other one watched on the far side of the room. The man's weight crushed her slim body, and she knew it would be a struggle to get out from under him. Even if she managed to bring a knee up into his groin, the other one would be right there to hold her down.

During the rape, the man with the scar tried to kiss her on the lips with his large and scruffy, nicotine-stained mouth. She wondered how a person could try being so intimate by kissing while raping?

When he lifted her shirt, he was delighted to find she wasn't wearing a bra. Voraciously, the man attacked her breasts with his mouth, and she averted her eyes. But she wasn't just looking away; she was looking around—around the room to find anything that might help her when she had a chance to make a move.

Her first glances revealed nothing that would be helpful. The place was just an empty room with covered furniture pushed against one wall. When the man with the scar pulled himself from between her legs, he held himself over her and brought himself to come on her with a loud series of grunts. When he was finished, he spit on her.

With a wide smile on his face, he motioned to the other one waiting his turn. The man with the scar then had grabbed her face to force her to look at him. Slowly and deliberately, she said, "Now go rape your sister, you sick fuck."

He smiled as he rubbed his large hand against her fine cheekbone. Forcing her to stand, he then knocked her down with a backhand to her face. He picked her up and threw her on a table that was covered with a white cloth. With a knife he had concealed in the back of his belt, he deftly sliced down her back on both sides of her body, cutting the cloth line of her panties.

Being bent over the table and before she could regain her wits, the other one straddled her from behind and forced himself into her. While fiercely pumping away, he reached his hands under her to forcefully squeeze her breasts. Seeing blood dripping down her thighs, she tauntingly asked him, "Do you like bloody pussy?"

The response she received was a powerful blow to the back of her head that knocked her unconscious for a few seconds. The man groaned in wild, animalistic pleasure as she felt like he was ripping her insides.

During this second rape session, the man with the scar stood right next to them, watching. Just as she felt the second man's pace quicken and his breath start to grow deeper, she glanced down and noticed something on the floor by the side of the table. A screwdriver.

Timing her move, she waited for just the right moment. In one fluid movement, she pulled herself from him, leaned down, and turned to stab him with the screwdriver, lodging it in his throat just as he was ejaculating.

She quickly pulled the screwdriver from his throat and rammed it into the skull of the man with the scar. She let him fall with the screwdriver still stuck deeply into the side of his head.

Glancing at the other one's body, she saw it twitching on the floor, penis still erect. The penis appeared to know this was its last time to be used, she thought.

After washing herself as best she could in the bathroom, she walked back into the room where the savages had raped her. For quite some time she stood, looking down at the two dead bodies. The fucking rapists got what they deserved, she said to herself. She wished she could have jammed that screwdriver into both of their asses while they were still alive.

But there was no time to dwell. She had to decide what to do next, and do it quickly.

She conceived an immediate plan. She decided to hitchhike up to the Côte D'Or, check herself into a cheap hotel under a fake name, and chill out on the peaceful beach until she could think things through. Hitchhiking had never been a problem for her. All she had to do was flash a little leg or stretch her shirt a little tighter and in no time some guy would pull over, pretending he would have stopped for anyone.

Before leaving the cottage, her eyes fell on the screwdriver in the scarred man's head and the knife still in his hand. As she closed the door to the small house, the two sharp objects had been moved to new final resting places—one each jammed into the groin of the two men's bodies.

* * *

ETA Suspect Escapes in France

A man believed to be a senior member of the Basque separatist group ETA has escaped from police custody in southern France. The suspect escaped from police headquarters in the town of Bayonne near the Spanish border. His arrest was seen as a landmark for cross-border cooperation in the fight against ETA.

He was arrested while driving a car with false number plates in France. His arrest led to seven more arrests of people Spain has identified as ETA operatives living and hiding in France.

The man is believed to be a logistics chief, responsible for organizing the backup for teams carrying out attacks. French authorities have launched a huge manhunt across the southwestern corner of the country.

21

Paris, France

SEBASTIAN PARKER LIT a cigarette as they stepped out of the Egyptian restaurant into the bright Paris day. Immediately, Parker noticed three of Nivelle's men, whom he had seen in the apartment the night before, spaced out alongside the crowded pedestrian road. He'd been counting on this predictability of Nivelle as he wanted to be followed.

He led Gibson through the Latin Quarter's winding streets, crammed with tables and chairs overflowing from the ethnic restaurants lined in rows next to one another. Exotic food smells lingered in the still air. Even though they had eaten a large lunch, both felt a touch of hunger again.

Smelling the air, Gibson caught a rich combination of smells, including sautéing peppers, cooking meat, and baking cakes. "Sure smells good around here," Gibson commented.

"This really is a great area for food in Paris." Parker's eyes fell on a girl, wearing a white buttoned shirt with a black skirt, approaching them from the opposite direction. From a distance, she looked like Alaitz, but as she got closer he noticed her knees were not bony like Alaitz's. He loved those bony knees. Taking a long drag on his cigarette, he tried to clear his head of thoughts about her. "Are they still following us, Gibson?"

"Yes."

"Perfect," Parker replied.

Gibson was dying to ask Parker why this was *perfect* and where they were going, but knowing him as he did now, Gibson assumed Parker wouldn't tell him anyway, so he didn't bother asking. He followed alongside, trusting the kid probably more than he should.

They turned from the small, winding road onto a wide boulevard. On this street, Gibson noticed there were more stores and shops of various kinds, interspersed between restaurants and cafés.

Parker touched his arm, indicating they were crossing the street. Once across, Parker stepped onto the terrace of a large café with red painted interior walls. The café was located on the corner of two intersecting streets and named the Café du Jardin. He deliberately made a point of seating himself facing the street and having Gibson staring back into the inside of the crowded café. A few minutes later, a waiter came to their table looking annoyed at their presence. Parker ordered two espressos. The waiter sneered as he walked away.

"I would have thought waiters in this city would be more appreciative of people who speak French," Gibson commented.

"I don't think waiters in this city really care. They're just assholes to everyone, regardless."

"How charming."

"Depends on how you look at it. You're just used to a culture where you're supposed to act pleasant all the time, even when you don't want to be." As he spoke, Parker noticed one of Nivelle's men taking post on the street corner a few yards from where they were seated. He had his back turned to them and was pretending to read a newspaper. "But we didn't come here to dispute cultural differences today," he added.

"Then why did we come here?"

Without raising a finger to point, Parker lifted his chin indicating something behind Gibson.

Moving his head slightly, Gibson caught a reflection from the café window, and then he saw what had smelled so good before they crossed the street minutes earlier. Directly across the street was a restaurant. Its front façade was similar to those he'd seen on farmhouses driving through the Basque Country.

There was the white stucco exterior ornamented by brightly painted green shutters and a plaque over the doorway. Though Gibson couldn't make out the name of the restaurant, he now could distinguish that it was something in Basque. Looking back at Parker, he beamed in approval. "You know, you're getting better at this, Sebastian. After this is done, maybe you should think about a career change."

The waiter reappeared and hastily set two small cups of coffee with tiny handles on the table along with a bill. Parker moved one of the saucers toward him. After peeling away the paper lining from a sugar cube, he gently placed it into the dark coffee and watched the white vanish. Then he quickly stirred it with the small spoon before knocking back the shot of fortified coffee. "A career change is definitely in the plans, but not that way," he responded, with an unreadable face as he pulled out a cigarette.

Gibson wanted to ask what he meant by the statement, but seeing the flame from Parker's lighter brought his mind back to the matter at hand. He did his best to survey everyone around them without making it obvious. He spoke to Parker barely above a whisper. "Two men just entered the café and sat down at different tables. I'm sure they are Nivelle's guys. There's the one behind us still, but also a street vendor who just pulled up to the side of the restaurant, and a guy, to the side of us, standing as if waiting to meet someone."

"Fantastic. I'm sure Lopé is living in one of those apartments above the Basque restaurant across the street. If we're lucky, they haven't moved him yet, but I'm sure they will soon after last night. I just wanted to come here in order to bring some of Nivelle's men along and not an entire brigade that would tip them off," Parker explained. His eyes darted to and from every face that walked by on the sidewalk.

Gibson drank his coffee straight. "But the problem is that they're watching us right now. Don't know we want them to watch for Lopé."

"Well then, it looks like we need to go buy a gelato from that vendor across the street," Parker said, rising from his chair and setting down a few coins on the table.

* * *

While Parker and Gibson were having coffee at the Café du Jardin, Lopé was waiting in a private room of an Algerian restaurant near the Eiffel Tower. He was there to meet one of ETA's senior members in the Paris cell.

The dim lighting in the room made him uncomfortable. He was seated alone at a table centered in the middle of the room, while two large men were seated like guards on each side of the doorway. They watched him in silence. It was impossible not to feel their large eyes boring into him. If it had been another situation, he'd have stood up and asked why they were staring at him.

After half an hour of waiting, a man stepped in the room. He was wearing a plain suit, was of medium build, and had a forgettable face. His shoes were even plain. Lopé had never seen this man before and felt a touch of pride as he realized this was due to the organization's ability to keep its top people secret.

The man nodded to the two guards at the door, then looked Lopé over, before sitting down in front of him. Once seated, the man's face, before having a look of indifference, turned into a bitter scowl. "Why are you here?" he demanded in French.

Lopé was taken aback by the question. Did this man, so high up in the logistical operations network, really not know who he was? He'd received a summons yesterday with no explanation from the messenger as to why he was called for a meeting.

"They brought me here from Madrid." He hoped he'd said the right thing. A second later, he realized he hadn't.

"I know that, you imbecile! But why are you here?" the man in the suit barked at him.

Lopé didn't like feeling cornered. Normally, when cornered, he reacted with violence; not an option in his present situation. He frantically tried to think of what he was supposed to say. He thought he had it. "I'm here because the totalitarian governments of France and Spain have ruled over our lands and people for centuries."

The man in the suit smiled at him and began to laugh. He looked back at the two guards behind him and they began laughing as well. Lopé smiled, not knowing if he was supposed to join in the laughter or not.

He wasn't.

"That answer may have been good enough for you to join us, but it means nothing to me," the man said. He slammed his fist into the table and leaned over the table to snarl at Lopé.

Feeling his pulse racing and his palms beginning to sweat, Lopé wanted to grab for the box of cigarettes in his jacket hanging on the chair. "I'm here because I hate the way the French and Spanish and English and Americans live, and I think that if we could rule ourselves, we would do better," he muttered, not fully cognizant of the words coming from his mouth.

The man in the plain suit sat, not saying a word. Lopé didn't know what to do, so he did nothing but meet the man's gaze across the table. All the while, he was careful not to show disrespect, but he also didn't want to come across as unable to hold his ground. The man in the plain suit stood up and looked down at him. He grinned. "We're going to be putting you back into action. You have too much promise to be stuck here."

Lopé breathed a sigh of relief, hoping he had not outwardly displayed his emotions.

"In a week, you'll be sent to a safe house outside Bordeaux. There you'll be joining a cell responsible for our top tier strikes. We have some high profile missions planned for the near future and you're going to be part of them. Take the next week to rest, Lopé, because you're going to need it." The man gave him a nod and rose to leave the room. Lopé felt the warm pleasure of pride flowing through his body.

As the man exited through the door, Lopé remembered something. "Sir, there's something I wanted to tell you." The two guards had risen to follow the man and now all three of them turned back to face him. "Last night I stopped at a store in Montmartre after meeting with a friend for drinks and I saw that bastard Nivelle."

"Did he see you?" the man asked in a grave tone.

"No." Lopé thought of mentioning his encounter with the young guy in the Monoprix as well, but quickly dismissed the thought as not being relevant. "I'm positive he didn't and no one else was with him, as far as I could see," he added.

"Good. This is interesting. I thank you for telling us. Fortunately, we aren't using any of our safe houses in Montmartre right now, but with this information we will be extra cautious before using one of them again since they may have gotten a lead on us. We also did not know Nivelle was back in Paris, so this is very good information. You are proving to be quite the operative, Lopé. Even though some may think you are sometimes out of control, many of us have high hopes for you."

"Thank you," Lopé said, holding back a smile even though this was one of the best moments of his life.

The man in the plain suit walked away from the door and began to slowly pace around the room. "Nivelle's return to Paris could mean he's given up on trying to find you and the girl…or it could mean he thinks one of you is here and he's looking for you." He stopped his pacing directly behind Lopé. "In either case, we can't afford to lose you and need to be extra cautious. I want you to go back to the safe house in the Latin Quarter and stay inside until someone comes to get you. Tonight, we will move you to a different location outside of the city."

Lopé nodded he understood. The man in the suit patted him stiffly on the shoulder as he walked by him to leave the room, followed by the two guards.

Lopé was left alone.

After waiting a safe amount of time, he rose to leave. Stepping into the mid-afternoon air he felt light, as if a load had been lifted from his shoulder. Ever since his return to the continent, he'd been concerned about his fate. His actions had been risky. He was well aware that failure to achieve the objective would have resulted in his death. From the beginning, he accepted the fact that even if they were successful, his life could be in danger. But after today's meeting, he felt assured of his position. Now he was on his way to the top of the ladder and intended to never stop climbing.

Instead of taking the Metro back to the Latin Quarter, he decided to walk and enjoy his new sense of security. The walk would take him easily over an hour, but he was in no hurry. After a few moments, he decided to find a good café on the walk and stop for a smoke and a pastis. Everything was finally coming into place.

* * *

It had been two days, and she'd not heard from him. He said he would call her the next day, but hadn't. He said he had to go to Paris for a few days. If anyone were to ask her where he'd gone, she was supposed to say nothing. He was so secretive now, whereas in the past he'd always been a blessing to her because she always knew everything about him. Now, when she looked into his eyes, she didn't see the same Sebastian Parker looking back into hers. Something had changed. Was it his job? Did he have a girlfriend back in America he didn't want to tell her about? Or had he finally realized she would never marry him?

Years before, when they were in lycée together, young and in love, he'd asked her to marry him. She remembered sneaking off with him over lunch period to stroll down the path that followed the Nive River from Bayonne to Ustaritz. They walked for hours, hand in hand, sometimes not bothering to return for the second half of classes. Sometimes they would pick up a baguette, sausicon, cheese, and a bottle of wine and have a small impromptu picnic on the side of the river, far away from the city among the gradually ascending hills and country houses. Sebastian would make her laugh, and she felt more comfortable around him than with anyone else. It was on one of these lazy afternoons, when they had walked for hours and then decided to cut off from the paved path and climb to the top of a nearby hill that he proposed to her.

From the ridge, there was a great expanse of countryside leading straight into a wall of low mountains in the distance. They were surrounded by the promise of life with tall grass swaying in the wind, birds chirping noisily, and insects buzzing around them. When they were seated, Sebastian rolled so that he was stretched on his stomach on the grass, with his head at her feet. Without any hesitation, he asked her to marry him.

If it had been anyone else, Alaitz would have laughed. But it wasn't anyone else. It was Sebastian. The problem was she did care for him more deeply than she could ever be able to describe—but she couldn't accept his proposal.

In many ways, she cared for him more than she ever would for another. But she knew she would not be good to him as a wife. From that moment, Alaitz knew it would never be the same between them. They would never be as comfortable together as they once had been. Seeing the hurt cascade through his entire body made her want to try and explain why she had to say no, but she couldn't explain even if she tried. Sebastian Parker was everything she could ever dream of for in a husband. It wasn't that she felt too young at eighteen to be married—she just couldn't possibly ever marry anyone.

Before the day on the mountainside, they had never had sex, but Alaitz didn't feel guilty about what she'd done. She loved him more than she loved anyone, and if this was one way to show him, then so be it. Although Sebastian had been gifted as an understanding person, she imagined he could never be quick enough to fully realize how much she cared for him.

Now she knew why he'd really returned and she hated him for it. She felt it was against his nature. She knew if he had been born in the Pays Basque, he would be a supporter of the Basque cause, even if he didn't have a touch of Basque blood in him.

Months and years had gone by with no contact between them. No phone calls, no emails, and no letters. She missed his letters most of all. She loved reading his messy scribbling that passed for handwriting. She loved the eloquence of his prose. He poured his heart out on paper when he wrote to her, and when reading his letters, she felt his warm breath whispering against her neck.

By being seen with him now, she realized she was putting herself in danger, but the risk was worth it. Over the years, she'd only seen him for brief moments at a time, but those times meant the world to her. But while she lived for those moments, she also felt as if she were dying while they were happening.

Alaitz sipped her glass of wine and felt tears building against her eyelids. The friends she was sitting with at a bar in Petit Bayonne had long since sensed her quiet disposition and left her out of their ongoing conversation. Vaguely, she listened to their gabbing about this *mec* or that one, and how that one was a moron but yet, they still liked him. She wanted to reach across the table and slap them all. Instead, she choked back the tears, mentally wished Sebastian well, and promptly finished off her glass of wine. She said a hurried *ciao* to her friends and stepped into the night.

Banners of small green and red flags had been strung across the roads from the buildings for the kick-off of the Fête de Bayonne tomorrow. As it did every year, the city had filled up with people for the five day festival, and despite the fact the fête did not officially start until the following night, the narrow streets of Petit Bayonne were already crammed with people from all over the world, downing ridiculous quantities of alcohol of all kinds. The streets were already littered with broken glass, bar fliers, and interspersed puddles of vomit. Normally, Alaitz went full throttle into the fête, dressing in the typical Basque attire of white pants and shirt topped off with a red scarf and beret. This year, however, she was not excited to see it come. Restlessness prevailed over her spirit, and she noticed her hands had begun to tremble slightly.

Wherever he was and whatever he was doing, she wished that Sebastian would stay away. She sensed something bad was going to happen.

* * *

They were instructed to enter the back of the building, just in case anyone was watching the front. It was thought to be a secure and safe location that had so far been undetected, but one could never be sure when considering the resourcefulness of organizations like ETA. And, like ETA, the DNAT had a tendency to sporadically change its various locations. These were the types of places that were never supposed to be found. Of course, not by terrorist groups, but also they were to remain hidden from journalists and the general public who, since the reports on the treatment of political prisoners during the uprising in Algeria, had taken a serious interest in semi-secret French policing activities.

For the purpose of holding suspected ETA and IK members, Nivelle had personally chosen this location. The right of habeas corpus did not necessarily apply for those held under charges of terrorism against France, and Nivelle took as much advantage of this well known fact as possible.

Nivelle had chosen the present site for his unit's interrogation facility due to its proximity to the Champs-Elysée. It was a Baroque style building that was situated directly behind the grand avenue itself. He felt certain not one of the millions of tourists and Parisians walking its wide sidewalks would guess that a quasi-military building was located just behind a Gucci gallery.

Earlier, Nivelle called Gibson on his mobile phone and only said that they all needed to meet as soon as possible. He said he would call with a location for the rendez-vous later.

Gibson asked for what reason, but Nivelle hung up before hearing the question. Mulling over the very brief conversation, Gibson had the distinct impression he'd just been given an order. He didn't like the feeling. In fact, he detested it. At the time of the call, he and Parker were seated in a pizza restaurant in what Parker called les Halles neighborhood of the city. They had spent the day walking the streets of Paris. With Nivelle's men in place keeping watch for Lopé, Parker talked Gibson into taking the afternoon to do a little sightseeing. If Lopé was still in Paris, they were going to catch him eventually.

Two large flat pizzas had just been set on the table in front of them when Gibson's phone began vibrating again. It was Nivelle. Gibson listened for a moment then hung up. He told Parker what Nivelle said, and Parker made a mental note of the address Nivelle told Gibson.

After concentrating a few moments on *la reine*, a pizza with ham and mushrooms, in front of him, Parker shrugged his shoulders and decided to eat. Gibson shrugged his shoulders in response as well, instantly glad no one observed his scarily similar shrug to Parker's, and looked down at the pizza before him. There was pepper, onion, sausage and pepperoni. The steam, lifting off the plate in front of him, smelled divine. However, one aspect of what he had ordered didn't look so appetizing to him. In the direct center of the pizza was a fried egg. He looked up from the steaming plate of dough, tomato sauce, cheese and toppings to cast an imploring glance at Parker.

Apparently, Parker had been watching him the entire time, as he was taking a bite from his own pizza, using a fork and knife. Parker shook his head, indicating that the fried egg was entirely normal. Gibson shook his own head and cut a ring around the center of his pizza, isolating the egg in the center. He could handle a lot, but messing with pizza by putting a fried egg on it was too much. Picking up a slice, Gibson took a large bite. It was delicious.

Parker commented on how the restaurant was located on the edge of a wide square where countless people passed by every minute and that it was too bad they would have to leave a great people watching spot in Paris.

"Why do you think Nivelle called us?" Gibson asked.

Parker responded by simply saying, "They caught Lopé." He added, "I led them directly to him."

* * *

Once at the fortress-like complex, they were escorted down a long, empty hallway by a stern, uniformed young man who refused to answer any of Parker's questions. What Parker wanted to hear was that Lopé had been caught because of him. Normally, it was not in his nature to be so arrogant, but in the current situation, he felt more reason to be acknowledged.

They turned a corner and found Capitaine Nivelle standing outside an unmarked door, clearly full of his own glory. Even from a considerable distance they could see the thin grin stretched across his face. Nivelle had a face too tight and drawn for grinning, Parker thought.

"So you actually listened to what I said this time and look what happened." Parker commented, instantly taking the offensive.

Nivelle's response surprised no one. He considered Parker's comment and casually brushed it aside, as if irrelevant how the suspect was caught. All that mattered was that was caught, and Nivelle's men were the ones to do it.

They caught Lopé just as he was finishing his walk through the city after his meeting. It was late in the afternoon by the time he made it back to the Latin Quarter, and the day's events still left the trace of a smile on his face as he continued the last stretch of his walk along the Boulevard Saint-Germain. He sensed nothing out of the ordinary, even though as far as five blocks from his place he was spotted and tracked. When Lopé stepped up to a *tabac* stand to buy a new box of Gauloises, they took him. His arms were locked in handcuffs behind him, and he was thrown in the back seat of a black car before the stand's owner could hand him back his change.

Not until hours later was he told he was under arrest for terrorism charges. Of course, they knew who he was, but he adamantly refused to give them the pleasure of responding to their incessant inquiries. In answer to his silence, he received repeated blows to the back of his head. When one of the officers threatened to go after his family if he didn't help them by giving them information that would lead to the arrest of other ETA supporters, Lopé spit in the man's face.

Instantly, the man reacted by placing both his hands around Lopé's neck. With Lopé's hands still bound behind him, the man literally lifted him out of the chair. While he was being choked, Lopé stared indifferently at the man. The other officers in the room pulled the enraged man off Lopé.

Sizing up the situation, Lopé saw hatred in the man's eyes fixed on him. He told himself that if he was to be killed, he'd take one of these bastards with him. Although he was tired, hungry, and thirsty, he tried to remain as attentive as possible. When he had a chance, he would take advantage of it. He needed to be ready for just the right opportunity, he told himself.

The moment Parker stepped into the room behind Nivelle was the moment Lopé was waiting for. Not only had the two officers standing on either side of his chair lessened their grip on his shoulders as their *patron* entered the room, but seeing Parker's face instantly made his eyes glaze with hatred. *The traitor bastard was working with Nivelle! He was one of them!*

In the time it took Parker to step through the doorway, a matter of two steps, Lopé swung his arms over the back of the chair behind him and covered the distance of the room in order to lunge himself at Parker. It was Lopé's intention to gain enough momentum so he could ram his head into Parker's face, smashing his nose, but Parker reacted quickly and side-stepped out of the way of the charging Lopé.

It was an ill-fated attempt that ended with Lopé ramming face first into the hard wall. When his body hit the floor, blood coursed from his broken nose. While he writhed and squirmed, he yelled as many curses at Parker in Basque as he could between spitting out mouthfuls of blood.

The two officers picked Lopé up and tossed him back into the chair. Gibson had entered the room right behind Parker and witnessed the debacle. Cautiously, he glanced at Parker, who met his concern with an appreciative nod.

Without another word spoken, Parker pulled a chair from the corner of the room and sat directly in front of Lopé. "You hate me now because you think I betrayed you," Parker said in Basque.

Blood dripped off Lopé's narrow chin onto his chest. Nivelle walked over to him, and the two officers standing beside Lopé tightened their grip on him as Nivelle pulled out a handkerchief from his suit pocket. At first, he acted as if he was actually going to help Lopé by wiping away the blood running from his now mangled nose. Instead, he took the handkerchief and roughly smeared blood all over Lopé's face until he looked as if he were wearing red face paint.

"People might actually think we broke your nose like that. Not many would believe someone would do anything as stupid as what you just did," Nivelle said in French, as he threw the sopping piece of cloth into Lopé's lap. Then he took a new one from his pocket and dangled it in front of Lopé's face.

Secretly, Parker wished Nivelle had not done the face smearing. Looking at Lopé had been difficult enough beforehand, just to see the burning anger in his eyes. Now the burning eyes were set in a blood-smeared face, and the overall effect was not easily digestible. It made Parker uneasy.

"You think I'm a traitor, when in fact I was never on your side," he said to Lopé in English. Lopé's head turned as if not understanding, yet his eyes remained glazed with hatred. "And I know you can understand English, because you were just in California," Parker added.

"I'll bet that nose hurts. It's aggravating, isn't it, when you have blood dripping from your face like that, and you can't do anything about it? We'll take you to get it taken care of after you tell us what we need to know. Otherwise, we'll just wait here until you do," Nivelle offered.

Nivelle walked behind Lopé, interrupting Parker's train of thought. He wanted to tell Nivelle to keep out of it for a minute, but a serious glance from Gibson told him not to. "Was it you who contacted the one in America to carry out this attack, or was it the other way around?"

The question seemed to surprise Lopé, and for a brief moment, he looked as if chewing on an answer. But then he grinned through the caking blood on his face. Parker sighed and leaned back in his chair. *What the hell am I doing? Interrogating prisoners isn't exactly in my job description.*

More in order to give himself time to think than anything else, as Nivelle, his officers, as well as Gibson were all in the room listening to him talk with Lopé, Parker pulled out his box of cigarettes and waved them at Lopé. Lopé nodded his head affirmatively and whipping out his lighter, Parker lit a cigarette for himself. He leaned forward, put one in Lope's mouth, and lit it.

Parker looked inquiringly over at Nivelle, who threw the handkerchief at Lopé's feet and motioned for the officers to undo Lopé's restraints. Slowly, Lopé bent down to pick up the handkerchief and placed it against his nose as he took a deep pull on the cigarette. As he did, he began to choke. He bent over in a fit of coughing and spit up blood on the floor.

When the coughing fit ended, Lopé straightened himself again in the chair and stared at Parker for a moment. "Who are you then?" he asked in thickly accented English.

"Who I am isn't important. *What* I am is the important thing in this situation," Parker said coolly, exhaling a stream of smoke into the space between them.

"*What* are you then?" Lopé asked, between sopping blood draining from his nose and trying to smoke his cigarette.

"You're looking at terrorist charges here in France and murder charges in the States. If you're helpful, I could possibly, in turn, be helpful to you."

"*Encouler, espèce de con!*" Lopé sneered at him, and one of the officers sharply slapped the back of his head. Lopé slightly flinched, trying to act as if the powerful hand slamming against the back of his head hadn't hurt. The officer was rearing back to hit him again, but Parker stood up. Silently, Parker met the much bigger man's glare, and the other lowered his arm and stepped back. "Let them hit me, you fool! I will be on the news tomorrow and all of France will see how they treat us."

Parker turned to face Lopé's determined demeanor. "No. You won't be on the news, Lopé. After keeping you here as long as they like, they'll move you to an undisclosed location. It will be months before they finally disclose that you've been captured, and even then, they will say you are being held somewhere a thousand kilometers from where you will actually be spending your days in a tiny, windowless cell."

Parker spoke with a quiet fierceness that shocked both Gibson and Nivelle. Of the two, however, only Nivelle knew Parker was not bluffing.

Parker smoked his cigarette casually while watching Lopé puff nervously on his.

"There's enough on you in the States to lock you away in one of the worst prisons over there and forget the key. Once you get done serving your sentence in a prison here in France, they will extradite your ass over there, and you're going to see what it's like to be the French bitch of some three hundred pound dude named Bubba who's going to make you scream in terror as he's having his way with your ass in the shower."

Lopé was trying to act tough and keep his expression stern, but Parker noticed the lines around his eyes were beginning to weaken and knew he was breaking him. He was mildly sickened by how these feelings of accomplishment made him feel somehow good. He quickly he dismissed this realization and continued to push his advantage. "So, Lopé, why don't we get to the point and you tell me what I need to know. Then we can see about keeping Bubba away from your ass."

Lopé let his cigarette fall from the corner of his mouth and they both watched it land on the dirty floor. As if he didn't want it to die, Lopé didn't move his foot to extinguish the ember. He lowered his eyes and bent his head forward. "If you know anything about her, you should know I would have no idea where to find her. She does her own thing, always has," Lopé said in Basque, just for Parker, then smiled at the thought of Graciana's recklessness.

He'd heard stories of what happened in the American prisons, and the thought made him wish he could say something, without really saying anything. "If she's out in the open, I would look for her for at a fête. She will always go to a fête, even if she knows she shouldn't," Lopé said before spitting blood on the floor.

Parker didn't want to waste the moment. "And what about the contact in America? What's the name?"

Lifting his eyes to Parker's, Lopé smiled, fully revealing his wolf-like incisors. He paused in reflection before answering. "I will tell you this: his name is not Jean Francois Goni, and he's not from Cambo." Lopé threw back his head and laughed. It was a piercing, almost eerie laugh. Then he was promptly smacked on the back of the head again. Lopé bit his lip until Parker saw a trickle of blood forming along Lopé's lower lip.

Parker placed another cigarette in Lopé's mouth and said, "*esker-rick asko*." Then standing, he nodded to Gibson and turned for the door.

Lopé explosively shot up from his chair. He moved so quickly his captors barely got a hold of him before he reached Parker. "They'll get you! You're going to die, *fils de pute*!" Lopé screamed as he was pummeled to the floor. With a knee jammed into the back of his neck, he managed to add, "When you find Graciana, they will find you!"

Parker leaned down and picked up the cigarette that had been knocked from Lopé's mouth. He walked over and bent down until he was directly above the now immovable Lopé. As he dangled the cigarette in front of Lopé's eyes for a few seconds, he wondered to himself, what would it be like to burn someone's face with the end of a cigarette?

Suddenly, feeling sick with himself, he threw down the cigarette and left the room. He stepped into the hallway where he began to pace and breathe deeply to hold down the acid he felt rising in his stomach.

When he looked up, Gibson was standing in front him, patiently waiting. "It's okay, Sebastian. Believe me—it's better when you still feel something than when you don't anymore," he kindly offered.

"How can you do this, Gibson? This is inhuman!" Parker spat out.

Gibson raised his hands, trying to calm the young man. "Try to relax, Parker. Unfortunately, this is how it is." Seeing the disbelief cross Parker's face, he tried to think of something more convincing. "Sometimes, in order to do good, you have to do a little bad."

"Then why do policeman arrest vigilantes?" Parker asked.

Gibson sighed heavily. "Why do you always have to ask such damn hard questions to answer?" Thinking for a second, he then answered, "We don't allow them to exist, because if we did, then we would have no power ourselves."

"This whole *putain* world is about fucking power! It's all about who controls who or who controls what. The French and the Spanish control the Basques, so why would they disgrace themselves by giving up that power?" Parker said, pulling out a cigarette. "The answer is that they won't." Gibson looked at him and lifted the corners of his mouth in a small smile.

Parker saw it and exclaimed, "What the hell do you think you're laughing at?"

Gibson broke into a laugh that riled Parker all the more. "I'm laughing because you're such a little asshole, Parker. Why do you always have to make everything so goddamn difficult?"

A scowl turned into a lopsided grin on Parker's face. He even produced a light chuckle. "Yeah, I guess you're right. No wonder I don't have a girlfriend, huh?" Gibson laughed harder and Parker joined him. "All right, old man, let's go. I need a drink."

"Honestly, so do I. Where should we go?" Gibson asked, between laughs, as they walked out of the complex.

"To the hotel to get our things and then to the airport. We've got all we're going to get here. I doubt Nivelle's men will get any farther with Lopé. Nivelle can either follow us or not. I don't think it really matters at this point."

Parker noticed the blank expression on Gibson's face. "Listen, back there he told me nothing, and he told me everything. I'll explain on the way."

"But where exactly are we going?"

"We're going back home, back to the Basque Country," Parker said absently, his thoughts already running ahead of them.

When they exited the complex, past the guards disguised in street clothes at the entrance, Gibson wanted to inquire on what exactly Lopé had added when he threatened Parker. But he didn't get the chance. After passing a group of African prostitutes, they were in the thick of the crowd parading down the Champs-Elysée.

* * *

Blast Rocks Spanish City

A bomb exploded in an underground car park close to government buildings in the northern Spanish city of Santander. There are no immediate reports of casualties, although a large cloud of smoke produced by the blast led to traffic being rerouted around the area.

Smoke was pouring from ventilation shafts in the car park and Spanish police were proceeding with caution because of fears of a second car bomb nearby. Police said a Basque newspaper alerted them forty minutes before the explosion, which had given time to cordon off the vicinity and evacuate the car park.

ETA has claimed responsibility for the bomb. The organization has injured more than 2,300 people since 1968 in its campaign for an independent Basque homeland in northwest Spain and southwest France.

22

Paris, France

PARKER TOOK A DRINK from a small glass of calvados. "You know the Fête de Bayonne kicks off tomorrow night," he said.

"I take it this is some other festival?" Gibson asked, lightly sipping on his beer.

"*Non.* It's not some other festival," Parker replied, mocking disgust. "This is *the* festival of the French Basque Country. It's la Fête de Bayonne!" He raised his calvados in salute and took a long drink.

"If Patrick hadn't known the owners of the hotel where we've been staying in Petit Bayonne, I doubt we would have been able to find a room in the city. When we return, the place is going to be a madhouse. I'm sure they are already pre-partying in the streets. Everyone knows about the Festival of San Fermin in Pamplona and the running of the bulls, but the Fête de Bayonne is the second largest festival in all the Basque Country."

"And you think we're going to be able to find who we're looking for in the middle of all that?"

"To be honest, I don't know," admitted Parker, lighting a cigarette. "But I think the temptation to be there will be overcoming for our *belle* Graciana."

"I still don't know how you expect to be able to find her in a crowd of people."

"I'm hoping we'll get lucky," Parker said, shrugging.

Gibson raised his hands from the table in astonishment and arched his eyebrows. "Great, Parker. I think I'll keep that one out of the report."

Parker drained his glass of calvados and rose to get another from the bar, not having the patience to wait for a waitress. "You won't, if we find her," he shot back as he walked away.

Gibson rolled his eyes and took a long drink from his *demi*, already feeling a touch of a buzz. He looked around the bar Parker had taken him to. After leaving the glamour and lights of the Champs-Elysée, they flagged a taxi to return to the hotel. They called the airline, but were unable to get on the last flight of the evening from Paris to Biarritz. In fact, they were unable to find a flight in the next two days.

Parker explained that this was because of the popularity of the festival in Bayonne. He said they would have wait until the morning for a train. Parker proposed they get drinks. Gibson agreed that it was not a bad idea.

The bar was stylish and trendy, a place he normally would never think of entering if not coaxed by someone else. Gibson noted the ceiling was comprised of exposed shiny piping and wooden rafters, the floor a patchwork of multi-colored tiling, and the walls painted purple, covered with Toulouse-Lautrec posters. Now, near eleven o'clock, the clientele was mostly flashily dressed twenty-somethings, but the place was far from crowded.

Parker commented that eleven was far too early for most Parisians to be out. Gibson thought it was likely he was the only person in the establishment, including the bartenders and wait staff, not smoking.

Having borrowed a tray from the bar, Parker returned to the table. On the tray were two draft beers and two short glasses of some other sort of liquor. He carried the tray loftily above his head and made an exaggerated show of placing the drinks on their table. The act made Gibson laugh and he played along, placing a dollar on the surface. Parker snatched the dollar saying he was a cheap-ass and returned the tray to the bar. When he came back, he instantly grabbed for one of the short glasses, explaining that it was liquor called Marc, known as the whisky of Burgundy. Still standing, he touched his glass against Gibson's, said *santé* and knocked it back in one easy swallow. He let out a deep sigh, indicating his approval, and sat back down.

Gibson watched this in amazement. "You're going to kill your liver before you're forty if you keep drinking at this pace," he commented.

"Oh, well," Parker darkly replied, grabbing for one of the glasses of beer.

Once again, Gibson felt concerned for the young man sitting in front of him, but he didn't know how to handle such a situation. He'd never been a father.

Fatherhood had always been in the back of his mind and he thought one day he and his ex-wife would have taken the step into parenthood, but his career had always put it off.

Putting concern aside, Gibson stuck with what he did know—his job. "Parker, what about whatever Lopé said to you?"

"I'm still thinking about that lovely riddle he left us. I'm sure the answer is there. It's just going to take some thought to figure out."

"That's very reassuring." Gibson finished off the beer he'd been working on and picked up the glass of Marc. He took a light sniff and quickly felt his nose burning.

Parker watched him intently. "Just drink it all in one shot."

Gibson raised the glass to Parker and drank the shot. As he set down the glass, he felt a burn run down his throat. He gasped for air and Parker laughed. Gibson shook his head, quickly reaching for the beer to wash away the taste of the Marc. He couldn't even taste the beer.

Still smiling at the expression on Gibson's face, Parker said, "Hold to, oh ye of little faith. I expect I'll have the puzzle figured out by tomorrow morning."

"You think you're going to find wisdom in the bottom of a glass?" Gibson asked. He took another drink of beer and tasted something different, like a fruit flavor. "What kind of beer is this?" he asked, examining the glass with a sour face.

"It's a *demi-pêche*. Basically, they put some concentrated peach syrup in a glass of draft beer. I think it has a nice taste. What do you think?"

Taking another swig, Gibson asked, "Who would ever think of ruining a beer by making it sweet?"

Parker ignored the beer criticism. "As far as finding wisdom, I could think of worse places to look." Parker took a swig of his *demi-pêche.*

"Listen, John. I've been thinking of something." Parker paused to formulate his thoughts. "What would you say to you and I coming back for a week or so when this is all done? We could stay in one of the hotels along the beachfront of San Sebastian and spend our days lounging in the sun on the beach watching the tight bodies of tanned girls that are even too young for me running around in string bikinis. Then, at night, we could have fantastic meals on the promenade. After that, we could try our luck at finding a couple of lady tourists. A nice, refined woman for you. And her daughter, hopefully one of those girls from the beach, for me?"

Gibson felt an unfamiliar feeling of warmth in his heart. "I'd like that, Sebastian."

They made a toast and finished off their beers. Parker was headed back to the bar for more before Gibson could say anything.

Two hours, and numerous drinks later, the two began staggering back to their hotel.

"I gotta take a leak," Gibson said.

"In France, men can duck into an alley or off into a small street and piss in the open as freely as they want and no one will think anything about them. In France, men may piss freely!" Parker proclaimed, waving his arms in the air.

Gibson laughed and called the French barbaric. But at the very next small side street, he told Parker to wait for him while he took care of some business.

He meandered down the narrow road until he found a suitable target area, the side of a white Peugeot van. He unzipped his fly and took a stance next to the back tire. Concentrating on the job at hand, he was just about there when he suddenly felt as if he was being watched. With his member in his hands, he glanced around.

He could no longer see Parker standing by the corner. All he saw was a poorly lit road with cars lining either side. The buildings bordering the street looked like low-rent apartment buildings. No light shone from the windows, making them look lifeless. Turning to look in the other direction, he observed the same bleak scene.

Trying to laugh off his growing anxiety, he returned to the task at hand. Then he thought of something that made his urge to urinate slip from his number one priority. *I can't remember from which direction I came.*

After seeing Parker standing in the open at the end of the street smoking a cigarette, he had let the drunkenness take him and walked down the narrow road, chuckling at things they had said earlier in the bar.

Quickly rearranging himself, Gibson zipped up his fly before moving into an opening on the other side of the van. A strong feeling of anxiety now overcame him. He was standing at an intersection of four small roads, which all looked the same every direction he looked. He couldn't recall how far he'd walked. He only remembered that he'd carelessly wanted to get far enough from the larger road so no one would be able to see him peeing like a dog on the street.

Not knowing whether it was the right decision or not, his thoughts clouded after what seemed like gallons of booze, he tried his luck and began walking down one of the roads.

After only a few steps, he knew he was lost. Still, he continued walking down the narrow road, figuring that he would have to end up somewhere to be able to find his bearings eventually.

Having finished three cigarettes, Parker began to ask himself where in the hell Gibson had wandered.

He'd watched Gibson meander down the street in his happy drunkenness. Thinking nothing of it, he'd not paid attention to how far Gibson had gone down the road. He considered that he could find a pay phone and call Gibson on the cell phone he had, but then he would have to head down the street a few blocks and Gibson might return and not find him. So he concluded that it would be better if he tried to find him first.

Peering intently down the road where Gibson had walked, Parker didn't see any sign of life. But he kept walking.

In the meantime, as Gibson walked briskly, the effects from the alcohol were quickly wearing off from the intensified fear mounting within him. He figured he could easily hop into a taxi once he hit a major thoroughfare and assumed, by saying the name of the hotel, he would get there without a problem. His rationale was that Parker would figure this out and would be sitting there on the front steps of the hotel smoking his brains out and polishing off a bottle of red wine he just happened to find on his own way there. Of course, Parker would surely give him shit for getting lost, but he could deal with it.

The problem was, as far as he could see, he was nowhere near a major thoroughfare. Every turn only revealed the same outcome of small dark roads. And the roads were not the linear roads he was used to in a place like DC. These roads wound one way for a block and then turned another direction. It was confusing as hell and he felt hope draining away. Under his breath, he cursed Paris for having so many damn obscure streets.

All he'd been looking forward to was a good night's sleep back at the hotel and now he was considering the fact that he may just have to keep walking all night until he could figure out what to do. And he wouldn't have been surprised if a thug jumped in front of him and demanded his money.

Yet, something about walking through the lonely, empty streets of Paris felt slightly comforting to him. The architecture of the low buildings was so old and distinctive and different from anything he was used to in the cities of America. Here one felt as if they were a part of history and not just passing through it. For a brief moment, he actually didn't feel panicked at being lost at all and enjoyed his momentary peace in the still night.

Suddenly, the snapping of a stick nearby somewhere near him quickly woke him from the brief calming sensation. Instinctively, he pulled out his .45 and held it against his waist.

After three blocks, Parker told himself he was pursuing a worthless endeavor. He fiddled with his lighter in one hand in an attempt to keep his mind occupied. He was feeling a touch badly at having coerced Gibson into joining him in a last round of shots at the bar. Clearly he'd pushed the old guy beyond his limits.

Though he didn't know where he was going, the cool night air felt good and he'd never minded walking the streets of Paris alone. After some thought, he decided if he didn't come across Gibson soon, he would just head back to the hotel, a mere four blocks away, and wait for him to either fall out of a taxi or call the front desk. Optimistic, he was sure it would all work out, one way or another.

Gibson saw a person coming down the road toward him and impulsively jumped into a doorway. He wasn't sure if he'd been seen. From what he'd glimpsed of the profile, he knew it was a moderately built man approaching. The straightness and light gait of the man's walk made Gibson believe it was a younger man. What worried him most though was the fact the man had something in his hand.

It was too dark for Gibson to see, but all his mind would let him believe was that the man was flipping around some sort of knife in his hand, something like a butterfly knife. Moving his gun from the front of his waist, Gibson held it at his side. *Let the punk try and fuck with me.*

As he walked, Parker popped a cigarette into his mouth and lit it with a lighter. The flicking sound of the lighter resonated through the quiet street.

Gibson heard the noise a few steps from him and knew the butterfly blade had been opened for action and that he was going to soon have the knife stuck in his gut. He raised the gun to the level where he imagined the assailant's head would be and quickly stepped out from the doorway to face the pending threat.

The next moment was one he would never forget.

His finger was on the trigger as he noticed the shocked expression on Sebastian Parker's face that was lit up by the burning cigarette between his lips.

Involuntarily, the cigarette fell to the pavement as Parker stared into the gun's dark barrel.

Registering his mistake, Gibson's muddled reflexes told his arm to lower the gun. He put his arm around Parker and held him tightly. It wasn't a moment for the word *sorry* to be expressed.

As they silently walked back to their hotel, Parker vowed to never smoke another cigarette again. He handed his box and his lighter to a homeless man sleeping on a street corner near the hotel. The homeless man was delighted to receive such a gift, but Parker didn't say a word in response. The tender fingers of death felt all too close and needed no further encouragement. He figured that if he considered himself to be as lucky as a cat with nine lives, then he'd just used up one. And that was in addition to however many others he'd already used.

They returned to the hotel and both passed a restless *nuit blanche.* Once morning was well underway, they gave up on the prospect of sleep and met for a late breakfast of coffee and baguette with butter and fresh blackberry jam in the hotel's crammed dining area. Afterward, they packed their bags and were off in a taxi for the Gare du Nord and a long train ride back to the southwest of France.

* * *

Thick gray clouds swallowed the land and made day seem like night. Rain came in spurts and showered the landscape in a thick downpour as they passed through it, moving at what seemed like light speed on the streamlined TGV train.

Gibson was amazed at the efficiency of the French train system. It made Amtrak look like a poorly run, dangerous carnival ride. He wondered how the French could be so backward in some regards, such as public toilets, but be so advanced in something as public transportation? It was a true anomaly. He didn't bother sharing his thoughts with Parker, who would surely find a way to defend the French in some way.

"Actually, we've been lucky. It's not at all uncommon to show up at a train station in France to find out that the SNCF, the organization responsible for rail service in the country, has declared *la grève* and decided to shut down rail service for a day or two. Sometimes they even pick certain lines on purpose in order to make rail travel all the more disruptive."

Parker laughed as he told a story where he'd been stranded in Bordeaux for two days not knowing how he would get back to his host family in Biarritz. Parker described how he'd attended a soccer match with friends and witnessed the glorious madness of a European football match. He and his friends got ridiculously drunk and ended up walking the streets and sleeping in the train station while they waited for the strike to end.

Parker seemed to think the story was hilarious, but it didn't sound at all humorous to Gibson.

The weather seemed to get worse the farther they got from Paris and the closer they got to the Basque Country.

* * *

She knew it was a bad idea. They would be looking for her at the festival. She told herself that she should forget about it and head for a friend's place in Amsterdam where she would be safe. But *should* was not a popular word with Graciana.

Fuck them. If they find me, they find me, she concluded. At least she now knew what they intended for her. In her mind, that gave her an advantage as she would never underestimate her status again.

And besides, with all of the different factions within ETA, there was bound to be some group that disagreed with whoever had ordered her removal. She would just need to find them. That faction would get her out of the country and set up with a new identity. They would be grateful for her sacrifice to the cause.

That was exactly what she'd do…right after the fête was finished.

* * *

The *gare* was nearly empty. A few employees of the train station could be seen, their faces long in despair at having to work on the first night of the city's grand festival. It was 8:00 p.m. and Parker told Gibson that most people would already be hammered.

"What about a taxi?" Gibson asked, but none were to be seen outside the train station.

"I never thought we would take a taxi. I figured the walk to the hotel was not too bad, provided we don't have to move through the crowd," Parker commented. Gibson didn't understand what he meant, but he was tired and didn't feel like asking for an explanation.

The long train ride was draining on both of them after the previous night and they weren't talking much anyway. Carrying their bags, they set off through the district of Saint-Esprit, which Gibson noted was a much rougher looking, run down area of Bayonne. The streets were empty of people and there were few cars on the roads.

Gibson found the lack of activity strange until they rounded a bend and stepped onto a bridge that spanned the river. Then he understood, first hand, why they had not seen anyone—the bridge was blocked off to vehicles and on the other side he could see a solid wall of people everywhere he looked. The noises of talking, singing, and musical instruments all blended together and Gibson couldn't believe he'd not heard it all from the moment the train pulled into the station.

Parker plunged into the mass of bodies and Gibson did his best to follow. He was fairly sure, under normal circumstances, he would be able to find his way back to the hotel in Petit Bayonne. However, in their absence, the City of Bayonne had transformed into another place. Whereas before it had been somewhat sleepy, now it was alive with a special kind of madness.

Faces leered all around him, contorted in varying stages of drunkenness. People raised glasses and smiled indulgently at them as they squeezed by with their bags. Some offered them the very glasses or bottles in their hands, but even Parker waved off the offers.

Witnessing this, Gibson wondered if Parker was ill. He was about to say so by yelling into his ear above the deafening noise surrounding them, when he noticed a still, concerned look come over Parker's face. Knowing they were in what was likely the closest thing to heaven on earth for Parker, seeing him looking so withdrawn troubled Gibson.

Making it to the hotel was no easy task. They were constantly slowed by unresponsive groups with red wine stains covering the fronts of their shirts like battle wounds. The dulled expressions they could make out staring at them under the glare of street lamps made Gibson laugh. At times they had to sidestep a line of young men singing and jumping in near unison in order not to get trampled.

Gibson gave up counting how many times drinks were spilled on him. One man ambled backward into him and almost managed to dump a bottle of red wine on him. Gibson's first instinct was to grab the punchy man and set him straight, but noticing the man was far from coherent, he changed his mind.

When they were close to the river they weren't even able to see the water due to all the bodies packed so closely together. It was like trying to push through a ridiculously over-crowded bar at the end of a night, yet they were outside in the streets and it wasn't even that late.

A sudden burst of fireworks made Gibson nearly drop his suitcase and reach for his gun. The crowd erupted into a soaring roar, louder than the explosives in the fireworks. Bright splotches of red and green spread out above them. The colors of the Basque country filled the sky overhead.

Feeling the pulsating drunk energy moving around him, and looking up at the brilliantly colored sky above, Gibson was surprised this place had not yet blown up into a full-scale revolt. The energy of the place was unlike any other he'd encountered.

Parker had given him numerous lengthy explanations on why the northern Basque Country had always remained relatively calm compared to its neighbor to the south, but those explanations didn't relate as he stood amidst the craziness of the Fête de Bayonne. It had the same crowded drunkenness of Mardi Gras in New Orleans and what he imagined, since he had never personally been, was a similar energy to the festival in Pamplona.

This Fête de Bayonne, however, had a palpable, underlying feeling of discontent in the air. It wasn't that people weren't having a good time, since at any given time he could spot either someone having too much of a good time and vomiting against the side of a building or on the verge to among the joyous faces surrounding him—but something unseen was present that weighed on him, pushing against him.

Most people they passed on their way to the hotel were red faced and happily drunk, but some seemed more than just drunk on booze. They were also drunk on pride, and Gibson had learned throughout his career that pride can be a dangerous drunk. These people were up to their necks, swimming in it.

If he and Parker were being followed, what would stop anyone from killing either of them? In the middle of this madness, it could be done clean and easy, leaving them bleeding to death on the ground. These thoughts made his arms tense and he kept one hand close to his breast, a quick grab away from his gun. Nothing ends the way you want it to, he thought, as they continued to push their way through the crowds.

After nearly an hour of muscling through hordes of bodies, they finally made it to their hotel in Petit Bayonne. When they pushed through a group of young men blocking the entrance chanting in Basque while they chugged bottles of red wine, the owner merely glanced at Parker, raised his filled glass of wine, and handed them the keys to their respective rooms.

Gibson thought it odd that Parker, of all people, was willingly stepping away from one of the wildest parties on the continent, but that's exactly what he did. With a somber expression on his face, Parker trudged to the door of his room and said *bonne nuit* before closing it behind him.

Gibson stood and stared at the grain of the wood in the door. He considered knocking to ask Parker what the hell was going on, but having had enough of Parker's moodiness for one night, he went to his own room.

If he is going to be that bitchy, at least it looks like he is staying in his room. This thought gave Gibson a touch of relief as he entered his room. He threw his small suitcase aside on the floor and flopped down on the bed. As he did, the weight of the day and the situation flowed from him. Within minutes he was snoring, fully clothed, on top of the bedcover.

* * *

Parker rose to answer the knocking on his door he could barely hear over the drunken pandemonium going on in the streets below his window. Opening the door, he found her standing in the hallway in front of him. She was as beautiful as the first moment he'd laid eyes upon her years before. Neither of them said a word. Parker silently opened the door wider.

Alaitz walked into the room and Parker closed the door behind her.

* * *

Sliding her naked body from the bed, Alaitz quietly picked up her clothes from the floor. She left his room without looking back.

Later, he realized that throughout the night neither of them had spoken a word. There are times when words are not necessary, he thought.

From the light outside his window streaking into the room, he caught glimpses of her savage eyes as their naked bodies moved in unison. In those revealing, brief moments, when her body was pressed against his while he was deep inside her, he looked into her opened eyes and saw the truth inside.

Perhaps she always looked at him this way and he'd never noticed. It was only at that moment, when all her defenses were down and she was surrendering herself to him, that Alaitz could look at him in the way she honestly desired. What he saw in the glimpses of her eyes was not only love—he noticed traces of fear, doubt, and pain. He felt her clench around him, holding him tightly inside her while her hands clasped on his shoulders. Her entire body shuddered like a small earthquake, and when it did, she looked straight into his eyes. Even with the lights of the room off, enough seeped in through the curtains so that they could clearly see each other's faces. A tear ran down her face. They held one another tightly until they fell over on the bed, exhausted.

When she rose from the bed, Parker awoke. Without saying a word, he watched the door close behind her.

* * *

Gibson opened the unlocked door and stepped into Parker' room. Parker did not bother to rise and lock it after Alaitz let herself out earlier. Gibson was clean-shaven, showered, and obviously ready to go.

Without a greeting, Parker glanced at the alarm clock on the bed stand and realized, with a shock, that he had been dizzily staring at the closed door ever since Alaitz closed it over two hours ago. This realization, accompanied by the unmistakable presence of Gibson, gave him no choice but to consider that perhaps Gibson was right to distrust women as much as he did.

"Parker! Get the hell up! We're not going to catch her staying in bed all day," Gibson demanded.

Parker raised a hand from under the sheet of the bed in recognition of the order. "Yeah, yeah. Just give me a few minutes," he muttered, letting his head fall back on to the pillow.

"I thought you weren't drinking? Why do you look like you had a rough night?" Gibson started to feel tense and he began to pace the room. "Did you go out last night after leaving me?" he cautiously accused.

Parker instantly shot up from the bed so his bare back was pressed against the wooden headboard of the bed. "No, I didn't go out last night. I just sort of worked out for a while after I got to my room." As he spoke, he felt a slow grin cross his face and he had to fake a coughing spree and bring the sheet to cover his mouth in order to keep from revealing it.

Gazing speculatively at him, Gibson said, "That's what you get for smoking like a goddamn chimney."

When he walked to the window, he pulled the curtain aside to look down on the street. He was surprised to see groups of people already on the streets, raising their glasses yet again in celebration. The area in front of the small hotel was nearly packed, due to the adjoining bar in the lobby.

"Jesus! Did these people go home last night and come back for more? Or did they just pass out on the streets and wake up again?" Gibson asked, not expecting an answer.

"I doubt they ever went home or passed out. They've probably just gone straight through. It's the outsiders that can't handle the Basque festivals. Why do you think it's always Americans that get pummeled by bulls in Pamplona? It's the Basques, and those fortunate others who live here, that really do the partying," Parker replied.

Gibson didn't like being lectured by a kid first thing in the morning and reacted defensively. "I'll bet you'd really like a smoke right about now, eh Parker?"

Parker also responded defensively, "And I'll bet you'd like to draw your big-ass gun on me too, eh Gibson?"

Piercingly, Gibson glared at him. *Watch out, young one.*

Parker didn't want to back down, but aware of the tension, he decided to change the subject. "So, I wouldn't mind smoking, and you wouldn't mind shooting someone…whatever. "Here's the deal for today. I think you should go with Patrick to wherever we should be going, and I'll stick around the fête and see what I can find."

"Where are Patrick and I going? Unless you had some inner illumination last night, we still don't know what the hell Lopé was talking about."

Parker hesitated before answering. He considered that, in a way, he had found illumination, just a different kind than what Gibson was referring to. Right now, he figured Gibson knew enough about his personal life. There was no need to say more on the subject. Instead, he said, "I just know he'll be able to figure out, at least part of it, before I do. The guy has lived here for twenty years and knows a lot about this place."

"But we took the rental car back, remember? And even if we could find a rental place here, there's no way we could get through these hordes of people filling the streets."

"He has a car and should be able to drive anywhere close. Why don't you let me get dressed and I'll give Patrick a call to meet us somewhere?"

"Fine. I'll meet you downstairs in the lobby in fifteen," Gibson said, quickly and sternly.

"You'd better watch out, John Gibson. I have the feeling you're going to kill someone today," Parker warned.

Gibson didn't respond and stepped through the doorway, closing the door behind him. Parker rolled his eyes. Suddenly, thoughts of Alaitz overwhelmed him and he fell on his side, smiling. For a splintering moment he wished he had a cigarette.

* * *

Closed Basque Paper Reappears

A Basque language newspaper, which was closed over allegations that it was linked to the armed separatist group ETA, has reappeared under a new name.

Earlier this week, *Euskaldunon Egunkaria* was shut down and the majority of its senior staff arrested as part of the Spanish government's crackdown on Basque separatism. The newspaper had a circulation of near 13,000 readers.

But the day afterward, its successor, *Egunero*, which means "every day" in Basque, was on sale at newspaper stands throughout the Basque Country with a headline reading: "Shut but not silenced."

The daily's assistant director told a Basque radio station the police had exerted pressure to prevent Egunero from being printed and distributed. An entire section of the daily was dedicated to the closure of *Egunkaria*, including descriptions of police raids on the offices and homes of its employees.

Spain's National Court Judge said the ban was temporary, while the fundraising network of ETA was probed. A march to protest against the newspaper's closure was immediately planned in the city of San Sebastian.

23

Basque Country, France

WHEN THEY WALKED INTO the dark bar in Saint-Esprit, Patrick Holm was seated alone at a table. Instead of immediately walking over to Patrick, Parker stepped up to the bar. He downed his own glass of Patxaran. When Gibson didn't pick up the glass placed in front of him, he downed his as well. Parker then motioned to the rough-looking bartender for another glass and as he did, Gibson noticed him glance in Patrick's direction. Their eyes briefly met. Something alluding to the fact that no apparent danger was present passed between. Parker quickly grabbed the two newly filled glasses from the bartender and headed to Patrick's table.

Since the normal bus lines couldn't run through the city due to the blocked-off streets, and since they would have no opportunity to drive out of Bayonne, Parker and Gibson had walked, once again, across the Adour into Saint-Esprit.

Parker felt good after his silent encounter with Alaitz. However, noticing that Gibson was in a foul mood, Parker tried to engage him in historical conversation as they wove their way through people and toward Patrick's table. He told Gibson, "In medieval times, Saint-Esprit was a haven for exiled Jews from Spain. They were the ones who had actually brought the secrets of making chocolate, for which Bayonne has since become acclaimed. The area of Saint-Esprit has always been a bit of a borderline area. It was closest to the port of Bayonne and thus always drew in the usual port crowds. Now it's an area of low income housing, dark streets, and a train station." After taking a sip of his drink, Parker continued. "The makers of Izarra had a factory for many years in Saint-Esprit that gave tours and a couple of shots at the end of the tour, but even that factory has closed and moved out."

Parker glanced around and then continued. "In a strange way, Saint-Esprit has still retained a certain vile charm that makes this little area unique. It's retained the same character for centuries. Five hundred years ago, if a visitor came to Bayonne and asked for the best place to find a good prostitute, the answer would have been here in Saint-Esprit. Today, that traveler's question would be answered the same way. The same question would be true if one asked where the best place to pawn stolen goods would be? The best place to buy drugs? The best place to rob someone in the middle of a street and get away with it?"

Parker had never trusted Saint-Esprit. Even walking through its streets in the middle of the day one couldn't help but feel on the defensive. A well known fact was that Nivelle and the rest of the French anti-terrorist and police forces thoroughly concentrated their efforts on seeking out any affiliated ETA partisans in Petit Bayonne. Parker did not deny that many did indeed hide out there, regardless of its highlighted attention. But to him, the more logical place to hide in the immediate Bayonne area was Saint-Esprit. It fit the profile of a place where one could disappear. The neighborhood was full of empty, unfriendly streets.

Since the Izarra factory had closed, there was not a single step outside the *gare* in Saint-Esprit where one felt welcome. He could think of many places in the Pays Basque where he didn't necessarily feel welcome, but Saint-Esprit was one of the few corners where he actually felt unwelcome. It was a place where everyone looked with questioning at all those who walked its streets. In his mind, he envisioned it as a place for pirates, both in the past and present. In many ways, he was right.

Arriving at Patrick's table, Parker pulled out a chair for Gibson and then sat down himself. Patrick motioned to the bartender, who took his time bringing over three glasses of Patxaran and set them on the table. He quickly snatched a bill from Patrick's hand as soon as it was pulled from his wallet. The bartender acted as if he didn't trust to be paid and scurried off without asking if change was needed. Patrick didn't seem to mind the rude gesture.

"I'm surprised you don't have a cigarette dangling from your lips yet," Patrick commented in English.

Parker and Gibson exchanged a quick, awkward glance. "I decided smoking isn't such a healthy idea," Parker said, uncharacteristically hurried and uneven.

Gibson felt uncomfortable as he remembered the night in Paris. He adjusted himself in the wooden chair. The chair squeaked with his movements.

The odd response to the comment didn't go unnoticed by Patrick, who quickly changed the subject. "Well, anyway, unless you have a plan, we're missing the fête and as you know, it's practically a sin to miss down here."

Gibson felt uncomfortable as he remembered the night in Paris. He adjusted himself in the wooden chair, which squeaked with his movements.

Parker clinked his glass against the one on the table in front of Patrick and poured his own down his throat. "We are missing the fête, but for good reason," he said wiping his hand across his lips deliberately, in order to give himself more time to consider how he wanted to phrase his next line. "I know you've done a lot for me, but I need to ask another favor."

Cold eyes stared back at him across the small table. Gibson waited, growing impatient at both Parker's slowness to come to a point, and the fact that he didn't know what exactly was the point. Patrick didn't need to speak. His gaze alone told Parker to continue.

"I need you to go with Gibson and look into something," Parker announced.

Patrick quickly drained a glass. "Go where?" he asked, after taking a drink.

Parker looked into his empty glass before responding. "I don't know." He looked up at Patrick to see he was receiving a blank look. "Someone told us something while we were in Paris that I'm sure is a clue. So far I just haven't been able to quite figure it out." He paused, once again, to look around the room before adding, "But I think you can."

"You know, it's getting more and more dangerous for me to be seen with you? One of these times, someone is going to see me with you two and put things together and then, not only will I be in danger, but my girlfriend as well. You don't live here anymore. You don't know what it's like. Some say they never notice them here, but if you pay attention, you cannot miss their presence," Patrick said forcibly, yet quietly.

"*Je sais. Je sais.* And I promise you this is the last one. Please, believe me. I wouldn't ask any more of you unless I really had no other option." Parker looked at Patrick and waited for a sign to continue.

Patrick felt anger coursing through him, but looking at Parker, the young man who he had befriended so many years ago, he gave in. Taking a deep breath, he asked, "What did this person say to you?"

"When I asked who I was looking for, he told me: 'His name is not Jean Francois Goni, and he's not from Cambo.' Now, what the hell do you think that means?"

"His name is *not* Goni, and he's *not* from Cambo," Patrick repeated. "That is interesting."

"Parker told me that Cambo is the name of a city near here, and my take is that the place to look for this person is not there," Gibson chimed in, happy to make himself a part of the conversation.

Patrick looked intently at Parker before responding, "No, I think Cambo-les-Bains is probably the place where we do need to go. The Basque people can be deceiving to outsiders, but it's always a subtle form of deception and not so obvious. I think our best bet is to go to Cambo and ask around about anyone named Goni."

Parker smiled a wide grin. "I knew you would be able to help," he said. The glass of Patxaran, sitting in front of Gibson, caught his eye. After getting an approving nod from Gibson, Parker grabbed the half-filled glass and split it between himself and Patrick. The two said *on egin* and downed their shots.

"*Bonne chance,*" Patrick added.

"Just what do you plan to do?" Gibson asked, with a touch of uncertain accusation.

"We're not going to find that girl by any conventional means. I know she's here, out there in the middle of it all, being beautiful and letting the fête love her. I can feel it." Parker paused, and both Patrick and Gibson looked at him questionably. For fear of what would be answered, neither said a word, as Parker seemed to be lost in his own thoughts. Suddenly, he snapped to attention. "To find her, I need to get out there too," he added.

Gibson shifted uncomfortably in his chair once again. "Are you sure that's such a good idea, Parker? I mean, we all know that this girl is dangerous."

At the bar, an animated patron spilled his glass of beer, resulting in a yell of annoyance from the bartender. Ignoring the commotion, Parker looked into Gibson's eyes. "This is a one shot deal, Gibson. We either do it, or we quit right now and give up."

The tone of his voice was deep and serious, unlike anything Gibson had heard in the short time he'd known Sebastian Parker.

Gibson knew he had a difficult decision to make and now was wishing he'd kept his drink. When he looked directly at Parker, he saw the burning determination in his eyes and knew the kid meant what he said. He admitted that he was beginning to think of Parker as real a partner. "All right," he quietly agreed.

Parker slammed his fist on the table. "*Allons-y*! We'll meet later in the hotel lobby."

After they exited the bar, Parker waited for Gibson and Patrick to round the corner to Patrick's car before turning to set out for the heart of la Fête de Bayonne.

* * *

The joint appeared in front of her face. Since it had already been passed around the circle of four people a few times, and since she hadn't smoked for weeks, she could immediately feel the hash taking a firm grip on her. First, her arms fell limp at her sides, and she began losing feeling in her legs. Ignoring her body's reaction, she concentrated on the joint and grabbed it carefully with two fingers. Bringing the joint to her mouth again took even more concentration, but once it was firmly in place between her lips, she pulled deeply until she felt as if her lungs could hold no more. Holding in the smoke, she did her best to pass the joint to the guy sitting next to her.

Graciana closed her eyes and felt the pressure of the smoke pushing against her lungs. Eyes still closed, she slowly let the smoke escape from her mouth and nose. Then she lethargically opened her eyes, surprised to find she'd fallen over on the couch. Vaguely, she realized the ecstasy pill she took earlier was now in full effect.

The other three people in the smoky room didn't seem to notice her condition. Since she was more comfortable with her head on the armrest of the couch, she didn't bother trying to move and straighten herself. Instead, she used what was left of her capable powers to summon strength and concentration in order to reach over to the low table in front of her and grab her box of cigarettes. After grabbing three times without coming up with the cigarettes, she managed to finally get a grip on the box and brought it close to her face. She held the box against her cheek and wished she could eat the cigarettes inside.

She was about to pull out a cigarette from the box, bring it to her mouth, light a match, and finally be able to inhale her favorite breath of air in the world. But the joint reappeared in front of her eyes. Glancing down, she noticed her girlfriend Cecile's fingernail polish, a light purple shade, more than she noticed the burning joint. Although they were never exclusive, Cecile was always ready to see Graciana when she called her.

When she didn't respond, the joint disappeared and was replaced by Cecile's lips. The lips, accented with light purple lipstick matching the fingernails, closed on hers and she suddenly felt a rush of smoke enter her lungs. She felt the flicker of tongue on hers as Cecile pulled away. Behind them, the two guys they were hanging out with howled out in pleasure at the sight.

Graciana blew out the smoke from her lungs and tossed the box of cigarettes at Cecile, mumbling for her to light a cigarette and place it in her mouth.

Cecile understood what she wanted, but when she leaned down again to set a lit cigarette between Graciana's barely parted lips, she lifted up Graciana's shirt and began to kiss her stomach around her belly button. The two guys moved in their seats to better watch the show.

Although Graciana realized what was happening, she didn't care. She felt no pleasure from it. Soon, her shirt and bra were pushed up to her neck and Cecile was kissing her bare breasts to the delight of the receptive audience.

The guys were students in Montpellier. They'd met them only moments before in a bar. Graciana and Cecile acted interested and invited them to their room, only because they wanted to smoke their hash.

Despite not moving, her body reacted and her nipples hardened. Graciana was more interested in pulling smoke from the cigarette than anything else. By now, Cecile had taken off her own top and the guys were trying to hide the bulges in their pants. Looking beyond the smoke of the cigarette, Graciana could see Cecile's thong poking out of the back of her jeans. Cecile had undone the front of her own jeans and had a hand jammed between her legs. Gently, Cecile pulled down Graciana's jeans and panties. Graciana looked away to the corner of the hotel room and watched smoke rise from her cigarette.

Sometime later, Cecile helped her to her feet. They were now both fully clothed and Graciana imagined the two guys from Montpellier had experienced accidents in their pants. *The dumb asses had probably thought they were going to get laid.*

As they walked out of the small hotel room into the hallway, Cecile put her arm around Graciana's shoulder. Graciana didn't like the feeling of having someone so close to her, but she was still flying from the effects of the hash and ecstasy, and Cecile's hold helped to keep her upright.

The door to the outside world opened in front of her. As they moved outdoors a bright light embraced her as if returning to a lover's embrace. For a moment, she felt warm.

* * *

Patrick drove as fast and wildly as Parker. They talked little, and Gibson didn't know if this was because they shared no love for one another, or if they simply didn't know what to say. He imagined a mixture of both. It didn't bother Gibson not to talk, and frankly, it was a relief. Most of the time, Parker didn't shut up. A break from him was kind of nice. Though Gibson was a little worried about Parker, he couldn't deny enjoying not having smoke or booze in his face, or Parker's smart-ass mouth yapping at him.

The car rounded a bend and climbed up a steep rise that took them above the city of Bayonne. He could see the piercing, darkened spires of the cathedral off in the distance.

Parker, once again, entered his thoughts. "Do you think Parker will be all right?" he asked Patrick.

Patrick took longer than was needed to respond. "He'll be fine," he muttered, his eyes never veering from the road in front of him.

"What makes you so sure?" Gibson prodded.

Tossing a quick, annoyed glance in Gibson's direction, Patrick said, "I say that because I don't think he'll ever find her down there." He motioned with a nod of his head back and to the right, in the direction of the now receding city limits. "As you've seen, there are thousands upon thousands of people down there. And what's more, it's one of the biggest parties in all of France, and I don't care if he did quit smoking, there's no way that guy will ever stop drinking." Patrick shifted gears as he slowed the car and then accelerated again when he rounded a turn-about and headed off onto another road. The road merged with a highway that cut through rolling countryside. "I wouldn't even be surprised if he sent you off with me just to have a couple of hours to party with some of his old friends," Patrick added.

Gibson's fists involuntarily tightened after Patrick's final comment. He shook the thought out of his head, but noticed that Patrick had been watching the displeasure he caused as much as he could while still driving. Turning in his seat, Gibson cracked the window to get some fresh air. When he took a deep breath, instead of fresh air, he got a nose full of pungent manure. Not wanting to give Patrick any more fodder, he held back from the reaction to gag and swallowed the deep lungful of air. Leaning back in his seat, he felt the .45 against his chest. Being reminded of his gun's presence calmed him.

Twenty silent minutes later, Gibson noticed the hills were growing both larger and closer to the road. The scent of the countryside was unmistakable and refreshing. Gibson noticed a few very strong and sweet smells in the air and asked what they were.

"It's the smell of wild plums and cherries of the Pays Basque. That smell in the air is mixed with the odors of grass, earth, and farm animals," Patrick explained.

Gibson decided he would tell Parker how much he enjoyed the smell of wild plums and cherries and sheep and cows in the air as soon as he saw him again.

Shortly after this brief exchange, Patrick turned off the highway onto a small, two-lane road that wound around a sloping hillside and followed along the Nive River. The road was lined with birch trees and sunlight danced through their green leaves. At times there was a break in the trees and one could see the rising hills in front of them that were covered with bright green, open pastures, and forests.

Just as they passed by a large estate that was cordoned off by a thick, cast-iron gate, Patrick said something to him about at the base of the mountains was where the Nive River was famous for being bluest. Patrick's referral to a famous line by a French writer fell on deaf ears.

When Gibson didn't even ask him what he meant by the comment, Patrick felt a need to educate. "Rostand was the writer's name who lived around here at the turn of the past century. He had moved to the area and built a grandiose, neo-Basque style villa on the Nive River with a fantastic garden offering views of the Pyrenees. The name of the estate is Arnaga. It's become a popular tourist attraction in the southwest of France."

Gibson still acted disinterested and unimpressed even though he was, in fact, hoping Patrick would continue with his dialogue. He found it strange that the longer he stayed in the Basque Country, the more he wanted to learn about it. The place had some sort of mystique that seemed unapproachable and enchanting at the same time. He thought he'd even buy a book about the region at some point.

"Wouldn't it just be easier to get a phone book for this city and look for our name?" Gibson asked.

Patrick nodded his head to acknowledge the question, but waited to answer until he maneuvered into the opposite lane and passed a car that was obviously driving too slowly for him. After he moved back into the proper lane of traffic and eased up on the gas petal, he responded. "We're not going to get a feel for what we're looking for from a phone book. We need to talk to people to get help."

"I'm not exactly sure that we really know what we're looking for," Gibson commented, letting his eyes fall on a group of cows that had wandered next to the road and were peering out from behind a low fence.

Patrick slowed the car and shifted into a lower gear when they came to an intersection. "I'm not entirely positive myself, and that's why we need to get into a place with the locals and see if we can get people talking." He turned onto a road and soon they were entering a residential area with newer looking houses that were all white with orange tiled roofs.

"Won't most people be at the festival thing back in Bayonne?" Gibson asked.

"Yes. But not the older people, and that's who we need to talk to. And a café bar is the perfect place for me to get someone talking." Patrick responded.

Gibson shook his head and rolled his eyes. "I see why you and Parker get along so well. You both think life revolves around being in a bar or café, as they seem to call the ones here that serve other things aside from booze," he commented.

The housing district gradually turned into the downtown area of the small and peaceful town. Patrick turned off the road and parked in front of a bakery that had a door open, letting the tantalizing scent of freshly baked baguettes bless the sidewalk in front of the building.

"Well, this is still France after all," Patrick said as he pulled back on the emergency brake.

* * *

A man, who'd obviously had his share of red wine judging from the deep stain down the front of his shirt, unsteadily rode a bicycle with the head of a bull on its front through the street. A group of children ran in front of the bicycle, cheering with joy, mocking fear as if a real bull crashed forward, ready to run over them. Perhaps some of them dreamed of running the loud and crazy streets of Pamplona one day, or even of facing a bull, eye to eye, in a ring surrounded by spectators.

Parker had done the first and loved the experience. The second would only remain a distant dream. Training to be a bullfighter was a lifetime pursuit and true talent was as distinguishable as any other sporting activity. A true bullfighter not only had skill and talent, he had the ability to be an artist in his performance through agility and grace.

Watching the spectacle of a group of running children passing by him, a little blonde girl wearing the traditional male costume of white shirt, white pants and red sash, ran into his leg. Parker leaned over to help the girl to her feet. When he tried to help her, she defiantly resisted and insisted she do it herself. Raising her sparkling green eyes, she looked up into Parker's face for a split moment. She couldn't have been more than ten years old, but Parker saw the reflection of the grown woman she would become some day. He turned to watch her run along, her ponytail bouncing behind her as she hurried to catch up with the other children. Inwardly, he smiled as he continued on his way.

If he knew Nicolas Leonis as well as he believed he did, he knew where he would be able to find him. The daily bullfights during the festival were popular events, and Nicolas would never miss them. Even though it was a few hours before the bullfight was to begin, Parker imagined Nicolas would be camped out in a bar somewhere nearby the stadium, quenching his early day festival thirst.

The stadium was located away from the business and historical districts, and even apart from the many parks and recreation areas that surrounded the city along the crumbling ramparts. It was in a residential area that, most of the year, was relatively quiet and calm. However, on bullfight days, and especially on bullfight days during the festival, the neighborhood's atmosphere turned to madness.

Bayonne was the first city in France where Spanish bullfighting occurred across the southern border. For hundreds of years there had been bullfighting in Bayonne, and none of its popularity had ceased. Every bullfight held in Bayonne pulled in a packed stadium.

As Parker approached the *quartier* of the stadium, he felt the day change, gradually ascending into something new and unique. The clamor of voices, or the sound of a distant flute, or the smell of red wine and dirt and animals had a way of raising the energy of the event to a new level that one couldn't quite compare to any other sporting spectacle. Parker was always reminded more of going to a crowded classical music concert than to a sporting event. But it would have to be a musical performance where, in the middle of a dramatic set, someone would pull out a canvas and paint a masterpiece on center stage. *Unique* was the word he was thinking of as he approached the friendly mayhem outside the stadium.

Makeshift vendors were on the sides of the road selling skinny Basque and Spanish spicy, hot sausages like hot dog vendors at a baseball game in the States. The two permanent bars outside the entrance to the stadium, which doubled their yearly revenues on the days of bullfights, were packed so fully that when you looked into their interior you could only see a wall of unidentifiable bodies. An area in front of the two bars was crowded with people sitting at tables and drinking red wine out of decanters and short wine glasses.

Someone had also made a wise business decision to open a drink stand off the street. Behind the long table stood two women and a man who all looked as if they were about to fall over from the constant opening of wine bottles and filling of glasses, or from the shots of wine they took themselves as soon as they could find an opportunity. The table was full of bottles of red wine and short plastic glasses and the line of people leading up to it wound back around the side of the stadium.

For as long as the line looked, compared to dealing with the crowds in one of the bars, Parker had to think the wait for the wine stand presented a faster option as far as getting a drink. He wished he'd brought a flask filled with Izarra, he thought as he fell into line behind a group of rambunctious men. Each of them wore red berets and the hats were bright in the now strengthening sun. Parker couldn't keep from looking at the deep red of the berets in the sunshine.

Somehow he needed to find Nicolas, but first he needed to get a drink. Since the line was so damn long, he planned on getting two.

He stepped away from the table with a plastic glass in each hand. When a man stumbled in front of him, Parker aerobically maneuvered to let the man fall on his face in the street and then brushed past him.

He looked down at the man trembling with drunken laughter as his two friends helped him to his feet.

Not wanting to take any more chances, Parker quickly downed one of his glasses of wine. Although he had drunk it far too fast, he still savored the taste of Irrouelegy in his mouth, long after the liquid had passed down his throat. The wine's tender bite was just about to consume his thoughts when a powerful shoulder struck his own. His remaining glass of wine spilled over his hand and arm, causing him to drop the plastic cup. He turned, ready to make his annoyance known. As he was about to explode in a tirade, he noticed Nicolas was staring at him. The expression on his face went from a broad smile to one of disbelief.

"You really want to hit someone over spilling your glass of wine?" Nicolas asked in English.

Parker took a moment to calm himself and shake off his dripping hand. "Sorry, buddy. I haven't been myself in the last couple of days." He tried to turn his look of anger into that of a smile, but only halfway succeeded.

Nicolas looked at him questioningly. "Yeah, well, you know very well that you're in the wrong place if getting bumped into makes you want to fight."

Shaking his head in approval, Parker replied. "You're right. So let's go get in line to get another."

Nicolas laughed and slapped Parker on the back. "You've been away too long, *mon vieux*." Nicolas leaned over, picked up the cup Parker had dropped, and nearly filled it with a bright deep green liquid that he poured out of a flask. He handed it to Parker and then filled his own cup half way.

Raising his cup to Parker, Nicolas took a drink. Parker did the same and felt the heat of the liquor work its way down his throat and into his body. The warmth of the liquor calmed him. A small band of three men moved down the street playing traditional Basque flutes. Everyone around them turned to watch the trio and show their respect for the music. Things could be worse, Parker thought.

As the crowd gradually moved toward the entrance of the arena, Parker and Nicolas joined the stream. Soon after, Parker found himself seated on a long wooden bench overlooking the light-colored dirt of the arena below. A musical group moved across the floor, blowing horns and flutes and banging drums. Looking around, Parker noticed the spires of the cathedral peering over the edge of the arena as if they too wanted to catch a glimpse of the unfolding spectacle.

By now, the sun had moved past a center position in the sky, and the partial overhang of the arena created a shaded area over half the seats. The line of the shade created an ominous boundary between the seats of those in the light and the seats of those in the dark. Feeling the sun on his face, Parker felt the energy emanating inside the arena moving through him. A combination of the sun, the cheering, and the music made him feel great.

At this moment, Parker was above his assignment. He was above what he was expected to do. He was merely a happy participant in what he could only describe as one of the most wonderful atmospheres he'd ever experienced.

This mood prevailed until he noticed *her* standing in one of the front row boxes.

At first, he wanted to tell himself that it wasn't her, and couldn't possibly be. But the more he looked, the less he could deny the fact he was staring directly at the person he had *said* he would find, yet deep down inside, had not actually believed he would.

There was no mistaking Graciana Etceverria in her full glory. She was wearing a short, tight white dress that left nothing to the imagination pressing against her torso and clinging to her waist.

Fascinated, he watched her chat, laugh, drink, wave her arms in the air above her head in order to make some point, and delicately smoke a cigarette. For as much as he wanted to believe she wasn't as bad as portrayed, something inside told him not to listen. Yes, Graciana was beautiful and sexy. She also was cunning and lethal.

Nicolas nudged him in the shoulder and passed him the flask of Izarra. Parker didn't even register the burn of the liquor this time. Noticing his preoccupation, Nicolas inquisitively asked if he was okay, "*Ça va?*" Parker answered with a nod, implying he was fine. Nicolas accepted the response, without truly believing it.

A solitary cloud passed in front of the sun, temporarily shading the world below. As the cloud moved by, it worked like a curtain about to be pulled back in order to reveal a stage. The music stopped. A feeling of quiet and intense anticipation reverberated through the charged crowd as all looked down onto the light colored stage of dirt that would soon be stained with blood. There was a strange, prickly silence surrounding the stadium as the anticipated scent of death slowly rose through the stands.

A wide board of wood was raised on the perimeter of the wall surrounding the ring. The black, powerful figure of a bull bolted out of the entrance into the sunlight and its last moments on earth. Collectively, the crowd burst into a joyous uproar at the sight of the bull. The crowd screamed and cheered on the bull. While the crowd wanted to see the bull die, it also wanted to see a graceful death.

Just as the man standing directly next to Parker jumped to his feet with the rest of the crowd at first site of the bull, the man dropped his cup of red wine. As the cup hit the ground the wine inside spewed out onto everyone in the immediate vicinity, including on the leg of Parker's jeans. No one except Parker seemed to notice the spill.

In full glory, the bull stomped to the center of the ring. The doorway through which it had come was quickly closed behind. The bull took little notice of the door's closing, or to the thousands cheering for its slow, bloody death. What the bull noticed was the first waving red flag that entered its field of vision. Almost without thought, he charged with thundering speed toward the flag and the man holding it. As the bull grew close, the flag waving man quickly darted behind a slim, wooden barricade attached to the wall of the ring.

Just as the bull was about to crash its deadly horns into the wall, another waving flag caught its dark eye. Quickly, the bull forgot about the man peering over the barricade wall at him and charged toward the new flag waving man. Over and over again the bull streaked across the ring in full glory, only to face the same outcome. After numerous trips around the ring, the bull became noticeably slower. His body heaved with strained breath, and his heavy breathing could be seen even from the top rows of the arena. Now that the bull was growing tired, it was time for the matador to enter the ring.

On queue, the matador entered the ring like a conqueror returning to the front lines of a battlefield. His tall, slender frame, tucked into a sequined outfit, rhythmically moved to the center of the arena. His movements were deliberately slow, exaggerated, and graceful. Once in the center of the ring, he removed his black hat and placed it on the ground in front of him. He looked up at the arena's President's box and bowed. As his back straightened and his shoulders rose, he placed his hat once again on his head and turned to face his foe, who had been breathing laboriously off to the side of the ring, never taking his eyes off the matador's shiny outfit.

Time to begin.

First, the matador attracted the bull's attention by dangling a large, purple flag by his side. The bull raced to him at top speed. A rush of bursting adrenaline took over the crowd and it roared in unison as the bull brushed by the matador with all its weight centered on the flag. The bull stopped itself before crashing into the wall and turned to look back at the deceiving presence standing before it. Theatrically, the matador bowed to the crowd. At the same time, the flagmen from the beginning of the event once again reappeared, both distracting and steering the bull toward a new set of characters that discreetly entered the scene.

These new characters were two portly men riding horses that were covered in thick padding to protect them from the bull's sharp horns. Adding to the drama was the fact that the horses were blindfolded and the men carried long lances. Between the matador, the flagmen and the horse riders, all the outfits seemed to sparkle together. The blues, reds, greens, gold and purple shone brilliantly in the afternoon sun.

As the bull was skillfully directed into the reach of one of the horseman, a lance was forced into the bull's strong back. Bright red blood spewed from the wound in the bull's back as it pushed uselessly into the padded side of the horse. When the bull pushed itself closer, the rider turned the penetrating lance repeatedly, grinding the blade into the bull's flesh. The crowd cheered louder with the site of more blood.

When enough damage had been done, the lance was removed, and again, waving flags distracted the bull. As the horse riders left the ring, a group of runners entered the stage. These runners quickly dispersed around the ring, causing the bull to glance frantically at the fast moving things surrounding him. The bull was both terrorized and angry as thick blood covered one of its sides. Taunting the bull, the runners moved toward him from different directions, calling to him in Spanish. As they called, one of them raised two short spears above his head and took off at a full sprint at the animal standing alone in the ring. The approach was orchestrated so that the runner could leap by the bull's head while, at the same time, forcing the two spears into its back.

The crowd roared in approval as the runner completed his brave task and left two spears protruding from the bull's back. As the bull kicked in pain, anger, and frustration, the runner bolted directly for the safety of a barricade. Then two more runners repeated the maneuver and the result was a fountain of blood pouring from the bull's back onto the ground.

Once again, the matador took center stage.

Red flag in hand, the matador again lured the bull past him. Now that the bull was severely weakened by a deadly mix of exhaustion and blood loss, the matador was able to bring the bull closer to him, where it appeared as if the body of the bull was brushing against the matador's leg. Again and again, the grand bull passed within inches by the matador's straight, balanced body. With quick flicks of his wrist and the red flag, the matador coerced the bull to fully circle him around and around without ever being touched. These movements were precise. Each time as the bull passed by him, he tauntingly called to it.

By now, the tension was palpable throughout the crowd as the music from the band rose to a crescendo. No one dared speak.

The matador displayed his years of training and experience through his connection with the bull. By understanding the animal, he knew where it would move, how it would respond. He was a teacher to the bull and would soon be his executioner. During this moment, the matador must feel godly, Parker thought.

After a succession of passes, the matador turned away from the bull with a strong, but delicate swipe of his now drawn sword. He bowed to an ecstatic crowd of onlookers, who were entranced by his performance. The clapping of hands now mixed with howls of appreciation and chants.

With a change of swords, the onlookers knew the matador decided it was now time to end the spectacle with one last action of grace. He approached the now unsteady bull. Standing quietly before it, he pointed the sword directly at the bull's eye level. Then, with a quick sidestep toward the unresponsive bull, he thrust the sword into the bull's spine.

How long the bull remained standing was entirely influenced by the precision of the matador's strike. An established matador could drop a bull within seconds.

The flag wavers returned to the arena and waved their flags around the bull's lowering eyes. During this ritual, the matador stood presiding over the bull, watching the once magnificent beast slowly expire. He waited for the exact moment he knew the bull would fall. At that precise time, he turned to the crowd and bowed, as the bull fell in a heap of flesh and blood behind him. Immediately, the crowd exploded and waved white napkins in the air.

The immense body of the bull was then ignominiously dragged out of the arena by two large horses and a small assembly of plainly dressed men. Part of the same group of men dispersed to gather the bloodstained dirt in baskets and remove it from sight as if the spectacle that had just taken place did not involve the spilling of blood.

As the dirty work of removing the executed bull and the blood-soaked earth was conducted, the matador toured the perimeter of the ring, bowing to the applause of the masses. The applause didn't quickly dissipate; it sustained itself long after the people's hands had grown tired of clapping. Flowers were thrown at the matador's feet and he politely nodded his thanks at the offerings. However, he momentarily stopped when his eyes met those of Graciana. Bending to pick up a white rose by his feet, with a smile, he casually tossed the flower up to her.

Even from a distance, Parker saw the elated expression on Graciana's face. Reluctantly, the matador moved on until he had made the full tour of the ring and then disappeared through a doorway. He noticed Graciana intently watching the matador the entire time and felt a bit of jealously.

Today the crowd had witnessed power, grace, beauty, and death. They left pleased, while Parker left feeling as he always did when he stepped away from a bullfight—utterly confused.

On one hand, he'd been swept into the emotion and excitement of the whole spectacle—the music, the cheering, the waving of white napkins in the audience, the brilliant colors, the strength of the bull, the graceful movements of the matador, and the dark blood on the ground. Then, on the other hand, he felt slightly sickened by the fact that minutes earlier, he'd eagerly cheered on a sick game of death that ended by slowly torturing a magnificent bull until it was killed.

Cruel beauty was how he best described the whole spectacle.

* * *

When they stepped into the interior of the café, they saw it was occupied by a young man standing behind the bar, two older men sitting at a table near the entrance, and a young teenage couple at a table near the back of the room. The older men, both wearing black berets, were staring out the window in front of the bar, seemingly bored. They had half-empty glasses of some sort of liquor on their table. In the back, the young couple looked nervous, as if they were afraid of being caught by their parents for doing something wrong. Behind the bar, the young man leaned against the wall, also staring out the window, watching life pass by, just like the old men at the front.

While they walked to the café's entrance, Gibson questioned the soundness of their plan. Wouldn't people automatically be suspicious of his presence?

Patrick boldly reassured him that Cambo-les-Bains was not as closed off as many other towns in the Pays Basque. He was sure that he would be able to make conversation with someone, as he knew many people in the area. He was also confident someone would be able to help. The only rule was that Gibson would have to sit on the side and wait. Once inside, Patrick handed him a Sud-Ouest newspaper he brought from the car and suggested that Gibson act as if he was reading.

On hearing the plan, Gibson pictured Parker chugging red wine and dancing in the streets of Petit Bayonne.

As he was about to open the door, Patrick remarked to Gibson that he was searching for older men to approach. Then they stepped inside.

Walking up to the bar, Patrick ordered a beer for himself and a coffee for Gibson. Then he left Gibson at the bar while he headed for the table occupied by the older gentlemen.

As ordered, Gibson opened the newspaper and blinked at the words on the pages he held. Then he found himself staring into the short tassel of coffee in front of him, hoping to see something in the thick, black substance that would answer the riddle in his mind. *"His name is not Jean Francois Goni, and he's not from Cambo."*

Gibson found the coffee strong, yet slightly creamy, and overall fantastic. The recognition forced him to smile inwardly as he considered how much of a hard time Parker would give him if he was there to witness that Gibson now preferred the French style of coffee.

Patrick laughed loudly with the men at a joke. Then he got up and walked to the bar and ordered beers. A song came on the speakers that Gibson thought was very sad sounding. He wished he understood the words. As the bartender poured the *pressions,* Patrick leaned closely to Gibson and told him that the song was about a bull being killed in a bullfight. Gibson nodded, his inward smile of moments ago now gone.

Before returning to sit back down at the table, Patrick gently nudged Gibson and with his eyes suggested Gibson join him in a light chuckle. He obliged, knowing it was a good tactic. As Patrick sat down at the table, a few nods were made to Gibson. Gibson had to assume Patrick was making the proper excuses for his friend not being very friendly, possibly telling them he was mute.

Again, Lopé's statement, *"His name is not Jean Francois Goni, and he's not from Cambo,"* echoed through Gibson's mind. A few minutes later, he overhead Patrick repeat the name to the gentlemen, who were noticeably enjoying a change in conversation and free beers. Not wanting to be seen watching them, Gibson raised the newspaper above the bar counter just enough so that he could see the table in his peripheral vision.

The two men each took a deep breath while pondering the name. Jean Francois Goni. Gibson watched their concentrated expressions.

One man shook his head and picked up his glass of beer, taking a long drink. Enough thinking for him. The other took longer to give up, but give up he did. Patrick shrugged.

When Patrick returned, he looked disappointed. He explained to Gibson, in a quiet voice, "I told the gentlemen I was looking for a distant relative by the name of Jean Francois Goni, who, I had been told might live in the Cambo area. Since they were of no help, let's move on to another place."

As they passed the men at the table by the door, Patrick gestured to them and they smiled in return while they took long sips of their beers. Just as Gibson and Patrick were stepping through the doorway, one of the men called to Patrick. Gibson didn't know what was said, but whatever it was made Patrick quickly return inside. Not knowing what else to do, Gibson stepped back inside as well, but kept a distance from the table. Patrick sat down.

Standing by the door, Gibson waited. Maybe it was good, or maybe the old guy just wanted another beer. After the old man recounted what seemed like a novel, Patrick rose from the table, thanked the man, and shook both their hands. He nodded to Gibson, who fell in behind him as they again exited. As Gibson opened the door, he looked over at the men and said *merci*.

* * *

Though too early to be thinking of eating, Parker felt his hunger growing. Normally, during a day of the fête, one wouldn't really eat until 8:00 or 9:00 p.m., after a full day of drinking. But Parker was thrown off his normal routine and was honestly not enjoying something he usually enjoyed more than anything else. The festival was happening all around him, with smiles and wine-stained shirts and red sashes and berets and scarves. It was above him with the raised arms holding drinks and below him in the puddles of spilled booze at his feet. Nicolas was still with him, but he had trouble paying attention to his friend because his eyes were focused on the head of blonde hair in front of him. The pretty head of blonde hair.

They were right behind her. He knew she'd not seen him. The rose given to her by the matador had long since been dropped, trampled on by hundreds, if not thousands in the streets. Observing her, Parker thought Graciana's attitude displayed that she didn't care what happened around her and probably didn't even care what happened to her.

Parker and Nicolas were crossing a bridge into Petit Bayonne and the further they progressed, the mass of bodies pressing against them increased. Nicolas said something, but Parker didn't hear him. He was focused. *I can't lose her now. Gibson won't be back until late, and if I return to the hotel to wait for him, I will lose her for sure. No, I can't wait. I'll have to confront her on my own.*

Parker felt a hand slap against his face. Every muscle in his body instantly tensed. He turned to meet whatever else was connected to the hand with a clenched fist.

"What the hell has come over you?" Nicolas asked in French, quickly moving away from Parker with a look of fear and confusion on his face.

It took Parker a moment to register that the slap had come from his friend. He took a deep breath, and then unclenched his fists, trying to force a smile. Quickly, he looked over his shoulder to see if he could still locate Graciana. She was ahead of them, about ten yards, and had stopped with her female partner to accept glasses of wine offered to them by four older, Spanish-looking men.

"I'm sorry, *mon ami.* There's something I need to take care of and maybe we should say *salut* for now," he said, turning back to face Nicolas.

A burst of loud chanting erupted from a group of people all sloppily drunk and stumbling out the front of a bar not far from where they were standing.

"I can't believe what I'm hearing!" Nicolas exclaimed. "You want to go by yourself? During the fucking Fête de Bayonne? We've always partied together during the fête!" Parker lowered his eyes to look down at the glass of a broken bottle of beer on the street. "Great! You do that! Have fun, asshole!" Nicolas replied in English. Insulted, Nicolas walked away through the enveloping sea of bodies around them. Within moments, Parker lost sight of him.

Looking back, he realized he'd lost Graciana as well.

* * *

Spanish Prime Minister Rejects Basque Devolution

The Spanish Prime Minister has strongly ruled out granting greater self-rule to the Basque region. The statement comes days after the Basque province's governor called for an early referendum on the issue.

The Prime Minister insisted that no part of the Spanish state would be able to break away and create what he labeled: "An illegal regime." On Friday, the Basque regional leader suggested a vote within a year on sharing sovereignty with Spain over the Basque provinces.

The Prime Minister stated that the priority for the Basque region should be to defeat ETA, accusing the ruling Basque party of repeatedly finding other priorities.

The Basque governor called for the vote, saying the Basque region's more than two million residents had the right to decide their fate. But the government insists the plan would violate the rights of non-Basques, who make up less than half of the population.

24

Basque Country, France

PATRICK HELD HIMSELF PROUDLY as they walked to the car. Gibson didn't want to ask him what happened back in the bar until they were inside. As soon as they opened the doors and sat down, he asked, "What did he say?"

"His name is not Jean-Francois Goni, and he's not from Cambo," Patrick said, turning on the ignition.

"Thanks," Gibson said sarcastically. "But please tell me you know what that means now."

As the engine rumbled to life, Patrick finally let a grin spread widely across his face. He met Gibson's stern gaze. "The old man back there told me he remembered his father talking with friends and mentioning a man by the name Jean-Francois Goni, who worked on a farm for an uncle of his just over that line of hills." Patrick pointed to the south, where a rise of green hills compounded on each other to form what resembled a natural southern barrier to the town of Cambo.

Patrick continued. "Now this Jean Goni apparently left, along with many other Basque herders, after World War I to go to the United States to work in the growing sheep industry. So, as he's talking about this guy, I'm thinking this is no big deal, because nothing is out of the ordinary. It's not out of the ordinary, because so many young men from the Basque country, both from France and Spain, migrated to the western United States to become sheepherders. And it's not even out of the ordinary that a good percentage of these that went to the U.S. became very wealthy men as they progressed from herders to owners."

Gibson was confused by Patrick's "became wealthy" statement, and his expression revealed his puzzlement. Noticing this, Patrick addressed Gibson's unspoken question. "You may not know that the Basques are famous for their determination and hard work ethic. I don't know if you could find a people in the world more dedicated to doing a job and doing that job right. They aren't necessarily the savviest concerning financial affairs, but they know opportunity. In the western United States there was the opportunity to find work when there was none to be found here. Once there, the opportunity to save money and invest in your own herd, or into an outfit, was also present. The Basques realized this and many pursued that opportunity. Thus, it was not odd to me when the man in the bar told me that Goni became a very wealthy man in California after a few years of grueling work. However, what was very odd to me, and to the old man, was that no one here ever saw Jean-Francois Goni again."

"Why is that odd? Maybe he liked California so much he wanted to stay?" Gibson commented.

"I'm sure that has a lot to do with it. Many of the Basques who went to herd sheep did end up staying because they liked it and because there was much more opportunity to earn a living. But, you need to understand, the Basques are a very closely knit group of people. Friends and family and birthplaces are sacred things to them. Those who went away did so because there was no work here, and they had to go somewhere, but the Pays Basque is so elemental to every Basque person that it's basically part of their religion. Many who went away to work in North or South America as herders or dairymen or something else, returned to live here after they made enough money to be able to afford taking a bride and starting a family. Others stayed longer and returned later in life, very rich men, ready to live out their golden years in their homeland. And for those who stayed abroad and never returned, nearly every one kept something to tie them to the Basque Country. Many wrote home, asking for Basque brides to be sent to them, and many would at least return for lengthy visits to the home country." Patrick put the car into gear and pulled out onto the street.

"Jean-Francois Goni did neither. In fact, he did what many considered the most sinful of all things—he changed his Basque name and took on a more American sounding name." Patrick paused. "You probably don't know this, but to the Basques, this is a serious offense. This guy completely turned his back on his family, friends and culture. The old man at the bar remembers the name from having overheard his father talking with his friends about how much they despised this character. Apparently, everyone in town knew the name Goni and shared the disgust. What was worse, according to the old man in the bar, was that the rest of the Goni family in the area also unfairly became acquainted with disfavor at the hands of Jean-Francois, and had to leave the area. The old man wasn't sure where they ended up, but he was fairly certain they felt they wouldn't be able to escape the shame that followed them anywhere in the Basque Country and had to move to the region north of here in France, the Landes."

Patrick switched gears. "Although I think we've unraveled the riddle, I'm not sure we've solved the mystery. What's this all mean?" He quickly accelerated, causing the gears to grind and the engine roar.

The jerk of the vehicle snapped Gibson's head forward and woke him from his pondering. He thought about Patrick's commentary and question for a moment. "Did the old man back there mention where exactly in California this Goni ended up? Or what Goni changed his name to?"

Patrick drove the car up the on-ramp and merged onto the highway, punching the small car forward. "He did mention Chico, but he didn't know what Goni changed his name to, and I doubt anyone here would know since the name became so blackballed." Lighting a cigarette, Patrick cracked open the window on his side of the car. "Does this mean we need to find the Gonis, wherever they may be now in France? Is that the answer to the mystery?"

"No. That's not the answer," Gibson quickly replied. Patrick waved a hand in an attempt to urge Gibson to continue. "That kid up in Paris knew he was screwed and wanted to sell someone out without actually doing it. I've seen this move a thousand times. He gave us that clue knowing we could eventually figure it out. It's a setback that we don't have the name, but I can get my people back in the States to look into the history of the name Goni in the Chico area. I'm sure it won't be long before they come up with something."

Patrick coughed out a cloud of smoke. "Back in the States? Wait, what does that mean?" With a straight face, Gibson gazed at him without responding. "Oh, c'mon. Do you really think I want to undermine your assignment when I'm the one who just helped you?"

Gibson rolled his head, cracking his neck. "All right, Patrick, but by telling you this, I hope you know that if, for any reason, I think you've betrayed us, I'm going to come back here myself and extradite your ass to the States."

No longer acting so enthused, Patrick agreed with a nod of his head. Gibson decided to trust him. "We've suspected from the beginning that there's a connection in the U.S. with this group. I didn't think we'd be able to get a lead on this anytime soon, if ever, but discovering this new information is a major development. Even if we never find the girl, now we have a lead on the U.S. connection and, to be quite honest, it's much more important."

"Why is it that much more important?" Patrick asked.

"Because by finding the U.S. connection, we can crack something that, in time, could escalate beyond our grasp. There is no record of ETA ever soliciting support from a source in the States until now. But, as you know, the U.S. is a wealthy country. If U.S. support began to finance ETA operations, or if ETA began to use the States more as a hideout destination, we could have a serious situation on our hands. This insurgency that's been going on here in the Basque Country, in Spain and in France, could double in a matter of years. Many believe the troubles in Northern Ireland lasted as long as they did due to the support the IRA received from U.S. sources. So, by nailing the source in the States now we could, in essence, be stopping a wave that is about to come crashing down."

Patrick reflected on Gibson's words. He took a last, long drag on his cigarette and let it fly out of the window, the ashes scattering behind as the cigarette hit the road. "Then answer me this, Agent Gibson. Why do you care? What I mean to say is that you've made it abundantly clear you really don't care for anything over here. So it makes me surprised that you would feel so passionate about stemming an uprising in a foreign country, when I assume you realize that no matter how powerful ETA may become, it would never be able to stand up to either the governments of Spain or France."

Gibson thought about the question. "I care because they committed a crime in the United States, and I was assigned to solve the case," he simply answered, noticing that, involuntarily, his hand had begun to rise toward his gun.

For a moment, Patrick considered pointing out to Gibson that his answer hadn't really addressed what he'd asked, but after glancing over and seeing tension stressed across Gibson's face, he decided to just drive.

* * *

Panic began to creep into him. Everywhere he looked, he couldn't spot her. He honed in on blondes he saw, but each time he got close, he would see it wasn't Graciana. A group of red faced men passed by on the street, arms on each other's shoulders, singing a Basque drinking song while they sucked away on bota bags filled with red wine. Years before, Parker would've joined the group and been accepted as if he'd been with them the entire afternoon.

Now the sun had set and darkness was beginning to overcome the sky above. The streets of Petit Bayonne were becoming even more crowded and active. Knowing that his task was soon to become much more difficult with darkness swiftly approaching and crowds swarming into the area made anxiety roil within him. Looking up and seeing the red and green banners strung from window sills across the streets reminded him of ropes trying to hold everything below in place. But how could all the energy, life, and culture emanating from the very cracks between the stones of the streets of the Basque Country be contained?

A high school aged girl, talking to a friend as they strolled down the street, ran into him. Though he'd seen it coming, he was unable to avoid the collision because of the pressing crowd on both sides of him. The collision happened in slow motion. Red wine, the drink carried by the girl, splashed against his chest and left a large red stain. Embarrassed, the girl looked at him and repeatedly apologized.

Parker told her in French to not worry about it.

The girl unashamedly invited him to join her and her friend at the nearest bar. This would not be difficult to do, as from where they were standing, there were at least ten bars immediately around them. Quietly he made his excuses and moved on, leaving the girl longingly watching him make his way down the street.

Wandering aimlessly, Parker eventually realized he was standing outside the Euskaldun. One quick drink won't hurt, he told himself.

He passed by a group of kids smoking cigarettes in front of the door and, once inside, was met with a wall of amplified noise from the combination of loud talking, singing, and Basque rock music playing over the stereo system inside. With determination, he forced his way through a gathering of English university students who were the only ones, aside from Parker, not wearing the traditional Basque outfit, all white clothing with red accents. One of them nearly burned Parker with a waving cigarette as he inched his way to the bar and ordered a Patxaran.

Everyone was smoking and for a minute, he felt an urge for a drag, but it quickly passed when the image of Gibson's gun pointed at him flashed through his mind. He toasted the fête and swallowed the drink in one gulp. But as he was raising his head to knock back the drink, his eyes looked into the mirror behind the bar. He saw Graciana Etceverria reflected in the mirror.

She was standing at the other end of the bar with a crowd of male admirers surrounding her. The girl Parker had seen her with at the bullfight was still with her. This one looked both bored and annoyed.

Wanting to get closer, Parker ordered another drink. Subtly, he moved nearer to Graciana, making sure not to lose track of her again. Grabbing his drink from the bar counter, he turned away to move closer. As soon as he turned, he found himself staring into Alaitz's eyes.

Parker noticed something different about her immediately. Her eyes, usually unreadable and detached, now looked warm and inviting. By the way she was holding herself, he could tell she was more than a little drunk. But there was something else. She was looking at him as she had when they'd been on the rocks together in the mountains—as if there was no one else except them. As if the entire festival, all the people, the music, all the singing and all the dancing were not happening. When she lowered her eyes to his chest, he saw a glimpse also of fear and vulnerability in them. Gently, she raised a hand and laid her fingers on the red stain. Leaving her hand rest against his body, she moved suggestively closer to him.

In his ear, she whispered in French, "I can't lose you again, Sebastian. I don't ever want to lose you. I want you to stay here and never leave me again."

Her body, now firmly pressed against his, trembled slightly. He felt her breasts press against him. One of her hands was still on his chest, the other rested on his shoulder. A warm tear ran down her face and dripped onto his neck. As Alaitz leaned into him and pressed her face into his shoulder, his eyes moved to locate Graciana. With a regret that emanated like lead in his veins, he noticed she was making her way toward the front of the bar to leave. The muscles in his arm flexed, and he clamped his teeth together. Placing his hands on Alaitz's shoulders, he gently pulled away from her. Her eyes were filled with tears. He didn't know if they were tears of happiness or sadness.

He had to lean forward to speak into her ear. "Alaitz, I don't know how to say this, but I have to go now." The words stuck in his throat. He fought back his own mounting tears.

She looked at him in disbelief. Two lines of tears streamed down the sides of her face. "What?" she asked incredulously, with no need to speak into his ear.

Parker had to swallow hard before he spoke again. "I can't explain, Alaitz. I do want to be with you and I will stay with you, but there's something I have to finish first. Please, understand. You have to let me finish this." Pulling back again, his eyes moved from hers to the doorway, where Graciana was about to walk out into the crowded street.

Alaitz's expression changed to anger. Rubbing the corners of her eyes, her hands fell from his body and her became taut. "Fine, go finish what you have to, but say *adieu* to me first, because you will never see me again."

Graciana stepped through the doorway. Parker took a deep breath and stared into Alaitz's eyes. "Alaitz, I love you more than anyone or anything else in the world, and you are all I could ever want. But, I have to finish this."

"Why? What makes you think you can finish it, Sebastian? You know as well as anyone, if not more so, that the troubles will never end here." Her eyes were now fierce and hard.

He tore his eyes away from her to see Graciana stepping into the street. Looking back for a brief moment, he leaned forward and said, "Because, if I don't, I'll never forgive myself. Too many people have died and she doesn't have to as well." As soon as he finished, he regretted what he'd said. The *she* hung in the charged air between them until a beer bottle was dropped somewhere nearby, exploding in a loud crash.

Her eyes focused on him in a deathly stare and she said in a cold voice, "Go then. You go find her and then you go to hell!" She spoke in anger and regretted every word. But the senseless anger she felt kept her from saying any more.

Parker looked at her one last time and then forced himself past the people blocking the way to the street. Once he was at the doorway, he noticed Graciana standing with her partner across the street, smoking a cigarette. He felt an overwhelming urge to look back to see Alaitz, but did not. As he stepped into his lonely night, he felt something he'd not felt in years—his own tears on his face.

* * *

Night's gentle darkness quietly crept across the Pays Basque. Patrick stopped the car at the edge of a blocked-off bridge. Without saying anything, Gibson opened his door and began walking to the bridge and whatever lay waiting for him on the other side. "Do you want me to come with you?" Patrick asked, hanging his head out the car's window.

Gibson looked ahead at the bridge crossing the river and at the pandemonium taking over the streets of Petit Bayonne on the other side. Looking back at Patrick, he said, "No. I'll be fine. I'll tell Parker to give you a call tomorrow. I'm going to meet him back at the hotel, tell him what we found out, call my boss back in the States to give a report, and try to get some sleep."

"Sleep? You guys are staying in the heart of Petit during the Fête de Bayonne. No one could sleep in there unless they were dead," he nodded across the river.

Gibson didn't hear Patrick's last comment. He was already turned and walking across the bridge.

* * *

She was standing directly across the street from him, smoking a cigarette and tilting back a cup of some sort of alcoholic concoction. Of course, she was on the receiving end of many male stares as they passed by, much to the obvious disgust of her companion. But her chilly demeanor kept any one from trying to approach her.

A handful of firecrackers were thrown out of the crowd into the street. They exploded in a series of loud bursts that reminded him of gunshots. Parker took a deep breath and began walking toward her.

* * *

Parker wasn't in his room. He wasn't in the hotel's bar. He wasn't standing idly at the front entrance waiting for him with his *I know more than you* smirk. He wasn't even on the street carousing in front of the hotel with passersby as he forced large quantities of booze into his body. Even the latter situation would have comforted Gibson far more than the reality he faced. Gibson couldn't hide the overwhelming feeling pulsating within him. The feeling was telling him that Sebastian Parker was in danger.

After a moment of reflection, Gibson decided he would have to go looking for Parker. He knew this was most likely a fool's errand. But he also recognized he wouldn't be able to relax by just sitting, waiting, and hoping, like a worried parent, that Parker would eventually stumble through the door.

Taking a deep breath, Gibson stepped into the night and forced himself through passing groups of people on the vibrant streets.

* * *

"Can I bum a smoke?" Parker asked in French, as he stepped close to Graciana. Even in the fragrant air filled with smells of tobacco, alcohol and sweating bodies, he recognized the scent of her from the day he sat with her on the hillside. It was something that he would label as being close to wildflowers, even though he couldn't think of what wildflowers actually smelled like.

She didn't bother turning from the conversation she was having with her friend to acknowledge the request. All she knew was that it was a male asking something from her—never a good combination. "*Va t'en*," she said, loud enough to be heard without turning around.

Parker laughed at her comment, then took hold of her arm. Immediately he felt a shudder cascade down her arm, and she turned quickly, ready to smash her free fist into his face. When she turned to see her assailant, however, she froze and slowly dropped her small clenched fist. Her eyes spoke to him, revealing more than words could convey. Though she was surprised to see him, she was pleased as well.

When he let go of her arm, she fumbled as she pulled out a cigarette and lit it with her lighter. She offered him one, but he politely declined. "What are you doing here?" she asked, after calming herself and blowing out a straight line of smoke.

He looked behind her at her companion before firmly responding. "I think you should have your friend go her own way for the rest of the evening."

Graciana's eyes widened with shocked amusement. "And why would I want her to do that?"

"Because I can help you. You're in great danger right now. They're coming for you, and you don't have anywhere else to turn." He paused, staring deeply into her eyes. "And they *will* find you, Graciana."

Her amused look transformed into an icy stare. She narrowed her eyes at him. Then, as if satisfied, or at least intrigued, she turned to whisper something in her friend's ear. Up until that point, her friend had been standing aside, smoking and trying to look as if not attempting to overhear their conversation. Whatever Graciana whispered into her ear made her friend's eyes widen in worry, but she eventually nodded in acceptance. Their lips came together in a prolonged meeting before Graciana pulled away to face Parker.

Parker noticed her friend hurriedly disappear down the alleyway. There was no way he could guess what Graciana told her, and he considered there was now a very good possibility he was in direct danger himself.

She looked at him inquiringly. "And why would I want your help?"

"I can be more help to you than the French authorities," he said to her in rushed words. "They don't care if you live or die. I do." He looked down. "There's no reason for you to die."

She laughed mischievously. "But what if I don't care whether I die or live?" Dropping her cigarette to the pavement, she stepped on the glowing ember.

Suddenly, Parker felt as if everyone around was not only staring, but also closing in. Furtively, he glanced around and saw an encroaching circle of faces—faces laughing, jeering, leering, and watching. It felt as if the temperature had risen twenty degrees in a matter of seconds and beads of sweat ran down his face from his forehead. She waited for him to respond, and as he looked, her face blended in with those surrounding them. He felt trapped, cornered, and alone.

The recent burning memory of Alaitz walking away from him flashed before him. He felt fear.

"Can we go somewhere else to talk?" he finally managed to force out. Seeing her disapproval, he added, "Please." She agreed by nodding her head.

They moved through the crowd, across the street and down an alleyway to a less crowded street. Graciana surprised him as while they were pushing through the crowds, she grabbed his hand. Parker pointed down the road, toward a wide alley off the street. He knew the area was primarily residential apartments, so there would not be as many people.

They walked next to one another in silence.

* * *

Gibson pushed his way down the street. The street was damp and sticky from a thousand spilled drinks. A group of hurried boys ran into him. They were carrying sandwiches that looked like baguettes split in half and filled with slices of grilled steak and fries. Any other time he would have stopped to inquire where they had found such wonderful looking sandwiches. His stomach growled, reminding him of his hunger. Nevertheless, he pushed on, darting in and out of random bars, hoping to catch a glimpse of Parker. He knew it was pointless to think he would find him with the thousands of people crammed into the small area, but he was determined to continue.

Even though he didn't have direct command over Parker, he thought of him as his responsibility. Yes, Parker was bright and worldly for a young man his age, but he was dealing with something different, of which he had no real comprehension. The world of covert organizations such as ETA was a world of dark, lonely corners. Gibson couldn't erase the thought that Parker was walking directly into one.

Not paying attention to where he was walking, Gibson walked into a man wearing a bull's head as a sort of a mask. Gibson expressed an apology, and the bull's eyes looked at him as if they were real. The bull lowered its head to him and Gibson moved on.

* * *

Parker stopped walking and released her hand to face Graciana while he talked. She looked at him curiously. As they were a little away from the lights of the main streets, a few stars were visible above the rooftops over their heads.

"So, how can you help me? I thought you were just a student," she said in French, interrupting the silence between them.

"I'll always be a student of the Basque Country." As he spoke, his glance picked up something on the wall behind her. He looked closer and realized they were standing in front of the demonic faced mural he'd first seen while strolling with Gibson. The sight of the face made him uneasy. "But I also can guarantee that you'll be okay if you help," he quickly added.

Graciana pondered his words thoughtfully. "And how is that?"

"Because I work for the U.S. government," he said.

"But the French government doesn't particularly like the U.S. government," she tartly replied.

Parker blew out a deep breath, trying to hold on to his composure. "Yes, traditionally that has been the case. However, if you haven't noticed, when it comes to the issue of Basque autonomy, both the

Spanish and French governments seem to become the most understanding in the world."

He kicked at a rock by his feet and it flew across the broken pavement. He was about to lose her patience any minute and he had to lay all his cards on the table to keep her attention. Because he had no desire to attempt to restrain her.

"I work for the CIA and with the FBI. If you help me identify whoever it was in the U.S. that organized the job, I can guarantee your safety." He instantly felt slimy for lying to her.

The look on her face changed from hard to inquisitive, but then returned to steely, as if she briefly considered something and then changed her mind. "I don't believe you. You Americans are all cowboys. You would like to see me hanged." She lit another cigarette.

"France no longer has the death penalty," he promptly responded.

Looking at him through the smoke from her cigarette, she said, "But you would have me deported back to America where they still do have the death penalty."

Parker shook his head in disagreement and in growing annoyance. "I wouldn't want that to happen. I would fully stand behind you being placed in a prison here in the Basque Country. If you help us, I think I would have great backing to enforce that promise."

She took a long drag off of her cigarette and let her eyes rest on the glowing stars over their heads. When she turned her face, she looked straight into his eyes. "Are you in love with me?" she curtly asked.

He couldn't imagine what kind of game she was playing, but he realized by the instantaneous response of his tensing body that he was nervous about her question. "What do you mean?"

Her eyes didn't move, didn't blink. "I mean just that. Are you in love with me? I want you to tell the truth."

Parker choked on his nervousness. "Well, I like you, and I think you're very attractive and interesting, and probably lots of fun and—"

"But are you in love with me, in any way?"

He bit down hard on his tongue, trying to think of a correct answer. "Yeah, I guess I am, at least a little, in some way."

She dropped the cigarette between her fingers and walked up to him, firmly pushing her body into his. Her arms wrapped around him and her hands pressed against his shoulder blades. The closeness of her gave him chills. Fiercely, she pressed her lips against his. Her sweet tongue flickered in and out of his mouth and across his lips. He closed his eyes. From the moment he first met Graciana, he'd thought about being in this position. Now that he was, he could only think of Alaitz.

Suddenly, she backed away from him, a hurtful expression on her face. "Liar. You are not in love with me. Your love is for someone else," she angrily said. He didn't know how to answer. "If you would lie to me about that, how can I trust you about anything?" Again, he didn't know how to answer. Before he could form any words, she was walking away.

The evil face painted on the wall watched his every move with its deep red eyes. He started after her. Just as he almost reached her, with his arm stretched out to grab her shoulder, he felt something touch his own shoulder and heard a loud noise.

Probably just some kids with fireworks nearby, he thought.

Sebastian Parker's body crumpled on the hard pavement. The face on the wall watched in indifference.

* * *

John Gibson had been around guns long enough to recognize the unmistakable sound of one being fired. If he had to guess, he would say it was a .22 gauge rifle. His heart sank when he rounded the corner and saw Parker's still body in the alley, surrounded by a pool of dark blood.

He looked up at the surrounding buildings to see if he could locate an open window or rooftop from where the shot originated, but he saw nothing promising. He held Sebastian Parker's in his arms and he was afraid.

Gently, he held Parker's head against him with one hand, as he used his other to put pressure on the bullet entry point in Parker's shoulder. Even with this pressure, Parker's blood spilled over his fingers.

For a few moments, Parker remained conscious. Then his eyes glazed as he looked up at Gibson. Having been in this situation before, Gibson knew time was short. He spoke Parker's name to him, but there was no recognition. "Parker, I know how to find the contact back in the U.S.," he struggled to get out. He saw no recognition of his words on Parker's stricken face. "Parker, don't go."

A loud screeching siren pierced the air and interrupted what he was going to say next. Gibson didn't really notice the new sound resonating through the night. It interrupted his thoughts, but the new noise was only an addition to the thousand noises already pulsating around him. Taking a deep breath, he forced his teeth together, now ready to continue saying what he'd begun.

Suddenly, a hand fell on his shoulder. Instinctively, Gibson pivoted with a drawn gun. When he did, he found himself looking down the barrel of his gun, aimed directly at the pointy nose of Capitaine Nivelle.

Nivelle didn't look surprised to find the gun pointed at him. "I don't think I am who you want to shoot, Agent Gibson," Nivelle said, in his usual steady, arrogant tone.

"I want to shoot all of you," Gibson shortly answered, turning back to Parker. "Do some good and call a goddamn ambulance!"

"An ambulance is on the way. Apparently, someone already called to report this, a few minutes ago."

Gibson looked up. "A few minutes? That must have been right after it happened. Did the emergency operator find out who made the call, or where from?" Nivelle shook his head. Gibson considered the possibilities, but it didn't take him long to deduce who had made the call—Graciana. It had to be her. Parker had found her. But had she led him to this end?

Regardless, she was now free.

The ambulance finally arrived. Gibson stood to the side and watched as Parker was given immediate medical aid. He was then loaded onto a stretcher and placed inside the ambulance. Gibson knew, judging from where the bullet hit him, Parker stood a decent chance of pulling through. *Maybe.*

"I'm truly sorry for your friend, Agent Gibson," Nivelle said to him.

Gibson held back from burying his fist into Nivelle's face. He ground his teeth as hard as he ever had. He caught one last glimpse of Parker's broken body before the ambulance door closed.

"His life is in their hands now. It's up to them," he said, turning away to walk into the night, alone.

25

Chico, California

Three days later

A COOL BREEZE SKIRTED AROUND the trees lining the streets of Chico, California. John Francis Garner, grandson of the late Jean-Francois Goni, sat in front of an upright piano delicately playing a nocturne. Inside, his house was not much warmer than outside, just as he liked it. The breeze caused the limbs of a small tree, on the side of the house, to dance upon its windows as the notes from the piano lightly filled the house. Garner finished a set and relaxed his hands on his thighs. He was pleased with his performance.

The front and back doors suddenly simultaneously crashed open as FBI agents stormed into the house. They moved so quickly he didn't even have time to rise off the piano bench. Before he could open his mouth to attempt to denounce the invasion on his home, he found himself forced to the ground, his face pushed firmly against the hard floor, his hands bound behind him. He was lifted to his feet where he stared directly into the eyes of Agent John Gibson.

Gibson smiled. "You've been bad, Mr. Garner. And you're a disgrace to the Basque people."

Garner winced at Gibson's words, but didn't say a word.

Gibson nodded to the two agents standing behind Garner. "Now read this murdering piece of shit his rights." He walked through the open front door and into the cool, refreshing breeze.

Gentle sunlight fell on him as he stepped outside. Quietly, looking into the distance he said, "Now the Basques can deal with the future on their own." Then his thoughts shifted to Sebastian Parker.

As he walked toward his truck, the dark shade of the trees blocked the sunlight, and he felt a chill move through him.

Epilogue

Washington, DC

JOHN GIBSON sat under the awning of a restaurant on the Georgetown waterfront enjoying an elegant lunch of raw oysters and seared Ahi tuna, accompanied by a glass of crisp Sauvignon Blanc. He felt he needed to pull himself away from his office and do something that Sebastian Parker always told him he needed to do more often—enjoy life. Even the seasoned Agent Gibson needed a break from report writing and status updates that had become his life from the moment he stepped off the plane from France.

It was a hot DC day. He'd found a shaded table on the restaurant's patio that was touched by a slight breeze blowing off the Potomac River. After taking off his suit coat and tie, undoing the top two buttons of his shirt, and rolling up his shirtsleeves, he found sitting outside actually pleasant. Idly, he watched kayakers spending their lunch breaks piercing through the calm water of the river. Tourists strolled along the waterfront's riverfront walkway. He considered maybe driving out to the Shenandoahs to do some hiking over the weekend.

Just as he was settling into his relaxing lunch, his cell phone sprang to life on the table in front of him. Promptly, he picked the phone up after noticing the number identified was that of his boss.

"Hello, Mr. Director," he jovially answered.

"Hello, John. Where are you? I expected to find you hunkered down in your office with a ham sandwich and pot of coffee," Director Smith replied with unveiled surprise in his tone.

"I felt the urge to get away for a little while to clear my head. So I came down here to the waterfront for lunch," Gibson replied.

"Okay, makes sense. I know you've had a rough couple of weeks and probably could use some time off. Maybe you should consider taking a vacation?"

There was no way of knowing if it was an actual offer or merely a formality, yet Gibson wasn't going to let it be left untouched. "Not a bad idea. Maybe I'll take you up on that." He paused, long enough to let his answer settle.

"Once you're back in the office I want to go over some of the details of your report on France and California. But while I have you on the line, I'd like to ask you a question or two."

Gibson figured he could imagine what his superior wanted to discuss. He would want to know more about how John Francis Garner had been connected to ETA. He would want to know if there were more people or cells of the clandestine group involved in California, or other places in the U.S. that needed to be further investigated. Such cells would be operating as promoters of Basque cultural or heritage activities, but would primarily be raising funds for ETA. Perhaps there would even be splinter groups, like Garner's, that had grown frustrated with the whole organization and decided to try and orchestrate activities on their own, such as assassinations of prominent Basque-Americans. Even though the Director had read Gibson's report, he would want to know if there was more for Gibson and the FBI to do.

Of course there was, Gibson said to himself.

"For instance," the Director continued, "how's the kid from the CIA holding up?"

"Oh, Parker is going to be just fine. He's a tough young man. I just talked to him earlier today and he sounded in good spirits. For his protection, they have a police guard on him at all times. He's even figured out how to talk a nurse into sneaking him glasses of wine." Gibson smiled at the thought.

"That's great news. Maybe we'll even try keeping this partnership between you two. Is that something of interest to you?" the Director asked.

"He may be young, and his methods may be a bit unorthodox, but overall, we wouldn't be where we are today without him. And I wouldn't want to stay on it without his involvement as well," Gibson replied honestly.

"Fantastic. I'll start the discussions and we'll see what we can do." By saying this, Director Smith implied that the usual bureaucratic hurdles would have to be jumped through before anything would happen—memos would have to be written, meetings would have to be scheduled, maybe even task forces would have to be assigned. It would be the typical DC obstacle course, but Gibson felt confident it would eventually work out in his favor.

"Stop by my office as soon as you get back and we can go over some of the outstanding issues," the Director added.

"No problem."

Hearing his boss hang up the line, he turned off his cell phone. He purposefully did not state a time for his return, as he didn't want to be rushed. After all, he was enjoying lunch.

The major *outstanding issue* to be discussed would undoubtedly be a particular young woman—Graciana Etceverria. The Director would want to know if Gibson felt they should continue searching for her.

Gibson already knew the response he would give, which was the same as his recommendation in his report. Graciana Etceverria had more than enough to run from for the rest of her life. She had, and he figured would always have, Nivelle after her. And Nivelle was about as determined as anyone Gibson had encountered. She would never be safe, as Nivelle would persist in his pursuit of her as long as it took—until he had his sharp teeth pierced into her neck. Unless she showed up in the States, which he seriously doubted, he didn't see any need to do more than occasionally keep in touch with Capitaine Nivelle.

After John Gibson leisurely finished his lunch, he decided to stroll across the bridge into Rosslyn to the Metro station, rather than the faster taxi option. Stepping into the bright sunshine, he stopped and took a deep breath before continuing on his way.

Amaiera
La Fin
El Fin
The End